Mosquito Lagoon

CODE OF MISCONDUCT III

C.A. Griffith

BRIGHTON PUBLISHING LLC
435 N. HARRIS DRIVE
MESA, AZ 85203

Mosquito Lagoon

Code of Misconduct III

C.A. Griffith

Brighton Publishing LLC
435 N. Harris Drive
Mesa, AZ 85203
www.BrightonPublishing.com

Copyright © 2016

Printed in the United States of America

ISBN 13: 978-1-62183-396-3
ISBN 10: 1-62183-396-8

First Edition

Cover design: Tom Rodriguez

Acknowledgements

THANK YOU TO MY INDEPENDENT EDITORS:

LYNDA COKER—CHIEF DEPUTY—COBB COUNTY SHERIFF'S OFFICE (RETIRED)

TRACI NELSON—COBB COUNTY SHERIFF'S OFFICE (RETIRED)

Dedication

For my beloved Grand Daughter:

Charlotte Adeline Roper

2 Peter 3:7 But the heavens and the earth, which are now, by the same word are kept in store, reserved unto fire against the Day of Judgment and perdition of ungodly men.

Chapter One

The whine of the Boeing 737 engines increased dramatically, alerting the weary travelers that it would begin to taxi soon. The passengers offered half-hearted applause in sarcastic appreciation. The forty-five-minute delay had elicited mumbled complaints and caused people to shift in their seats. The General Ulpiano Paez Airport was in no way comparable to Hartsfield-Jackson in Atlanta, O'Hare in Chicago, JFK in New York, or LAX in Los Angeles where delayed departures were expected. The irritating cry of a child near the rear of the aircraft was now muffled by a high-pitched scream as the engines strained to drag the forty-five ton aircraft from a dead stop to the taxiway. The engine noise subsided once the wheels surrendered to the thrust and began their forward roll.

Jay Taylor was momentarily startled awake by the sudden throttling of the engines and forward motion of the jet. He had been snoozing with his arms crossed. His knees were crammed against the seat in front, and his head was tilted slightly back against the headrest. He was in an aisle seat with two men seated to his left. One was dressed in casual business attire and the other wore shorts with a preppy pink pullover. Both had given Taylor a quick look and then just as quickly cut their eyes away as the dark-skinned, muscle-bound Taylor approached them wearing his white muscle shirt, black parachute pants, and wraparound sunglasses. Taylor was accustomed to such reactions and took little note as he eased himself into the cramped economy seat, effectively trapping the two men against the bulkhead. Taylor suspected they would hesitate to bother him to take a restroom break, so he'd eased his head back for a quick nap for the hour delay.

His good eye was closed again, but he knew it would instinctively open when the pilot powered up for takeoff. He had heard the majority of crashes occur during takeoff, and if that was to be the case today, he would rather witness his final moments. And maybe it would be his fate that day, as payment for some of the pain he had inflicted on certain people in the past. But hadn't they deserved it? Hadn't they had it coming? Not those he fought in his martial arts career. Those were fair fights, and his opponents knew full well they could be injured. Taylor's vengeance spewed only to those who inflicted pain for self-gain or self-advancement, like the optometrist who blinded him for money, the billionaire who paid the money, and the one man who professionally benefited from their actions and won the world Ultimate Fighting Championship title.

Now it was over. Just payment had been delivered and received. Taylor felt satisfied, but not to the level that he'd hoped. Maybe he should have listened to his employer and best friend, Grey Colson.

"Let it go," Colson had told him on multiple occasions.

He had also said that vengeance belonged to God, but Taylor would just chuckle and tell him he was a fine one to be saying that. Taylor dismissed the memory and summoned images from the previous day: the beautiful, tropical scenery of the Ecuadorian coast and the beautiful women wearing only a suggestion of clothing. Taylor loved being Grey Colson's roommate in his Daytona Beach condo, but every beach was different with its own unique offering of beautiful places and people. But after his one-night mission, it would not have been wise to hang around and play tourist. The pleasant memories of the previous day were interrupted as his good eye opened again in response to the continued mumblings of passengers around him.

The mumblings quickly changed to sharp complaints as passengers pointed and craned their necks to look through the small windows on the left side of the aircraft. During his light slumber, Taylor hadn't realized that the jet had never made it to the runway, but instead had turned around and was nearing the same gate from where they had boarded.

Becoming irritated himself, Taylor leaned over the preppy man to his left to confirm the comments he was hearing around him. As he focused his good eye on the dirty concrete runway below, a Humvee shot into his line of sight and then out of view toward the nose of the aircraft. It was not the civilian type of Humvee built on a Tahoe chassis, common in the States. That baby was a military version from the Desert Storm era.

Several passengers stood and clicked open overhead compartments and then hastily began pulling down bags before they were halted by a male voice on the intercom.

"Please be patient and remain seated. This will only be a five-minute delay, and I assure you we will be departing as soon as possible." The same voice spoke a second time in Spanish, which Taylor suspected was the same statement. Taylor's seat was three-quarters the distance to the tail of the jet, but he was still able to see activity near the cockpit. A middle-age man dressed in a white pilot's uniform stepped from the cockpit and was looking down at a paper handed to him by a flight attendant. He appeared to be studying the paper and speaking to someone to his right at the forward hatch where Taylor couldn't see.

A few moments passed, and then the pilot moved down the aisle. As the pilot made his way through the first-class section, a man in a military uniform stepped into view from behind the bulkhead wall and followed. Two younger military men carrying AK-47 assault rifles joined the parade. One soldier had his AK slung over his shoulder with the muzzle pointed at the floor of the plane and the other's rifle was slung in a similar fashion with the muzzle aimed at the ceiling. A collective gasp rose in the cabin from startled passengers who were apparently petrified at the sight. In response, the pilot tried to suppress their shock by pushing the air down with both hands, nodding and making smiling comments to passengers on both sides of the aisle as he walked by.

The military men behind the pilot did not mimic his actions. They were strictly business as they scanned the passengers and were on alert for any sudden movements or threats. Taylor remained stoic in his seat, having no clue as to what their mission was. But he found out soon enough. The pilot checked the paper five seats ahead of Taylor and stopped in his tracks. He briefly glanced in Taylor's direction and snapped his head around to the lead soldier. Whatever he said made him quickly shoulder his way around the pilot. He took two large steps and stopped directly in front of Taylor, invading his personal space. The two other soldiers stayed behind the lead soldier and adjusted their rifles to port arms. Taylor stared at the trio through his sunglasses.

"Senor Taylor," the lead soldier said in a thick Latino accent. Taylor sat silent. The soldier smiled from behind his own sunglasses and continued. "Oh, it is you without question. You need not speak now. We have time," he said while glancing at his wristwatch. "But we don't want to keep these nice tourists waiting, do we?"

Taylor shrugged. "I'm not keeping them waiting. You are."

"You must come with me, Senor Taylor," the soldier said and pulled a folded document from his inside his shirt. "I have a warrant."

"For what," Taylor said.

The soldier responded with an exaggerated sigh. "Senor Taylor. We can discuss the matter in private. You wouldn't want your dirty laundry aired in public."

The two soldiers on either side of the lead man leveled their rifles on Taylor. The cabin had fallen totally silent. Even the crying baby had been silenced. Either its mother had calmed the child down or it had sensed the thick tension hanging in the cabin and hushed instinctively.

"I have a right to know," Taylor said evenly.

The lead soldier chuckled. "You are not in America, Senor Taylor, but if you insist," he said and referred to the document in his hand. "It concerns an incident just last evening involving a Senor Clayton Haggart."

Grant Parker typed a sixteen-digit password into the rectangular white field below his personal e-mail address. He was satisfied that Spidersilk was the most secure service. Their advertisement claimed that just as a fly could not escape a spider's web, a third party could not remove their customers' data. They even claimed the National Security Agency couldn't hack their service, but Parker seriously doubted that. It was a necessity to utilize data storage, and Spidersilk was the best money could buy.

Parker turned thirty-nine years old the day before, but no one in his quiet office at the National Aeronautical and Space Administration knew it or would even care. He never made a big deal about his birthday, or slipped little hints to his coworkers, or took the day off to celebrate. Parker had been working for NASA for almost seven years and on his current assignment for six months. Although it was not his dream assignment, he understood that all staff members had to do their time and build seniority. But Parker wasn't certain he would still be employed if NASA discovered what he was going to do that day.

Parker loved his work, and it had shown love in return with a six-digit salary, annual bonuses, and a car allowance. He expected as much after investing years to attain a PhD in statistical science. At six-one, he was taller than his current colleagues, and his slender frame and muscle tone made him attractive to women. Not that he was a woman chaser, but his dark curly hair and slender build had made him the pray instead of the predator with a few aggressive females. Especially when they discovered Parker had a passion away from computer code and numbers and analysis. He was an outdoorsman during his off time. Not a hunter or fisherman, but a survivalist. He felt he was as good as any reality show contestant—probably better than most.

Parker needed fresh air now more than ever. Recently, he'd begun to feel a degree of disappointment in his career. The disappointment had turned into a realization of betrayal and finally grew into hatred. He had grown self-conscious and felt he wasn't sufficiently concealing his true feelings. He knew people had taken notice, which made him more nervous. The nervousness had grown into paranoia. He was now paranoid to the point that he was losing sleep, and the lack of rest made him extremely irritable. The growing combination of unhealthy emotions and reactions to normal, day-to-day stimuli would be impossible to hide for long. What he was planning to do, he would have to do that day. He was expected to pass off the hard drive tomorrow.

Parker knew enough about computers to get by, but he was no expert. There wasn't time to seek advice, and he most certainly wouldn't ask the computer gurus at NASA. But he was highly intelligent and could learn new skills quickly. He pulled up a new e-mail and typed the date and time in the subject line. He then drug a file from his desktop screen and dropped it in the e-mail as an attachment and then sent it to himself and one other recipient. He stuck a flash drive into the USB port and copied the same file there. He then removed the hard drive from the rear of his computer tower and replaced the cover. It was all about redundancy. If anything happened to the flash drive, there would be the hard drive. If anything happened to both, the e-mail file would be the last and final backup. One single e-mail sent to two addresses. He alone knew the login and password to his account, and he was satisfied that his contact was just as cautious. *Maybe being paranoid can be a good thing*, he thought. *It can make you crazy, but it can also keep you alive.*

The main laboratory Parker's specific group utilized remained spotless, but maintained an aroma so distinct that Parker had never experienced it before or anywhere else. The group, jokingly called GWOAN, or Group without a Name, consisted of six scientists who split shifts. Three worked day shift and the other three worked evenings. The seventh man was considered the boss and wasn't a scientist but a bureaucrat named Maxwell Rollins. Nice enough guy, but he rarely spoke or interacted with the group. Grant was number eight. He wasn't considered a scientist for the purpose of that specific group, but rather an expert auditor of sorts. He analyzed data gathered by the others and prepared reports. The group name, GWOAN, was more of a running joke and not the group's official title because it had no official title. When he first heard others refer to the group by that name, they sounded like six-year-olds trying to pronounce, GROWN. Parker had chuckled then, but the joke quickly became old.

Parker slid his white lab coat on a hook inside his office door and headed toward the front office. He had deliberately waited until 6:10 p.m. to avoid the foot traffic of the other NASA employees. At 5:00 p.m., the rush of the entire facility staff resembled a fire evacuation. He had made it within five feet of the laboratory exit with his computer bag in hand when he heard Rollins's voice.

"Grant."

Parker spun on his heals to see Rollins standing outside his office door, running his fingers through his hair. Rollins wore a smile but appeared disheveled, with the sleeves of his dress shirt rolled to his elbow and the knot of his black tie loosened.

"Sorry, but do you have a minute before you go? I just have a question about that last batch of data you sent me."

"Ah, sure," Parker said after a brief hesitation. Rollins would know he didn't have an impatient wife or children waiting at the dinner table for him. Rollins waved him into his office, and they sat opposite of each other. Rollins was behind his desk, and Parker was in an armchair with his computer case resting in his lap. Rollins flipped open a file in front of him. He slipped on a pair of tiny reading glasses and looked over them at Parker.

"You've done a great job with this data, Grant," he said. "Oh, would you like coffee?" Rollins snatched the half-full pot from a table behind him and held it at eye level.

Parker shook his head. "No thanks, I'm good."

"Bottle of water?" Rollins said, now gesturing to the small fridge on the floor to Parker's left. "Grab one," Rollins said insistently.

Parker shrugged and pulled a bottle from the microfridge. He wanted to get going, but Rollins was the group supervisor and couldn't be ignored. His counterparts would occasionally say, "He thinks he's the only GWOAN up here." Still not funny.

Rollins considered the file and took a sip of his coffee. Parker snapped off the bottle cap and took a swig of water as he waited for Rollins to say why he had summoned him. Parker took a peek at his watch. It was 6:25 p.m.

"These new sets of readings, measurements, or however you refer to them," Rollins said. "They don't seem to have varied much from the readings from last month."

Parker leaned forward in his chair as if to examine the document upside down. "I thought I adjusted them appropriately as instructed, sir, as we discussed before."

Rollins responded with a quick nod. "Yes you did, Grant. Just not enough, and I have to have this report curried to Washington by tomorrow afternoon."

"Of course," Parker said respectfully, "First thing in the ..." He trailed off as the room, Rollins, his desk, and the coffee pot appeared to move quickly to the left and snap back to the right, and just as quickly jerk to the left again. Parker felt as if he had been dropped into a spinning clothes dryer like a pair of dirty socks. He instantly became severely nauseated, dropped from his chair to his knees, and vomited on the computer case now lying on the floor between his knees and the front of Rollin's desk.

Totally disoriented and violently ill, it's not at all surprising that Parker had no idea when the two men wearing white lab coats moved into the office behind him.

"Grab his keys," the taller man said to the shorter one.

"Why me?" asked the shorter man.

"Because you're closer to the floor," the taller man said with a smirk.

Parker wouldn't remember Rollins's last statement before he blacked out either.

"No, Grant. I think we need to get these readings adjusted tonight."

Code 7 Police Supply on International Speedway Boulevard in Daytona Beach services Volusia and the surrounding county sheriff's offices and multiple municipal police departments. Their staff of fifteen employees stayed extremely busy with the number of orders flowing in for uniforms and equipment for law enforcement new hires, not to mention the number of replacement uniforms required every year. Eleven of the fifteen employees worked in the rear of the building behind commercial sewing machines tailoring uniforms and attaching patches and rank insignia. In addition to uniforms, Code 7 supplied belts, gloves, boots, and weapons, both lethal and nonlethal, as well as ammunition at a discounted rate to departments and officers with the proper credentials, of course.

The young man working the counter was twenty-five-year-old Troy Smith. Troy was a former juvenile delinquent and die-hard pothead, although he masked it better than most. His father had arranged the job at Code 7 for him three years ago and demanded that he cut his stringy hair and straighten his life out or he would throw his lazy ass out on the street. Troy hated his name, but loved the expensive sound system in his tricked out Honda. His weekends were spent cruising Daytona Beach, blasting rap music to the annoyance of anyone within earshot, and trying in vain to pick up young girls. His friends began calling him Tune instead of Troy because of the ridiculously expensive sound system, and he liked it. He insisted that everyone address him as such, but his boss and father refused. But to everyone else, his street name was Tune Smith.

The owner of Code 7 and Troy's boss was a fiftyish man named Paul Rehorn. He was speaking with the off-duty officer who guarded the door and checked the credentials of customers who entered. Walk-in traffic was minimal, so the officer often chatted with Paul to pass the time. Paul appeared a little nervous about something as he shifted his feet and looked past the officer toward the parking lot and then glanced at Troy behind the counter.

Grey Colson eased his Daytona Blue C7 Corvette Stingray to a stop in a parking space at the front door of Code 7 and reached in the center console for his ASP expandable baton. Collapsed, the baton was a little under eight inches long and slid easily into the side pocket of his battle dress uniform. A stainless steel Smith & Wesson .38 caliber revolver lay beneath the ASP. He grabbed it and slid it in the opposite pocket. He then lifted a slim case file folder from the passenger seat and stuck it under his arm as he stepped out and eased the door shut. He saw the owner and officer peering out of the glass door, more so at the Stingray than at him. He had bought it brand new just a month ago after his old Corvette met a sad demise. Colson had driven a rental for the three months before allowing himself to spend the money for a new one. It gleamed like a polished blue diamond. He allowed himself a stretch and looked over his shoulder as two Volusia

County Sheriff units sped down the street. Colson turned back and grinned at the two men's thumbs up of approval as he stepped to the door. Life's too short, he reminded himself.

Colson opened his wallet for the officer to glance at the deputy sheriff major badge and credentials given to him by Volusia County Sheriff Langston and headed straight to the counter. Troy had his elbow on the counter and one side of his face in his palm as he flipped the pages of an *Audio Tech* magazine laying in front of him. Oblivious to Colson's presence, he didn't bother to look up until Colson slapped the case file on the counter next to him.

Troy bolted upright and shot Colson an annoyed glare. Colson stood silent and watched Troy's eyes as they appeared to process information. Colson allowed him extra time than normal, as he understood that the electrical signals in the young man's brain would be required to detour around the abundance of dead brain cells to reach their destination. But it didn't take too long. Troy's glare morphed into surprised recognition. Colson smiled but remained silent. He didn't often see the look Troy was expressing, and he wanted to relish it. Troy looked over Colson's shoulder to the entrance where Paul and the off-duty officer stood and then returned his undivided attention to Colson. He leaned forward and spoke in a loud whisper.

"What are you doing here, Greg?" Troy asked.

Colson leaned in a few inches himself and whispered his response. "It's not Greg. It's actually Grey. And you're not Tune, but actually Troy."

"Whatever," Troy snapped but maintained the whisper. "What are you doing here?"

"Just this," Colson said, slipping the .38 from his pocket and laying it on the counter at an angle, with the barrel pointed toward the far wall. "I decided I didn't like this gun and would prefer a larger caliber. I also began to feel bad that this wasn't your gun at all, but belonged to that fellow Paul behind me. It just wouldn't be Christian of me to keep his stolen property."

Troy stepped back from the counter. "You don't know what you're talking about, old man. You a cop or something?"

"Something I guess," Colson said. "Retired cop, but smart enough to figure out that you've been stealing from this business, little by little, for the entire time you've been working here." Colson nodded to the parking lot. "Most likely to turn that Honda into a ghetto boom box and buy wacky weed. You know, you really shouldn't smoke that crap in your car. It ruins the resale value. Just ask Cheech and Chong."

Troy took another step back, shook his head, and pointed a scrawny finger at Colson. "You can't do shit to me man. You ain't no cop, and I ain't saying anything to you."

Colson slid the file across the counter to Troy. "You can have that if you like. It's a copy with photos of us talking at the beach, recorded conversations of you talking about getting your hands on any gun I need. The digital recording from the hidden camera I installed in the storage room of you slipping it out of the incoming delivery and hiding it in your floppy pants pocket. Oh, and the other video of you setting ammo out by the dumpster to pick up at night. Really, must I go on?"

Colson saw Troy's eyes glance at the gun laying on the counter. Colson knew he could see the rear of the cylinder and the brass casings of the .38 shells. He had no idea if Troy would go for it or not, but by now he had probably realized that Colson wasn't a cop and chances were pretty good that he would. Colson slipped his right hand around the ASP in his pocket.

"I wouldn't do that," Colson said, watching Troy's eyes flash back down to the gun.

Here it comes, Colson thought as he jerked the ASP from his pocket and extended it with an upward snap. At the same moment, Troy's hand shot for the gun. Colson whipped the ASP downward and caught the top of Troy's forearm just as he wrapped his hand around the butt of the gun. Troy instantly screamed and released the gun. He stumbled backward and screeched like a baby with diaper rash as he clutched his right forearm with his left hand. Troy began bending up and down repeatedly at the waist like the toy birds you find at truck stops that stoop over to dip their beaks in the water.

Colson glanced over his shoulder during Troy's screaming tirade. It would be a minute before he calmed down. He couldn't remember if there had been customers inside when he walked in, but there were absolutely none now. Paul stood away from the door with his hands on his hips and a mild look of shock on his face. The off-duty officer began walking toward Colson, but stopped when Colson held up four fingers to keep him back. All cops want to back up fellow cops, and Colson understood that. He knew that code 4 in Volusia County meant the same thing it had when he'd worked in Clay County.

Colson said, "Everything's OK."

"You broke my arm, man," Troy screamed.

"You should have thought of that before you decided to go for that gun," Colson said as he narrowed his gaze at Troy. Then he lifted the gun from the counter and pointed it at the center of Troy's chest. Troy's eyes shot wide open for the second time, not in surprise, but in horror. Colson wasn't certain if it was Paul or the off-duty officer who yelled "No" from behind him as he pulled the trigger.

The sprawling NASA facilities located in Titusville, Florida, covers an area of 144,000 square acres on the Atlantic coast. Also known as the Kennedy Space Center and, more recently, the Space Coast, it has been the primary launch center for human spaceflight since 1968. Vital research is conducted by a multitude of scientists in a wide range of programs. But with the budget gutted in recent years, funding for many programs had been delayed or eliminated. Recently, Washington had announced a new mission, part of which was for NASA to acknowledge Muslim achievements and their contributions to the math sciences and engineering. The new mission directive left many in the scientific community scratching their heads in wonder.

Grant Parker had been furious with NASA's latest directive, but it was the last thing on his mind now. He was in a bright room, and the glare of fluorescent ceiling lights hurt his eyes. He rubbed his temple and tried to massage the pounding away. He closed his eyes and tried to remember. The room smelled industrial. Clean but not a hospital clean or a residential clean. And it wasn't his bed he felt beneath him—or his pillow. He opened his eyes a slit and waited for them to adjust to the light. His mouth was dry, and the faint taste of vomit made him nauseous.

Parker drove his elbow into the mattress and began to push himself up. He'd made it only halfway when the room began to spin and forced him to drop back to his side.

"You need to lie down and you'll be fine," came a man's voice from the foot of his bed. Parker looked down past his feet at Max Rollins. He was sitting on a stool with his hands on his knees while twisting lazily side to side as if he was a doctor explaining a minor medical procedure. His tie was loose around his neck, and his sleeves were rolled to his elbows. Parker breathed hard through his nose and waited for the nausea to diminish before trying to speak.

"What happened? Why am I here? What do ...?"

"Hang on," Rollins interrupted and rolled his stool to the side of the bed. "I need to warn you that any attempt to sit up or stand will make you violently ill. We can talk as long as you remain prone. No one here wants to harm you or keep you any longer than necessary. And it goes without saying that I would prefer that you not puke in every office at NASA."

Parker eyed Rollins for a long moment. Through the subsiding fog in his head, he only remembered Rollins asking him into his office and setting his computer bag down. Parker stiffened at the recollection of the events. Without moving his head, he swept the room with his eyes.

Rollins grinned and waited to speak until Parker's eyes landed on him. "Lose something, Grant?"

Parker lay silent as Rollins continued. "Look, Grant. I'm not here to play games with you as long as you give me the same respect." Rollins stood and gently pushed the rolling stool against the wall. "I'm no bad guy, Grant. Hell, I'm not even a scientist. I'm simply a supervisor, an overseer if you will. And I know you're not a bad guy either, but what you were trying to do can't be overlooked." Rollins put his hands on his hips and stared down at Parker. After a beat, Rollins pointed at the wall. "There are people out there who want nothing more than to ruin all the good we've done and put all of us out of business. And you," Rollins said, now scolding Parker, "You are ... were a vital part in the success of the program." Rollins turned and walked to where the stool rested against the wall. "You disappoint me, Grant."

Parker eyed Rollins back. He had regained his equilibrium but dared not move. "But what you're doing is *not* good," Parker said evenly. He flinched as Rollins kicked the stool and toppled it over on the polished concrete floor.

"You have no idea what you're talking about," Rollins shouted. "And it's not for you to decide regardless of what you think. This project is far bigger than either of us, and it will not be undermined by you or anyone else."

Rollins lifted the stool and rolled back to his position next to Parker. His voice returned to its previously bureaucratic tone. "You can recover from this, Grant. I have been authorized to offer you the opportunity to resign after you are debriefed and I obtain your signature on a sworn, non-disclosure agreement. A man with your experience and education won't have any problems finding employment elsewhere."

It didn't sound like a bad offer to Parker. But it was too big of a deal to trust on some non-disclosure agreement. He was not that stupid and Rollins wasn't either. What Parker had planned to turn over was not the recipe for Coke or the secret ingredients in Kentucky Fried Chicken batter. It couldn't be that easy. A slap on the wrist and a visit to the unemployment office? He knew it was very possible that Rollins may have been told such a deal would be accepted, but Rollins was nowhere near the top of the government food chain. He even admitted that neither he nor Rollins could undermine the program. No, if Rollins was telling the truth, he was only being afforded plausible deniability. He nodded slightly as if seriously considering Rollins's proposal.

"And what will you do to me if I refuse?" Parker asked.

Rollins chuckled and spread his arms. "Nothing, of course. I told you I'm only a supervisor. Just an overseer. So whatever happens to you won't come by my hand. I'll just watch."

Chapter Two

A screaming Troy threw both arms in front of his face an instant before he heard the hammer drop with a click. There was no sound of the .38 discharging, but it made Troy flinch and excrete a half cup of warm goo in his underwear. He immediately turned and ran down the length of the counter and shoved open the stock room door and disappeared to the back.

Colson felt the presence of someone to his right. He turned to see the off-duty officer breathing hard and leaning against the counter. He was staring a hole through Colson and shaking his head from side to side. With a broad smile for the officer, Colson turned the .38 up and released the cylinder, dropping the five empty brass casings on top of the display counter. He laughed as the brass bounced and rolled around on the glass.

"You're letting him go, Colson?" Paul shouted while running toward the stock room.

"It's fine, Paul," Colson assured him. "He's not going anywhere."

"Well, he just did," retorted Paul as a loud squealing noise emitted from the storage room. "He's pushed through the back door and set off the alarm bar."

Colson gathered the spent .38 shells and dropped them in the large side pocket of his BDUs. "One thing you always do when serving a warrant is cover all exits."

Colson eyed the variety of merchandise in the display case for a moment and then started for the front door with Paul and the officer trailing behind him. They stepped out into the hot Daytona sun as two Volusia County Sheriff's units swung from behind the building and came to a stop in front of the trio. The deputy driving the lead car dropped his window and glared at Colson.

"The guy says you broke his arm," he said.

Colson could see Troy clutching his bicep in the rear of the cruiser as he mouthed muffled complaints from behind the cage. He turned his attention back to the deputy. "He's lucky I didn't break his neck."

"And he shit himself," the deputy added.

Colson shrugged, ignoring the complaint. "You have the warrant, right?"

The deputy nodded, "Yeah, I got it, but now I have to detour to the hospital before I take him in. I honestly don't know why Sheriff Langston puts up with your crap, Colson," he said and immediately drove off with the other cruiser on his tail.

"So you had those guys waiting out back," Paul said from behind Colson.

Colson looked over his shoulder. "That's how it works," he said with a wink.

"I never would have hired that boy if I'd known about his record."

"Not your fault. You couldn't have known. Juvenile records are sealed."

"Thanks, Grey," Paul said and started for the door. "It's hotter than hell out here."

"Paul," Colson said, stopping him in his tracks. "Was that a tomahawk in your display case?"

"Yeah. The military uses them, and a lot of police departments issue them now. They call it a tactical tomahawk. That particular brand is called a Shrike."

Colson squinted. "A Shrike? I guess I'm behind the times."

"It's not as compact as the ASP you carry, but a hell of an effective and versatile tool for cops," Paul said while stepping through the door.

Colson's cell phone started playing Steely Dan as he opened the car door. He pulled it from his pocket while punching the Stingray's start button. A few seconds later, the AC was blowing cool air in his face. The heat was much more bearable on the balcony of his fifth floor, oceanfront condo where a constant sea breeze would buffet against the white stucco exterior, all but eliminating the effects of humidity.

It had been four years since he'd lost his wife, Ann, to cancer and relocated to their oceanfront vacation home. His almost three decades with the Clay County Sheriff's Office seemed like a lifetime someone else had lived. He'd had mostly good memories and interesting experiences, but there comes a time in most cops' lives when they realize it's time to lay the gun and uniform aside. In Colson's case, that realization snuck up on him when he didn't even expect it. Being a major on command staff of any law enforcement agency is a privilege, especially one the size of Clay County. He didn't regret his career at all, but his world changed after

Ann's passing. His only real regret was that he hadn't retired earlier and spent more time with her. There had been men he worked with who seemingly cared more for the job than their families. Colson never understood that mentality, but ironically, most of them still had their wives waiting for them at the end of shift.

Colson had found new love in the years that passed in the Fulton County Coroner, Beverly Walls. The only problem was the long distance relationship with her working in Atlanta and Colson piddling with petty theft investigations in Daytona Beach. But it wasn't Beverly's fault. She had invested too many years of study and hard work to simply walk away from her career, and unless the old Volusia County Medical Examiner kicked the bucket, it was doubtful she would consider the move. Colson's private investigation business had tried to take off, but he had refused to allow it to. Although being a full-time beach bum would have most likely driven him insane, he was not going to allow himself to take on too much work.

Colson was in excellent shape for a man of fifty-three. At 5′ 10″, he was not the tallest dude on the beach, but he exercised and worked out regularly to maintain a thick chest and broad shoulders. He knew if he worked full time, he might let the exercise slide and his gut grow. He knew crime and criminals and the law well. He didn't have to buy advertisements for his private-eye business. Word of mouth sent business owners' out of the woodwork with complaints about employees stealing them blind. Even if he wanted the extra cases and more retirement money, there was only so much that he and his sole employee, Jay Taylor, could do. And Jay had been out of town for over a week.

Colson checked his phone but didn't recognize the number. In fact, it didn't look like any phone number he had ever seen. He looked at the 0-98-9272-700 number and for a moment thought his phone had been hacked. Then he remembered Taylor was out of the country.

"Hello?" Colson said into the phone.

There was a low hiss on the line. Colson turned the air conditioner fan down and strained to listen. It just made the hissing noise more prominent.

"Hello," he said again, raising his voice a notch.

"Grey?" came the reply in the middle of Colson's hello. He realized there was a delay like you see on the news when an anchor is talking to a reporter on the opposite side of the world.

"Taylor?" Colson said and waited through the five-second delay.

"I'm in some trouble, Colson," the distant voice responded.

"What's going on Taylor? You OK?"

The hissing and delay were becoming irritating. Colson stuck a finger in his opposite ear and almost shouted into the phone.

"I said what's going on Tay—"

"Senor Colson."

It was a different voice with a Latino accent. Colson's first fear was that Taylor had been abducted by a drug cartel. That's one reason he never ventured outside the continental United States. He and Ann had considered it several times, but Colson could not stand the thought of anything happening to his wife just because they were curious to see another country. The world was getting worse every day, and the only quasi-safe place to be was America. Sure, it had been safer in years past, but it was still the safest. He'd tried to convince Taylor not to go to Ecuador, but there was no convincing his once-famous, one-eyed friend of not doing anything he was determined to do.

"Senor Colson, are you there?" came the voice again.

"Yes, who am I speaking with?" Colson said respectively. It would do Taylor no good if Colson acted like a smartass at that point, whether he was in trouble with the bad guys or the good guys.

"My name is Colonel Guerra with the Policía Nacional del Ecuador. Your friend, Senor Taylor, is under arrest for assault of an aggravated nature."

Colson rubbed his temples. At least it wasn't the bad guys. Nevertheless, he never had much faith in most foreign law enforcement agencies. The lion's share of them were corrupt. He wasn't necessarily talking to a good guy, but probably not one of the worst guys. Colson had never had to deal with a close friend being in jail, but from working in a jail off and on over the years, he knew how things worked—at least in American jails. Methods may vary, but the release procedures were pretty standard and straightforward. But aggravated assault? That's a pretty big-time offense in the States. Taylor must have had no trouble finding Clay Haggart and exacting the revenge he'd wanted so badly. Colson worried that he might not be able to help Taylor, but not trying was out of the question. The man had literally saved his life twice. Colson maintained a respectful tone for his friend's sake.

"How can I help?"

"I'm afraid his charge is very serious, Senor Colson. He blinded a man."

Colson tilted his head back against the seat and blew out an exasperated breath. Of course Taylor did. "I understand that it's serious, but of course he has not been convicted yet. Can you tell me if you are investigating the incident? What if it was self-defense? Were any witnesses interviewed?"

Guerra's tone turned very official and impatient. "I'm not at liberty to discuss the case, Senor Colson. Now, do you want to assist your friend? This call is very expensive."

"Of course, Colonel. What is his bail amount?"

"One hundred thousand US dollars"

Colson might have fallen over had he not been seated already. A hundred grand was ludicrous. He had seen bond amounts of ten or twenty or even fifty thousand for aggravated assault in the past, but double that was rare. Taylor might as well not even have a bond. Colson glanced around the cabin of his new Stingray. The interior was two-tone blue, and the new car smell was intoxicating. He wished Taylor had either done his deed when he had Haggart in the United States or better still, had listened to him and not gone looking for Haggart at all. He would have put off buying his new toy and used the ten grand he put down to bail out his best friend. Now he would have to think of a way to put his hands on bail money or tap into his retirement. He needed some time.

"I'll need to put together the ten percent for the bondsman," said Colson. "It may take a few—"

"Ah, no, Senor Colson," Guerra interrupted. "That will not be acceptable in this case."

Colson was quickly running low in the respect category. Taylor might as well have been captured by a drug lord. In some ways, corrupt government officials were worse. This so-called Colonel didn't want bail money. He was asking for ransom. Colson kept a measured tone.

"Why is it not acceptable?"

"You were a police officer, Senor Colson. I am surprised you do not understand that it is very likely your friend will flee the jurisdiction of the court once he is released. We must have the full amount in cash for assurance that he will return for trial."

Colson understood only too well. People jump bail all the time. In those cases, the court is more than happy to keep the bail money and issue another arrest warrant. Nine times out of ten, the suspect is rearrested and the court gets a double whammy: it keeps the money and still prosecutes. In this case, Colson had no illusions about the outcome. The good Colonel knew Taylor would be back in the States before one dollar of the ransom was disseminated to all the players, if there were any other players. The court and justice system had nothing to do with it. He would have to be careful how he played this guy.

"And I hope you would know, Colonel, that I'm a retired police officer and have never seen that much legitimate money in one place."

"Of course I understand," Guerra said with a chuckle. "It would take most people time to arrange such a transfer."

"What do you mean by transfer?" Colson asked.

"When you have the full amount, I will give you the routing numbers for the bank transfer."

"Colonel, just as you require an assurance that Taylor will return to trial, what assurance do I have that he will be safely released?"

"My friend, is there no trust between officers of the law? We have no desire to detain your friend any longer than necessary."

Colson's knuckles were turning white from gripping the leather-bound steering wheel in front of him. He wasn't talking to a fellow lawman any more than he was talking to Elvis Presley. Now this so-called Colonel was insulting his intelligence. Colson just wished he was close enough to reach out and touch him with his ASP. Colson needed time to think. The longer he talked to the slug, the more of a chance he was going to say the wrong thing and get Taylor killed.

"How can I get in touch with you when I arrange the bail?"

"That will not be necessary, senor. I will be back in touch with you."

"Please let me speak with—"

The hissing background noise abruptly disappeared before Colson could finish his sentence. He sat thinking for five minutes with the air conditioning blowing in his face. Every thirty seconds he could hear the radiator fans spin to life until they sufficiently cooled the 6.2-liter V8 to the appropriate temperature. Why would that imbecile think he had a hundred grand or would be able to raise it? What could Taylor have possibly said to make him believe that? Or is it a case of believing that all Americans are filthy rich and can get their hands on that amount of money at the drop of a hat? Colson sat for another five minutes with both hands gripping the steering wheel and stared straight ahead at nothing. It was a situation Colson had never prepared for and the solution would have to be as unconventional as the problem.

He turned off the ignition, slid out of the car, and walked back into Code 7 Law Enforcement Supply. The off-duty officer gave him a nod as he stepped up to the counter. Paul was stacking new uniform shirts in a neat column on the counter.

Colson tapped on the glass at the object below with the corner of a credit card. "Does a sheath come with that tomahawk?"

"The Shrike?"

"Whatever," Colson said.

Paul looked up from his task with a grin. "For you it does."

"Put it on the card."

Colson walked back to his car and dropped the Shrike on the passenger floorboard. He had no intention of sending anyone a hundred grand, especially Colonel Guerra.

Grant Parker knew he had been held captive for two days despite his bouts of nausea. The slim window near the top of the ten-foot wall was about one-foot high and six-feet wide. It was the only source of light in the drab room, but it did allow him to tell day from night. Parker didn't wear jewelry or watches and had depended solely on his cell phone for the time of day, but Rollins had relieved him of it.

He stood, stretched, and yawned. It was a relief to feel quasi normal again. He would put on his "sick" act for Rollins when he returned to the room. He had visited him twice yesterday and promised Parker he would regret not revealing whom he was passing the data to. During his visit the previous evening, Rollins had waved around a printed copy of the e-mail he had attempted to send and demanded the identity of the account holder behind the e-mail address rainbow316@safemail.com. He sarcastically exclaimed that they had been on to him for weeks and had only waited to pounce when Parker took overt action. He claimed that they prevented the e-mail from being sent. Maybe they had. Parker had no idea how long Rollins had suspected his plans to expose the purpose of GWOAN, but it didn't matter now. The only question was what they were going to do with him.

Parker wondered why they hadn't used some exotic truth serum to make him reveal who he was working with. Maybe they already knew or suspected. Maybe this was just punishment for being a traitor to the cause. But Parker figured the "who" didn't really matter because it would be no different than a drug dealer calling the police after some thief stole his stash. Rollins knew full well what they were doing was wrong and obviously didn't care. Parker's very existence was their biggest problem at that point, and that's why he had to get out that night.

He'd finally figured it out the night before after one of the white-coat guys, the shorter one, had dropped a Subway bag on the foot of his bed. Parker had been so nauseated, the last thing he'd wanted was food. But he gradually felt better over the course of two hours and eagerly scarfed down the entire sandwich. He had dug in his pocket for the one thing they hadn't taken from him: a plastic toothpick. Being obsessive compulsive about hygiene, Parker always kept one on his person. Picking his teeth had always helped him think.

He had sat at the foot of the bed and searched his memory. They had not given him a shot or other form of drug since he drank the bottled water from Rollins's office. And unless they'd tapped the water supply, what he'd drunk from the small sink in the room where he was being held had been normal tap water. It just didn't make sense. He had refused to eat or drink anything they had brought him until that point. If it was indeed the food or water, he could count on another long night of torturous stomach cramps and a spinning room. The thin Subway napkin had slipped off the side of the bed and floated to the floor. As he bent to pick it up, it slid from his reach across the floor and stuck flat to the vent at the corner of the small room. Parker laid what was left of his sandwich on the plastic bag and shot to his feet. He knew it was not an intake vent because he had laid on the floor earlier for the cool air to blow in his face during one of his violent stomach cramps.

Parker stretched his body out on the floor to examine the vent. He almost missed it. It was a transparent, flexible tube that would be invisible if one wasn't looking for it. But what was its purpose? He dropped to his back and rubbed his temples. Why was the vent blowing into the room at times and sucking air from the room at other times? The cool air had not relieved his cramping earlier, but seemed to make it worse. Parker sat up and stared at the vent as he tried to clear his mind. It had taken him another ten seconds for the pieces to fall together. That was why he had begun to feel better approximately an hour before Rollins's interrogations. They were pumping noxious gas or some other chemical agent into the room to keep him curled up and completely immobile in between interrogations. Whatever chemical agent it was, they literally had to evacuate it from the room before Rollins came in. And it had to be very concentrated, because the small tube was no larger than ...

Parker jumped to his feet and grabbed the plastic toothpick off of the Subway bag. He squatted in front of the vent, broke the toothpick in half, and then pushed the fattest end into the tube. It was snug, but otherwise a perfect fit. Parker first thought Rollins was just being cruel and punishing him. But, no, the gas was to keep him immobile and too sick to attempt escape. He looked around the room. The walls were Sheetrock, the floor was concrete and the door was made of steel and had a dead bolt. This wasn't an impenetrable jail cell, but a run-of-the-mill storage room or office converted into a makeshift holding area.

"Number one," he whispered to himself, "it's always Rollins and his two minions during the interrogations, so it's just a handful of people who know I'm here. Number two. They are keeping me sick so I can't leave. They must realize this room could not hold a grown man in good health. Number three. No one is monitoring the room when they're gone."

Parker glared at the door and gritted his teeth. "Well, I won't be sick when you're gone next time, Rollins."

⟨❀⟩Chapter Three❀⟩

Agents Mcilwain and Strickland had been partners for over a year and had investigated numerous cases, but none had ever brought them to the Kennedy Space Center. All they knew about this particular case was that the special agent in charge of their field office had sent them and ordered them not to let any grass grow under their feet getting there. That always meant important people were involved.

Mcilwain was thirty-nine years old and had been with the FBI for a dozen years after serving two tours in the army military police. In that time, he'd never had a partner quite as beautiful as the thirty-year-old Myra Strickland. He glanced at her through his dark sunglasses and offered a slight grin as the tall buildings of the space center came into view. It was as if a billionaire had constructed a strange and isolated city on a sandy coastline without regard for building placement. The structures had a sterile appearance and sat in random clumps as if they had been dropped in a haphazard fashion from the sky. Strickland was dressed in a navy-blue pantsuit and white blouse, and Mcilwain was dressed in a medium-gray suit, white dress shirt, and gray tie. The heat of the Atlantic coastline was simply too intense to wear the classic FBI black. Strickland returned Mcilwain's grin and shrugged.

"What do you think this one's about?" she said.

Mcilwain responded with a shrug of his own. "You never know. But we are the two most qualified agents for the job."

"And how would you know that if you don't even know what it's about?"

"Well," Mcilwain began with a serious tone, "we're both Star Trek fans, so ..."

Strickland chuckled. "Speak for yourself."

A mechanical voice came from the smartphone on Mcilwain's belt. "In five hundred feet, turn left onto Saturn Causeway."

Mcilwain drifted the black government-issued Charger into the turn lane on Kennedy Parkway and took the left as his phone had instructed. A white guard booth with a red-and-white striped gate arm appeared directly in front of them. Mcilwain slowed to a stop under an awning where an older security officer gave them a serious look over a pair of reading glasses from behind a sliding window. Mcilwain passed his and Strickland's badge cases over for examination and said, "FBI Agents Mcilwain and Strickland to see Director Danz."

The security officer tilted his head back to read the credentials through the bottom of his bifocals and passed them back without a word. The officer lifted a cordless phone, pressed in a short series of numbers, and said, "Two FBI agents to see the director."

The gate arm lifted silently, and they eased through. Once they passed Contractor Road and then Instrumentation Road, the smartphone announced, "Arriving at destination on the right."

From the air, the Operations Support Building II or OSB II would appear to be a right-angled triangle with a pregnant hypotenuse. Driving or walking toward the building, the sidewalk stretching away into the distance was indistinguishable. But from above, the walking path would be clearly recognizable as a full-scale outline of a space shuttle.

Mcilwain ignored the large parking lots to his left and parked the Charger in the circular drive near the front doors. After discreetly offering the front attendant their credentials, Mcilwain and Strickland rode the elevator to the top floor. A set of double doors guarded an inner office as they stepped from the elevator, and a modest black placard stuck to the right of the doors read Earth Science Division in four-inch white lettering. In slightly smaller lettering beneath the sign was Dr. Nicholas Danz—Director. A professional photo was stuck to the wall above the placard. The man half-smiling in the photo had short dark hair and a slender face.

After showing their credentials a second time to a middle-aged woman at the reception desk, Mcilwain and Strickland took a seat in the silent waiting area. Mcilwain took inventory of the rather large room. There were eight steel-framed chairs with black leather upholstered seats and backs sitting in pairs and facing the center of the room. Brushed steel and glass side tables sat between each set of chairs with chrome lamps centered on each. There were no magazines, no pamphlets, no canned music, and no flat screen on the wall. The only wall decoration was a four-foot square frame containing a large photo of the earth from space.

They had been seated for less than a minute when the secretary told them Dr. Danz would see them. She opened the door, and Danz crossed the room from behind his desk. After a short professional greeting and handshake, they sat across from the director of the Earth Science Division in the same type of steel-framed chairs in the waiting room. Danz didn't offer a smile or small talk. He was a slender man. He wore his dark-blue suit well, and his hair was cropped in a high and tight military fashion. The photo Mcilwain examined of Danz in the lobby could have very well been taken that day. Danz reminded Mcilwain of an astronaut from the late sixties, but Danz was obviously too young to have been part of the original, "Right Stuff."

Director Danz removed a flash drive from his inside coat pocket and held it at arm's length across the desk. "This is all we have, and it's all you should need," he said flatly.

Mcilwain leaned forward to retrieve the flash drive and turned it over in his fingers to examine it. He looked up at Danz. "I apologize, Director, but we haven't been briefed on this case."

Danz flattened his cream-colored tie against his white shirt and sighed. "My complete summary is the first eighteen pages of the file, but I'll give you the Reader's Digest version if it helps. From my experience as a military intelligence officer, that file contains everything required. It's a prosecutor's dream reduced to the size of a thimble. All you have to do is cut a case number and lay it in front of a federal judge."

Mcilwain cleared his throat. "I'm certain your report is sufficiently comprehensive, sir, but if you wouldn't mind, my partner and I may have to ask a few questions if you can provide a short synopsis."

"Very well," said Danz. "We're missing a scientist, well, more of an analyst in his current job description."

"A missing person's case? Have the local authorities—?"

Danz raised his hand to interrupt. "Let me finish. His name is Grant Parker. A seven-year employee we trusted. He was recently assigned to a highly sensitive group that collects and analyzes top-secret information and then produces a report that is forwarded to Washington where it is referenced to make vital national security decisions."

"How long has he been missing?" Strickland asked.

"Today will be four days."

Mcilwain looked at the date on his watch. "Four working days?"

"No, the past four days."

"So that means Saturday through today. Did anyone check with family or friends? Have the county cops done a welfare check at his house? I mean, this is only the second working day and—"

Danz stood and placed his palms flat on his desk. "Agent Mcilwain, we are wasting precious time here. Yes, we checked with his emergency contact. His mother. He told someone in the group he was going to a family reunion in Georgia over the weekend, but he didn't show. But to be frank, I couldn't give a damn about his welfare."

Mcilwain and Strickland momentarily glanced at each other in mild confusion and surprise. Danz sat back behind his desk and continued.

"That's why I said everything is in the case file. Parker was providing the Chinese and other foreign governments with top-secret information about early warning systems, satellite tasking, methods for retaliating against large-scale attacks, and communications intelligence information related to major elements of defense strategy."

Mcilwain glanced at the flash drive in his hand as if it were plutonium. "So Parker is a spy for the Chinese government."

Danz sighed loudly and shook his head. "He's no spy, Agent Mcilwain. You give him too much credit. Spies are ruthless, cunning, and well trained. Parker's selling vital and sensitive information for a profit. He's nothing but a low-life traitor."

Colson had been on the phone all morning. His first two calls were to friends in the FBI. They listened and acted sympathetic about Taylor's predicament, but said there was very little if anything they could do to help and referred him to the State Department. Colson didn't know anyone in the State Department, and it frustrated him to no end. Even the people he knew from his law enforcement days were drifting into retirement, if they weren't there already. He had been out of the game too long, and his favors were drying up.

Colson walked past the flat-screen television on the wall. It was an election year, and the president was standing behind his podium for the fifth or sixth time in as many days, spouting something about his so-called accomplishments and his concern about the need for a $15-per-hour minimum wage and how the world would go down in flames if his opponent was elected. Colson snatched the remote off the kitchen counter, killed the power, and flung the control across the room where it bounced and settled on the couch. Colson was very concerned about the economy, national security, and politics in general, but he was sick of the entire last year being filled with candidates' promises and the never-ending campaign commercials.

He stepped onto his fifth-floor balcony and eased down on the cushion of the closest chair. The curve of the earth lay before Colson and continued as far as he could see to the north and south across the vast Atlantic Ocean. It was early October and the throng of Daytona Beach sun bathers, Frisbee throwers, and novice surfboarders had waned in the last two weeks as children headed back to school. Families were winding up their vacations as fall set in and turning their thoughts toward pumpkins, turkey dinners, and Christmas shopping. But summer couldn't last long enough for Colson. Winters in Daytona were not nearly as cold as those he had endured in Georgia, but it still grew cooler than he preferred.

It was an overcast day, and Colson felt helpless. There may have been two to three hundred people on the beach that he could see from his fifth-floor view, but how many hundreds, or maybe even thousands, of Americans were being held captive by corrupt foreign government officials? Even if he'd had a personal friend at the State Department, there wouldn't be an ice cubes chance in hell that he would have enough leverage to negotiate Taylor's release unless it was politically expedient to a high-ranking political figure. He doubted the president himself could make it happen—or would even try.

Colson's cell phone started playing Steely Dan from the kitchen counter. He had never gotten around to changing the ring tone. He hustled up and answered, thinking just maybe one of the last favors he'd called in would be good news for Taylor.

"Mister Colson?" a female voice asked.

Colson didn't recognize the voice and was prepared to snap an insult if it was another sales pitch, female caller or not. He wasn't in the mood for a polite response, but he decided he'd play nice, for now.

"Who's calling?"

"My name is Lisa Riley and my family needs your help."

Colson breathed a sigh of relief. At least it wasn't some idiot congratulating him on winning a seven-day cruise to the Bahamas. He turned and walked back inside.

"Miss Riley, I'm sorry about whatever problem your family is involved in, but my work is strictly limited to corporate and small business theft and fraud."

"Please, Mister Colson. My half-brother is missing. Our mother is elderly and very sick. I'm afraid his disappearance might kill her if you don't help us. You were very highly recommended."

Colson had heard that before. Most likely the first two private investigators the woman had reached out to, had turned her down for the same reason and had cheerfully referred her to Colson. Finding a missing person could be a very expensive and laborious job. In most cases, missing adults didn't want to be found for one reason or another. A miniscule percentage were abducted or dead in the middle of nowhere. If the person was dead because of a car accident, he or she would be found soon enough. But in most cases, they were missing from people they wanted to be missing from. Their reasons could be a dispute between siblings after the death of a parent and the division of inherited property, an ugly divorce and subsequent child custody disputes, or mounting debt and the embarrassment of bankruptcy and foreclosure. Colson's policy to stay away from domestic cases was a no-brainer. Thirty years as a cop and dealing with such messes had been quite enough.

"So," Colson said, taking the bait, "who recommended me to you?"

"Well, you see, I work for the Fulton County Clerk's Office in Atlanta and the coroner is a family friend."

Colson sat back down in his PVC chair and dropped his head into his free hand. "Don't tell me Beverly told you to call me," he said with his eyes closed.

"Yes. She said you'd be happy to help my mom and me. She said you were a wonderful man. If not, she wouldn't be dating you."

"I'm sure she did," Colson said, not bothering to mask his sarcasm.

"I'm flying down in the morning," Lisa said with the confidence of a fisherman reeling in a giant marlin. "I'll give you the address of my brother's townhouse. Could you possibly meet me there around noon?"

"Do I have a choice?" Colson said more as a statement than a question.

Within sixteen hours of leaving the space center, Agent Mcilwain had obtained a warrant and entered it into the National Crime Information Center or NCIC. The special agent in charge had the affidavit waiting for him at 8:00 a.m., and then he found himself sitting in front of a federal judge as fast as Mcilwain's government-issued Dodge Charger could get him there.

Mcilwain felt as though he was just going through the motions. His boss had never prepared an affidavit for him or anything else for that matter. He hadn't even had the chance to go over the documentation Danz had given him. His only concern was that he was signing an affidavit of probable cause without even knowing what the probable cause was. If and when Grant Parker was arrested, there would eventually be a trip to testify before a federal grand jury and subsequent trial. If the probable cause was weak or not accurate, Mcilwain would get the blame, not his boss. All he knew was that someone important and powerful was greasing the wheels and wanted Parker in custody—yesterday.

Mcilwain studied the affidavit before signing it. What Danz had told him was very well articulated in the document along with the addition of specific details such as dates and times and delivery methods. Parker typically copied classified information on flash drives and dropped them surreptitiously at various locations. Other times he would e-mail certain sensitive documents to himself and an unknown third party. At that point, it didn't matter who the unidentified third party was because sensitive information was classified, and it was a violation of federal law to forward it to private servers. Even to oneself. Mcilwain rubbed his chin as he thought about Parker's motive. He never thought people smart enough to be rocket scientists would be that stupid. Didn't this guy watch TV and notice how government employees, with the exception of powerful ones, got jammed up for e-mailing classified information?

It was obvious to Mcilwain that someone was looking at Parker closely and even conducting surveillance if they'd observed him dropping the flash drives. If it had been agents with his field office doing the surveillance, they had kept it a very good secret. Did they send a bunch of scientists or astronauts to conduct their own surveillance? Maybe those NASA security guys? Surely not. Mcilwain had dismissed his speculation, signed the affidavit, and obtained his warrant. Strickland was waiting for him when he stepped off the elevator.

"You get the warrant?" she said.

Mcilwain held the document in front of his face. "The quickest I've ever gotten a warrant in my life."

Strickland stepped closer to Mcilwain and whispered, "Why is this such a drop-everything-else-and-haul-ass case? Is this guy some sort of terrorist?"

Mcilwain shrugged. "You're talking to the great ill informed, Myra. I haven't even opened the file Danz gave us yet. The only thing I know for sure is this Parker guy has seriously pissed off the pope."

"I've been reading the file, and I suggest you do the same while I drive," Strickland said.

Mcilwain gave her a confused glance. "While you drive where? I haven't even had breakfast."

"I would plan on a long day if I were you, and it won't be spent turning over rocks looking for this guy. It will be a long interrogation process if you ask me. Parker's not AWOL anymore. He must not have realized they were on to him and actually showed up for work. The SAC says NASA security has him in a secure area until we can get back there and transport him to the Marshal's federal holding facility."

It wasn't exactly the escape Hollywood would make a movie about. It had been around ten hours since Parker's last interrogation by Rollins with his two, white-coated nerds silently framing the doorway with smirks on their faces. He thought he had played a pretty good part, acting as though he couldn't steady himself while sitting up in the bed. In reality, he wasn't acting all that much. Whatever gas he had been inhaling was taking its sweet time finding its way out of his system, but with every breath expelled, Parker felt a micron better than the moment before. The vent had begun blowing cool air into the room only moments after the Rollins trio shut the door.

It had become a laborious routine. The same questions followed by the same answers, but then it became glaringly obvious. They were stalling. Rollins's final comment removed any doubt. He had said, "We're getting nowhere with this, Parker. But don't worry, soon enough you won't be my problem." Rollins had given him a chuckle as he left the room with his nerds in tow.

Parker had always tried to stay fit, and he was successful for the most part. That meant he rarely became ill aside from the occasional sniffles. He had never been so sick and disoriented as he had been in the last four or five days. He had lost count. They didn't need to watch him constantly or restrain him. The gas had done all the work for them. He constantly checked the tube to make sure the pressure of the gas hadn't blown the toothpick out. At eight o'clock, he had lain down to sleep and conserve energy. He wasn't sure of the time he stirred awake, but estimated he had slept for six hours. There had always been some noises, whether it was the faint sound of a door closing or the muffled voices of people walking somewhere beyond the door. Then there had been distant sounds of vehicles passing outside or the beeping of heavy equipment backing up. Some of those exterior sounds would last late into the night but weren't as distinguishable during the day due to normal human activity. He estimated it must have been about 3:00 a.m. The witching hour.

NASA was just an extension of the government, and he had grown to know the staunch habits of government employees. That meant if a scheduled work day was from 8:00 a.m. until 5:00 p.m., his counterparts were on the elevator at 4:45 p.m. and on the way to their cars. That's how government workers are. He had stood and walked to the door, placed his ear against the thin cold steel, and concentrated. As Parker had expected, there were no sounds of voices or footfalls. They would expect a nauseated and disoriented Parker to be curled up in a fetal position on the verge of projectile vomiting, not preparing to charge the door at full speed. But that's exactly what he had done. After three solid kicks just to the right of the dead bolt, he stopped and placed his ear against the door. Again, he heard nothing—no running feet or raised voices.

A strong fourth kick seemed to weaken the lock. Parker could push it outward about a quarter inch, but the bolt still caught against the jamb. He had placed his back against the far wall and charged the door for the fifth time, throwing his shoulder into it, and it flew open.

A spacious yet dim storage room welcomed him. The fluorescent fixtures held one tube each. File boxes were stacked floor to ceiling against one wall, and a canvas cart half full of black mesh bags sat on casters. There were metal shelves against the far wall labeled A though Z that were also piled with black mesh bags. At a glance, shelves Z, I, and Q had no bags sitting above them and only one sat above V. Parker had hoped there would be a pipe or stick or anything he could use to defend himself, but nothing caught his eye. He checked the bag above V and found orange construction jumpsuits folded in a square. A tag was attached to the bag that read "Vasquez, Jesus" in permanent marker.

Parker suddenly realized the room's purpose was for the drop off and pick up of laundered uniforms. He loosened the string from the mouth of the bag and pulled out an orange jumpsuit. It was not the optimum color for an escape, but he hoped they wouldn't scrutinize a construction worker if searching for someone dressed in typical scientist attire.

He spun on his heels and dropped to the floor to slip off his shoes. That's when he saw it. Against the wall and about eight feet down from the now ruined door was a clothes rack with uniforms draped in clear plastic. These weren't construction uniforms that a person would fold and drop in a mesh bag. He stood back up to take a closer look. White uniform shirts and black pants, again grouped and twist tied together on hangers with paper labels with handwritten names. Round patches were sewn on each sleeve. The unmistakable emblem he had admired all of his life: a dark-blue, round backdrop of stars with a red comet tail and the white acronym, NASA, embroidered across the middle. Embroidered on a thin patch above the NASA patch was the word, "security."

The first pair of pants was too large and there were no belts lying around to cinch them up. It took Parker three tries to find a pair that wouldn't fall around his ankles. He tucked in a baggy uniform shirt. There was no time to worry about winning a fashion show. The door leading out of the room opened into a long hallway, which was also dimly lit until a motion sensor somewhere brought all the lights to life. At first the lights startled Parker and made him worry that a motion sensor would activate an alarm, but he didn't hear any bells or a claxon. At the end of the long hallway was a door with a red illuminated "exit" sign attached to the ceiling above it. Parker ran to the door and stopped short. A sticker spanned the length of the push bar. It was white-and-red striped with the word "emergency" written through the design. He subconsciously held his breath and pushed his way out. That's when the bright lights of the security vehicle nearly blinded him.

The Cloverleaf Condominium complex was located just a few miles south of Colson's condo on A1A. All Colson had to do was swing his 'Vette left out of the parking lot and drive straight until he arrived at 3 Oceans West Boulevard in Daytona Beach Shores. Parker's half-sister was wrong about him living in a townhouse, or she didn't know the difference.

Colson had driven past the property dozens of times but had paid it no attention. It was usually on the few weekends when Beverly was down for a visit and they would drive to Inlet Harbor in Ponce Inlet for dinner and dancing. On those occasions, his focus was partly on the road, but mostly on her. Beverly was an excellent medical examiner with a rare talent for investigating and determining causes of death. He didn't expect her to drop her profession and move in with a beach bum, and she didn't expect him to dust the sand off his feet and drift into retirement obscurity as a suburban house husband in Atlanta. The arrangement had worked well enough thus far.

Colson was immediately impressed when he turned into the front parking lot. The seven-story complex was laid out in a practical design that consisted of four separate living structures set at forty-five degree angles and joined by a seven-story parking garage in the center. Each individual condo had wide glass doors leading to large balconies—larger than Colson's at the Sundowner. Colson estimated the cost of the smallest units facing A1A to be no less than a half million and didn't even venture a guess about the largest units with an ocean view. He suspected there weren't any makeshift PVC chairs on any of those balconies. He spotted the blue Prius parked near the office and pulled into the space next to it. An earlier text he'd received from Lisa Riley had described the rental car.

Colson stepped out and tapped on the driver's side window of the Prius, causing the distracted fortyish woman to flinch. She had been focused on her cell phone. She smiled and rolled down her window.

"Grey, right?" Lisa said with a half-smile.

Colson returned her smile. "That depends. Do you work for the IRS?"

"Beverly showed me a photo of you two." Lisa was a pleasant-looking woman but it was obvious she was weary from the short flight and probably had not slept. Colson understood that there's no such thing as a short flight anymore when you have to show up at the airport two hours early to make it through TSA and get to your gate on time. Not to mention the hell on earth that is currently called metro Atlanta traffic.

Colson squinted. "If she was in the photo with another man, I may have to find him and tune him up a little."

Lisa chuckled and brightened a little. "You wanna follow me up the parking deck? Grant lives on the seventh floor. The code at the garage gate is 0-1-0-1."

Colson followed Lisa's rental in a slow arcing circle up the seven floors of the deck. The wide tires of the Corvette created a light squeal on the slick concrete all the way to the top. They met at the back of her car and shook hands. She then pointed down a line of mostly empty spaces to a black Dodge Challenger parked next to a small minivan on the outside wall. Most other vehicles were parked against the inside wall.

"Well, his car's here," said Lisa.

"The Challenger?" Colson asked while walking toward it with Lisa trailing behind. Colson stuck his hands in his pockets and circled the muscle car while peering inside. There was no trash on the floorboards, nothing in the side storage pockets of the door panels, and no briefcase or books or files. It was very clean. On the back was a specialty Florida tag. It was yellow, blue, and white, and Colson had seen hundreds of them since moving to the state. The bulbous sea otter–looking creature depicted between the numbers and letters was supposed to be a manatee. It looked like it had been drawn by a second grader. "Save the Manatees" was written at the bottom of the plate.

"Have you tried calling him this morning? If his car is here, there's an excellent chance he's in his condo."

"No," Lisa said while pulling her cell from her purse.

"Has he had this car long?" Colson asked as Lisa raised the phone to her ear.

Lisa sighed. "Straight to voice mail again. He's had the car at least two years. I remember how he talked about it at the family reunion that year."

"What made you suspect he was missing or that something happened to him?"

Lisa walked to the driver's door and bent to look inside. "This past Saturday was our family reunion. We spoke just last Thursday, and he was excited to see everyone, especially our mother who is too old and disabled to get out. We both talked about how this was probably her last reunion." She turned and looked at Colson to emphasize her point. "He *never* missed a reunion. *Ever*."

"Anything unusual about the car? Let's not touch it yet," Colson said.

Lisa shook her head. "He always keeps it this clean."

"Well," Colson said, "how about we knock on his door?"

Lisa nodded. "Yeah. Sure."

The parking deck door opened and a bald man wearing a bright-yellow T-shirt and sunglasses smiled and held the door for them. They stepped into a wide, terracotta-tiled hallway. Colson followed Lisa while admiring paintings of beach scenes, boats, exotic birds, and tropical foliage in the foreground of a remote waterfall. Each painting was the same size and hung midway between the units. Eight wall sconces illuminated the doorways of the units. Four left and four right. Lisa had already walked past three, meaning Parker had an end corner unit, probably with balconies off the main living area and the bedroom. Colson hadn't even been inside the unit and was already willing to trade his for it. If Lisa stopped at the door on the right, the bedroom would have a beach view to the side, but the front would face A1A. If she stopped at the door to the left, both views would be of the ocean. She pivoted left in front of Colson and stopped. Yep, he was ready to trade.

"So, you have your own key?" Colson said.

"It's a combination." She said and started punching in numbers on a box below the door handle. "He made me put it in my phone the week he moved in. Just in case."

"Any roommates or girlfriends?"

"No," she said and pulled the door open. "Grant," she called from the doorway. "Grant."

There was no answer.

Colson followed Lisa through the door into a large foyer. The thick terracotta tile from the outer hall continued inside and covered the entire area. Lisa flicked a switch, illuminating a small chandelier above. Colson estimated the ceiling height at twelve feet, which was unusual for the condos he had seen. They walked past a hallway to their right and into a spacious living room where three enormous glass doors provided a breathtaking view of the Atlantic below. To Colson's left was a nicely appointed open kitchen with stainless appliances, commercial stove with six burners with a pot filler faucet mounted above. The cabinets looked like solid mahogany, and the counters were a polished tan granite. Colson turned back to the ocean view and crossed his arms. Lisa's voice came from behind him.

"What are you thinking, Grey?"

"I'm thinking I need to do some serious renovations at my condo."

"I mean about finding my little brother."

Colson spun around. "I know, sorry. Can I look around? I mean drawers, closets, papers—everything."

"Of course. That's why we're here."

Lisa walked toward the dining area and through a door, and Colson backtracked to the front door and down the first hallway they had passed. He pushed open the first door to his right. It was a half bath with a toilet and pedestal sink. Clean and tidy. He stepped out, moved down the hall and opened the door to what he concluded was the master bedroom. It was large enough for a king-size bed and sitting area. A leather couch sat at the foot of the bed facing the opposite wall where a sixty- or seventy-inch flat screen hung. There was no need to turn on the lights since, as he suspected, large glass sliding doors led out to an equally large balcony. The bright Daytona sun provided all the light needed. The bed was made with a two-tone gray comforter stretched tightly across it. Above the bed hung two boat paddles in the shape of an X.

Colson checked the dresser drawers and the bedside tables. He found nothing but a couple packs of chewing gum and sales receipts from a sports equipment store and the Home Depot. He moved on to the walk-in closet. Suits, dress shirts, and ties hung on one side of the closet. A neat row of dress shoes sat on a rack beneath them. The opposite side was all casual wear: jeans, shorts, and drawers with socks and underwear. Cargo pants, coveralls, and a variety of T-shirts completed the rack. On the floor beneath the casual clothes sat three sets of tennis shoes and two pairs of hiking boots next to an upright vacuum cleaner. Two ball caps hung from the back wall. One was dark blue bearing the Atlanta Braves logo and the other was orange with a logo that read, Mosquito Lagoon.

The letters were randomly tilted on a background that resembled old weathered planks flanked on either side by a trout or a bass. Colson wasn't a fisherman and couldn't identify either for certain.

Colson walked back into the bedroom, squatted next to the bed, and flipped up the comforter. A green canvas bag had been shoved underneath. He slid out the three-foot-long bag and pulled the zipper open. He found tent poles and nylon tent material. He stood and ran his hand through his hair. Nothing so far. He walked back into the hall and found a laundry room on the right across from the half bath. He wanted to look in the half bath again. A cop's intuition. He checked behind the hanging mirror above the sink and felt around the back of the sink pedestal. Nothing. He knelt and run his hands around the back of the toilet but again felt nothing. He then stood and lifted the tank lid and turned it over in his hand and there it was. A small black vinyl pouch stuck to the bottom of the ceramic lid.

Colson pulled on the pouch, but it had apparently been hot glued to the surface. He knew what the pouch was because he'd used one almost identical to it for his flash drive. This one was empty. By itself it wasn't really significant. If he had found it in the closet or a dresser drawer, he would have dismissed it as having no value. But who hot glues one to the underside of a toilet tank lid? Especially when the person lives alone.

"Grey," Lisa called from down the hall. "Find anything?"

Colson sat the lid back in place. "Ah, nothing yet."

Colson didn't know the significance of the pouch under the toilet lid, but it *was* significant. A flash drive pouch without a flash drive. He had to ask himself a question. Should he tell Parker's half-sister? Absolutely not. At least not right yet. Colson would have rather found a printed, online receipt for a sudden business flight to Houston that would explain the whole thing, but there was no immediate reason to give Lisa and her mother a mysterious clue. It would only lead to additional worry. They met back in the living room.

Colson said, "You find anything unusual in the other bedrooms?"

"Not that I would call unusual. They've probably never been used except when Mom or I visit, and Mom can't travel anymore." She held out a key fob with two fingers. "His keys are here. That's about it."

"Care if I hang on to them for now in case I need to check his car later?" Colson asked.

Lisa shrugged and dropped them into Colson's hand.

Colson said, "Anything you think should be here that isn't?"

"No."

"Can I ask you some questions about Grant? Some may be personal."

"Whatever will help," Lisa said.

"You said he had no girlfriends?"

"None currently. He would have mentioned something."

Colson shrugged. "Well, maybe or maybe not. I'm just speaking from a guy's perspective. How about male friends?"

Lisa looked down and to the left, indicating to Colson that she was attempting to recall anything Grant had said about guy friends.

"The only thing I remember is him talking about camping and hiking and kayaking."

"I know," Colson said. "I found the tent under the bed. Does he do that often? Go camping I mean."

"He loves the outdoors. Who would ever think a NASA scientist would be a survivalist on the side?"

"What kind of a scientist is he?" Colson asked.

"Statistical."

Colson reached over to a small drop-leaf table shoved against the wall and picked up a photo. A curly haired man wearing tan cargo pants, an olive-colored T-shirt, and ball cap stood with his hand resting on a large piece of driftwood on the sandy bank of a waterway. The driftwood was at least as tall as the man, and it was twisted like it was formed by a category-five hurricane.

"I take it this is Grant?"

Lisa nodded, "Yes."

"Do you know where this was taken?"

"No, but I'm sure it was on one of his excursions."

"Look," Colson said and held the photo up to Lisa's eye level. "I guesstimate that Grant is standing twelve to fifteen feet back in this picture. You can see his entire body and six feet of the sandy bank in front of him."

Lisa took the picture from Colson and studied it as if she was missing something. "What does that mean?" she asked.

"It means he wasn't alone on his excursion. It's obviously not a selfie. Someone was with him."

"Do you think that has anything to do with what happened to Grant? Is it important?"

"Everything's important right now. We have to consider anything there's not an answer for and discard it later if it's not relevant. Have you made a police report?"

"That's where I'm going when we finish. They told me to wait until after the weekend because we were probably overreacting and he would call or show up. I told them I was flying here to check myself. They said I could go by a precinct to make a report if he hadn't contacted us by today."

"OK," Colson said. "I'll go with you. You can follow me. Can I keep this photo for now?"

"Anything that helps," Lisa said.

Lisa made sure the condo door was locked and then followed Colson back to the parking garage. They walked side by side and talked about Grant's likes and dislikes, his habits, places he had visited, and his limited social life. Colson had no idea if he could locate Parker or not, but it wouldn't be from a lack of trying. There was no doubt Beverly had bragged about his abilities as an investigator. But that was just her perception. Colson knew she was the actual smart person in their relationship, and he often reminded her of that fact. In reality, he was just a concoction of curiosity, suspiciousness, and determination with a dash of sarcasm thrown in to taste. Colson realized Lisa had stopped talking and walking. He turned to see her staring at the Challenger as if she had seen the ghost of Grant Parker at the wheel.

"What is it?" Colson asked.

"You said everything is important?" she said, keeping her eyes on the car.

"That's right."

"There *is* something. Grant was anal about this car. About everything. That's what made him a great statistician. It was at the reunion when he first showed us the car. It took me by surprise, but he let me drive it down the street and back. Of course he had to ride with me. Then he almost lost his mind when I started to pull into a parking space. He made us swap seats, and he backed it in."

Colson shrugged. "I do that most of the time myself. Some lunatic almost took the rear off my 'Vette in the parking lot when I was backing—"

"You don't understand," she said, interrupting him, "he was absolutely obsessive compulsive about it. I'm not exaggerating."

Colson looked back at the car nosed into the parking space and realized what Lisa was suggesting. He stuck one hand in his pocket, took out a toothpick with the other, and wedged it against the back tread of the front tire and the concrete slab.

"What are you doing, Grey?"

"I understand what you're saying, Lisa, and I agree. Grant didn't park this car."

Chapter Four

ny Daytona Beach resident would ignore the bald man in the black Tahoe across from Grant Parker's Challenger. He wore a bright-yellow T-shirt, tan cargo shorts, and tan boat shoes. His T-shirt sported a Margaritaville screen-printed logo covering his entire chest. In some respect, he was a tourist. He had frequented the Daytona Beach area for the past year but it was not for pleasure. His current home was in Virginia, but his Tahoe was registered in Ontario and displayed an Ontario license plate. He had been waiting in the Tahoe for over thirty minutes with the engine off and sweat running into his eyes. The parking garage was covered, but humidity still won the day. During his wait, he briefly thought about babies dying after being left in hot cars. He had heard the stories on the news every summer. It was somewhat of a consolation in knowing that if the garage wasn't covered, he would be as well-done as a barbequed steak by now.

The bulk of the man's thirty-minute wait was spent in the rear luggage area of the Tahoe. He had pulled his nine-millimeter Glock from his waistband and stuck it in the middle console before climbing between the front seats and over the rear bench seat. He now sat with his legs crossed, facing the rear dark tinted window with his cell phone in hand. He waited and thought mostly about his luck of not being discovered in Parker's apartment when the man and woman went in. He had just left the apartment and opened the door of the parking garage when the couple walked in. He had thought nothing of it at first, but something about the look on the woman's face stopped him before he got to the Tahoe. Her eyes were puffy and tired, not vacation rested. He had trotted to the door and eased it open an inch. They had walked straight through Parker's locked front door.

But they would find exactly nothing, just as he had. No signs of struggle, no suicide note, no disheveled furniture, no obvious clues, no Grant Parker, and, almost as importantly, no flash drive in the toilet tank. There was no choice but to wait until they came out. He had already jotted down their tag numbers, but one was a rental. Either way, the tag registration doesn't always identify the person driving. He had just dried his face, neck, and head with a towel when the man and woman finally stepped into view. They stopped for a minute. The woman gestured toward Parker's car and spoke to the man, but not loud enough for him to hear what was being said from within the humid Tahoe.

The man lifted his smartphone and snapped photos of the two talking and their individual close-ups and texted them to a pre-set contact along with the tag numbers. By the time the man crawled over the rear bench seat and squeezed between the front two seats, the Corvette and Prius had disappeared from view down the spiral garage exit. The man started the engine and cranked the air conditioner to the highest setting. He pulled a notepad out from under the Glock in the console and began to make a note when his cell phone rang.

"Yes," he said.

"Any luck?" asked the male voice on the opposite end.

"No. Nothing."

"What's the significance of the photos you sent?"

"Those two were here and in the apartment thirty seconds after I left. When you find out who they—"

"We already know who they are."

The man now cooling in the driver's seat of the Tahoe raised his eyebrows. "That was fast."

"It's early October." The voice of the man on the other end of the line was controlled but his urgent tone was unmistakable. "We're running out of time."

The Volusia County Sheriff's Office is divided into six districts with offices spread across the county from Daytona Beach to New Smyrna Beach to the county seat of DeLand where Sheriff Stuart Langston's office is located adjacent to the courthouse. However, that was not Lisa and Colson's destination. Lisa trailed Colson as they merged onto Interstate 95, heading north to International Speedway Boulevard and then left onto Indian Lake Road where they parked at a boxy two-story building in what looked to Colson like an industrial park.

"Where are we?" Lisa asked as they stepped out on the hot asphalt.

Colson motioned Lisa to follow. "When you make a report about a missing person, the uniform officer sends it to the detective division, in this case the operations and investigations division of the sheriff's office. We might as well cut out the middle man and go straight to them."

"We can do that?"

Colson held the glass door open for Lisa as she walked in. "I have a feeling we can," he said with a wink.

A small reception area greeted Colson and Lisa. A young female sat behind a tall half-moon-shaped desk. Her dark hair was rolled into a bun, and she wore a white golf shirt with an embroidered sheriff's star on her left breast. On the wall above her head in large gold relief lettering was "Volusia County Sheriff's Office." Beneath was the wording, "Operations and Investigations Division" and "Stuart Langston, Sheriff" in smaller lettering. Two wide-screen computer monitors sat at forty-five degree angles in front of the young lady, and she was speaking into a small microphone attached to a headset.

The woman gave Lisa a brief glance, but continued her conversation. She then saw Colson and offered a grin and a wave. Colson pointed to the glass door to the left of the desk and mouthed, "Is he in?"

The girl nodded and pressed an unseen button from under the desk. A mechanical click sounded at the inner glass door. Colson pulled it open and waved for Lisa to follow.

"I think Beverly knew what she was doing when she recommended you. These people seem to know and trust you," said Lisa from behind Colson as they walked down a long corridor of office doors and photos of police and detectives in various poses hanging on the wall in cheap plastic frames.

"They have tolerated me for the past few years," Colson said as he stopped at the last office on the right. "But you never know how many times you can go to the well before it runs dry."

Colson knocked and stepped in the office. Lisa moved in behind him where she saw a chubby man with thinning blond hair standing behind a desk and looking down at a computer with his hands on his hips.

"Lieutenant Cantrell," Colson began. "I haven't had the chance to congratulate you on the promotion."

"Yeah, well," Cantrell said as he eased himself into his chair. "It's not all it's cracked up to be. Instead of investigating, I'm having to help the operations captain figure out this election security schedule."

"Tell me about it," said Colson. "Can you help out a friend and fast-track a case? This is Lisa Riley. Her half-brother didn't show at their family reunion in Georgia, and they haven't been able to contact him since."

Cantrell turned his focus away from the computer, stood, and extended one hand while pressing his tie down with the other.

"I'm sorry. I thought Colson was here to beg me to get his butt out of trouble again."

"Really," Lisa said. "You get in trouble often?"

"Are you kidding?" Cantrell said with a snort. "He's a walking crime scene, and I usually get dispatched to clean it up. And instead of running Mr. Sarcasm out of town, what does Sheriff Langston do? Gives him a major's badge."

"I thought you were retired," Lisa said, turning to Colson.

"I am," said Colson. "The sheriff was just being nice."

Cantrell chuckled. "Nice, my ass. He is just tired of getting called in the middle of the night about something Colson was involved in. This way, he can just badge himself out of trouble. Now, tell me about your brother."

Lisa repeated everything she told Colson to Cantrell, including the empty apartment and her suspicion about the brother's car being parked by persons unknown. Cantrell was polite as he jotted down notes and nodded his head. Whether he was interested in Lisa's story or not, or thought she was overly suspicious and paranoid, he remained professional and half interested. That's what Colson liked about the man. It is far easier to teach professionals to be hard-asses the 5 percent of the time they need to be than to teach complete hard-asses to be polite the 95 percent of the time they need to be. Cantrell finished by asking Lisa for all the personal information on Parker. She gave him Grant's birth date and social security number, as well as a full physical description. Colson trotted back to his car for the photo and gave it to Cantrell to scan into their system. Cantrell called in a uniform officer to transcribe his notes into a formal report, cut a case number, and enter it in NCIC.

"What's NCIC?" Lisa asked.

"The National Crime Information Center," Cantrell said. "If law enforcement has any contact with him and runs his information, we'll know about it within five minutes. But I'd like to suggest that you try to relax. We'll check out every possibility, but almost all of these cases have a logical explanation. Chances are good he'll show up soon. You should stay somewhere in town, and I'll call as soon as anything turns up."

Lisa took a Kleenex from her purse and dabbed her eyes. "Thank you, Lieutenant."

"Ah, you said he worked at NASA?"

"Yes, he's a scientist."

"A scientist," Cantrell said, apparently trying to lighten the mood of the room. He turned to Colson. "You see, Grey. You should have stayed in college, and you could have been a NASA scientist. You could have made the big bucks and still be a beach bum on the weekends."

Colson caught Cantrell's attempt at levity. "I'd rather watch wrestling."

"I'm shocked," Cantrell said. "You'd rather watch wrestling than become a scientist? I didn't even know you liked wrestling."

"I hate wrestling," Colson said evenly.

The uniformed officer stepped in and laid a computer printout in front of Cantrell and left. Cantrell studied the document and swiveled his chair to face the computer. He moved his mouse around and clicked. Then he entered several characters and pressed enter.

"I apologize," Cantrell said. "I had to send an e-mail. If you don't mind excusing us for a minute, Miss Riley, I need to ask Colson a few questions about another case. You are welcome to grab a bottle of water in the waiting room."

"That's OK," Lisa said. "If we are finished, I'll going back to my hotel and get some sleep."

All three stood and shook hands, and Lisa walked out. Colson and Cantrell sat. "I was coming by to see you anyway, Lieutenant. Taylor got himself locked up for assault."

"Well, I can see which assistant D.A. the case has been assigned to and—"

Colson raised his hand to stop Cantrell. "It's more complicated than that. I only *wish* it was here. He's in Ecuador."

Cantrell held out his hands, palms up. "You mean like the *country* Ecuador? I'm afraid that's a little outside my jurisdiction and even farther out of my reach of influence."

"I know, I know. I just need a good contact number for someone with the State Department. Someone who'll actually talk to me about options."

Cantrell tapped the top of his desk with his index finger as if trying to summon information. "I can call over to organized crime. I'm sure they've had to deal with them. Can you not just make his bond and skip the country?"

"They don't want bail, they want a ransom," Colson said.

"I see."

"Thanks for the help," Colson said and leaned forward in his chair. "Now, I know you've got a lot irons in the fire, but are you going to actively look for this Parker guy, or am I going to have flash my honorary major's badge all over Florida and find him myself?"

Cantrell gave Colson a long look. "As a matter of fact, we are. I plan on assigning four investigators immediately. As many as we need actually."

"Don't BS me Cantrell. If I tell his sister that, she'll be expecting a miracle."

Cantrell didn't reply, but turned his computer monitor around one hundred and eighty degrees so Colson could see the screen. The web page was mostly white with a blue header and eight pull-down tabs. In the middle of the header was a blue and gold Department of Justice seal. Beneath the seal and left of center were two rows of five photographs. The top-left photo was highlighted and enlarged to the right of the screen. It appeared to be a driver's license photo, and the man pictured was a dead ringer for the man in the driftwood photo Colson held. He looked at the photo and back to the screen. It *was* the same man. "Grant Parker" was typed in bold white lettering against the blue background under the photo.

Cantrell turned the screen back around. "That's why I asked the sister to step outside. It's not every day we have the opportunity to search for one of FBI's top-ten, most-wanted fugitives in our own backyard. Let alone one charged with espionage."

Taylor stirred awake and sat up on the thin, musty mattress. He'd spent another night of occasional dozing on the hard floor of the damp, six-by-eight cinder block cell. He hadn't shaved in a week, and he felt sticky from head to toe. His own body odor was nauseating. There was no ventilation, not even a cell door with bars to allow at least a fraction of air movement. He was fed a dry meal of beans and rice twice per day and given a scoop of water with each bowl. He knew he had a flu or a virus, most likely from the water they gave him in a nasty tin cup. They had switched to giving him bottled water as his condition worsened. He suspected it was to keep him alive just long enough for them to get their money, but neither he nor Colson had that kind of money.

He had been in a cell with two others until the day before. They were both drunk Latino males. They stank from a combination of tequila and vomit. Taylor would have been fine if the two had minded their own business and shut up for a solid hour. Their yammering in Spanish for hours on end and blowing their hideous breath in his direction eventually took its toll on his patience. He had asked them to stop talking in the most polite tone he could muster, and every time they would respond by laughing and pointing at him, obviously commenting about his dead eye. Taylor had no idea if they understood his requests, and he really didn't care. But he had tried.

He had been desperately trying to sleep on his paper-thin mattress. Sleep was the only escape from feeling sick and being cognizant of his situation. Taylor had been literally feeling his muscles atrophy in his chest and arms and legs, and he was becoming weaker by the day. He had propped himself up on one elbow and looked at his two cellmates chattering and cackling in the far corner.

"Por favor, be quiet please," he had said over and over and over. "I need sleep por favor."

Then it had happened. They finally shut up for a long moment. The two had looked in his direction. Their grins and joking had vanished. They looked back at each other and back to him once again. Then the one leaning against the back wall spoke in the most even voice he'd heard from either man.

"Apesta el muchacho Negro."

Taylor didn't know much Spanish, but he recognized the last word. The two men had stood quickly, and the one who had made the comment produced a switchblade from nowhere. The guards had strip-searched Taylor before leaving him in the stinking cell. He guessed fellow countrymen didn't require the same special treatment. The man began the classic switchblade weave around the cramped area of his corner and repeated the comment. Taylor felt a sudden burst of adrenaline he thought had long since gone and shot to his feet in the classic stance of a mixed martial arts championship contender.

Taylor had kept his focus on the man with the switchblade and the other man in his limited peripheral vision. The man with the switchblade was grinning from ear to ear in eager but ill-advised anticipation of taking Taylor on. The second man wore his own grin and switched his eyes from his cellmate to Taylor repeatedly. The man with the switchblade continued to bob and weave. He had no way of knowing whom he was up against. Taylor bided his time and watched as a pattern in the man's movements became predictable, but he would not be the first target. He kept his eye on the man with the knife and lunged at the second man the moment he was focused on his knife-wielding friend. The hit bounced the second man's head off the concrete wall, and he dropped to the floor like a dead man.

Taylor had felt a burning sensation as the short blade sliced a three-inch long gash just below his left breast. They had been too confined in the cell for him to prevent it. His focus was now on the man with the switchblade. He had faked with his right while cocking back his left fist. The man with the switchblade had taken a swipe at Taylor's right arm but missed. Taylor fired his punch to the man's jaw. It had knocked him to the back wall where he dropped the blade and slid down to his butt. However, it hadn't knocked him cold. Taylor knew the only reason the punch hadn't killed the man was due to him be 70 percent weaker than he could ever remember.

Taylor had bent down and lifted the switchblade from the floor. The man on the floor was groaning and holding his jaw. Taylor hoped he had broken it. The one he had shoved against the wall was still in dreamland, so Taylor grabbed the collar of the knife wielding man and jerked him to his feet and spun him around. He dropped the man's head in the crook of his arm and squeezed his carotid artery until he went limp. He had dropped him to the floor like a Mexican sombrero but hadn't had the strength to dance around him in celebration.

Taylor had pressed his hand against the cut on his stomach to slow the bleeding while he thought about where to hide the switchblade. The cut was much longer than it was deep. The bleeding ceased within five minutes. The metallic sound of a large key sliding into the lock brought him back to the present.

A guard shoved the solid door open and stood aside for Colonel Guerra. Taylor propped himself against the wall and gave the man a one-eyed stare. Guerra's uniform looked like something a third-world dictator would wear. He had jet-black hair and his thick dark moustache drooped over the corners of his mouth to his chin. His ridiculous tan uniform was a hodgepodge of pins and dangling medals, and his frilly shoulder boards and gold cords looked like they had been fashioned from the drapery of an eighteenth century brothel. Guerra was slender and could not have weighed more than 140 pounds. Even in his weakened state, Taylor knew he could pound him and his flunky like he'd done his two former cellmates, but the pistol strapped to Guerra's hip kept Taylor silent and still. Guerra stepped close to Taylor's mattress, but not too close. His grin raised the corners of his thick moustache.

"I understand you are famous, Senor Taylor. I should address you properly. Jay 'the Terrible' Taylor."

Taylor kept silent and his eye on Guerra as he continued.

Guerra lifted his right hand and exposed the broken blade of the switchblade he was pinching between his thumb and index finger. "You are lucky those two men are not dead. You're bail would have been much higher."

Taylor suddenly shoved himself a few inches higher on the wall, causing Guerra to flinch and take a step back. He returned Guerra's snarky grin and crossed his arms.

"If I had wanted them dead, you would have already hauled them away in the back of a pickup. I only needed them to shut the hell up for a solid hour so I could sleep."

Guerra's grin vanished. "I'm not a greedy man, Senor Taylor. There will be no additional bail as long as your friend transfers the required amount in the next ten days. I will be contacting him again soon. By then he should have had more than enough time to rearrange his assets."

Taylor chuckled and pointed to his lifeless eye. "Didn't you notice I'm half blind? Colson's just a retired cop, and I've been out of the UFC for almost five years. You're a fool if you think either one of us have that kind of money."

"*You* are the fool if you underestimate me, Taylor. Compared to my pension, retired policemen in America live like kings. I know far more than you give me credit for. I have many contacts in America. I know you live with Colson in an expensive beach house—"

"It's a condo," Taylor injected.

"Silence," Guerra barked.

It didn't escape Taylor's attention that Guerra had dropped the courtesy of addressing him as Senor Taylor. The man was becoming enraged, so Taylor decided to back off for his own good. There would be another, more appropriate time to deal with the good Colonel.

"Do not interrupt me again. Colson drives a sports car that is worth ten times the annual salary of any man here. One cannot doubt that your combined assets could more than pay your bail. You see, we may be a small nation to you Americans, but we have contacts and comrades the world over."

Taylor remained silent. He rested his head back against the wall and looked at a spider web in the corner of the yellowed plaster ceiling, stained by decades of cigarette smoke. There would be no reasoning with a narcissist like Guerra. He decided to save every ounce of strength and fortitude he had left for getting out of this hellhole.

Guerra turned and mumbled in Spanish to the guard and then looked over his shoulder at Taylor who was still surveying the ceiling.

"It has been fascinating to have an American celebrity guest, but if your friend does not make payment, it will be *you* who will be leaving on the back of a truck."

Mcilwain and Strickland were back in the waiting room adjacent to Director Danz's office in forty-five minutes with warrant in hand. As before, the secretary told them they could go inside. Danz was on the phone as they walked in, and he motioned for them to sit. He swiveled away from them in his chair, spoke for a few more seconds, and then swiveled back around.

"Did you find the file comprehensive?" Danz asked.

"Ah," Mcilwain began, "I'm still…"

"It covers all the bases, sir," Strickland said over her colleague.

"May I see the warrant?"

"Ah, certainly," Mcilwain answered and handed it over.

Danz slipped on a pair of reading glasses and took longer than Mcilwain expected to read it. Most people would glance at the charge and be satisfied. Warrants were not extremely detailed. There was only a brief synopsis of an unlawful act or acts, a section for the charges and their respective code sections, a case number, a space for the names of the case agent and witnesses, and a federal judge's signature beneath an order to arrest the individual. Most federal warrants do not list a bond or bail amount. That would be determined at an arraignment. Danz examined every word on both sides of the warrant and then handed it back to Mcilwain.

"So it appears Mr. Parker was not aware that you were on to what he was doing?" Strickland said.

Danz slipped his glasses off and dropped them on his desk.

"Frankly we were quite surprised he showed up today. I would have thought he'd be well out of the country by now. He obviously felt he was more intelligent than we were."

"In the file I noticed that your tech people notified you when they discovered Parker was downloading data onto an external hard drive, and that's when they dug deeper, correct?" Strickland asked.

"Yes. We didn't want to be premature. For all we knew at the time it could have been a recipe for a pot roast."

Strickland nodded. "I see."

Danz said, "When will he be able to communicate with the outside world? Phone calls or other outside communication?"

Mcilwain was somewhat puzzled by Danz's interest in detention procedure. The main interest of most complainants and victims was usually getting the perpetrator out of their sight and off the property, not how many phone calls they could make from jail. Mcilwain had not been involved in espionage investigations in the past but had in other sensitive criminal matters. The answer was obvious to him but not so much to a NASA director.

"Certainly not before our interrogation and his arraignment before a judge," Mcilwain said. "The judge will probably allow his attorney to notify his family of the arrest, but this is far more sensitive than a shoplifter calling dad to get him out of jail."

"Sir, it would be best for us to transport him to our office for an interview before he has time to formulate and practice any lies," said Strickland.

It appeared that Danz was about to ask another question, but he stopped, held up a finger, and spun back around in his chair to a large window with the view of a massive white building with a NASA logo and American flag on its side. Mcilwain had seen it in space movies but had no idea of its size in real life. He estimated it was at least fifty stories high, dwarfing every building surrounding it. Danz pulled a humming cell phone from his pocket, held it to his ear, and shot to his feet.

"Lock down everything and find him," Danz barked into the phone.

Mcilwain and Strickland stood and glanced at each other as Danz dropped the phone on his desk and turned back to them. "Is there a problem?" Mcilwain asked.

Danz began breathing hard through his nose, clearly exasperated. "Parker's gone."

Mcilwain slipped his cell from his jacket and began punching the screen. "How long?" he asked.

"We don't know. Could be hours."

Strickland threw Danz a puzzled look. "I thought you said he just showed up this morning," she said and checked her watch. "It couldn't have been more than an hour. Two tops."

"I know what I said," Danz snapped and then glared at Mcilwain. "Who are you calling?" he demanded.

"The office. They'll send more agents and bring in the marshal's fugitive team with a K-9 tracking unit."

"No marshals," Danz said. "This stays inside the FBI, specifically the two of you."

Mcilwain lowered his cell and met Danz's stare with one of his own. Danz was not his superior, and he was growing tired of being talked down to like a rookie just out of Quantico. Danz was obviously a NASA big shot, but that didn't mean a hill of beans to Mcilwain. Politicians and executives love to stick their noses into investigations because most are micromanagers, but they are clueless when it comes to law enforcement. Mcilwain knew he still had to tread lightly with Danz. He was no doubt a very powerful and politically connected guy—no different than a "made man" is in the mob. Mcilwain would remain a diplomat, but he could not suppress a chuckle at Danz's ridiculous demand.

"With all due respect, sir, we are going to need more personnel. You can't conduct a manhunt with just two agents."

Danz sat and pulled his collar away from his neck with his finger, loosening his tie a fraction of an inch. He clasped his hands together on the desktop and released a long breath.

"Well, Agent Mcilwain, that's the reality of the situation. The attorney general is having the judge sign a gag order today, and no one aside from your boss and the two of you are to know the specifics of this case."

"We never discuss or reveal information about cases we are working, gag order or not," said Mcilwain.

"It's a permanent order, Agent Mcilwain. You can't talk about this one until the day you die."

"Has your security set up a perimeter?" Strickland asked. "Is his car here? Is he on foot? Do any of your people have any information other than the fact that he's gone? Mr. Danz, it's going to take more than Mcilwain and me to find Parker now that he knows he's wanted."

"Not to mention," Mcilwain said, "he's already in the system and on the FBI website. There's nothing we can do about secrecy if he's stopped for a traffic ticket and snatched up by a state trooper."

Danz stood and met the agents in front of his desk. "We'll cross that bridge if we get to it. And, yes, Agent Strickland, a perimeter is being established, and they are searching for his vehicle on the facility grounds as we speak. Now, I'll have a security officer escort you to Parker's office if you want to start there. Nothing's been touched, and it's sealed off. You can get more information from his immediate supervisor, Max Rollins. You're wasting time standing here. Do I need to call your supervisor for you two to get busy?"

Mcilwain couldn't believe what he was hearing. Plenty of people have been prosecuted for espionage, and the public heard about it for weeks and sometimes years on television depending on the situation. Movies are even made about high-profile spies who have been caught. Governments worldwide have suffered the embarrassment of such cases, so why was this one so hush-hush? NASA had suffered the loss of life and humiliation from space craft explosions due to faulty equipment in the past. This situation paled in comparison. It baffled Mcilwain as to why a scientist selling information to China would be more damaging. He once again told himself to be the professional diplomat.

"That won't be necessary, Director. If I'm going to be yelled at, I'd rather it be in person. Let's go," Mcilwain said to Strickland as he jerked his thumb toward the door.

At a distance of three miles, the Vehicle Assembly Building looked like a white monolith against the blue midmorning sky. At the moment, Mcilwain and Strickland were climbing into their car, Grant Parker was looking in their general direction, but at that distance he could only see deep-green foliage and the top three-quarters of the massive assembly building. Parker knew that as long as he kept the building behind him, he was going north. The coast would be a couple of miles east, so he adjusted his heading twenty degrees to his right. He estimated his heading would eventually end at his destination. If he miscalculated and arrived at the coast too far south, he would stay hidden in the thick undergrowth and trudge north. Walking a mile through the dense marsh was more arduous than walking fifteen miles under normal conditions. Moreover, the temperature and humidity were climbing rapidly.

Parker had thought it was over when he stepped out of the fire door and into the headlights of the security vehicle. If he had run, a dozen security officers would have rounded him up within seconds, so he had resisted the urge and threw his hand up in a wave while pivoting to his right and walking down the sidewalk of the operations building. He suspected it was close to shift change and the bored officer behind the wheel would be thinking more about getting home than chitchatting with another security officer. The white security vehicle had made a slow wide arc and left the parking lot.

Parker had crossed the circular drop-off lot at the front of the building, moved through the main parking area, and then across the main four-lane road appropriately named Saturn Causeway. He walked along a six-foot fence that separated the two main parking lots of the Vehicle Assembly Building and cut left to Utility Road, which was flanked by two sand packed tracks for hauling rockets and the space shuttle on a crawler-transporter vehicle. Once on the far side of the enormous building, Parker found another fence running parallel to the road. He jogged parallel to the fence line until he crossed over Launcher Road and disappeared into thick trees and undergrowth north of the facility. He had not expected to encounter an electric fence with razor wire, and he was correct. NASA was not a prison, or at least that was not the original intent. At over 140,000 acres, it would be a budget killer to fence in the entire area. If any unauthorized person wanted to enter surreptitiously, they would have to do so in the same manner that he was getting out. Through the snake and alligator infested marsh.

Parker was not immune from the fear of snakes and alligators. He had already seen two snakes and counted over a dozen alligators of various sizes that morning. He hadn't moved far during the night in fear of stumbling over one. What *was* actively attacking him was not alligators and snakes, but mosquitoes. They were relentless. Once he'd pushed through a hundred yards of foliage, he climbed as high as he could in a tree and waited for dawn. Parker remained quiet and still in his perch while a helicopter circled above. The *whop-whop* of the aircraft would grow in intensity, fade, and grow again until it faded away after what seemed to be two hours.

Parker slithered down the tree and crossed a large clearing. He loved the outdoors but not in his current unprepared state. This was the first excursion he had not spent hours planning for. No one had ever chased him like an animal before, and certainly not federal authorities. If he could not make contact and deliver the stolen data, he would probably never see his elderly mother again. Now Parker faced a body of water he wasn't certain he could safely cross. An island sat about a hundred yards offshore. Parker knew he had the physical ability to cross it, but his concern was running across a hungry 300-pound alligator along the way. He took off the security officer uniform shirt and slipped off his shoes and socks. Like Moses at the Red Sea, there was no turning back, and the people after him were just as dangerous and relentless as the Egyptians of the Old Testament. He just wished the swamp waters would part. That's when he saw it. It was just a glint of light. There only for an instant and then gone. He looked up and saw what was reflecting the noonday sun. He estimated it to be at least five hundred feet above him, but not knowing the actual size of the object made it impossible to know for certain. The high-pitched hum could barely be heard over the wind and chorus of wildlife chirps and mosquitoes buzzing around his ear. Parker put aside any thoughts of 300-pound alligators and dove into the murky water.

Danz paced in his office, occasionally stopping in front of the window to look at the Vehicle Assembly Building and beyond. He regretted involving the FBI and wished instead that he had taken Max Rollins's advice and dealt with the problem internally. It was too late to worry about that now. The portable radio sitting in its charger on his desk chirped, breaking the silence and his concentration.

"Command post to all units, status check," came a female voice. The security officers began responding in succession.

"Units one through four still checking the south and east sectors. No contact at this time."

"Units five through nine checking north and west. Same traffic."

A final male voice transmitted, shouting over the brutal thumping of a helicopter rotor. "Helo one checking north near Pad 39B. No visual on subject."

Danz picked up his buzzing cell phone and turned the radio volume down.

"Danz," he said.

A monotone male voice addressed him. "Have you located Parker?"

"I have my entire security force searching right now," Danz said, avoiding the direct question.

"So you haven't then. Do I actually have to explain how upset the committee chairman is right now? He'll have your head if this all goes south."

Danz resumed his pacing. "This is insanity. We had everything under control until he insisted on involving the FBI. It could have been over with by now if we hadn't waited days to fix it."

"What do you expect? He's a politician. He wanted to make an example out of him for anyone else thinking about sabotaging the research, not have a dead body tied to the program."

"It's still a risk," Danz countered. "If the feds find him, he'll run his mouth about the data."

"And," the voice said, concluding Danz's sentence, "we will debunk what he says as we have done many times before. He has no proof, and even if he does, we'll respond that he manufactured it. You know how it works."

The radio chatter caught Danz's attention. It wasn't the even tone of units checking in. The low voices contained an element of excitement. He asked his caller to hold on and turned up the volume.

"Helo one to last unit. Repeat your traffic."

"I say again, command post to all units, the eagle has located the subject approximately two miles north of the complex."

"Helo one to command post, give me the coordinates."

"Coordinates are currently twenty-eight degrees, thirty-six minutes, twenty-two seconds north by eighty degrees, thirty-nine minutes, thirty-four seconds west. Repeating. Twenty-eight, thirty-six, twenty-two north by eighty, thirty-nine, thirty-four west."

"Helo one, copy. Turning west."

"Command post to units five through nine, converge on those coordinates."

The remaining units began chattering and coordinating their response as Danz expelled a sigh of relief and lowered the radio volume.

"We found him," he said into his cell in a confident tone. "I told you we could handle it."

"Good. It's time you called your two agents and get him in custody before he slips through your fingers again."

"Listen," Danz said. "Talk to the chairman again. Now is our opportunity to fix it. The FBI knows he is on the run. For all they'll ever know, Parker's attempt to evade justice resulted in him becoming an alligator's appetizer."

There was a long pause on the line. Danz thought he'd lost the call. "Are you still there?"

"And if they find the body?"

"Do you really think they will search a hundred and forty thousand acres of swamp to find him?" Danz answered. A second long pause followed.

"Just remember, this is on you. Another slip and you're done," said the caller a half second before the line went dead.

Chapter Five

C olson had spotted the black Tahoe in his rearview mirror ten minutes earlier. There was nothing really unusual about a black Tahoe, but this one was fifty yards behind him and matching his speed like it was attached to the Corvette by a steel cable. He decided to give the Tahoe driver a simple test. If he was being followed, Colson would soon know. Their distance from each other would allow a small mistake by the Tahoe driver without him thinking Colson had noticed. He drifted into the left lane of Dunlawton Avenue as he approached the next major intersection and toggled his left turn blinker. He checked his rearview mirror and drifted into the left turn lane. And then there it was—a cardinal sin when tailing someone. The Tahoe's left turn signal started blinking. Colson jerked the Corvette to the right and continued through the intersection. The Tahoe had not yet arrived at the turn lane, so the blinking stopped, and it slipped through the intersection. The driver was an amateur. You never telegraph your intentions during a surveillance unless you want to get burned.

Colson had no idea who would be tailing him or why. He suspected it was possibly an angry ex-employee he had made a theft case on. People had a strange way of blaming him when they got caught red-handed and then fired or prosecuted. It was the way a criminal mind worked. But they had nothing to gain by following him. If confrontation was what they wanted, there were plenty of opportunities. Colson did not live the life of a recluse and never would. He was confident the driver of the Tahoe was not trying to intimidate him or he would be right on his tailpipe. That would be futile because there is not a Tahoe on the planet that could keep up with the 460 horses under the hood of his Stingray. Colson decided it was time to solve the mystery.

Colson did not want the driver to believe he was suspicious or expected the tail. He wanted to know who was following him and why without spooking the driver. However, he wouldn't make it easy. He drifted into the deceleration lane and turned right on Nova Road. The clock on his dash screen read 11:10 a.m. Time for lunch. He checked his mirror and watched the Tahoe make the right, but it had dropped back to nearly hundred yards. Colson turned left into the corner lot of Giuseppe's Pizza. It was a one-story, tan-colored structure that looked more like a mechanics shop than a restaurant, but the hot wings were famous. Colson had eaten his share of them during their yearly vacation weeks when Ann was alive, but he had not given the place a thought since he became a permanent resident. It would have brought back memories he would rather leave in the past.

Colson backed into a space near the entrance and casually climbed out and stretched. He adjusted the ASP expandable baton in the deep side pocket of his BDUs and then walked to the door of the restaurant. The place had not changed since his last visit years ago. There were already a dozen vehicles parked along the front of the building and a handful on the side gravel lot near a deck with round tables and umbrellas. Colson pushed through the door to the familiar aroma of Italian food. The interior of the restaurant had not changed its Pittsburg Steeler's theme. Football memorabilia decorated almost every square inch of the walls with several old license plates from all over the country thrown in for good measure. Football jerseys that had been stretched over the cheap ceiling tiles dangled overhead.

A young girl with a dark tan stepped around the end of the bar with menus in hand and greeted Colson with a smile.

"How many in your party?"

"I'm thinking just two. It may be a few minutes. Is this table OK?" Colson asked, gesturing to a booth in the corner. The girl nodded and sat a menu on the table. Colson slid in the booth against the wall where he could see out of the window on the opposite wall. He knew the layout of the restaurant from eating there every year for three decades. Colson had made a point to survey his surroundings in case he had to act or take cover or get Ann and Nicole to safety. Every cop he knew sat with his or her back to the wall to maintain a view of the entrance whenever possible. Colson took it a step further and deliberately visited the restroom of every restaurant to identify escape routes.

Right on cue, the Tahoe appeared in the gravel lot, made a wide arc, and nosed into a spot. Colson slid the ASP from his pocket and laid it against his right leg on the booth. Whoever was driving would be watching the Corvette in the rearview mirror. One thing Colson knew about all surveillances was that they grew boring very quickly if one was not accustomed to them. Colson checked his watch and decided to give his shadow forty minutes. It only took twenty-five.

Colson was working on his eighth hot wing when a bald man wearing a bright-yellow T-shirt and tan shorts stepped from the Tahoe and slipped on a pair of sunglasses. It was the man who had held the door for him and Lisa at Parker's condo. Colson looked around his section of the restaurant. Most of the patrons were on the deck devouring pizza and wings at wooden round tables beneath yellow and red umbrellas. Only one other couple sat in a booth against the far wall, totally oblivious to Colson. Over his shoulder the young waitress stood at the bar folding napkins around sets of forks and spoons. He stood with the ASP concealed in his palm against his leg and walked to the bar.

"See the guy coming in?" Colson said to the girl, pointing through the large window.

"Sure. Is that your friend?"

Colson nodded "Uh-hu. I gotta hit the rest room. Would you point my booth out to him?"

The girl smiled. "Of course," she said and slid out another menu.

"He won't need that. He's not eating, but you could grab us a couple of drafts. Just point the table out to him please."

The waitress shrugged and continued wrapping silverware. Colson walked toward the back of the restaurant and turned around just out of the waitress's sight, but where he could watch the entrance. The bald man stepped in and removed his sunglasses. He began scanning the interior but was met by the waitress who pointed to Colson's booth. The man threw the waitress a puzzled look as she walked back out of view. The man began walking slowly in the direction she had indicated, turning his head from side to side as if expecting a trap. That's exactly what he got.

Mcilwain slammed the driver's door of the Charger after dropping in the seat next to Strickland. He pushed the start button, snatched at the seatbelt, and then dragged it across his body. It was one thing to be ordered around by his group supervisor or the SAC, but something entirely different to be bossed around by Danz. If he had wanted to work for NASA, that's where he would have applied. He was an FBI agent and only took orders from FBI superiors.

"It pisses me off too," said Strickland as Mcilwain jerked the gear into drive and barked the tires as he launched the Charger toward the exit. Mcilwain sat silent, eyes forward.

"Look," Strickland continued, "we're both going to get our asses chewed if we go back to the office instead of looking for this guy, especially if you approach the SAC fuming about Danz. Chances are ten to one he's already called to complain."

Mcilwain turned right on Kennedy Parkway and gunned the Charger northbound. Strickland was making sense, but he still didn't like it. It wasn't until they crossed the bridge over the Indian River and into Titusville that he spoke.

"Tell me something, Myra."

"What?"

"In your training and working with other agents before me, have you ever—and I mean *ever*—gone to arrest someone without uniformed backup unless there were no other options?

"No."

"OK," he said and held up his left hand as if taking an oath. "And tell me, Agent Strickland, can you swear that you have never located a dangerous criminal charged with espionage and failed to call in for more agents, including but not limited to SWAT?"

Strickland was silent as she looked to her right at the traffic Mcilwain was speeding past. Mcilwain looked to his right for the first time since leaving NASA. "Agent Strickland. The court will hear your answer."

"No," she snapped. "I've never even arrested a documented dangerous person, let alone one charged with espionage without uniformed backup."

Mcilwain slapped the dash with his hand. "I rest my case, your honor. Don't feel bad. Neither have I, unless you want to call a few counterfeiters and tax evaders dangerous enough to warrant a SWAT call out."

"Rest your case? What's your point?" Strickland asked.

"My point *is* that they could have assigned this case to any of the forty-plus agents in our office. A couple of those ex-seals would have made more sense if they wanted a black operation. But who do they send? You and I, who have been working white-collar crime for the past half-dozen years."

"But this guy *is* white collar. A NASA scientist, for heaven's sake," Strickland said.

Mcilwain swung the Charger out of the lane and shot around a tractor-trailer truck. "No disrespect, but you don't seem to understand. If Parker is truly involved in espionage with foreign nations, he's not simply a scientist. There's more than meets the eye here, and he should automatically be considered armed and extremely dangerous."

"Maybe," Strickland said evenly.

"Maybe, hell. There are only two reasons why we've been dragged into this mess. One being that they know he's already vanished and out of the country." Mcilwain paused and wondered if he should even offer the alternative.

Strickland adjusted her frame to face Mcilwain. "What's the other reason?"

Mcilwain shrugged. "Just between us?"

"Of course."

"They don't want him found. Neither the FBI or NASA."

Strickland spread her hand. "Then why all this? The warrant and top-ten, most-wanted list? It doesn't make sense."

Mcilwain checked his mirror and changed lanes again to pass a school bus. "It makes sense if you want to vanish someone and make the world believe he fled for the hills because he's an international fugitive. Everyone would forget all about it in a week, and life would go on as usual, but no more Grant Parker."

Strickland shifted back in her seat and dropped her head back with an exasperated sigh.

"So what are we going to do?"

"Our job," Mcilwain said. "They want us to go through the motions, fine. We'll go through the motions, but we won't find Parker, because they don't want us to."

Strickland said, "And if we do, even accidentally?"

Mcilwain gave her a serious stare. "If we even stumble on a scent of Parker, I'm calling in reinforcements from everywhere. I'm talking animal control all the way up to the marines if I have to. No matter what kind of shit storm they've stuck us into, none of it is worth our lives."

"When you say we go through the motions—"

Mcilwain raised his hand to interrupt and pointed at the file on Strickland's lap. "We start at the obvious starting point. His residence."

Colson waited until the man turned to walk in the direction of the booth before picking up his pace and moving in directly behind him, fast and silent. He stuck the blunt end of the collapsed ASP in the man's lower back at the same instant that he rested his hand on the man's left shoulder. The man immediately stopped, and his body became ridged. He started raising his hands.

"Don't raise your hands," Colson said. "We're just going to have a seat and talk. On the other hand, if you move for the gun, I'm going to ruin everyone's dinner here, including mine."

The bald man shook his head and said, "No problem." Colson checked the couple in the far booth out of the corner of his eye. Their attention clearly remained on each other. He slipped the Glock out of the man's waistband and dropped it in his deep pocket while sliding into the booth. Colson gestured for the man to sit. He did so reluctantly. They remained silent as the waitress slid two beer mugs in front of them.

Colson released a sigh. "You can have the rest of these wings. I've had enough already," he said, sliding the bowl across the table. The bald man's puzzled expression didn't surprise Colson. Then the man glanced at the bowl and back at Colson.

"Don't worry," Colson said. "They're not poisoned. If I was a killer, you'd already be dead."

The man narrowed his gaze at Colson. "How did you know?"

Colson held up his index finger. "Number one. That's a government-issued Tahoe outside if I've ever seen one. Could be local, state, or federal, but my guess is federal. Number two," he extended a second finger, "it's not federal law enforcement you're involved in because my grandson could conduct a better surveillance." Colson extended a final finger, "Number three, you're working alone unless you have a partner who's a complete slug since he's not covering your back. And number four, didn't you realize I would recognize you from the Cloverleaf condo parking garage. *Really?*"

"And how do you know for sure I'm alone, Mr. Colson?" the man asked, revealing his own ability to deduce accurate information about his presumed opponent. Colson ignored the question.

"So you know my name? Inspector Colombo would be proud."

The man lifted a wing from the bowl and took a bite then sipped his beer. He spoke as if reading a resume. "Greyson Walker Colson. Retired major with the Clay County Sheriff's Office where you served with distinction for nearly thirty years. Specialized in undercover narcotics operations, internal affairs investigations, and, finally, on command staff as operations and investigations watch commander. You are currently a private investigator with a commendable, however rambunctious, reputation in Daytona Beach and the greater Volusia County area."

"Don't forget Atlanta as well," Colson added.

The bald man smiled. "Of course not. How you dodged federal prison is comparable to a Houdini act."

Colson returned the man's smile and spread his hands on the tabletop. "Well, you know so much about little ole me. Don't you think it's rude not to formally introduce yourself?"

The man gave Colson a long look before responding. "You can call me Rob for now. I admit I do work for the government, but that's all I can tell you."

Colson chuckled. "I can tell you from personal experience that no one *works* for the government. They're just employed."

The bald man shrugged. "That's all I can say."

"Well, *Rob*," Colson snarled. "Let me make this as clear as the air that swirls around where your brain should be. If I don't want you following me without a good reason you can explain, you'll never get within ten miles of my tail. And if you don't let it go right now, you better make sure your emergency contact information and life insurance policy are current and valid."

Colson slid out of the booth, keeping his glare on Rob. "Your government-issued Glock will be in the bottom of the trash can outside the door. I suggest you finish your lunch and not step a foot outside until I'm long gone. You really don't want to find out how rambunctious I can be when people screw with me." Colson took five steps before Rob spoke and stopped him in his tracks.

"It's about the disappearance of Grant Parker. I'm trying to find him and would appreciate your help."

Colson spun on his heels and studied the bald man who called himself Rob. Colson had dealt with plenty of federal agents in his career, and most of the experiences weren't fun. Rarely did any of them request assistance from a retired local yokel. Most only tolerated county cops because they had to or were ordered to by their superiors for political reasons. Otherwise, they preferred not to lower themselves. Colson knew he was not a human lie detector but considered himself a pretty good judge of character. This guy didn't fit the profile of a federal agent. He was something else, and there was a mysterious reason why an amateur was sent to do the job of a seasoned investigator. Colson enjoyed mysteries as long as they didn't endanger people he loved.

For a moment, Colson considered turning back around and dropping the man's gun in the trash as he had promised. He had already driven to the hotel to break the news in person to Lisa Riley about her half-brother being a fugitive and had dreaded it as much as he would have making a death notification. It's not much easier to hear that a loved one is wanted for espionage and on the run than it is to hear that he is dead. She had cried and denied Parker could ever be involved in such a crime, and Colson had comforted her as if she was his own sister. He told her there was no reason for him to continue the search and explained that if anyone could find him it would be the FBI. She had tearfully said she understood. Lisa had her bag packed and boarding pass in hand ten minutes later, and Colson had escorted her to the rental car. She had thanked him again before she left for the airport. For the same reason Colson had driven to the hotel to break the news, Lisa wanted to be face-to-face when she gave the news to her elderly mother.

Colson knew the man who knew so much about him also had to know the FBI was involved. So why was he wasting his time recruiting a retired dirt-road deputy? Maybe Lisa Riley was right about Parker. Maybe he was not a criminal after all. Maybe Colson would like to find out. Maybe he would regret it. But maybe, in return, the man could help him with Taylor's predicament. A little tit for tat.

"Don't call me Greyson," Colson said and nodded toward the door. "Let's go."

Director Danz stood with his arms crossed, looking at a computer screen. Max Rollins was seated in front of the screen moving a wireless mouse around and occasionally clicking until a page appeared with two blank fields. The office was bug proof and soundproof, as were all the offices in the group unofficially known as GWOAN. Danz was no longer wearing his jacket and tie. He had been sleeping in his office for the past three nights, but he wouldn't call it sleep. It was just hours of dread occasionally interrupted by moments of unconsciousness. As opposed to counting sheep, Danz was unwittingly warding off sleep by counting the congressmen and senators who would be grilling him over an open flame if Parker ever surfaced and ran his mouth. As if Parker wasn't enough, now there was this.

Rollins said, "Give me the coordinates."

"What?" said Danz before noticing the Bluetooth device in Rollins's ear.

Danz watched as Rollins typed in longitude and latitude coordinates into the two fields and hit enter. A blurred image appeared and quickly resolved to crystal clear: the view of earth from space. A moment later, it was as if they were on the nose of a rocket plummeting to the ground at warp speed. It made Danz's stomach flinch. Then, just as quickly as the view zoomed in it came to an abrupt halt. Danz was looking at a satellite view of a bridge over an inner coastal waterway from a height he estimated at about five hundred feet.

"Why are you not watching the marsh area?" said Danz. "There's no way Parker is that far inland."

"We are," said Rollins. "We believe we've discovered Parker's contact. I should say we *know* for certain after our friends at the NSA came through."

"I'm listening."

Rollins cracked his knuckles and kept his eye on the monitor. "NSA pulled records from Parker's cell phone and identified a Virginia number that came back to a Robert Bankston."

Danz shrugged. "What's the significance of that?"

"Look," Rollins blurted and pointed to the monitor. He hovered the mouse over zoom and clicked. The image jumped from five hundred feet to one hundred feet. He then clicked an icon labeled "track." A small red dot appeared center screen, and Rollins adjusted its position with the mouse until it centered on the roof of a moving vehicle and then clicked again. Danz bent down to get a closer view. The red dot remained locked on a black SUV behind a bright blue sports car."

"Where is this," Danz asked.

"Port Orange. The Dunlawton Bridge where it spans the Halifax River. Robert Bankston is driving."

Danz checked his watch. "Tell me the story, Rollins. I don't have all day, and you need to get back to finding Parker. It doesn't matter who his camping buddies are, we're both going to be up shit creek if we can't get Parker back under control and stuffed in a federal penitentiary."

Rollins shook his head but kept his eyes on the monitor. "He's not a camping buddy. Robert Bankston works for the Department of Justice out of Washington. NSA says Parker's relationship with Bankston began only six months ago. Bankston has no reason to be in Daytona except for Parker. Today he met with a private investigator by the name of Colson who was hired by Parker's sister. It's obvious they have joined forces to locate him."

"That doesn't make sense," said Danz. "The Justice Department wouldn't be investigating our work. The administration would literally be shooting themselves in the foot."

"They're not," said Rollins. "The NSA and Justice believe Bankston's gone rogue. None of his activities have been sanctioned by the Department."

"What's his motivation? Why?"

"*Because*," said Rollins, drawing out the word as if attempting to explain gravity to a child, "the NSA has identified numerous communications over the past year between Bankston and Franco Livigni." Rollins clicked the mouse again, pulling the view back to two hundred feet. "And... here it comes," he said pointing again at the monitor. Danz saw a black semi without a trailer a half mile behind the black SUV, switching lanes and closing in fast as the vehicles approached the crest of the bridge.

"Who is Franco Livigni?" Danz asked.

Rollins took his eyes off the screen for the first time and cocked his head at Danz. "I swear, Danz, you need to get out of that office more often and catch up on current events. Livigni is next in line for chairman of the RNC if the right wingers pull off this election."

Danz stood with a blank stare. He never paid much attention to politics and was a little more than put-off by the expression of shock on Rollins's face. He knew Rollins was big into politics but there was no reason for his condescending tone.

"The Republican National Committee," Rollins said, emphasizing each word. He turned his attention back to the monitor shaking his head. "It's a good thing they're letting me take care of the details."

Danz had just about had enough. Insubordination has a way of eliminating the symptoms of sleep deprivation. Rollins had to be reined in. Danz knew if he barked at Rollins, he would realize it was fake. That just wasn't Danz's personality.

He was not a thug, but a scientist—a scientist with strongly held beliefs no matter which political party was in charge. Those beliefs were far more important than politicians who were no more than schoolchildren arguing over a football. He controlled his tone, even though his emotions begged him to scream.

"There is no 'they' to it, Rollins. I selected you out of three other political hacks because you were highly recommended to oversee our group's progress. Don't make me regret that decision. I may not be able to bark orders like some of your military buddies, but I can damn sure write like Shakespeare and can have a memo drafted in three minutes that will send you back to wherever the hell you're from."

Rollins appeared to lose his concentration and freeze. He swiveled in his seat and held his hands up in surrender. "OK, OK, sorry. I've just got a job to do."

"What exactly is the job you have to do with this Bankston character? He's just Parker's contact."

"If we cut off his lifeline, Parker has no one else to turn to. Like I said, they are rogue players with no official ties."

Danz turned and started for the door. "Then just do what you have to do," he said without looking back.

"Hey," Rollins said, "you don't want to see—"

"No," Danz said, throwing up a dismissive hand. "I have my own job to do. And it's *Director* Danz to you. Don't make that mistake again."

Colson hoped his new acquaintance, Rob, had noticed, but he doubted it. Colson had made casual note of the big rig on his way to Giuseppe's. It had been parked in the parking lot of the ABC liquor store on Nova Road. He couldn't resist the satisfaction of seeing the establishment previously known as Cash's Liquors transformed into a reputable business. And there would be nothing out of the ordinary about a big rig parked in the lot if it had a trailer attached for delivery. But even then, smaller trucks usually deliver inventory to package stores, not big rigs. He had dismissed his curious analogy until he caught a glimpse of the semi making a wide swing out of the parking lot after the Tahoe fell in behind him.

They turned south on Dunlawton and crested the Port Orange Bridge. Colson kept one eye on the road and the other on his side mirror. The semi vanished from sight for a few seconds once they crested the bridge, but then reappeared and maintained a constant distance. Colson couldn't decide if the follower was now being followed or if his paranoia was kicking in. There was only one way to know for sure, but the Tahoe was too close behind. Colson dropped the gear into forth and mashed the accelerator. The sudden jolt of speed reminded him he was no longer driving his twenty-year-old, three-hundred-horsepower machine. The blue Stingray shot forward as if the Tahoe had stopped in the middle of the road. He eased off the accelerator and swung right into a vacant lot at the foot of the bridge next to the Bikini Company Swimwear and Hair Waves beauty shop. The Tahoe pulled in after Colson swung the car around so they would meet driver's door to driver's door. Colson waited for the Tahoe's dark tinted window to slip down.

Rob said, "What are we doing?"

Colson stayed silent until the black semi rolled past the lot and continued through the intersection and turned right on A1A. He looked up at an obviously exhausted Rob with his head laying against the headrest. Colson estimated the man hadn't had a decent sleep in days.

"Is there any reason why someone would be following you?"

Rob looked down at Colson through his sunglasses for a long moment and finally nodded. "Sure. I'd be surprised otherwise."

"Then you need to fill me in, Rob, or whatever your name is," Colson said.

"I would, but it's literally a national security issue."

Colson chuckled. "A national security issue? I don't buy that crap for a second."

Rob shrugged. "It's the truth."

"Listen, *Rob,*" Colson said mockingly, "I used to send no fewer than five agents on low-level dope deals, and you're trying to tell me the government sent one shot-out dude dressed like he's going to a Jimmy Buffet concert to track down some number-crunching NASA nerd and calling it a national security crisis?"

"I never said the *feds* sent me."

Colson glared at Rob, seeing only his reflection in the man's sunglasses. He touched the temperature icon on the dashboard screen and set it to sixty degrees. The sun was high and hot and so were the waves of heat and vehicle exhaust rising from the concrete three feet below his open window. He wanted to be sitting under his beach canopy enjoying a cocktail instead of playing mission impossible with a self-appointed secret agent man. Twenty-five years ago, he would have felt very different about such cloak-and-dagger adventures, but they didn't hold the same appeal now. There were legitimate, well-paying cases on the backburner that needed his attention. Colson slid the gear into first and held down the clutch. If he didn't get the right answers to the next three questions, he would release the clutch and be gone so fast that Rob would think he had been parked next to the loudest booster rocket ever made by NASA. Colson needed to watch Rob's eyes.

"Take off your glasses," Colson said flatly. Rob complied and slid them on the dashboard.

"Is Grant Parker a traitor?"

"No."

"Did you search his condo when you were there?"

"Yes. Just moments before you and his sister arrived."

"Did you find the flash drive?"

The question clearly threw Rob. Colson saw his eyes widen slightly. Pay dirt. Colson was not supposed to know anything about a flash drive, but now he not only knew about it, but he also knew its significance to whatever was going on. If Parker wasn't selling secrets, he was a whistle-blower. In that case, Parker's situation just became much more dangerous. Traitors risk prison. Whistle-blowers risk assuming room temperature in remote locations or being launched into orbit with the next deep space probe. Rob took a deep breath and finally answered.

"No. That's the extent that I can answer now. If you don't want to help find Parker, that's fine, but there's nothing else I can tell you now. If you are willing, you'll be compensated of course."

"I don't want the kind of compensation you're talking about."

"You want something though, right?"

"I want a private plane to Ecuador and back. I'll need it for three days. And the trip cannot exist… officially."

"Why?"

"Hey," Colson said with a shrug. "You have your secrets. I have mine."

Rob nodded. "Done."

Colson said, "You know, it sounds to me like you're working off the grid. That can be just as dangerous as whatever your elusive Mr. Parker was doing. It reminds me of someone who's gotten his ass into a crack or two multiple times."

Rob said, "Who might that be?"

Colson slid off his sunglasses and winked. "Me."

Colson turned right out of the lot with the Tahoe on his tail. They cruised under a green sign hanging above the road that read, Wilbur-by-the-Sea and Ponce Inlet, as they approached the traffic light at A1A. Colson never tired of the sights and sounds of Daytona Beach, although he wondered if he would after being a permanent resident for almost four years. One such sight was at the foot of the Port Orange Bridge and South Atlantic Avenue. As a tourist, he looked forward to that particular intersection. The inner coastal waterway beneath the Port Orange Bridge was a beautiful and welcoming sight, but it wasn't until you coasted to the light that it hit home. Dunlawton Boulevard continued past the light, but only for parking and beach access. Just across the intersection, the pavement was covered with a layer of beach sand and the great Atlantic Ocean lay just a hundred yards beyond.

The memories of years gone by swept through Colson's mind in the form of still photos and video clips, such as Ann and Nicole chatting and laughing in celebratory fashion following the long drive. They would point at people and places as if they had never seen the area before in their lives. Mike's Gifts was on the right corner where they would shop on warm evenings after dinner for knickknacks and swimsuits and finish with a stop at Cow Licks ice cream. It had been a family tradition.

Colson almost forgot about the Tahoe behind him and the rogue government agent behind the wheel. Trusting this *Rob* could turn out to be the biggest mistake of his life, but he needed to get to Taylor, and there was no legitimate, aboveboard, or legal way to do so without help. If it meant commandeering a black helicopter gunship from CIA headquarters, he would try it—for his friend.

Colson checked his rearview mirror and could see Rob rolling his fingers on the steering wheel. The Tahoe inched up behind him just as Colson noticed the green left turn arrow had illuminated. He slid the gear into first and pulled into the intersection just one second before he regretted it. Somewhere buried deep in the photos and video clips in his mind emerged a memory of teaching his sixteen-year-old, Nicole, how to drive.

"Even if you have the green light, look both directions before pulling out," he'd reminded her many times.

The traffic on A1A to his right was usually light because there was no outlet, only residential areas and a few restaurants. You were either a millionaire going home to your beach house, or a tourist visiting one of the bars in Ponce Inlet. In fact, Colson had seen no vehicles waiting at the light whatsoever. Now, in the middle of the intersection and a tenth of the way through his left turn, it was as if a solid black wall of death had appeared from nowhere at his passenger side door.

Colson had seen the commercials before. A woman and child riding along, sometimes singing, or listening to the radio while the child played with a doll in the seat next to

Mom. You don't realize the purpose of the commercial until, out of nowhere, the car is obliterated from the side by another car running the stop sign. The screen would go black followed by a warning about distracted driving or driving under the influence or not wearing seat belts. Watching for the first time would at the very least cause a person to flinch. But this was real life, and Colson didn't have time to flinch or think. There was no time for planning or weighing options or considering a clever idea. Only a bolt of lightning would be fast enough to save him, and that's what he got. Electric pulses shot from his brain to his extremities without pausing for Colson's permission or approval, driving his right foot down on the accelerator and jerking his left hand down hard on the wheel.

Still in first gear, the 460-horsepower engine transferred its energy to both of the wide rear tires that instantly bit into the hot Daytona asphalt and shot the Corvette forward as if it had been rammed in the rear by a locomotive at full speed. However, Rob and the Tahoe were not so lucky. Above the howling Corvette engine came a sound that Colson felt just as much as he heard—a sound that no expensive theater surround sound system could ever duplicate. The front grill of the black semi caught the Tahoe dead center, nearly shearing the engine compartment from its chassis.

The Corvette crossed A1A and pirouetted through a double 360 spin as the wide tires lost their bite on the sandy pavement of the beach access road. For a quarter second through the first spin, Colson caught a glimpse of the Tahoe inverted in mid-flight above the lead car at the light. The driver's brain in the stationary car had likely not processed the impact in front of him or the fact that a five-thousand-pound sport utility vehicle was five feet above his head at that moment in time. Through the second spin, Colson got a snapshot of the Tahoe on its passenger side and Rob's body folded in flight like a pocketknife as he was ejected butt first from the driver's window.

The tires of the Corvette spinning on the sandy concrete made the sound of two giant pieces of sandpaper rubbing together. After two revolutions, the spinning slowed and suddenly stopped. Colson shook off a moment of dizziness and jumped from the car. He could see the Tahoe had come to a rest on its roof at least twenty-five yards from the point of impact. People stood on the sidewalk and next to their cars in shock. Others gazed and pointed from behind the plate glass of small businesses along A1A. He didn't see anyone running to help. Professional bystanders. Several were shaking their heads, murmuring, and taking videos with their cell phones. Colson looked north on A1A and caught a glimpse of the semi a quarter mile away, weaving through traffic.

Colson sprinted to the wreck, looking for Rob. A small knot of people stood where the gutter met the sidewalk thirty or so feet beyond. Colson ran to them and found Rob lying motionless. One heavyset man wearing a blue tank top and black shorts cradled Rob's head in his hands. Colson knelt next to him and pressed two fingers against Rob's carotid artery. The man in the tank top looked at Colson.

"He's still breathing."

Chapter Six

Grant Parker had survived day two of his escape. He moved quickly to the opposite side of the small island and took cover once again. The helicopter and drone sounds increased in addition to the new sounds of fast-moving fan boats and speedboats. He had collected small vines as he made his trek, jerking them free from trees and undergrowth, and found a tall live oak to climb. He knew the boats would cease circling the island soon enough, and the searchers would come aground. But the sun would be setting within an hour, making a foot search through the thick undergrowth a difficult and time-consuming task. Then there were the mosquitoes that would begin to swarm for their nightly feast. Parker's best guess was that they would set up a perimeter offshore and wait until morning. They had to know he was completely trapped and surrounded.

In the limbs of the live oak were bushels of Spanish moss, drooping off its long limbs like dreadlocks. Parker had set to making a blanket, weaving the vines through clumps of the prickly moss until it resembled a sloppy, misshapen pancake. The sun sank and the burnt-orange glow of the atmosphere slowly morphed to a deep blue and finally to the black of night. The sound of the boat engines offshore had gone from idle to off, but they were still there. The moon was bright with a few passing clouds at first, but as the night progressed, the clouds moved in and he heard the distant rumble of thunder. He would count the seconds between the quick flashes of lightning and the sound of the thunder. One-thousand-one, one-thousand-two, one-thousand-three. Boom. The count had shortened every few minutes and rain would soon be closing in. He waited while the sprinkles became drops, the drops became fat drops, and the fat drops grew in number to a full-on deluge.

Before nightfall, Parker had scoped out the opposite side of the island and determined where he would go. It had to be northeast. The main marsh area appeared to be farther away from the opposite side of the island, but manageable. He had waited thirty minutes after the hard rain began and made his way to the bank alongside a fallen tree trunk. One of the speedboats was at his eleven o'clock position, about a hundred yards out. They would not be able to keep a visual on the entire island if they were in too close. He wondered if the NASA security officers had thought to bring their rain gear with them. If not, they were going to be as soaked and miserable as he was. He waded waist deep next to the log, dragging his Spanish moss blanket behind him. Once neck deep, he pulled the blanket over his head and commenced his slow swim to the distant marsh. North and east. A half-mile distant. He said a prayer of thanks for being spared the mosquitoes during his submerged escape and then said a second prayer, pleading that the alligators and snakes would not be interested in a midnight snack.

Twenty hours later, Parker had plodded another four miles through the thick brush and over streams where his feet sank in a sandy mush, creating a strong suction every time he lifted his feet. He was hot, sweaty, and thirsty. He drank as much rainwater as he could catch in his mouth and then slurped the rain caught on every wide palm leaf he passed. He climbed another oak and waited for the sun. Parker reacquired his position of northeast and continued. He had no way of knowing for certain how long it would take, but guessed another two days before he arrived. It was almost impossible to estimate. Twenty minutes by car, maybe a full day if he walked a flat road, but in the marsh where every plant was an obstruction and the spongy soil was a hindrance, it was just a guess. However, Parker knew if he could get there, he would no longer be a nerdy statistician on the run. He would be king.

Agent Strickland and Mcilwain arrived at the Cloverleaf Condominiums at 10:00 a.m., trailed by two additional agents in a second unmarked Charger and two marked Volusia County Sheriff's Office units. One of which stopped behind Strickland and Mcilwain as the other unmarked Charger and sheriff's unit continued to the parking garage. They walked into the ground floor lobby where a fiftyish woman stood behind a long counter with a dark wood countertop. Her hair was fashionably short and white, and her skin was well tanned, but not wrinkled. She was reading something out of view on the counter and peaked over her small reading glasses as the two official-looking types and a uniformed deputy approached. She offered a nervous smile. The Cloverleaf was a respectable community not known for trouble.

Mcilwain and Strickland returned her smile, but the deputy remained stone-faced and came to a halt in an interview stance to the side. Mcilwain read the gold plastic tag on the woman's blouse. Her name was Mona and the word "Management" was stenciled beneath it. They produced their credentials and held them close enough for Mona to examine. She tilted her head back slightly to read through the lower portion of the bifocals. Mcilwain glanced at Strickland and nodded for her to make the introductions—woman to woman.

She said, "I'm Agent Strickland, and this is Agent Mcilwain with the FBI, Mrs..."

The woman hesitated for a moment, not recognizing the prompt at first. "Oh, Parks, but everyone just calls me, Mona. Is everything OK?"

Strickland said, "I'm sure it is. Are you the manager?"

"Day manager, yes."

"Is your security on duty?"

"If he hasn't gone to lunch. I'll radio him. Are you sure there's nothing wrong?" Mona reached for a walkie-talkie and pressed a button on the side. Strickland didn't reply. After a short *cleek* sound, she said into the radio, "Johnny, can you come to the office?"

"Ten-four," came a static reply and within five seconds, a young man around the age of nineteen popped through the door wearing dark-blue uniform pants and a white shirt with blue patches on both arms displaying an eagle with wings spread and the word "security" beneath. The young security officer stopped on a dime at the sight of the uniformed deputy and the two agents. Mcilwain shook his hand. The boy probably wanted to be a cop but was still too young to carry a gun. They needed all the cooperation they could get if they were to find Parker, so Mcilwain wanted to make the young man feel like he played an important part.

"I'm Agent Mcilwain with the FBI," he said and held up a folded document. "We need your help today."

The boy looked at the deputy and back to Mcilwain and pointed at his own chest as if amazed an FBI agent would give him the time of day and said, "Me?"

"I need the override door lock code for condo seven zero eight. We have a search warrant."

Day Manager Mona spoke up. "That's Grant Parker's condo. Is he OK?"

Strickland said, "We hope so ma'am. We're here to check."

Security Boy Johnny looked at the deputy. "Can I do that?"

The deputy responded with a stone-faced nod.

Mona said, "His sister's been calling, and we sent John up to check, but there was no answer. And his car hasn't moved."

Johnny eagerly jumped back into the discussion. "I've been checking every day. I even checked the hood of his car to see if it's warm. It hasn't moved at all."

Mcilwain gave Johnny a quick nod, but the kid's enthusiasm had already become a little irritating. Then again, if swearing him in as a junior detective was required to keep him on his toes and on constant look out for Parker, he'd put up with it for now. He pulled a notepad from his coat pocket, clicked open his pen, and handed them to Johnny.

"Good work, Johnny. Now the master override code, please."

Johnny eagerly wrote down the number.

"Just one more thing," Mcilwain said, handing both Mona and Johnny a business card. "Well, maybe two things. First, it is extremely important that you contact me immediately if and when Mr. Parker returns."

Johnny took the card, pinching it by its corners with both thumbs and index fingers as if reading his favorite novel or studying the curves of a Playboy centerfold. He said without looking up, "What's the second thing?"

"This deputy is going to stay here with you until we get inside and make sure everything is OK. I'll radio him once we do, but in the meantime, neither of you are permitted to make any phone calls."

Without another word, Mcilwain and Strickland spun on their heels and marched to the elevator.

A fire truck, a boxy fire rescue vehicle, two ambulances, and two Volusia County Sheriff's Office units had the intersection of Dunlawton Boulevard and A1A totally shut down for two hours. Two sheriff's STEP units, or Special Traffic Enforcement Patrol, were on the scene to gather physical evidence of the hit and run, and to interview witnesses. What would have been typical, lazy beach traffic on a normal day became complete bedlam. One sheriff's unit was parked sideways on Dunlawton, directing all traffic descending the Port Orange Bridge to turn around while drivers on A1A were forced to take it upon themselves and turn around whenever they were able to inch out of line. Rob had been placed in a neck brace, hoisted onto a gurney, and then rushed from the scene under a screaming siren that alternated in tone and pitch as it weaved through the line of traffic. The remaining ambulance workers and paramedics checked those in close proximity to the accident. The older man who had the misfortune of driving the car the Tahoe flew over was bleeding from the head after a side mirror had been sheared off and rocketed through his windshield in an explosion of glass. Two young bikini-clad women on the sidewalk had caught safety glass shrapnel in their bare arms and legs. All looked as if they were suffering from shock while their wounds were being bound with gauze.

A wrecker arrived and unceremoniously flipped and dragged the Tahoe onto its side with heavy chains. The screeching protest of metal against concrete was sickening. The flip had flattened three of the SUV's tires with the remaining wheel and tire resting in a crater it had created in the hood of a KIA parked in the Dolphin Beach Club condos. The two STEP deputies stood ten feet apart with semicircles of witnesses giving their eyewitness accounts of the incident. Colson stood to the side, knowing he should have joined one of the semicircles. The only information he could offer was a snapshot of the collision and the fact that they would have had to call the meat wagon if it had been him instead of Rob. The pedestrians and other drivers witnessed far more than he had, but there was a small piece of information no one else was aware of: that they had been followed and stalked, and the attempt on their lives had been deliberate. The attempt would have been successful if the semi had hit both vehicles as intended. Colson took a step toward the closest semicircle and stopped. Maybe he would just listen. He could always inject his story later.

He took another step to get closer, just like the busybody bystanders who always make him sick to his stomach. The deputy was asking the group to not all speak at once. He took the logical approach and started with the lady on the far left and then worked his way around. She was holding a child's hand and fanning herself with the other.

"We were just waiting for the light to turn so we could cross. He was going so fast. He could have killed my granddaughter."

The deputy didn't look up from his pad. "Did you see the driver or a tag?"

"No."

A man wearing prescription glasses, a plaid shirt, tan shorts, and a floppy hat spoke up. He stood next to the woman and put his arm around her. "There was no tag or markings or numbers anywhere on the truck."

The deputy nodded and made a note. The man added, "But there *had* been letters."

The deputy looked up from his pad. "What do you mean there *had* been letters? Either there was or there wasn't."

"And the semi has not always been black. It used to be white," the man continued.

"I'm not following you, sir."

"Son, I've worked on cars all my life. Mostly body work. If you're going to paint anything with stickers or decals, you have to heat them off or the paint job will look like crap. After it hit the SUV, it lost its top coat of paint in several places around the grill, and I could see the white base coat."

The deputy scribbled on his pad and said, "What about letters? What and where were they?"

"Just below the side door in the bottom left about eight inches high. I didn't notice them until it went past and the sun caught it just right. The outline of letters 'ESD' stood out like a sore thumb. Someone was lazy and did a sloppy job."

Colson made a mental note and stepped back to the curb. He knew he could confide in Lieutenant Cantrell and Sheriff Langston, so there was no need in telling the deputy. He played the conversation in his head. *Yes, I had just met the driver who called himself Rob at a pizza place and found out he was a secret federal agent and then this mysterious, black semi followed us and tried to kill us both.* The deputy would write out a police officer's committal and ship him off for evaluation at the county loony bin. Maybe the letters meant something. Maybe they meant nothing. But a wise man would want to find out before surrendering himself to the men in white coats.

Colson walked back to his car and eased onto A1A north. At least the direction he needed to go wasn't blocked. He felt bad for Rob, or whatever his name was, and any family he had. Maybe he would make it and fill him in on the grand conspiracy, but his recovery didn't look promising. It was back to the drawing board for his ticket to Ecuador. He had almost had it in his hand.

Mcilwain followed Strickland off the elevator and down the hallway to condo 708. The two additional FBI agents and uniformed deputy stood near the door chatting in low inside voices. Three white mail delivery boxes they had commandeered from the field office sat stacked inside each other at Parker's front door. The top box contained stacks of yellow envelopes and plastic evidence bags of various sizes. The voices of the men at the door trailed off as Mcilwain and Strickland stepped up.

Agent number one said, "Parker's car is on this floor in the parking garage."

Strickland said, "Does the hood feel warm?"

"No."

Mcilwain said, "Was a nineteen year old boy's palm prints all over it?"

"What?"

Strickland said, "He's just trying to be funny."

Mcilwain stood off to the side of the door with Strickland behind agents one and two and the deputy behind her in a proper tactical entry formation. Mcilwain knocked and waited and listened. Nothing. He repeated the process twice more and added a verbal announcement.

"Grant Parker, FBI. We have a search warrant. Please come to the door." He glanced back at Strickland, nodded, and punched in the numbers Security Boy Johnny had provided and pushed the door open, gun at low ready.

They took little note of the terracotta tile or high ceilings or the chandelier or the ocean view that Colson had admired. Their mission was far different than looking for a misplaced brother. They were conducting a search warrant to find or determine the whereabouts of a potentially dangerous traitor. Mcilwain broke left and Strickland broke right, followed in the same fashion by Agent 1, Agent 2, and the deputy. It took a total of five seconds to clear the living room–kitchen combination. Mcilwain and Agent 1 cleared the bedrooms on the left while Strickland and Agent 2 cleared the master bedroom and bath. The deputy dragged the white boxes into the room and stood guard at the front door.

Twenty-two minutes into the search, Mcilwain heard Strickland call his name. They met back in the living room. She was holding a ceramic lid.

Mcilwain said, "I'm not so certain I'd consider a toilet lid as evidence unless it was smeared with the blood of a murder victim."

Strickland flipped the lid over. Mcilwain took a step closer. "What's that?"

"A flash drive case without a flash drive. Looks like it was hot glued to the underside."

Mcilwain shrugged. "A lot of good that does us. But take it anyway. At the very least, it shows he was hiding something and will demonstrate to the jury that the something he was hiding was the information he was selling. Are you done with your side? Haven't you found anything else in the bedroom? Notes, records of any type, checkbook, bank statements—anything?"

Strickland shook her head. "Not even a laptop. Just a tent under the bed and a bunch of outdoorsy type clothing, boots, and a vacuum cleaner. The guy is a clean freak."

Agent 2 said, "No porn or girly pictures, no huge ticket items, no computer tablet or smartphone. No nothing. It's almost *too* clean. I don't know how much your guy was getting paid to sell secrets to the Chicoms, but they either weren't compensating him well, or he has an account in the Caymans. Have you looked there? He's probably on the beach sipping a cocktail and laughing his ass off."

Mcilwain said nothing. Strickland stepped over and laid the toilet tank lid in the top white box. She brushed her hands together as if she had completed an enormous task and said, "Looks like we brought too many boxes."

Mcilwain just stood there thinking and not responding. Then he said, "We're not finished. We're doing it again." Agent's one and two groaned. "Except we switch." He pointed at agent number two. "You and Strickland search the area we searched, and we'll search yours. We missed something."

"Like lunch," Agent 1 said sarcastically.

Mcilwain said, "Let's go."

Thirty minutes later, they stood facing each other in the living room. Mcilwain and Agent 1 now stood on the side where Strickland and Agent 2 had stood earlier and vice versa.

The deputy leaned up against the front door with his arms crossed, looking on.

Strickland said, "Anything?"

Mcilwain stood with his hands on his hips and blew out an exasperated breath. "No. Same as you found. Outdoor clothes, shoes, boots, a tent, and a vacuum cleaner. Nothing in the boots or shoes or under the sheets or shoved between the mattress and box spring. Nothing."

Strickland said, "I tell you the guy is a clean freak. There was even a vacuum cleaner in the guest bedroom."

The deputy pushed off the wall and stepped closer into the room. He said, "I know I'm sticking my nose into your business, but if I could suggest—"

Mcilwain raised his hand to stop him. "Thanks, but we're done here. I don't know why we've busted our ass this much. Let Stan or Danz or whatever the hell his name is find his boy." Mcilwain threw his hands up while walking past the deputy and then snatched the condo door open. "They obviously don't want *us* to find him." He paused and pulled a copy of the search warrant from his jacket, tossing it inside like a badly folded paper airplane. "Put the copy on the coffee table. Be sure to write down that we took his damn toilet tank lid."

Strickland trailed behind Mcilwain, followed by agent number one. As Agent 1 walked through the door, the deputy said, "What's his problem?"

Agent 1 slowed, but didn't stop. "It's an FBI thing. You wouldn't understand."

Agent 2 stayed behind to note what had been taken on the search warrant copy and collected the boxes and envelopes and toilet tank cover. Mcilwain shoved his way through the parking garage door to check Parker's car for himself. Next to the car sat a white golf cart and next to it stood Security Boy Johnny. Mcilwain marched toward the car while looking the garage up and down.

He said to Johnny, "As nice as this complex is, I can't believe they didn't install security cameras."

Johnny smiled. "They did."

Mcilwain stopped and turned in circles and then settled his gaze back on Johnny. "Really, 'cause I haven't seen any anywhere."

"That's right. It was our security chief's idea. He said that exposed cameras get vandalized or avoided." He pointed upward. "They are in some of the fake sprinkler heads and in all the exit signs hanging at the hall doors. There's over fifty of them."

Mcilwain's mood brightened. "Are they recorded to a hard drive?"

"Yep."

"What's the retention?"

"The what?"

"How far back. How many days until they overwrite themselves?"

"Thirty, I think."

The door to the hallway swung open and Agent 2 walked out wearing one blue surgical glove and carrying the white mailboxes. He wore a smirk as he walked toward Mcilwain. Strickland was saying something to Johnny about the cameras. Agent 1 was walking around Parker's Challenger, either admiring the sports car or looking for clues. Mcilwain called to him.

"Don't bother with a tow truck and don't start an impound yet. Forensics will have it picked up and work on it later when it can be moved to a clean environment."

"Got it," he said, still walking around the car.

Agent 2 stopped in front of Mcilwain and sat the boxes on the concrete without a word. The agent eyed him for a long second until Mcilwain lost his patience and held his arms out wide.

"What?" he blurted.

Agent 2 said, "Well, after you guys dressed down the deputy and walked out, I asked him what he was going to say."

Mcilwain dropped his arms to his side. "And?"

"He thought having two vacuum cleaners for a condo that size was strange. Said he was out with their narcotics guys on a search warrant about a year ago and they couldn't find any dope although they had just sent in a credible CI who came straight out of the crack house saying he had seen plenty inside. It was exactly thirty seconds later that they busted through the door down and couldn't figure out where the dope was. They were all scratching their heads until one of the narcs remembered a vacuum cleaner in one of the closets. When they rolled it out to the living room and unzipped the catch bag, a hundred crack rocks fell out. The vacuum in Parker's bedroom had one of those clear canisters, but the one in the guest bedroom had a regular bag."

Agent 2 squatted and reached into the top mailbox and pulled out a manila envelope. With his gloved hand, he reached in and produced a small, inch-long, black stick. Mcilwain's impatience evaporated the instant he realized what he was looking at.

"A flash drive?"

Agent 2 nodded. "The flash drive case under the tank lid was either a decoy to make us think nothing was there or it held a backup copy."

The deputy walked into the garage and headed toward his marked unit. As he opened his door, Mcilwain called out to him.

"Ah, thanks deputy." The deputy eased himself behind the wheel and gave Mcilwain a lazy glance.

He said, "No problem. It's a street cop thing. You wouldn't understand." The deputy clicked the door shut and started the engine. Mcilwain turned to where Strickland and the boy were still chatting.

He said, "Myra," and held out the flash drive. "Can you get this to forensics ASAP? I'll call for an agent to pick me up later. Officer Johnny and I have about a week's worth of surveillance video to watch."

A touch of fall was in the air. Colson knew the temperature in Clay County Georgia would be at least fifteen degrees cooler with crisp mornings and cool afternoons. The weather lady said the temperature in Daytona Beach would reach eighty-four that day, and if it wasn't for Taylor's predicament and mad scientists and mac trucks and secret agents named Rob, he would be enjoying another visit with Beverly on the beach. Colson loved Daytona at that time of the year. The water might be turning a little too cool for a dip, but the afternoons were always warm, and the beach was a wide-open playground with all the kids back in school.

Colson propped his heels up on his balcony railing and pulled up Google search on his tablet. With very light vehicle traffic on the beach and fewer boom boxes playing, or whatever they called them now, the sound of the surf was not as muffled. Colson heard the sad tinkling sound of the ice-cream truck as it trolled slowly south to north on the sandy beach road. He couldn't identify the tune, but it wasn't "Twinkle, Twinkle Little Star" star. It almost sounded like a dark tune from a mystery movie. He wondered if the selection of forlorn music was deliberate due to his waning seasonal business, or if it was a random selection from his subconscious mind.

He chose a website to define acronyms and typed ESD. The results were quick but numerous. Easily over a hundred suggestions including *electrostatic discharge, electronic software division, executive staff director, energy spectral density, estimated start date, epilepsy spectrum disorder,* and on and on down the page. Colson closed the tab and sat the tablet on the plastic side table. He rubbed his eyes. For all he knew, the acronym could be a specialty restaurant's slogan: *Eat Snails Daily.* The only logical thing was it involved Grant Parker not being found. At least not found by the wrong people such as Rob... and presumably himself.

Colson grabbed his phone and pulled up recent calls then touched the call icon. After three rings there was an answer.

He said, "Lisa, this is Grey Colson. How are you holding up?"

Her voice seemed measured with the excitement of possible good news, but deadened with the likelihood of bad news. "Did you find out anything?"

"Only that us and the feds are not the only people looking for Grant. Did he ever mention an acquaintance named Rob?

"Not that I remember. Does he have any information about where Grant is?"

"Not that he's letting on. I'll tell you more about that later but I need you to try and think about anything Grant may have said about his job."

Lisa sighed into the phone. "I really don't know any more than what we talked about in Daytona."

"Do you remember if he ever mentioned ESD? Maybe as an acronym for anything?"

The line was silent for a few seconds as if Lisa was searching her memory. "I've never heard anything about ESD. I have no idea. Is it important?"

"Like I mentioned, everything is important, but it's possible ESD, whatever it is, has nothing to do with it. Did he ever mention coworkers or who his supervisor is? How about his attitude toward his work assignment?"

"It only seemed like he wasn't as happy as he had been when they hired him. But aren't we all that way? He never talked much about work when he visited other than telling Mom he was doing well and making plenty of money. He was a loner for the most part and didn't socialize with coworkers. At least, not that he talked about."

"So he didn't praise his boss or complain about him?" Colson asked.

"No. No complaints and no compliments. He didn't mention a name. Wait. There's a business card on Mom's side table. Let me get it."

Colson could hear Lisa moving through the house. She mumbled something, and Colson heard a feeble female voice respond. Grant's and Lisa's mother no doubt. Lisa came back on the line.

"OK, I have his business card if that'll help."

Colson pulled the phone away from his hear when an incoming call alert beeped. He looked at the number and then got back on with Lisa. "I have to take this call. Can you take a clear photo of the card and text it to me?"

"Sure," she said, and Colson touched the screen to switch calls.

Colson said, "Hello," and heard the hissing and popping he expected.

Colonel Guerra said. "It has been yet another three days, Senor Colson. Only a few remain if you want to help your friend."

Colson said, "You told me ten days. I'm working on it."

"A friendly reminder is always helpful, wouldn't you agree?"

"I would agree that you are desperate, Guerra. You're acting like the money is yours for the taking, not the courts. And I use the term 'court' loosely."

Guerra ignored Colson's poke. "I simply offer a kind reminder because your friend, Taylor, is not in the best health. The sooner you wire the funds, the sooner he will back home and resting in his own bed."

Colson said through clinched teeth, "Allow me to offer you a kind reminder, *Colonel*. An inmate in the custody and care of any institution is that institution's responsibility. I will hold you personally responsible for his safety and—"

"Let me assure you, Mr. Colson. Taylor is quite safe. As a measure of good faith, Taylor has been transferred to the finest medical facility at Quito Prison. But the sooner you—"

"Don't cut me off, Guerra. If anything happens to Taylor, you'll be getting no money whatsoever. And if that does happen, you won't be getting a wire transfer, but a personal visit from me, and you won't know how or when to expect it."

Colson pressed the "end call" button before Guerra could respond and stared out at the Atlantic thinking. The waves piled over themselves and onto the beach in constant rhythm. He would gladly pay Taylor's ransom if he had it, but he didn't. If only he hadn't retired and still had the active contacts he used to have with almost every state and federal agency. But if he hadn't retired, he wouldn't even know Taylor. There was always a give and take or tit for tat or quid pro quo that he could have used. Nothing illegal, but a system of scratching one back to expedite this or that in return for the same courtesy later. However, thinking about the bad old days was a waste of time. The only option at that point was going to Ecuador and making his plea to the US Embassy directly. He would complain about the exorbitant bail and convince them to demand Taylor's release or a more reasonable bail amount. At least he could make the effort. His frustration with Guerra had made him forget about Lisa's call.

He grabbed his phone and pulled up his text messages and then touched the photo to enlarge it. It was a white business card with the blue-and-red NASA logo at the top left. Centered below in all capital letters was "National Aeronautics and Space Administration." Beneath was the location without a specific address: "Kennedy Space Flight Center." On the bottom to the left was written, "Grant Parker, PhD" with the single phrase "Research and Development" shown beneath his name.

R&D thought Colson. Research and Development. There were too many acronyms to keep up with, like the hundred-plus acronyms that made his eyes hurt earlier. Even his old agency used them. There was CCSO for the Clay County Sheriff's Office, SWAT for Special Weapons, and Tactics and CID for the Criminal Investigation Division. More than Colson could remember. But then something caught his eye. On the right bottom portion of the card, there was a name. Just as Colson's sheriff's name used to be displayed on his own business cards: "Representing Sheriff Neil Warren." The man listed on Parker's card would be his top boss. "Dr. Nicholas Danz, Director." But the name was not what caught his eye. It was what Danz was the director of: the "Earth Science Division."ESD.

Florida Hospital Oceanside was located on South Atlantic Avenue or A1A in Ormond Beach. It was a straight shot north of the Port Orange Bridge and a solid twenty-five-minute drive in normal traffic—ten minutes when riding in the rear of an ambulance running lights and siren. Two paramedics rolled Robert Bankston's limp body through two automatic sliding glass doors with his neck brace, an oxygen mask over his mouth and nose, and an IV hanging from a shiny steel hook attached to the gurney. They quickly followed a nurse down a short hall into triage where a trauma surgeon had just scrubbed and stood ready after snapping on a pair of blue nitrile gloves.

A trickle of blood ran from Bankston's mouth and nose, and bright-red road rash trickled blood from the exposed areas of his right arm and leg. Otherwise, he did not appear seriously hurt, suggesting his injuries were more internal due to severe blunt trauma. The surgeon looked on as the nurse and an attendant cut Bankston's shorts and Margaritaville T-shirt off with safety scissors and a third nurse pealed the backs off of probes and stuck them to his chest. His breathing was dangerously shallow. The surgeon probed Bankston's body with his hands, checking for broken bones. He had seven at first count. He inserted a ventilator tube and ordered an emergency x-ray and MRI. A female in scrubs and blue gloves hustled into the operating room and prepared her weight calculations for anesthesia in the event Rob survived long enough for surgery.

A uniform Volusia County deputy stood in the threshold of the trauma room making notes on a small pad, seemingly oblivious to the surrounding activity. He looked up when the surgeon spoke.

"Do we have his name?"

The deputy flipped back a page in his pad. "From his license at the scene, it's Robert Bankston."

The surgeon turned his attention back to his patient and lightly patted his cheek. "Squeeze my hand if you hear me, Robert?" Nothing. That was no surprise at that point.

The surgeon said, "Has his family been notified?"

The deputy shook his head. "None have been identified yet."

The surgeon straightened his back as they rolled the gurney out. "My suggestion is that you continue trying."

Colson took the same route Mcilwain and Strickland had taken to Operations Support Building II. It had been easy enough to find Director Danz's office number on the Kennedy Space Center website. He didn't know that much about the space center but he had enough sense to know it covered a lot of ground. Since no specific office location for Danz was listed on the official website, he needed to improvise. Colson knew that NASA was not the NSA or CIA, so inquiring about specific office locations over the phone shouldn't be that big of a deal. On the other hand, terrorism was on everyone's mind and some nobody calling and asking for directions might raise suspicion. So he had to act like a somebody. Not someone famous but someone expected. He counted on a secretary screening all of Danz's calls. He was correct, and she happily gave directions to him, the lost UPS driver that he claimed to be.

Colson turned left off of Kennedy Parkway and encountered the guard shack with its overhang, sliding window, and red-stripped arm blocking the road. The older security officer slid open the window and looked at Colson over his bifocals, but only after taking a long look at the gleaming blue Corvette.

The guard said, "Help you?"

Colson already had his wallet out. He smiled and handed it to the guard without a word and let his arm hang out over the door. The guard took it and tilted his head back to read. Colson knew he would see his driver's license behind a clear plastic sleeve and a small flap of felt on the opposite side. He counted on him being thorough. At least curious. The guard flipped the felt flap aside. He would see the badge given to him by Sheriff Langston.

Colson finally said, "Grey Colson to see Director Danz."

The guard handed Colson the wallet back and hesitated before raising the gate arm, giving the Corvette another once-over.

He said, "The sheriff must be paying you guys good money these days."

Colson patted the driver's door and said, "Courtesy of your local drug dealer." The guard half smiled and touched something out of sight that raised the gate arm. Colson pulled forward and caught the guard in the rearview mirror, punching numbers into a cordless phone. He took the same route as Mcilwain and Strickland had past Contractor Road and Instrumentation Road. Since he didn't have government plates, Colson didn't park in the front circular drive, but found a parking space on the side lot among several official-looking sedans, all with government plates. He removed his ASP expandable baton from the center console and slid it in his deep side pocket. He felt naked without it. As Mcilwain and Strickland had done, he got past the scrutiny of the ground floor receptionist and up the elevator to the double office doors. He paused at the placard with Danz's name, title, and photo before pulling one of the doors open and walking up to the secretary. Colson smiled but didn't present his ID. It was becoming a pain.

He said, "Grey Colson to see Director Danz."

The secretary was several years older than the receptionist. That made sense: more senior, higher floor, better job, and better pay. She was not so old that she wasn't attractive, but old enough not to be silly or flippant. She was probably in her forties. Her hair was in a bun, and she sat in front of a wide-screen computer wearing a blue pantsuit. Sitting proudly at the edge of her desk was a nameplate engraved with Deborah Blackwell in gold against a black background. She didn't look up, but said, "You don't have an appointment."

"That's correct."

"May I ask what this is regarding?"

"He seems to have misplaced one of his scientists, Grant Parker, and I'm here to help find him."

The secretary looked up from her computer. "Please take a seat, and I'll see if he can speak with you."

Colson decided instead to stroll over and examine the large wall photo of the earth from space. He counted the seconds in his head. How long would it take Danz to decide to speak with him or not? The secretary had already called and mumbled into her phone and immediately hung up. If he was in a meeting, he would expect her to tell him right away and be rid of him, but almost a minute had passed and nothing. A minute and fifty seconds passed and then Colson heard the double doors swoosh open behind him. Colson glanced around at a man who walked in and took a seat in one of the steel-framed chairs without speaking a word to the receptionist. He wore dark dress pants, a long-sleeve white dress shirt with the sleeves rolled to his elbows, and a loosened tie.

Colson turned his attention back to the photo. Thirty more long seconds passed without the secretary or the man with the loose tie saying a word. The only sensation he had was the hole being bored into his back by the man staring at him. Colson adjusted his angle and put the man in the reflection of the glass covering the large photo, thus confirming his suspicion. With the exception of checking his watch every three seconds, he wouldn't take his eyes of Colson's back. He was becoming fidgety, adjusting in his seat, and began looking from Colson to the double doors and back. He wasn't looking at Danz's office door in anticipation of an appointment, but at the doors leading to the elevator he had walked through four minutes earlier. He was waiting for something or someone else. At four minutes and five seconds, a soft beep came from the secretary's phone. She picked up. There was more mumbling and then a loud and clear, "Yes, sir." She called out to Colson.

"Mr. Colson. He should be able to see you in the next ten minutes."

"Fine, thanks," he said, not taking his eyes off the man's reflection. The man seemed to relax in his chair, stopped checking his watch, and rested his arms on the chrome framed armrests.

Colson had interviewed countless suspects in his three-decade-long career and had been able to glean as much information from their body language as from what they'd said. A person normally didn't walk into an office and plop down on a chair without having any interaction with the secretary or the person he obviously came to see. Even if that person was expected, there would be some type of interaction, if nothing more than "I'll be right with you" from the secretary. Colson spun on his heels and glared at the man who instantly jerked his eyes downward, but he was a fraction of a second too late. He then looked over to the secretary and said.

"You know, I forgot I left a casserole in the oven. Tell Nick we'll talk later."

The man with the loose tie checked his watch again as Colson walked past and pushed through the double doors and then walked to the elevator. He pushed the button for the lobby and rocked back and forth on his heels. The man would have to wait a few seconds or his attempted subterfuge would be painfully obvious. The elevator could be anywhere between the lobby and the top floor, so there was no way to estimate when it would arrive, but he suspected Mr. Loose Tie couldn't wait more than five seconds. It didn't take even that long. Colson heard the door open behind him and felt the man stop at his side. Colson slipped his hand around the ASP in his pocket. The man was breathing audibly, as if he had just climbed a flight of stairs.

The man wiped his brow with the back of his hand and said, "Whew, it's been damn hot today. Where's the water cooler?"

Colson heard a door opening at the end of the silent hallway. Two nerdy-looking guys in white lab coats stepped out. A soft *ding* and an illuminated green arrow above alerted Colson that his ride had arrived. The two men began walking quickly toward them as Colson stepped on the elevator and pressed the "L" for lobby. He turned to see the man with the loose tie looking in the direction of the approaching nerds instead of stepping in behind him.

Colson said, "What was your question?"

The man jerked his head in response. "What? I said where's the water cooler?"

The elevator doors began their mechanical slid inward. The man stood motionless with his arms dangling stupidly at his side. Colson gave him a smirk, and as the final inch of open space disappeared he said, "In Canada."

Max Rollins stormed past Danz's secretary and into his office with the two nerds following in their white lab coats. Danz sat on the corner of his desk with a blank look on his face. The two nerds stood just inside the door. Danz waited until the door was closed completely before he spoke. He turned his palms up and said, "Why did that Colson guy come to see me?"

Rollins spread his own arms wide, palms up and said, "How the hell should I know?"

"You told me you took care of it."

"I did. There was always a chance we wouldn't get both at once."

"But you could have gotten him just now and you let him go instead. He was giving himself to us on a silver platter."

"Look, Director, there was no reason to think this Colson would ever follow up with you. You have to understand, if we could have made a move in the office we would have."

Danz pointed a finger at Rollins. "You *were* in the office with him," he said and nodded toward the door. "But you felt you had to wait on Frick and Frack to get here, and he got away from you."

Rollins sat in one of the chairs in front of Danz. "You didn't see how big he was. We would have wrecked your office fighting if it had been just me going one-on-one with that guy. We have to be careful. It's not like everyone outside of our group knows about the project. Drugging and dragging a limp body across the main lobby or the parking lot would draw attention. That's the type of attention we don't need right now. Besides, there's no chance he knows anything. And make no mistake, I'd like nothing more than to take out that smartass."

Danz said, "You're not a scientist, but I am. There's nothing absolute in a fluid situation. You can't measure and predict the actions of a human with free will like you can predict the actions of protons and neutrons."

"Just use the FBI to shut him down. They won't like Colson poking around their manhunt any more than we do."

Danz nodded and said, "I'll consider it, but if Colson finds Parker before we do, it could get ugly."

"I don't see it being possible. He's one man against the FBI and our search teams and technology."

"Your search teams and technology haven't found Parker yet," Danz said.

"They will… if he's lucky enough to be alive. It's been five days, and he doesn't have fresh water or food, unless he's eating his way out of the marsh like a goat. I have four men, twenty-four hours a day, watching real-time satellite imaging of a five-square-mile area from where he was last seen. Not to mention fifty patrol units. Nothing has moved. Nothing and no one has gotten out of that godforsaken place. I guarantee it."

Danz scoffed. "You guarantee it? That's a dangerous word for a politician."

Rollins stood and walked toward the door. One of the nerds opened it for him, but he stopped halfway and turned back to Danz. "I've got five hundred that says Parker is a half-eaten corpse by now."

Chapter Seven

The temperature was 89 degrees but the 90 percent humidity pumped the real-fell heat index to 103 degrees. The johnboat coasted into the Indian River on idle. It was a drab olive color and carried one occupant. NASA Security Officer Ray Skibba sat at the rear of the boat with one hand on the outboard motor tiller and his eyes fixed on the bank. It was his third six-mile patrol, which began at the most southern point of Max Hoeck Back Creek and into the Indian River. His assignment was to round Pelican Island and return to his starting point. It was twelve miles round trip. His instructions were to scan the banks for any sign of Grant Parker, the once beloved NASA scientist, now regarded as an enemy of the state. He was given a laminated photo of a slender-faced man with dark curly hair, age thirty-nine, and 6′ 1″ in height.

Skibba wore a duty belt with a radio holder, handcuff case, and holster that held his issued Smith & Wesson .40 semiautomatic handgun. The coiled microphone cord attached to his radio stretched across his back and over his left shoulder, where it was clipped to the front of his shirt. He checked his G-Shock watch, killed the outboard motor, and drifted forward into the mouth of the river. It was12:58 hours. Skibba could not help but notice that the occasional drops of sweat dropping from the bill of his ball cap had grown into a steady stream. He slid off his sunglasses and took off his hat.

Not only was it completely soaked, but a starburst design had developed across the top from the body salt that had secreted from his brow. A female voice came over the radio, right on time.

"Thirteen hundred hours. All patrols acknowledge."

There were fifty total patrols scattered over the northern half of the two-hundred-square-mile federal property. Some were in jeeps, some on foot patrol, and the rest on the water. The voice on the radio informed them that Parker had been first sighted north of the facility and would not likely backtrack into their hands. If that were the case, the officers on station would intercept him. Skibba was assigned to Patrol 17.

The first patrol officer responded with his status and coordinates, "Patrol one clear. Twenty-eight, forty-six, fifty-three by eighty, forty-five, thirty-six."

The first twenty-five units cleared at the top of the hour and the rest at the bottom. If not, it would take forever to get through the list of units and coordinates. To account for all units, the responses would be in numerical order. If they heard Patrol 10 clear and the radio traffic went silent, they knew there was a problem with Patrol 11. Skibba grabbed a towel off the top of his tackle box and dried his face and head as he waited for his turn. He paused for a count of three when it was his turn to respond, knowing someone was furiously typing the coordinates from the last unit into a program that updated their map positions. A supervisor would be standing by to make any needed adjustments to the dragnet, as if he were a giant alien moving chess pieces across the planet. Skibba held a hand over his GPS unit to cut the glare and keyed his microphone.

"Patrol seventeen clear. Twenty-seven, forty-seven, forty-seven by eighty, twenty-five, fifty-six."

Skibba wished with all his heart he could have responded, "Patrol seventeen. Contact made with suspect, twenty-seven, forty-seven, forty-seven by eighty, twenty-five, fifty-six." He had been with NASA for twelve years and was passed over for promotion three times. There was nothing more demeaning than training three rookies only for them to end up as your supervisor. The first one he had trained had been promoted two additional times and was now in a cushy administrative job with a take-home car. After making what he thought were respectful inquiries about why he had been passed over, he was given the same old answer. His time would come. He was good officer, and they needed to maintain good line staff to bring up the rookies in the way they should go. But after a few years of pressing the issue, the real reason was given: he was a little too aggressive and not a "company man." Skibba interpreted that to mean that he wasn't an ass kisser. Since then he was determined to prove his worth. If he could reel in Parker, they would have no choice but to reward his effort.

So he sat in the johnboat and listened intently. The only sounds were of birds, the water sloshing lazily at the bank, and the occasional *plop* of water when an underwater critter broke the surface. Four more round trips should end his twelve-hour shift, and if Parker wasn't found, he'd repeat the same process beginning at 6:00 a.m. the next day. He cranked the outboard motor and puttered slowly, examining the shoreline. The radio chirped again at the bottom of the hour and the remaining twenty-five patrol units gave their status in order. There was still no sign of Parker. He throttled down the engine fifteen minutes later, turned the tiller left, and coasted twenty feet to a small sandy bank where he killed the engine and dragged the boat onto the sand. He stood and listened for anything that sounded human but heard nothing. He reached into the tackle box, retrieved a roll of toilet paper, and disappeared into the thick undergrowth.

If Parker had a GPS at his disposal, he would have discovered that he had covered a little over seven miles in four days. It was a distance a runner could accomplish in an afternoon wearing a good pair of running shoes on an unobstructed landscape while occasionally gulping from a water bottle. He survived day four by eating sea grapes he had gathered from a crowd of shrubs in an opening next to a creek bed. Using his stolen uniform shirt as a sack, he plucked as many as he could carry and flung the makeshift bag over his shoulder. The relentless rain the night before had provided enough life-sustaining water to keep him alive for at least another thirty-six hours or so. And that should be enough if his calculations were correct.

Now it was day five, and Parker was thirsty again. The sea grapes weren't bad, but he needed more protein. He found another opening and checked his bearings against the sun. It was another steam bath today, but he was thankful the sun was visible and kept him on track. Parker felt like a crossbreed of Moses and the Creature from the Black Lagoon. His head was covered with a portion of his torn shirt, which he had fashioned into a type of turban. He had found a long, slender piece of driftwood to use as a walking stick, and the exposed parts of his body were caked with mud partly for camouflage and partly to protect him from sunburn and to act as a barrier against the mosquitoes. It worked part of the time.

Parker had been walking since first light. He estimated it had been five hours or so, and it was extremely laborious. He likened it in his mind to walking in mushy sand against the ocean tide, waist deep in water. His legs, arms, and chest stung where briars and thorns had scratched him. He had never seen two-inch thorns protruding from tree trunks in his life, but he was becoming very acquainted with them now. Ahead and through another line of trees, there was either another clearing or body of water, so he decided to walk another hundred yards to find out.

It was a body of water. Not the football-field-size ponds Parker had avoided or creeks he was forced to cross. This had to be the Indian River due to its size. He sat on the bank and dropped his head in his hands, thinking. His bearings had held true, and he was where he needed to be, but he was exhausted and had to get out of the scorching sun and regain some strength. He tried to pull the map up in his mind. Parker knew he must be at the most southern point, so he still had about eight miles to cover, and it would have to be along the eastern shoreline of the river. Most likely, it would take him another three or four days at his current speed. He scooted to the nearest tree, leaned against it, and closed his eyes. That's when he heard the sound and scrambled up the tree as quickly and as high as possible.

Officer Skibba put his hands on his waist and rotated his torso, popped his lower back twice, and then repeated the process with his neck. He walked into the undergrowth and found a dry opening to conduct his urgent business. When finished, he dropped the used toilet paper on his mess and jerked up his sweat-soaked underwear and clammy uniform pants. He then proceeded with the arduous task of strapping on the heavy belt and securing it to the under belt with four belt keeps and sliding his radio back in its pouch. He momentarily thought about kicking sand over his deposit but decided against it. His supervisors were so strict about their rules and policies and procedures, he was surprised they didn't have a written procedure about how to cover crap properly in the marsh. He trudged back to the shore, shoving waist-high weeds, limbs, and briars out of his way.

Officer Skibba could see the opening at the shore and the johnboat. He was five feet away when the radio chirped at the top of the hour.

"Fourteen hundred hours. All patrols acknowledge."

Skibba had plenty of time to get to his GPS and be ready to announce his status by the time Patrol 16 spoke up. There was no reason to crank the outboard motor until then. He announced his status and coordinates and then took his seat at the tiller. That's when the dirty white object caught his eye. Clearly out of place among the green foliage, dirty sand, and murky water was clothing of some sort, waded up at the base of a nearby tree at the bank. It was not very surprising. He couldn't begin to count the beer cans, discarded potato chip bags, and assorted trash he had seen washed up along the twelve miles of shore, but something was vaguely familiar about the spot of blue on the filthy rag.

Skibba climbed back out of the johnboat for a better look. He slipped on a pair of leather patrol gloves and lifted the cloth at one corner. A dozen or so large grapes rolled out in a clump at his feet. What he thought he recognized from the boat was confirmed: a torn uniform shirt with a blue NASA security shoulder patch. It initially puzzled Skibba. Had a security officer been attacked and eaten out of his shirt by an alligator? He hadn't heard about anything worse than one of the guys getting a rug burn from wrestling with a drunk trespasser. And what would they be doing out here this far unless they were looking for...

He froze and jerked his head from side to side. His heart raced. Skibba felt it beating in his throat as he took two deliberate steps back and pulled the Smith & Wesson from his holster. Then he heard the crack from a limb directly above him. The adrenaline rush was like nothing he had felt before. Years of checking doors and watching monitors and writing parking tickets had made him soft. Complacent. The excitement of being a cop had faded over the years into visions of lofty promotions and take-home cars. Long dormant instinct instantly alerted him to what was happening, but years of a lukewarm attitude and the rut of routine had left him totally unprepared, incapable of logic, and devoid of sound judgment.

Skibba raised his pistol and found the source of the sound in his front sights twenty feet above his head. The filthy, mud-caked figure with a dingy rag wrapped around its head stared wide eyed at him as he pulled the trigger once... twice... three times.

Colson turned left out of the Operations Support Building parking lot onto Saturn Causeway, checking his mirror for a tail or security vehicle every two seconds. He was certain he could have gotten the best of the man with the lose tie and rolled up sleeves, not to mention the two nerdy guys in the white coats. He was also certain that they wanted him for some reason, and it wasn't to recruit him for the next space flight. On the other hand, maybe that was exactly the reason. What better way to get rid of a body. Colson had no idea what they were up to, but they were out of their league in the wet-work business. Thriving criminal enterprises hire tough, solid men and jackbooted thugs to take care of curious people who threaten to throw a monkey wrench into their devious plans. He ran down the list of possibilities in his mind. Those preppy types wouldn't be involved in the typical criminal enterprise involving drugs or guns or prostitution or fraud. They didn't fit the profile. The only thing Colson knew for certain was that it involved the dark side of the federal government, and confronting them on their own turf was not a good strategy. For one man to do so was insanity, but their actions had confirmed their involvement, and that's what he needed to know.

The amateurs Colson had just avoided were not following him, and he didn't see any security vehicles. Ahead was the lonely guard shack but he wasn't going to pass by just yet. He turned left on Instrumentation Road and took another left next to a smaller white building. The parking lot he had seen from the OSB building had to be directly behind it, so he snaked around the building and found the entrance. At the rear of the lot he could see the entrance of the OSB building and parking lot. Colson parked in a vacant space between a minivan and a pickup. The clock display on his dash read 4:11 p.m. There was no chance of pitching his tent on the beach today. He removed a small pair of binoculars from the console, switched the satellite radio to '70s on 7, and made himself comfortable. Time was getting short for Taylor, and he needed to come up with a solution. He grabbed his phone and redialed the number Lieutenant Cantrell had sent him and got the same result as yesterday.

"You've reached the desk of Dan Rutledge with the United States Department of State. Please leave a message or press one for the office secretary."

Colson dropped the phone on the seat. He had already left two recorded messages and two with the secretary without a callback. There was very little they could or would do to help Taylor, but he needed to try the legal route first. During his ruminations, he almost missed Danz. From the distance of two football fields, it would have been easy to do, but the foot traffic in and out of the OSB was minimal at 4:30 p.m. It was a male figure walking toward a line of cars nosed in at the side walkway. The man stopped at a car on the nearest end—a bigwigs' parking space. He brought the binoculars to his face and adjusted the focus. It was Danz. The same face as in the photo above his wall-mounted nameplate.

Danz slipped off his suit coat and flung it in the back seat before lowering himself behind the wheel of a sliver Jaguar. Colson pushed the gear into first and then shot out of the parking space and back around to the entrance at Instrumentation Road. He backed off the gas and coasted toward the stop sign on Saturn Causeway. His timing was right. The Jaguar had already stopped and was pulling away. Colson kept a respectable distance and followed Danz north on Kennedy Parkway to State Route 402 West and over the Indian River to Titusville. A green sign at the foot of the bridge proclaimed the road as being the Max Brewer Memorial Parkway. Whoever that was.

At the foot of the bridge, the Jaguar turned left on South Hopkins Drive and continued for four miles and seven traffic lights. The right turn blinker came on just ahead of Country Club Drive where Colson followed it into the parking lot of La Cita Country Club. Danz stopped the Jaguar under a portico and a young man wearing a white shirt, dark slacks, and a tidy haircut opened the driver's door. Danz slid out and disappeared behind a dark stained door. The structure appeared to be everything a person would expect a country club to look like, from the tan stucco siding to its Spanish tile roof. The finely detailed columns supporting the portico would make Julius Caesar envious. Through the sea of palms to his left, Colson could see huge private residences of similar design sprinkled at various angles with perfectly manicured lawns and bright flowing shrubs. He imagined the fairways and fast greens of a golf course stretching out from behind the million-dollar homes that appeared to be built at deliberately haphazard angles along the course, as if they were an afterthought.

Colson had no intention of allowing a valet to drive his car and found a space at the rear of the lot. He wondered what kind of grief he would get for wearing a golf shirt and BDUs in the establishment but suspected he'd get by without too much attention. He gave the valet a nod as he walked past and got a blank stare in return. He opened the door and stepped into a lobby of sorts. To his right were double doors identical to the ones he'd just walked through with the exception of the placement of rectangular glass panels where solid wood inserts had been in the exterior door. A young man wearing a jacket and tie stood behind a slider lectern. He looked up at Colson with another blank stare and said. "May I help you, sir?" Colson gave the young man a half smile.

"I'm here to meet a friend. Nicholas Danz."

The young man looked at a book on the lectern and back at Colson as if he needed to see if Danz was there. The man had walked in less than thirty seconds ago. The young man acted as if he had never encountered such a quandary. Colson wasn't familiar with country club living but suspected most members invited guests frequently. What good is a country club membership if you can't show off to your less fortunate buddies? The young man must have snapped out of his coma. He said, "Mr. Danz didn't mention a guest joining him."

Colson shrugged and said, "Maybe he thought it was none of your business."

The young man narrowed his eyes without responding to the slight. "Are you a member with us, sir?"

Colson sighed and pulled his wallet to flash his badge. He took a step closer to the young man and lowered his voice.

"Now, you see, that's why you don't need to know everything. Mr. Danz's troubles are his own personal business, so I have to insist that you say nothing about this."

The young man's eyes widened, and he offered a quick nod. Colson patted him on the back as he walked past and pushed open the door. It was happy hour at the bar. He counted six people scattered at tables and two male and female couples seated in booths. Not traditional booths, but little individual rooms cut into the walls. The floors were dark wide-plank hardwood with a hand-hewn finish, and the walls had an expensive looking stucco finish and were painted a distressed tan color to resemble age and weathering. The stucco was missing in several random places on the wall, exposing brick beneath. At the very back of the room was a baby grand piano where a young woman in a glistening gold evening gown sat playing lightly. So lightly that Colson couldn't recognize the tune. Old black-and-white photos of men in baggy clothes standing proudly in the foreground of manicured fairways hung here and there on the stucco. Some were smiling with their elbows resting on golf bags and others were caught in the follow through of their swings with serious concentration on their faces.

Colson looked to his left where a long mahogany bar lined the wall. A slightly plump bartender stood with his arms crossed, looking up at a football game on a flat-screen television. Danz sat with his back to Colson watching silently along with the bartender. Colson walked over and sat next to Danz on a wooden barstool with a dark leather cushion attached around the sides with bronze nail heads. A small tumbler sat in front of Danz containing ice cubes and amber liquid. The bartender started toward Colson.

Colson said, "I'll have what he's having."

Danz glanced to his left at Colson and did a double take. He looked past Colson and took quick inventory of the bar before half whispering, "What are you doing here, Mr. Colson? What do you want?"

Colson dropped a ten-dollar bill on the bar as the bartender placed his drink on a napkin and turned his attention back to the game.

Colson said, "It's amazing you know me when we've never met, but we'll discuss that later. I just came to ask some questions about your missing scientist as I had planned on doing at your office before you called in a couple of pencil pushers to escort me out or whatever they were planning to do."

"What? That's ridiculous," Danz said.

Colson sipped his drink and nodded. "I agree. That's why I didn't let them."

"You obviously have a serious problem, Mr. Colson. I believe they call it paranoid schizophrenia."

"What it's actually called is being smarter than the director of the NASA Earth Science Division. And I do have a problem with simply trying to talk to a man who has a mutual goal and he tries to avoid me at best, or at worst has something more sinister in mind."

"What mutual goal could we possibly have?"

Colson chuckled. "Finding Grant Parker of course."

Danz gave Colson a flat stare. "If you're smarter than me, Colson, then you already know the FBI is working on that." His expression suddenly changed. It was as if he remembered the name of a song he'd been trying to recall for hours or the solution to a complex equation. He glared at Colson.

"Wait. You can't even be in here. You're trespassing. The security here won't put up with your smartass."

"Does that mean you won't sponsor me through astronaut school?" Colson asked.

"Just get out."

Colson stood. "Fine by me, but just one unrelated question. Just pretend I'm one of the taxpayers that chipped in to buy your Jaguar."

"That depends. What?"

"I noticed the space center is really out in the middle of nowhere. You bring equipment and rocket fuel in on big black semis or what?"

Danz picked up his glass and looked down at it while swirling its contents. "I would have thought you were more observant than that, Colson. If you had bothered to notice when you came to interrupt my work earlier, you would have seen that all of our vehicles are white. Now good day, Mr. Colson."

Colson started walking away and then gave Danz a backward wave. "Thanks, Director. Catch you later."

Colson stepped out where the young man in the jacket and tie stood behind the slender lectern. He paused to peek back through one of the glass door panels. Danz still sat at the bar with his back to door. His elbows rested on the rich mahogany bar. His forehead rested in his right hand, and he held a cell phone to his ear with the left.

Port Canaveral is situated sixteen miles south of Titusville as the crow flies. Cargo and cruise ships can be seen many hours of the day navigating through its massive shipping channel. If viewed in a satellite image, the channel would resemble a straight road cut into the landscape with three short cul-de-sacs known as the West, Middle, and East Turning Basins. Major cruise lines predominately use the West Turning Basin, leaving the Middle and East Basins for commercial traffic.

A massive warehouse the length of five football fields is located at the northern point of the Middle Turning Basin butted up to a dock of the same length. On the eastern end of the warehouse are offices, sleeping quarters, a modest kitchen area, and a rather large break room with long folding tables, a commercial coffeemaker, and a flat-screen television hanging on the back wall.

A short man of Latino descent walked into the break room wearing gray coveralls. He sported a pencil-thin moustache and black hair slicked back with Brylcream. He poured black coffee into a flimsy Styrofoam cup and picked up a clipboard from the counter, examining columns of numbers, destinations, and departure times. He ran his finger down the list and found the number he was looking for, T-6917; ran his finger to the destination column, Lumberton, Mississippi; and finally to the departure time in the far right-hand column, 11:30 hours. He checked his cheap digital watch, sat the clipboard back on the counter, and stepped into the main warehouse while sipping his coffee.

He walked past seven semi-trucks and found his on the far end where a second Latino man squatted at the front driver's corner, running his hand along the fender. The second man stood as the man with the pencil-thin moustache approached.

The second man said in a thick Latino accent, "It is ready. The paint is good."

Thin moustache said, "I leave in five minutes."

The second man scratched his head and said, "What did you hit?"

"Nothing."

The second man gave thin moustache a long look and nodded. He said, "Did they dock your pay?" Thin moustache silently climbed up the step to the driver's door and slid onto the seat. The second man watched him close the door, crank the diesel engine, and lower his window. Thin moustache offered the second man a weak wave of his hand and said, "They did nothing."

Two minutes later, the garage door in front of the black semi rolled slowly upward. The Florida sun reflected off the concrete like a field of new fallen snow. The man with the thin moustache slid on a pair of sunglasses, dropped the gear into first, and then slowly departed the warehouse pulling a forty-foot long steel tanker.

A branch exploded two feet from Grant Parker's face. He couldn't believe the guy was shooting at him—trying to kill him. He swiveled his body around the trunk trying to place it between him and the madman with a gun. He literally felt the second shot fly past his ear. The blasts from below were deafening. Parker felt panic rising as he hurriedly repositioned himself while trying to maintain his footing. If they wanted him dead, why didn't they kill him when they had him locked down at NASA? Why the kill order now?

Parker had seen cop shows and movies. They always gave commands to stop or to put your hands up or lay on the ground. This maniac hadn't said a word or given a warning command. It wasn't until he scrambled up the tree that he had noticed that he'd left the shirt on the ground with the grapes.

Parker had watched the man get out of the boat. He had been convinced that the man had heard or seen him before he came ashore. He felt somewhat relieved when he saw the man disappear into the brush with the roll of toilet paper and then heard the sound of the man grunting in mid-dump.

Parker had then held his breath when the man returned, but he flinched with the unexpected voice on the radio. The man had said, "Patrol seventeen," and something else that was too muffled to make out. He didn't know what to expect when the man returned and picked up the shirt, spilling the grapes at his feet. The man appeared to be in deep thought and then suddenly became rigid as if he had been shot. The next instant is when he looked straight up and they locked eyes. The instant after that was when he had started shooting without a word of warning.

Two shots had already been fired and the man was circling the tree, pointing and moving, and moving and pointing as Parker kept circling the trunk, denying him a target of opportunity. He knew he couldn't keep it up forever. He would rather give up than be shot dead in the marsh. The man was still circling the tree and not speaking, but that didn't mean Parker had to remain silent. He would tell him he was giving up.

"Hey," Parker yelled down a fraction of a second before it felt like a snake had bitten his left hand. The pain was immediately followed by the fourth blast coming from below. He instinctively jerked his hand to his face, lost his grip, and fell backward. His mind canceled the pain in his hand and replaced it with the fear of falling to his death. Parker flailed his arms and felt flimsy branches slapping against his back as he descended. His hands were catching nothing but air.

A moment later, it was over. It had ended. Parker felt no pain. He was neither hot nor hungry nor thirsty. He was no longer exhausted. The last sensation Parker knew was a dull thud on the back of his head.

Agent Mcilwain walked into the Orlando FBI Field Office at 2:00 p.m. after spending half of the previous day and all morning reviewing security camera recordings. He dropped a file on his desk and stuck his head around the corner where Agent Strickland sat typing on her computer.

Mcilwain said, "Did you get that flash drive to the IT guys?"

"Yep," she said without taking her eyes of the screen. "They already have results."

Mcilwain's eyebrows went up. "Really? Why didn't you call me?"

"I thought you were busy reviewing security footage."

"I was… all evening and half the day. Fast forwarding and scanning until my head hurt. You should spend eight hours with Security Boy Johnny and his constant jabbering about wanting to be an FBI agent and asking more questions than a three year old. I was standing around with my gun in my mouth after the first thirty minutes."

Strickland turned one corner of her mouth up in a half-amused grin. "See anything interesting?"

"You first. What did they find on the flash drive?"

Strickland held her hand above the computer screen and made a circle with her index finger and thumb. Mcilwain released a sigh and said, "Nothing? They didn't find anything at all. Did Parker wipe it?"

Strickland shook her head. "According to the computer gurus, it's never been written on. It's as if Parker had taken it brand new out of the package and stuck it in the vacuum cleaner bag."

"That's stupid. Why would he do that?"

Strickland shrugged. "Maybe it's another decoy like the pouch under the toilet lid. You know how those scientists are. Think they're the smartest guys in the room. Would he really leave national security secrets in a toilet tank or vacuum cleaner bag for us to find? Now *that* would be stupid. For all we know the information is on a microchip injected under the skin behind his ear." She pushed back from her desk and said, "So what did you come up with?"

Mcilwain ducked back into his office and grabbed the file from his desk. He opened it on the desk in front of Strickland and spread out four eight by ten photographs and a blank DVD with a case number written in black permanent marker on the front. The picture on the far left was of a hallway and a bald man at the door of Parker's condo. The second was of a man and woman at the same door. The third pictured the rear of a blue Corvette and blue Prius in the parking garage, and the last was a photo of a black Tahoe leaving the garage.

Strickland laid the photos in sequential order according to the date and time stamps on the top-right corners of each and said, "So all these people were in Parker's condo before we executed the search warrant?"

Mcilwain nodded. "Right."

"Maybe that's your answer about the missing and blank flash drives. Whatever evidence was there is certainly gone now."

Mcilwain pulled a chair next to Strickland. He said, "This is where it gets interesting."

"How do you mean?" she asked.

"I don't believe the first bald man and the couple knew each other." Mcilwain tapped the DVD with his finger. "On the video you see the bald man leave the condo and walk into the parking garage right when the couple went down the hall toward the condo door. You don't see the bald man leave in the Tahoe until the couple comes out almost thirty minutes later. The man and the couple didn't interact at any point." He pointed at the Tahoe photograph. "That's him leaving ten seconds after the couple pull out and go around the first turn."

"Did you run the plates?"

"Are you kidding? I just walked in from my morning torture session with Security Boy Johnny."

Strickland chuckled. "No problem. I know who they are already."

"How would you know that?"

Strickland clicked the mouse to open a file on her desktop and pointed at the man in the photo standing next to the female. Mcilwain looked at the photo and then read the driver's license on Strickland's screen.

He said, "Grey Colson?"

"Yes. The woman is Grant Parker's half-sister, Lisa Riley, and the bald guy is Robert Bankston. He worked for the Justice Department."

"What does he do now?" Mcilwain asked.

"Struggles to breath, I guess. He was the guy involved in the hit and run we heard about on the news. If he survives, it'll be nothing short of a miracle."

Mcilwain sat back in his chair and thought for a moment. He said, "That Grey Colson guy. His name sounds vaguely familiar."

Strickland clicked the mouse again and an FBI case file filled the screen. She said, "A little over three years ago Colson was involved in the death of Martin Cash after Cash's son kidnapped Colson's daughter."

Mcilwain's expression changed, and he leaned forward in the chair. "That's right. That was Frank McCann's case. He was exonerated wasn't he?"

"Yes, and he runs a small private-eye business now."

"I still don't understand how you figured out his connection with Parker."

"I didn't until now. I was called into the group supervisor's office while you were out playing with Security Boy Johnny."

"And…"

"*And…* you need to grab your beach towel and flip-flops again."

"Why?"

"Because the group supervisor got a call from the SAC who got a call from Danz. We've been instructed to go back to Daytona and, I quote, have a face-to-face with Colson and order him to cease and desist his harassment of Director Danz and his interference with a federal investigation, unquote."

Parker opened his eyes and instantly grabbed the back of his aching head. Not only was he hot, thirsty, hungry, and exhausted again, but it felt like someone had hit him in the head with a baseball bat. His body was pitched at an awkward angle, and his vision was blurry. He was lying on something that elevated his rear end, as if someone had shoved a sack of potatoes under the small of his back. He rolled to his right and pushed himself up on his hands and knees.

Parker pressed his hand against the sore spot on the back of his head and tried to rub the pain away. His roll maneuver had made his head spin, and he dry heaved, but nothing escaped his mouth but soured sea grape saliva that he spat on the mushy sod between his hands. He lay on his side, closed his eyes, and took deep breaths. His mind insisted that he jump up and run, but his exhausted body begged him to remain still and either surrender to authorities or surrender to death. It was several minutes before the blurry images began to sharpen. He glanced to his left.

The crumpled form of the man with the gun lay in an awkward lump two feet away from Parker. The man's head was tilted backward as if he was straining to see a movie screen in the front row of a theater. His eyes were open—staring but not seeing. There was no visible sign of blood. For an instant, Parker scooted away from the glaring gunman before his brain registered that he was dead. He crawled back and read the name stenciled on the man's shirt. R. Skibba. He placed his hand under Skibba's right ear and lifted his head. It moved freely in his hand. Parker tilted Skibba's head from side to side and heard bones in his neck crunching against each other in protest. He dropped the head and rubbed the back of his own head again. The pain had somewhat subsided to a dull ache. Parker concluded he must have been more of a hardhead than the dead security officer.

Parker stood and gave the body a final look. He felt no remorse. He had not intended to kill anyone. It was the security man who had been trying to kill *him*. He wrestled the shirt, pants, shoes, and duty belt off of Skibba. The pants were baggy, so Parker pulled the Velcro belt to its limit around his waist. A stream of sweat dripped from his nose as he struggled with the duty belt and snaps. The weight of it surprised Parker. It was hot enough without the equipment, but he could make use of it. Skibba's boots were a size too large, but that was better than being too small. He slid the radio in its pouch and snapped the Smith & Wesson in the holster. He was too dehydrated and weak to drag Skibba's body, let alone bury it. He instead pulled Spanish moss from the nearby trees and covered the body the best he could.

Parker stood quietly at the shore and listened for other boats, but there was no man-made noise to be heard. He climbed into the johnboat and slipped on the dead officer's ball cap. He flipped open the tackle box and smiled for the first time since the beginning of his nightmare. Parker couldn't have been happier if he had won the lottery. Next to a multipurpose Leatherman tool was a flair gun and an insulated bag. Inside the bag was a wrapped sandwich, a bag of potato chips, and two large bottles of water, which were still cool to the touch. He couldn't waste time, but he also couldn't resist his frantic desire for food and clean water. Parker devoured the sandwich and chips and gulped one entire bottle of water in less than sixty seconds.

Parker shoved the empty plastic bottle and sandwich bag back inside and tilted his head back, closed his eyes, and released a satisfied sigh. He stared the outboard engine and pointed the boat northeast. Pelican Island was in sight, but it was not his final destination. Parker was silently thankful for the food, water, and the boat. He had to put more distance between him and those hunting him. Thirty minutes later, Pelican Island was behind him and a second, larger island lay ahead. Parker dismissed his earlier calculations. Instead of another three days of hiking around the perimeter of the river, he could be at his destination in a couple of hours. That is, if he lived long enough. Now that he was out on the open water, the trees and underbrush no longer shielded Parker. There were no convenient trees to climb, and jumping in the water was out of the question in the uniform, boots, and twenty-pound belt strapped to him. He would sink like a rock. He spotted another small boat in the distance, but the figure sitting with a floppy hat had a fishing pole in his hand and shouldn't pose a threat He adjusted the tiller, giving the small boat a wide birth, and continued north. Parker pulled the second bottle of water from the tackle box and rolled its cool plastic surface on his neck and face. He resisted the temptation to drink it and started to slip it back in the bag for later when he flinched at the piercing voice that seemed to come from directly behind him.

Chapter Eight

Colson threaded the fourth plastic steak through a loop in the canopy anchor rope and hammered it into the sand with a small rubber mallet. He stepped under the canopy to his rolling beach cart that had two fat plastic tires designed for pulling it through the thick sand. A bungee cord held a folded beach chair against its frame. He unhooked the cord and pulled the chair from its hook; then he situated it in a spot that would remain shaded for the next two to three hours. Colson laid the cart flat next to his chair with the table side exposed. There were two cup holders cut in the tabletop resembling pool table pockets, except they were nylon mesh instead of leather. He sat a small cooler on the opposite side of his chair and removed his smartphone from another mesh compartment. Colson flipped open the cooler lid and grabbed one of the water bottles standing next to his Glock .45-caliber semiautomatic and settled in.

It had been a ritual for the past thirty-three years: the canopy raising, the chair unfolding, and the placement of the cooler. The bulk of the time, Colson had been with his late wife, Ann, and his daughter, Nicole. Now as often as possible he performed the ritual with his current love, Beverly. But it was not as often as he wished. Colson kicked off his sandals and set his sunglasses on the table next to a bottle of water in the other mesh cup holder. Under the canopy, it was neither hot nor cold. The ocean breeze was light and the sky was cloudless. The beach traffic had increased when the kids were paroled for fall break, but it was relatively quiet again and back to the normal fall season. The die-hard beach goers still rode their bicycles, the joggers continued to jog, and sunbathers still soaked up the rays, maintaining their greasy-bronze appearance.

If Colson had his way, and the beach police wouldn't arrest him, he would set up a permanent office tent on the beach. Maybe even a gazebo. There was work to do but nothing said he couldn't do it fifty feet from the water. He woke his cell phone from its slumber and typed "Quito, Ecuador" in the search engine box. He touched a link and a map filled the five-inch screen with a red indicator in the middle. Another link gave details about the capital city of Ecuador, which is found in the northeastern region of the country, twenty-five kilometers south of the equator with a little over two million residents living at a whopping 9,350 feet above sea level. According to one writer, that region had only two seasons: rain and no rain.

Quito Prison. That's where Colonel Guerra said they had transferred Taylor. It was over 350 miles from Salinas, Ecuador. Instead of being held in a local jail, they went to the trouble of sending Taylor halfway across the country to the capital city. That meant Colonel Guerra was quite powerful and influential in their world of law enforcement. And their world of law enforcement was completely foreign to Colson. It was a place where corruption, intimidation, bribery, and brutality thrived on the wrong side of the bars. Colson set his phone in the side table and admired the gentle curve of the earth where ocean met sky as he searched his memory. Of all the people he had met and worked with in his career, he could not recall a soul who could help him fix Taylor's royal screw-up in South America.

Colson was momentarily distracted by a young couple walking along the shore. The girl was too young for Colson's taste, but she was perfectly shaped and wore her medium-tanned skin exceptionally well. The most distracting thing about the couple was the pale-skinned, bone-skinny, longhaired, and bearded slug the girl was holding hands with. The boy was wearing only long black swim trunks that hung well past his knees, making his already pale skin resemble that of a corpse. Colson followed the couple's progress northward through his sunglasses as they walked in ankle deep water and disappeared in the distance. When Colson looked back south, he saw another couple that was even stranger still.

There was a young woman, but not a teenybopper like the girl out walking her corpse. She was slender with short brown hair and probably thirty years old or so. She wore a blue pantsuit and sunglasses. The man was maybe forty and wore a medium-gray business suit and tie. And sunglasses of course. They stood just outside the canopy to his right, apparently waiting to make eye contact before they spoke.

The man said, "Mr. Colson?"

Colson leaned slightly forward and set his elbows on knees. He said, "Allow me to cover all the bases to save everyone some time. If you're Jehovah's Witnesses, I'm Baptist. If you are collecting for the needy, I'm *still* Baptist and donate at my church. If you're the police, you already know that I'm Mr. Colson, and if you're animal rights activists, I'm already a proud member of PETA, which is an acronym for People Eating Tasty Animals. I've been studying up on acronyms lately."

The man and woman slipped off their sunglasses and simultaneously drew small black wallets from their suit jackets as if choreographed. They opened them with the same exact precision as the man spoke.

"I'm Agent Michael Mcilwain and this is Agent Myra Strickland with the FBI. May we have a word?"

Colson leaned back in his chair and said, "Thank God you're not Jehovah's Witnesses. You can come in out of the sun and tell me what you need but I can't guarantee you'll get a word back."

Mcilwain and Strickland stepped under the canopy. Strickland slipped off her sunglasses and said, "I would think a man with as many years in law enforcement as you would be eager to assist fellow officers."

Colson nodded. "Typically, I would, but lately it seems that my *fellow officers* at the federal level have either ignored me or declined *my* request for assistance. Your office is not the same since Frank McCann retired."

Mcilwain said, "I'm afraid I don't know what you're referring to."

"I'm certain you don't," Colson said.

Strickland said, "We're here regarding your contact with Nicholas Danz at his country club."

Colson chuckled. "That's a federal crime?"

"You were trespassing."

"Which is *not* a federal crime. The FBI doesn't respond to trespassing calls. Even if they did, you wouldn't have the jurisdiction to make a misdemeanor arrest any more than you could write a speeding ticket. So why don't you tell me why you're really here."

Mcilwain said, "Mr. Colson, Danz said you were harassing him, but the main reason we came to speak with you is about your efforts to locate Grant Parker. We know his half-sister hired you to find him."

Colson said, "That's right, and when I find him, you'll be the first to know. Hell, I'll wrap him up like a Christmas present and send him to you by same day mail if you like."

Strickland said, "No matter who hired you, we cannot permit you to interfere in our investigation. Now that *is* a federal crime."

Colson said, "You're not conducting an investigation, you're on a manhunt. And where I'm from, the more people looking for him the better."

Mcilwain said, "Look, Mr. Colson, we are doing everything we can to locate Parker. I want to appeal to you as a fellow law enforcement officer. Call it a professional courtesy if you will. I'm sure you had supervisors and you supervised a lot of people. Well, we also have supervisors, and we're just trying to do our job. We've been told to warn you about your continued involvement in this case. Let us be able to tell our boss that we did our job and you cooperated fully."

Colson pointed his finger at Mcilwain and looked at Strickland. "Now *that's* how you do it, Agent Strickland. You're partner knows the limits of his authority and the law. He's polite and persuasive and knows how to empathize with people." He looked back to Mcilwain. "You were in police work before working for the feds, right?"

Mcilwain nodded. "Two tours in the army. Fifteenth Military Police Brigade, Fort Leavenworth."

Strickland snorted. "Polite, persuasive, and empathetic? This from a guy with the biggest smart mouth on the beach."

"I'm retired. I had to restrain myself for thirty years, and I'm trying to make up for lost time."

Mcilwain extended his hand and said, "Please, Mr. Colson. Shake on it?"

Colson gazed at Mcilwain for a long moment and then stood but didn't take Mcilwain's hand.

"Hold that thought for a moment and let's see if we can come to a mutual agreement."

Mcilwain dropped his arm to his side and gave Colson a puzzled expression. Strickland crossed her arms and leaned her shoulder against Mcilwain's as if to impart a secret, but she didn't whisper.

"He wants money, Mike. You know, to buy him off like some low-life informant," she said.

Colson didn't give Strickland the courtesy of a glance. His eyes stayed on Mcilwain until a look of understanding crossed his face. Mcilwain said, "Of course. I can see that. We're asking you to quit a paying gig. I can't guarantee how much, but I'm sure we can reimburse you for a portion of your fee."

Colson said, "You can do more than that."

Strickland appeared astonished and then just plain mad. "You think you can shake down the FBI?" She stuck her sunglasses on her nose and grabbed Mcilwain's elbow. "To hell with him, let's go. We'll just arrest his ass for obstruction if he gets in the way again."

Mcilwain said, "Hang on a minute. What are you talking about, Colson?"

"I was attached to DEA for almost five years and I know the FBI operates just like they do. And it's that time of year where you have to spend money or lose it, but money is not what I need." Colson glared at Strickland and said, "And if you paid me the fee for this investigation it would be exactly zero because that's what I was charging Parker's sister."

Mcilwain said, "So what are you asking?"

"I have a good friend who got locked up in Ecuador on an assault charge. My employee, Jay Taylor."

Mcilwain shrugged. "I honestly don't know how we can help you with that. I mean, if he was in a US jail, then maybe we—"

"I know you can't. That's not what I need."

"Why not make his bail? Didn't they give him a bond?" Mcilwain asked.

"What they gave him was a ransom."

"How much?"

"A hundred grand."

Strickland said, "But you said you didn't need the money. Even if you did, there's no way the FBI is giving you a hundred grand."

"All I'm asking for is transportation—a small plane to land on a private strip and then transport both of us back in a couple of days."

Strickland said, "That doesn't make sense. Why not fly commercial?"

"Because they wanted the money wired. I don't trust them. I don't believe they'll release Taylor. It has to be a flight that doesn't exist or their crooked immigration officials will seize what little cash I can scratch together before I have a chance to pay the ransom."

Mcilwain said, "How do you expect to get them to release him?"

Colson shook his head. "I'm not sure, but I have to try. Offer them a settlement. Bribe a politician or a higher-ranking officer maybe. Picket the American Consulate until they intervene. Whatever I have to do."

Mcilwain shrugged. "All I can do is make the request, but I can't promise anything."

Colson stuck out his hand. "That's all I'm asking."

Mcilwain shook Colson's hand and said, "I do need to ask a couple of things. Did you or the sister remove anything from Parker's apartment?"

"Nothing helpful. The sister gave me his photo so I'd know who I was looking for."

"Just one more question for now. Why did you confront Danz? If he had any idea where Parker is, he would have told us, and he'd be in custody by now. The government is the victim in the espionage case, but NASA is the agency that dropped the ball, and they want Parker found to save face."

"With all due respect, Agent Mcilwain, NASA is not the only intended victim in this case. Have you heard of a hit-and-run accident involving a semi and Tahoe that happened here several days ago? It was on the local news."

Mcilwain and Strickland looked at each other. It seemed they were silently asking if the other should say anything. Colson said, "So you *do* know what I'm talking about."

Mcilwain finally spoke. "Yes, we heard about the accident."

Colson said, "And you know the man who called himself Rob was also looking for Parker. I'm curious, was that his real name?"

Strickland said, "We are not at liberty to say."

"Of course not."

Mcilwain said, "I'm not following you. How are you connected with that man? It was a terrible accident and only coincidental to this case.

"You may not be following me, but Rob was… in his Tahoe at the time of the accident, or I should say, the murder attempt. Danz is a problem because he or someone else with NASA tried to kill both of us."

Strickland snorted. "That's ridiculous."

Colson shrugged.

Mcilwain handed Colson a business card and said, "I'll let you know what I find out about your request if you'll do us both a favor and cool your heels for now."

Colson nodded and said, "I'll expect a call by the morning. That's plenty of time to ask your boss a question."

The agents plodded their way through the sand in their dress shoes and disappeared up the stairs at the sea wall to the parking lot.

Colson had little hope that Agent Mcilwain would call him with good news. He didn't expect an answer of "No," but, "Hell no." He knew federal law enforcement agencies well enough to know if it doesn't further their investigation, mission, or agenda, it wouldn't happen. And if the female agent, Strickland, had anything to do with it, the answer would most certainly be "No." Colson took no pleasure in butting heads with women, but Strickland was obviously a college graduate who was waiting tables one week while finishing up her degree and in FBI training at Quantico the next. Mcilwain was a different breed as a former MP. He didn't look down his nose at local cops.

Colson knew he would have to keep working on the problem. If Mcilwain came back with good news, wonderful, but he would need a plan B and time was running short. He scanned his phone for old contacts from A to Z. He was relieved he had resisted the temptation to clean the slate and delete his old contacts. Colson slowly scrolled down the list twice and came up with nothing. He had plenty of old friends and colleagues, but not any with the political pull or resources he needed.

Colson sat his phone on the side table, stepped out into the Daytona sun, and stretched. He could hear the faint whine of a speedboat a quarter-mile offshore, pulling a couple lofted high above in parasailing harnesses. Then he heard the more pronounced buzz of a Cessna 150 approaching from south to north, with its wings tipping slightly downward to one side and then the other in the warm updraft. Behind the two-seater aircraft flew a long advertisement on a netted background that read, "Visit the Historical Old Fort in St. Augustine."

Colson had been there years ago, just forty-five minutes north of where he now stood. He recalled the tour guide saying St. Augustine was the oldest city in the nation, and it was named in honor of a Catholic saint, but that was the extent of his memory. The Cessna made its pass and continued north toward the main pier. Colson stepped back under the canopy and grabbed his phone for a third time. The ice-cream truck passed by playing a cheerful, tinkling tune he didn't recognize, but it made fewer and fewer stops as the month progressed with fewer families vacationing and Halloween approaching. Colson wondered how the man made a living when there was no one buying his ice-cream sandwiches and snow cones. The thought of snow cones and St. Augustine reminded Colson of something. It was a long shot, but it was the only shot that remained.

He sat and opened his contacts and scrolled to the name under "A." He touched the contact and waited. The line was picked up on the second ring and a female voice said, "Drug Enforcement Administration, Buffalo Field Office, how may I direct your call?"

Colson caught himself holding his breath. It had been over four years and his chances of contacting his old acquaintance would be rather slim. He said, "I'm trying to reach Group Supervisor Donnie Augustine, please."

"Sir," the female said with a hint of annoyance, "Mr. Augustine is our special agent in charge. Who's calling please?"

The voice Parker heard was loud, but it wasn't coming from directly behind him as he first thought. It was coming from the microphone clipped on his shoulder. "Sixteen hundred hours. All patrols acknowledge."

Parker maintained his speed and northerly course as the patrols started sounding off "clear," followed by a series of numbers. He had heard the same voices responding earlier, but had paid no attention at the time since he was too busy dodging bullets. He pulled the radio from his belt, turned the volume down, and held it close to his ear so it would not draw the attention of anyone who may be lurking near the shore. He listened as patrols one through sixteen cleared and then there was radio silence until the female voice returned in a half-irritated, half-concerned tone.

"Patrol seventeen, advise your status."

Parker froze. Had that been what the dead security officer had said? Had he been Patrol 17? Parker jerked his head around 360 degrees to check his surroundings. He had left the lone fishing boat behind the last bend. No johnboat patrols were in sight, and there was no movement on the shore. The voice came again, sharper than before.

"Patrol seventeen, advise your status."

Parker pressed the side button and said into the face of the radio, "Patrol seventeen clear," as the others had in sequence before him, but the response seemed too short. What else had the other patrols said? What were the numbers they had rattled off?

Clearly agitated by now, the voice returned. "And your coordinates, Patrol seventeen."

Coordinates? How could I know my... Parker thought before noticing the small GPS unit mounted by the tiller? He quickly cupped his hand over the unit to shield the sun's glare and read off what was there.

"Ah, twenty-eight, forty-five, fifty-three and eighty, forty-five, fifty-six."

"Clear," came the agitated voice. The remaining patrols then followed until it ended with Patrol 25 and the radio fell silent again.

Parker breathed a sigh of relief one moment and then he was frightened the next, realizing he had given them his exact position. But surely they wouldn't know it was him. Not at that moment. But would they know when Officer Skibba didn't return, and how long would that be? He maintained a steady speed and a northerly course. It seemed as though another thirty minutes passed without seeing another human being or boat, or hearing the *whoop-whoop* of helicopter blades. Directly ahead, a group of small islands came into view and grew larger as the minutes passed. Parker smiled to himself. He knew what they were. He gunned the outboard motor and headed directly for them.

Mcilwain turned right out of the Sundowner complex toward International Speedway Boulevard. Strickland had not said a word since she slammed her door in the parking lot and jerked her seat belt across her lap. She had her elbow perched on the door panel where it met the window glass and chewed on a fingernail. Mcilwain recognized her behavior immediately. He had two ex-girlfriends who had exhibited the same silent behavior.

Mcilwain swung the Charger east when the green arrow appeared and said, "What?"

Strickland didn't take her eyes off the small shops passing to her right and said, "You let Colson basically insult me and didn't say a word. I thought we were partners."

"We *are* Myra. But you have to admit, you were a little testy yourself."

Strickland said nothing.

Mcilwain shrugged. "Look, he knows the law and the fact that we couldn't order him to not work with Parker's sister to find him. I talked to Agent McCann and he vouched for him. If there was a reason to think Colson was aiding or abetting Parker, it would be a different story."

"Whatever," she said. "You can go to the boss with his demands if you like, but leave me out of it."

"I'm not going to anyone."

Strickland finally looked at Mcilwain and said, "What do you mean? Why'd you tell him if you weren't going to ask?"

"I guess just buying time. I might not be the hard-ass you would like, but I'm no idiot either. If I told the group supervisor what Colson's condition was, he'd throw me out the window. Besides, it's not the FBI that wants Colson to stop looking for Parker. It's Danz."

Strickland said, "So you buy us twenty-four hours, then you know what will happen. Colson will be sticking his nose into the case again, Danz will call the supervisor, and we'll both get screamed at."

"I don't know what to tell you, Myra. I can't lock Colson up for something he hasn't done. We're just between a rock and a hard spot for now. I suggest we stay out of the office and work on finding Parker and hope Colson will stay far enough out of the picture that Danz won't complain again." Mcilwain paused a moment before changing the subject. He said, "Do you think there's anything to what Colson said?"

"About what?" Strickland asked.

"About someone trying to kill him and Robert Bankston."

Strickland threw Mcilwain a puzzled look and said, "Seriously? Colson must be senile."

Mcilwain shrugged. "You could be right. I mean, you *are* the one with the psychology degree."

"Think about it," Strickland said. "Colson was a local cop and dealt with local offenders. Drug dealers, shoplifters, wife beaters, right?"

"I suppose."

"You know he did. It's perfectly logical that the thugs he locked up would threaten him on a daily basis, but we're not talking about run-of-the-mill street thugs at NASA. We're talking about a bunch of pencil necks crunching numbers, solving equations, and planning light-speed space flights to the Andromeda Galaxy."

"You're probably right," Mcilwain.

"You *know* I'm right."

They drove in silence for several minutes. The Daytona International Speedway slipped past them to their left, and they were caught by the red light at Thames Road. They were in the thick of the shopping district with restaurants, sporting goods retailers, and clothing stores. The traffic exiting the shopping centers on both sides of the road was a steady stream, nose to tail for the next three minutes. Mcilwain sighed and shook his head at the delay. He finally moved the Charger forward again when the light decided to turn green.

Strickland broke the silence. "I have my own suggestion."

Mcilwain said, "Hey, I'm open to anything."

Strickland pointed ahead and said, "Go south on I-95."

"Where are we going?"

"Back to see Danz. We've done what he wanted with Colson. Maybe we can reason with him and keep him off our backs."

"What's this *we* business. He hates me."

Strickland smiled and patted Mcilwain's shoulder. "You just sit in the car. I can take care of Danz."

The NASA Mobile Command Post, or MCP, sat in the center of a long parking lot directly off Playa Linda Beach Road on a narrow stretch of land bordered on the west by the Max Hoeck Creek waterway and on the east by the Atlantic Ocean. At the MCP's location, the distance from river to ocean was less than 350 feet on either side. Directly across from the entrance of the parking lot is a hard-packed sandy access road to a natural boat launch into the Max Hoeck Creek. The berth was shallow, but deep enough for small craft, including johnboats.

The NASA security lieutenant assigned to evening watch arrived for duty at 17:30 hours with a large Styrofoam cup of coffee in hand for the twelve-hour tour. Being fall, the night was arriving a minute earlier each day, making the night shift seem even longer than it actually was. The lieutenant had been having difficulty sleeping during the day. Until the manhunt started, only sergeants worked evening and morning watch. Now every officer was stuck on twelve-hour shifts until further notice. The only consolation was the overtime pay and knowing that as a lieutenant he was not required to walk the marsh or pilot a johnboat or drone all night long.

The lieutenant paused next to his car and gave the ocean a look while taking a sip of coffee. He'd rather spend the entire night lounging in an Adirondack chair in the sand, but duty called. He turned and climbed three steps to the side door of the MCP and stepped inside. To his right was the empty driver's cabin. He turned left down a hall that ran the length of the MCP and passed the small restroom door. Radio equipment and flat-screen monitors neatly tucked inside custom-made, built-in cabinets were ahead of him. The rear of the MCP opened to an oval couch surrounding a small oval conference table bolted to the floor. On a normal night, the only personnel in the MCP were the radio operator and the day watch commander. They both would have reports already written and their lunch boxes ready to go at their relief time, which was fifteen minutes before the hour. The day watch commander may have written information on the pass-on log or not depending on if anything other than time checks had occurred during his shift. The radio would be silent since it was a quarter to the top of the hour. But that night it was different.

The lieutenant stepped in the rear of the MCP, but found nowhere to stand around the conference table. The radio was a buzz with voices that he couldn't understand over the chatter of the day watch commander and the two sergeants crowding the room. The day-shift lieutenant raised his voice over the others.

"Hang on," he blurted, "Just hang on a minute. What other boats are in his area?"

The radio operator looked at the monitor to his left and ran his finger down a spreadsheet. He said, "Patrols thirteen and fifteen are the closest to his last location."

The night-shift lieutenant spoke up from behind the four officers. "Have they found Parker?"

The day-shift lieutenant spun on his heels. "I wish, but no. One of the patrols is forty-five-minutes late clearing his status."

"Which boat is it?"

The radio operator referred to his spreadsheet again and said, "Officer Skibba."

The night-shift lieutenant set his coffee on the small conference table and shook his head. "Why am I not surprised? He ignores policy like I ignore my mother-in-law.

Either that or he forgot to change his radio battery before his shift. He's done that before too."

The day-shift lieutenant said, "All I know is I'm gonna chew his ass if he makes me work past midnight to round him up."

The night-shift lieutenant waved his hand dismissively and said, "You guys get on out of here." He checked his watch. "Don't worry. Its five minutes until shift change, and he'll be motoring up right on time. Believe you me. Skibba's never late to clock out."

At 19:00 hours, Skibba was an hour late. At 20:00 hours he was two hours late and still not answering his radio. The night-shift lieutenant had sent three of his evening watch patrols along Skibba's assigned route with no success. The half cup of coffee in the night-shift lieutenant's cup was ice cold and legitimate concern was setting in. It had been a quandary of events. It was either call his chief of security and pull him away from dinner when Skibba would most likely arrive before the chief did, or risk being demoted for not calling the chief when a man was missing. He knew he better make the call before the chief went to bed, so he did, and the chief was pissed and on his way. He ran through a list in his head. Had he done everything he could have done to find Skibba to that point? If not, he would have to before the chief arrived and asked him why the hell he hadn't.

"OK," the lieutenant said to the night-shift radio operator. "We have three patrols running his route in a staggered pattern, right?"

The radio operator nodded affirmatively.

"Did you tell them to run their spotlights like I ordered?"

"Of course... I mean, yes, sir."

The lieutenant ran his fingers through his hair and stared at the spreadsheet on the computer. "Pull the day-shift spreadsheet back up."

The radio operator clicked his mouse once and the old spreadsheet took the place of the new one.

The lieutenant said, "What time was his last transmission again?"

"Sixteen hundred hours."

"Okay, and what were his coordinates at that time?"

"Twenty-eight, forty-six, fifty-three by eighty, forty-five, fifty-six."

"All right. Show me where that is along his route and send two additional boats to that exact location."

The radio operator turned to the screen to his right, typed in the coordinates, and waited. He adjusted the zoom out and studied the screen for a long moment before zooming back in. He right-clicked on the screen and selected a distance marker. He then clicked on the coordinates given and dragged the line south to a second point, leaving a solid white line between the two points divided by small hash marks and numbers.

The lieutenant said, "What are you doing?"

"Ah, this top marker is on the coordinates Skibba gave at sixteen hundred."

"What's the southern point?"

"Well, sir, that's Pelican Island. His turning point."

"What?"

"I'm just imputing the coordinates he gave, sir."

The lieutenant leaned forward to see the small numbers by the hash marks and said, "Why would he be nine miles north of his route? Surely, he's not that stupid. Where exactly is that?"

The radio operator zoomed the satellite image back in and a name appeared across the water. The lieutenant bent closer still and read the name over the radio operator's shoulder. He said, "Why the hell was he in Mosquito Lagoon?"

Among fishing and bird watching enthusiasts, the Indian River Lagoon system is a well-known destination. At its northern point, Mosquito Lagoon divides the city of New Smyrna Beach and extends from Ponce de Leon in Volusia County to the north end of Merritt Island. Situated next to the Canaveral National Seashore on Cape Canaveral and the Merritt Island National Wildlife Refuge, Mosquito Lagoon is a broad, shallow body of water acclaimed to provide some of the best inshore fishing on the east coast of the United States.

Grant Parker breathed a sigh of relief at the sight of Middle Island. He was close to where he needed to be. He had considered dropping the irritating radio in the shallow water, but that would not have been a smart decision. Shortly after he failed to respond as Patrol 17, the chatter had gone from half-hour checks to frantic communication between the patrols and the radio operator. He also resisted the urge to use the spotlight laying at his feet, instead depending only on the reddish glow of dusk to navigate.

Parker aimed the johnboat a few degrees to his left and motored around to the west of Middle Island, and Plantation Island came into view. Two dim points of light became visible as he closed the distance. He knew they were campsites. The young man called Chris Roper at the fish camp had given him a map two years ago when he first visited. It was the perfect getaway for someone like Parker, even though fishing wasn't his forte. Roper had indicated on the color-coded map the islands where camping was permitted and the ones where camping was restricted. Roper hadn't clarified why some were off limits, and Parker hadn't bothered to ask.

Parker's first weekend excursion was on Plantation Island where the two dim campfires were now burning in the distance. They would remain in the distance as Parker pointed the boat west once again to avoid being seen or heard. Parker had enjoyed that first weekend. For the most part, the three fisherman camping nearby had left him alone, but he felt obligated to interact with them in passing and that's not what he had come for. Parker was a loner, simple as that. So he had studied the map Roper gave him and spent the entire following weekend exploring the islands where camping was prohibited. He was not the type to break the rules, but it wasn't like he was hurting anyone. If a National Park Ranger or game warden told him to leave, he would have politely and respectfully obliged. But they never had for almost two years of weekends on the forbidden Gaines Island.

Parker twisted the outboard motor throttle to full speed once clear of Plantation Island. Darkness had overcome the dusk, so he risked flicking the spotlight on and off to stay on course. He guided the johnboat toward an inlet on Gaines Island and left the spotlight on steady to find the familiar landmark. The spotlight illuminated it fifty yards or so away, at the farthest end of the inlet. He stopped short to be certain the johnboat would make it to the open river and not hang up on either side bank or stall in the tall grass at the mouth of the inlet.

Parker stepped out when the nose of the boat slid onto the short, sandy bank. He grabbed the spotlight, lunch sack, and the security officer's sweat rag and set them on the ground. The radio on his belt was still active with chatter, but the transmissions were broken and garbled. He considered keeping the bulky device. Maybe he could move to higher ground and keep up with the movements of the security patrols, but the battery indicator had gone from green to a yellowish orange. It would soon be turning red and then go dead. The thought then occurred to Parker that they may be able to track the radio's location. He pulled the radio from the belt pouch and dropped it in the boat. He stepped into the water and pointed the boat southwest. He turned the throttle to medium speed, locked it in place, and gave the boat a shove toward the mouth of the inlet.

Parker stood and watched the johnboat's progress until it disappeared into the darkness. He flashed the spotlight twice to be satisfied that it had cleared the inlet before walking to the landmark. With the exception of a few stars peaking from behind a mostly cloudy sky, he walked in total darkness along the bank. Although he felt quite hidden from view, Parker only used the spotlight sparingly to check his progress. Once he arrived at the landmark, Parker permitted himself a short rest and placed his hand near the top of the cold, dark wood like it was an old friend.

Parker clicked on the spotlight and illuminated a small gap in the thick brush ahead. He wrapped the security officer's sweat rag over the lens, which allowed only a pale glow to escape. The ambient light could not be seen offshore and was perfect for walking the trail he had committed to memory months ago. He arrived at a familiar stump and turned slightly to his right, two o'clock position. Parker counted his steps until he reached forty-six and stopped at the base of a medium-size bolder, where he changed direction once again, this time to what would be his three o'clock position. He counted once again until he reached sixty steps and stopped. Parker slipped the sweat rag off the lens of the spotlight and aimed it dead ahead. What the light illuminated made him smile. He had made it.

Chapter Nine

Colson made a mental note of the departure time from the Orlando Airport to Atlanta International and powered down his tablet. Following the short hop to Atlanta, he would board an international flight for the five-hour-and-fifteen-minute trip to Quito, Ecuador. He walked to the bedroom, dragged a small duffel bag out of his closet, and unzipped it on his bed. He turned to the sliding glass doors and took a long look out across the expanse of the Atlantic. He slid open the door and inhaled a deep breath of salty sea air. The morning was bright, and the humidity was low. The beach had yet to be driven on, and the high tide had left the sand as smooth as a tabletop.

Colson loved the beach but there had been little time to enjoy it. Yesterday was no exception. He had spent three hours racking his brain for a plan to help Taylor. He'd spent another four hours debating with the two FBI agents and making more phone calls. Colson had not been surprised that his old DEA acquaintance, Donnie Augustine, couldn't provide the transportation he needed, but instead vowed to do anything else within his power to help his old undercover buddy. Colson didn't hold it against him. He would have probably said the same thing had the situation been reversed. At least he offered Colson a satellite phone that was overnighted and delivered an hour ago. A lot of good it would do, but he could at least let his daughter know he was never coming home if the situation went sideways on him. Augustine had also given him an address of a mail drop in Quito, used infrequently by the DEA attaché in Columbia. Colson considered himself lucky.

Colson slid the door shut and locked it. He grabbed a change of clothes and tactical boots, and shoved them in the bag. He checked his nightstand and found his passport. He flipped it open to the one and only foreign country stamp. He and Ann had been on a cruise eight years ago and went ashore in Jamaica. They had never been outside of the United States and wanted to know what all the hubbub was about. It was like an expensive trip to the mall. They saw none of the interior of Jamaica due to the warnings about being accosted by every dope-smoking hoodlum outside the protective zone of the shopping district. Even the supervised tours were rumored to be dicey. From that point on, they never left the country again, and Colson vowed never to renew the passport. It would expire within two years. At least it will be good enough for this one, final use. He still had not worked out how to return undetected, but they would cross that bridge if they miraculously got to it.

Colson carried the duffle bag into the kitchen and set it next to a sealed cardboard box addressed to the Quito mail drop. He powered on the satellite phone and tested it by dialing his old cell number. The knock came at the door before his old phone had a chance to play its Steely Dan tune. He killed the call, looked out the peephole, and opened the door to Agent Mcilwain.

Colson said, "You didn't call this morning."

Mcilwain said, "May I come in?"

Colson pulled the door open wide, and Mcilwain stepped in and walked to rear glass sliding doors. He turned back to Colson and said, "Nice view."

Colson ignored the compliment and said, "Where's your sidekick, Elvira?"

"Her name is Myra."

"Sorry. She reminded me of the mistress of the dark."

"She's a good agent."

"I'm sure she is. She didn't like me much."

"You could say you didn't impress her."

Colson sat on a stool at the breakfast counter and said, "Who's trying to impress anyone? I've only had to impress a couple of women in my lifetime. When you get it right the first time, you don't have to worry about impressing anyone else."

Mcilwain stood silent for a moment as if processing Colson's point. He lowered himself on the living room couch as Colson continued, "So what's the occasion today? If it's about your illusive scientist, you have nothing to worry about. I'm not looking for him today."

Mcilwain said, "Your flight has been arranged."

Colson stood and gave Mcilwain an even stare. "You could have called to tell me that."

"There's no official record of the flight. That means no monetary paper trail, no tickets, no boarding passes, and certainly no phone records for the NSA to find. It leaves late tonight from the Daytona airport, nonstop to Quito. I'll be here at nineteen hundred hours to drive you if you're still determined to go. I highly recommend you reconsider."

"And leave Taylor in prison?" Colson said.

"Chances are good they'll release him in several months if they don't get the ransom."

Colson shook his head. "Unacceptable. He won't survive."

Mcilwain leaned forward and emphasized each word. "This Colonel Guerra is a bad actor with a lot of equally bad connections. I can't be specific, but I strongly suggest you let this play out."

Colson said, "I appreciate the concern, and I don't doubt your information is accurate. If you had all day, I could tell you what I owe Taylor. You're right. I may not have a snowball's chance in hell, but I have to try."

Mcilwain pushed himself up off the couch and smoothed the wrinkles from his suit jacket. "OK, I just felt it was the right thing to do to warn you. You remember the condition?"

"Let me guess," said Colson. "I stop looking for Parker or digging into the case, right?"

Mcilwain nodded.

Colson said, "I already told you I would. How did you pull this off, if I may ask?"

"I didn't. Strickland made the request."

"That's hard to believe. She despises me."

"She has more pull with the SAC. Believe me, she only did it so we could accomplish what we were told and that was to encourage you to stop interfering. There's just one more thing."

"What? When I get back you want me to help Agent Strickland find a personality?"

Mcilwain said, "Not quite. You wanted three days but you only have twenty-four hours. You have to do whatever you're going to do and be back on the plane no later than nineteen hundred hours the following day. Deal?"

Colson took one last look at the beach from his perch on the barstool and turned back to Mcilwain.

"Deal."

Colson spent the rest of the afternoon searching for images of Quito Prison and the surrounding area on the Internet. He found one. It depicted the main entrance, which was unexpectedly elegant. The structure sat high and directly above the roadway on what appeared to be a man-made plateau. A ten- or twelve-foot-high wall constructed of cinder block jutted skyward at the edge of a road. To the far right appeared to be the top of a heavy door in the wall surrounded by stone. The wall was topped by a fence made of decorative iron pickets held in place by tall square columns eight to ten feet apart and painted white with a yellow band of trim finishing off the top. Mounted atop each pillar were bronze decorative lights resembling old train station lanterns.

Set several feet back from the fence stood two tall polls of the same bronze finish. What appeared to be spotlights were directed toward the building, and security cameras were mounted beneath each light. The main building sat probably twenty feet back from the spotlights. It consisted of two buildings painted off white with a line of yellow trim at the top to compliment the fence columns. The two separate structures were joined in the middle by a grand entrance that was a patio with three arches supported by wide columns. Above the covered patio was a deep balcony with a white-and-yellow-trimmed railing to finish out the design. The rounded archways complimented the eight arched windows, four running along the second floor of each building. The first floor windows were rectangular. All the window glass sat behind substantial-looking burglar type bars.

Colson suspected they were the administrative offices and also where Guerra's office would be, most likely centered in the middle structure with access to the large balcony. Colson pictured a pergola perhaps, built above comfortable patio furniture where Colonel Guerra could entertain his cohorts and enjoy a Cuban cigar. Colson also strongly suspected the cheery façade would be the only elegant part of Quito Prison—something for residents and tourists to admire instead of recoil from.

Colson entered variations of key search words but couldn't find more images. He suspected why. It was for the same reasons that the Clay County Jail had been set back from the main roadway. Policy had been written to restrict the public from taking photographs of the building from within the guard line. The intent being to prevent escape plans from being formulated by family members or criminal associates. The photo he was seeing was from the street where anyone could take a photo. That meant they were not concerned about the administrative offices. There were no prisoners there. They would be held in structures out of the public's line of sight. And theirs would be far less luxurious accommodations.

He checked the time. It was 16:00 hours or 4:00 p.m. He was getting cheated out of his twenty-four-hour window since the flight itself would take almost five hours. Colson grabbed the box with the Quito mail drop address off the counter and made his way to the elevator and down to the parking garage. Thirty minutes later, he squealed back into his parking space, frustrated. The original plan of staying at least two days had been shrunk to nineteen hours of operating time. Even at the exorbitant price of over $600.00, the express mail service couldn't get the package to Ecuador overnight. It was fast approaching 5:30 p.m., and Mcilwain would be there to pick him up in less than an hour. He would just have to chance it.

Colson was waiting in the guest parking area when Mcilwain turned his Charger into the lot. He almost missed Colson standing in the shadow and hit the brakes abruptly. The trunk lid popped up, and Colson set his duffle bag and box in the back. He caught a glance of Mcilwain watching in his side mirror. Colson dropped in the passenger seat and jerked the door closed. Mcilwain put the car in gear, made a circle around the middle isle, and then nosed up to A1A. Traffic was light, but Mcilwain didn't pull out. Colson noticed the agent glaring at him.

Mcilwain said, "What's in the box?"

Colson said, "Just equipment I might need."

"Equipment? I can't allow you to take any guns—"

"It's not a gun," Colson interrupted.

"Look, Colson. I can't allow you into another country with any offensive weapons."

Colson turned in his seat and pointed a finger in Mcilwain's face. "You didn't totally live up to your side of the agreement. Instead of two or three days, I'm stuck with twenty-four hours, less flight time, which leaves me with nineteen hours *at best*. I appreciate the ride, but I'm not in the mood to be bickering with you about my luggage. So are we going to meet this flight or are you going to let me out so I can go buy a membership to the country club and become golfing buddies with Director Danz? I told you I'm not taking a gun."

Mcilwain slightly recoiled at Colson's outburst, but otherwise seemed to keep his composure. He said, "I understand your plans got changed, but it isn't because of me. I have a boss just like everyone else. I'm just saying I can't *knowingly* allow you to transport any offensive weapons into Ecuador."

Colson stared at Mcilwain silently for a moment and then said, "You're *already* allowing an offensive weapon into Ecuador."

"How do you figure?"

"You're sending *me.*"

Max Rollins had a pounding headache. He was mentally and physically exhausted. The tie he had worn loosely around his neck for the last three days lay abandoned and crumpled on his office desk, his dress shirt was as wrinkled as the face of a ninety-year-old man from days of wear; and his undershirt was clammy and stuck to his armpits. He had spent the past twenty-four hours at the mobile command post with the security chief. He knew nothing about police work, security operations, or coordinating search patrols, but as the de facto civilian in charge of the NASA security force, he had to act like he did.

The methods of search deployment, as the security chief termed it, sounded like nothing more than controlled chaos to Rollins. The entire situation with the escape of Parker and now the missing security officer was becoming an endless nightmare. Rollins occasionally dismissed the extent of damage Parker could inflict if he ever surfaced in public. Parker was a nobody. The machine he would be up against was too massive to take down. If he was a famous journalist or author or celebrity, he could potentially make a lot of noise, but even then it would be nothing more than a blip on the screen at best or a short-lived scandal at worst.

Rollins craved a shower, fresh clothes, and a decent meal, but Danz was calling him on the carpet for a full debriefing that morning—in person of course. The security chief had called for one of the officers to drop him off in front of the Operations Support Building. He straightened and tucked in his shirt and tried to flatten most of the wrinkles with his hands as he rode the elevator to the top floor. He prayed Danz's secretary had made coffee. Thankfully, she had. He poured a Styrofoam cup full, composed himself, and then walked into the director's office.

Danz stood in his typical position with his back turned and his hands on his hips as he gazed at the Vehicle Assembly Building in the distance. He said nothing as Rollins walked in and stood behind the chair across from his desk. Rollins hated it when Danz was quiet. They had given him oversight of this project, and he knew Danz was losing confidence in him. If he couldn't produce positive results soon, his career would evaporate. He tired of standing and decided to sit and take a sip of coffee. Danz didn't turn from the window, but finally spoke.

"I was beginning to think you were right," he said.

Rollins shifted in his seat and took another sip of coffee. "About what?"

Danz turned and sat at his desk. Rollins wasn't expecting Danz's demeanor to be calm. Then again, Danz was not typically confrontational. Sometimes the quiet ones were the worst. You never knew where you stood with people like Danz. That type of treatment was usually reserved for people one was about to fire. One of those, "Sorry, but we're going to have to let you go," moments.

"About Parker," said Danz. "That he was most likely dead by now. I even had the chairman convinced. Do I now have to let them know that the problem is not resolved?"

"No," said Rollins. "The disappearance of the security officer is a coincidence."

"And his missing boat?"

Rollins grinned. "It was found not ten minutes ago. The radio call came in just as they dropped me off here."

"And the officer?"

"No."

"Where was the boat?"

"About three miles north of his route."

Danz slid a notepad in front of him and began jotting notes. He said, "How do I explain that?"

"Simple enough," said Rollins. "He dozed off and fell overboard or he was bitten by a snake or capsized by an alligator, and the boat drifted for hours away from his route. One of those options is likely true anyway and has nothing to do with Parker."

Danz sat in silence writing notes. Rollins gulped the remaining coffee in his cup and waited. Danz stopped writing and began tapping his index finger on the desk as if working out an equation in his head.

Danz looked up from his notepad and said, "We have to be prepared to submit this month's data. Do you have that covered?"

Rollins wasn't expecting the change of subject. He adjusted his posture in the chair. As it was turning out, this was not the, "Sorry, but we're going to have to let you go," moment he was expecting. The coffee was doing its job, and his headache was subsiding.

He said, "Yes, sir. I have one of the other group scientists accumulating the data. One with conviction, not conscience."

"Very well," Danz said flatly.

"And," Rollins continued, "I'm working on another angle to deal with the private investigator."

Danz made a dismissive wave with his hand. "No need. I had the FBI take care of that."

"Really," Rollins said with a tone of satisfaction. "So we're good then?"

"Not so fast, Max. We're not out of the woods yet. You have to keep Parker contained for the next few weeks. After that, I couldn't care less what he does or who he talks to. It'll be too late for him to do any damage by then."

Rollins slumped back in his chair. "So we keep looking?"

Danz stood and crossed his arms. "*You* let him go so *you'll* keep looking until he is either found or midnight strikes on Election Day. Whichever one comes first. Now go take a shower and get some sleep. I can smell you from here."

Agent Mcilwain turned left on Nova Road off of International Speedway Boulevard and then right on Bellevue Avenue. Colson had been in silent thought for ten minutes. He needed time to plan and identify options, and to prepare for contingencies. There were very few things worse than charging into an operation blind and unprepared. That is precisely why cops have pre-action briefings before conducting search warrants or attempting high-profile arrests or hostage rescues. Everyone would know the plan, the layout, and the sequence of events. Colson was one person alone, with no backup, no blue prints, no firearms, and no specific plan. Mcilwain had cranked up the air conditioning, but the collar of Colson's shirt was moist with sweat as anxiety was getting the better of him. He drew a deep breath in and out in an attempt to expel the uneasiness.

He finally noticed the residential road they were on and turned to Mcilwain and said, "Do you know where you're going?"

Mcilwain nodded, "Yep."

Mcilwain slowed and turned right on Clyde Morris Boulevard, drove another tenth of a mile, and then turned left into what at first appeared to be a well-manicured business park. They passed a large rectangular blue sign with a three-dimensional aircraft model set at an angle in a circular cut out. The sign read, Embry-Riddle Aeronautical University.

Colson said, "I seriously doubt I have time to get a commercial license and fly myself."

Mcilwain half smiled. "You said you wanted a flight that doesn't exist, didn't you?"

Colson shrugged.

Mcilwain snaked the Charger through a large parking lot and emerged at the rear of the complex next to an enormous metal structure. White lettering along the top eve read, Fleet Maintenance Hangar. On the far side of the hangar, the main terminal came into view off in the distance. They were technically at the airport, but at the end of the main runway. A long line of small Cessna's and Beechcraft planes filled spaces to their right. To their left was the open door of the hangar with a sleek Cessna Citation backed in and partially shadowed in the cavernous space. Mcilwain pulled the Charger into the shadows alongside the jet and shut down the engine. Colson stepped out and admired the sleek design. A thin ribbon of alternating green-and-gold stripes spanned the fuselage from nose to tail with a matching design on the engines mounted at the rear of each wing. He made a mental note of the tail number, which was painted on the rudder to match the green stripping: N950P.

A slender man wearing black pants, white shirt, and airline captain's hat ducked from under the nose of the jet and walked to Agent Mcilwain with an outstretched hand.

"Agent Mcilwain," the man said, shaking Mcilwain's hand.

"Captain," Mcilwain replied.

Turning to Colson, Mcilwain said, "This is Grey Colson."

The pilot and Colson shook hands. The pilot said, "I'm Captain Robert McCollum."

Colson chuckled. "Nice to meet you. Mcilwain and McCollum, huh? Don't tell me the in-flight meal is McDonalds?"

"I'm sorry," the Captain said, obviously not understanding the joke. "Ah, there's no in-flight meal."

Colson threw Mcilwain a sideways glance. "Figures."

Colson grabbed his bag and box out of the Charger, climbed the steps of the Cessna, and ducked inside without another word. Captain McCollum followed and disappeared into the cockpit. Colson heard muffled clicking noises and then the high-pitch whine of the twin jet engines spinning up. He had his pick among six rows of wide leather-appointed seats. Three rows facing three rows. He selected one at the rear with his back to the bulkhead. There were no announcements and no safety instructions given by a stewardess with a fake smile as the jet slowly emerged from the hangar, just the variation in the pitch of the engines as the jet gained momentum and taxied left toward the runway.

The Cessna paused for what seemed like five minutes, apparently awaiting clearance for the non-existent flight. It eventually rolled to the end of the runway and pivoted to the right. After a brief pause, Colson heard the engines throttle to full, and he was pulled into his seat as the small jet shot down the runway and lifted into the darkening Daytona sky. Colson reclined his seat as the jet banked south. He had checked and found that Ecuador was in the same time zone. But nineteen hours was still just nineteen hours. With luck, he would land by 1:00 a.m.. It was time to sleep.

Parker looked skyward as the jet rose in the distance flying southward, with its red beacon fixed on one wing and a green one on the other. A white strobe on the belly of the craft blinked rapidly as it flew directly overhead. The sound of the jet turbines increased and quickly faded as it ascended and disappeared into the night. In all of his excursions to Gaines Island, he had never seen aircraft on a flight path directly overhead. And it was at a very low altitude, as if it was trying to sneak below the radar. It was momentarily distressing, but he quickly dismissed the possibility that NASA was searching for him with a corporate jet.

Parker turned his attention back to the massive, hundred-year-old oak tree. The flashlight gave its trunk a haunting glow. To the right of the oak was a slender cedar tree, dwarfed by its larger neighbor and deprived of full sunlight by the oak's huge canopy. Parker walked to the cedar tree and reached for a vine that was looped around its lowest branch. With a quick jerk came the sound of a bushel of leaves falling to the ground. It wasn't leaves, but a length of rope that had been secured to a branch high above the mossy ground.

Parker had been a latecomer, born fifteen years after his older brother and sister. Possibly a surprise to his parents, but never treated as such. His father had been a veteran of World War II and had died when Parker was twenty-seven. He clearly remembered his dad telling him about the war and the global scare of nuclear weapons that followed until the Reagan administration's "peace through strength" policy crushed the Soviet Union. Survival in the old days consisted of nuclear fallout shelters in the backyard, stocked with nonperishable food and water. Parker thought it was still important today, even if people laughed at the notion. But in the days and years following 9/11, and the growing terrorist threats around the world, he felt the threat was even greater than in the brave years of the greatest generation. At least then soldiers fought a nation within set boarders and proudly flew the flag of their home country. Now there were no recognizable borders, no honorable rules of engagement, and no bounds to which the radical idealists would go to kill civilians, or, as they were called, "infidels." Parker was convinced that 9/11 was not the end, but just the beginning.

There was obviously no backyard to dig a bomb shelter behind his condo. On his first excursion to Gaines Island, the idea came to him almost immediately, and it had taken until just a month ago to complete. Parker walked to the base of the old tree and shone his light upward. Large branches were woven in chaotic angles where they sprouted smaller branches and then smaller ones still, with Spanish moss hanging and swaying gently in the light evening breeze. He clicked off the flashlight, stuck it in his back pocket, and climbed the seventy-foot rope through the thicket of limbs to a solid bed of Spanish moss. The rope disappeared inside the moss and into a hole in a solid plank. It continued through the plank where it was tied off and nailed to a large unseen branch above.

Parker wrapped his legs around the rope for stability, pressed a free hand against the bed of moss, and pushed upward. The surface above the moss was solid and didn't budge. He spun slightly to his right and pushed upward once again. This time the moss and solid surface above gave way. He gave a third push and the hatch flipped over and out of sight, leaving a square opening of pitch-blackness.

Parker pulled himself into the tree house, flipped the hatch closed, and felt relatively safe for the first time in days. He sat silently in total darkness, slowed his breathing, and listened. He pulled the flashlight from his pocket and pointed it in the direction of the faint scratching noise he heard. He risked clicking it on and released a sigh at the sight of a small lizard tail disappearing through a crack in the far wall. He took a quick survey of what previously was his eight-foot-by-eight-foot sleeping quarters, now a hideout. It had taken the better part of eighteen months of surreptitiously transporting small amounts of lumber from the storage unit to the fish camp to the island—two boards here and three boards there. But it was worth the patience and effort once he completed his home away from home. It was a task that would have been easily completed in a weekend with one trip to the big home improvement store, but that would have defeated the purpose of subterfuge. No one knew his hideaway existed and never would if he had his way.

Parker almost forgot the most important task. He grabbed the rope, pulled it furiously through the hole in the floor, and bundled it in the corner behind him. A hammer, ax, folding shovel, and handsaw hung from nails on the wall to his left. On the wall across from Parker hung a hooded raincoat next to an ammo box he had purchased from an army surplus store and a crossbow was propped in the corner with a half-dozen short arrows. Parker had always been fascinated with the crossbow, but had only used it for target practice after ordering it online three months earlier. He had been surprised by its accuracy.

Two foam beach floats lay stacked on each other and pushed against the wall to the right with a sleeping bag roll resting on top. At the head of the makeshift bed was a boxy item the size of a Kleenex box with a small headlamp attached to the top and a small crank on the near side. Parker had seen it on an infomercial and thought a lamp he could power by cranking it was perfect for a survivalist application. It had worked for an hour at a time as advertised, so he ordered the crank powered weather radio, which sat next to it.

Gallon jugs of water sat against the wall behind him next to a portable gas hotplate and two small tanks of propane. Not the dream survivalist situation, but a far cry better than the accommodations for the contestants on reality shows. A thatch roof covered the structure and rectangular size holes were cut into each wall at the top for 360-degree observations.

He found the small LED light strip at the foot of his foam bed. He turned it on and the flashlight off. The ambient light from the strip would be all he needed for the moment. He popped open the ammo box and grabbed a MRE, or "meals ready to eat." Parker savored the freeze-dried meal as if it was his mom's Thanksgiving dinner while taking swigs of water from one of the jugs. After trying to sleep in trees and moss beds for days, the foam floats felt like a cloud beneath the sleeping bag. The night was still too humid to crawl inside the thick bag, so he lay on top. He felt like he could really rest that night, but his thoughts began nagging at him. Parker lifted his head for a long moment to listen to the new sound of helicopter rotors that grew louder for several seconds, but eventually faded.

He exhaled and dropped his head back, thinking, *Now what?*

Colson couldn't sleep or even catnap. The cabin was quiet, and he rather liked the hum of the jet engines on each side of the fuselage. White noise in the background made him sleep like a baby, but he wasn't the type who could sleep just anywhere. Even fully reclined with his feet resting on the seat facing him, it wasn't his bed. He slipped his seat into its full upright position and flipped a small table up from the side of his seat and over his lap. The setup was like a small restaurant booth. He lifted the box at his feet and opened it on the tabletop.

A pair of black BDU pants was neatly folded on top of cash bundles. It was all the money Colson could put together. Two $10,000 cash advances from credit cards made the first $20,000 and $10,000 from his savings account brought him up to $30,000. The credit union would allow him only $35,000 against a refinance on his practically new Vette, which Colson griped about, but finally gave in to. And $7,500 added to the pile out of his private investigation operating fund came to a grand total of $72,500—exactly $27,500 short of Guerra's ransom demand.

Colson pulled the BDUs out and ran his hand along the edge of the box, under the cash bundles, and grabbed a small round plastic package. He laid the pants on the table, opened a small pocketknife, and began methodically plucking at the threading on the left leg inseam from the crotch area to just past the knee. Using the same knife, he sliced open the plastic package containing a roll of fabric Velcro and cut a section the length of the open portion of the inseam. He separated the Velcro with a *rip* and removed the clear film to expose its sticky side. He carefully placed the pieces along the length of the open inseam and pressed it back together.

Satisfied with his amateur alteration, Colson dropped the pants and remaining Velcro back on top of the money, flipped the box lid closed, and set it back in the isle next to him. He flipped the tabletop back up and let it drop back in place, and then propped his feet back up on the facing seat. He closed his eyes and rewound old drug deals in his mind. One could insert almost any item in place of drugs when conducting deals, such as bootlegged cigarettes, counterfeit money, stolen firearms, or hot cars, and the result would be the same. In this case, it would be a human being. There was certain protocol followed worldwide, regardless of the nationality or ethnicity or tongue, from the common thief on the street to the leaders of third-world countries. It all boiled down to common sense, and the bad guys usually counted on those they dealt with not having any, which is why the smart ones typically won the day, the cash, the women, and the power.

Colson hoped he could count on an attribute he had observed in others over the years. He felt certain this one attribute was as universal as the commonsense protocols the bad guys followed. That would be complacency. He had no doubt Colonel Guerra controlled his own little world and would be in his comfort zone. But what about his soldiers or deputies or turnkeys, whatever he called them. Colson was almost always impressed with those who worked for him, but there was always a small percentage who became complacent, especially if they stayed in the same routine and did the same job day in and day out. That's what he would be counting on because he had no intent on Guerra keeping a dime of his money.

Colson's thoughts were interrupted when Captain McCollum emerged from the cockpit. He walked toward Colson and stopped, resting his hands on the back of the seat Colson's feet were propped on.

McCollum checked his watch and said, "Two hours until wheels down. You good back here?"

Colson offered a small grin. "Sure. You want me to drive for a while?"

McCollum raised one hand. "No, thanks. I'm good."

Colson dropped his feet to the floor and leaned closer to McCollum. "I may need a couple of extra hours. Let's say nine in the evening?"

McCollum shook his head. "It's not up to me. I was told wheels up at seven, no exceptions. We'll be on a remote, private airstrip, and I have no desire to get caught up in whatever you're doing. I don't even want to know. I have a family to get back to."

Colson said, "Yeah, well enjoy them while you have them. Thanks for the ride anyway."

McCollum nodded, turned, and made his way back to the cockpit. Without turning around he said, "There's supposed to be a car waiting for you when we land."

"I'm curious," Colson said, which stopped McCollum in his tracks. "Not asking you to divulge any state secrets, but how do you pull off a flight that doesn't exist?"

McCollum looked back at Colson. "Not such a big deal in this case. After we cleared the Florida coast, we had to give Cuba a wide berth, but then we stayed on a flight path over international waters in the Caribbean."

Colson leaned forward and looked out the window. "What's that land mass?"

"We have to pass over Costa Rica to get to the Pacific side for the last leg of the flight."

"They'll know we're here won't they?"

"No way around it without creating an unnecessary international incident. They are friendlies for the most part. There's too much tourism from the US for them to get their backs up too much. We're listed as a diplomatic flight."

"So I finally achieved diplomat status?"

McCollum made a deliberate show of rolling his eyes. "Hardly. And you're certainly no diplomat in Ecuador, so you better watch your ass."

"I appreciate the sentiment, but my ass will be fine. You sure you don't want me to drive for a while?"

McCollum cocked his head and turned back to the cockpit door. Colson sat back as it clicked shut. He supposed he should be happy to have pulled off the private flight. One moment he was going to have to risk being listed on the manifest of a commercial airline, and the next moment he was awarded with a covert flight that couldn't be traced or tracked, which was exactly what he needed—exactly what he'd demanded in exchange for doing nothing. Simply stop looking for some scientist that... Colson felt a sudden chill shoot up his spine. He reached into the side pocket of his cargo pants and pulled out the satellite phone. It took a minute to find the message icon since he hadn't used it before. He found Augustine's number, typed in a message, and hit SEND.

Agent Mcilwain stood from behind his desk and arched his back, popping a couple of stiff vertebrae. The Parker investigation was essentially at a standstill. Wherever Parker was, he was not using his credit cards, pulling money out of an ATM, renting a car, buying a plane ticket, or checking into a hotel—anywhere on the planet. The FBI database was the most sophisticated in the world unless the

NSA or CIA had something better. He knew he would never know for certain. One moment Parker was the biggest game in town, and the next moment it was no longer a priority. The file now lay in his "pick up in case of boredom" stack, and he was fine and dandy with that. It wasn't even the FBI's primary function to hunt down fugitives. That task was best left to the deputies of the United States Marshal Service.

Finding Parker would no doubt have been a feather in his cap, but Mcilwain would give up all his feathers if it meant not having to deal with Director Danz again. He had felt at the time as if he and Strickland had been on loan to NASA like a couple of rent-a-cops. He had flat out refused to meet with Danz after leaving Colson's condo and told Strickland she could take her best shot as he stayed in the car and held their parking spot at the curb. She had returned with a sly grin, saying that Danz was satisfied with the warning given to Colson to stay off his back. Of course, Strickland was a talker and could convince a turkey it could fly. Mcilwain knew that was what got under her skin about Colson. He wasn't a pushover like most common men are when being chastised by a very confident female FBI agent. And how she was able to convince the SAC to fly Colson to Ecuador was anyone's guess. He would just rather not know.

A new file was handed to him during a lunch debriefing. It was his and Strickland's new case: two eighteen-year-old high school students with a newfound interest in Syria and the terrorist network. The latest Facebook photos were of them standing in full Arab garb and sporting the beginnings of dark, wiry beards. The question was had the two up-and-coming Muslim terrorist sympathizers bought into the seventy-two virgin promise of eternal sex or were they just a couple of misguided youths with little or no adult supervision? It was Mcilwain and Strickland's new task to crawl up their backsides with a microscope and find out before the duet decided to stroll into a school or the nearest convenience store with a couple of AK-47's slung over their shoulders.

Mcilwain dropped back in his seat and flipped the new file open when his desk phone chirped. The name across the caller ID was "Shawn Cannon," the resident tech hound. He lifted the receiver to his ear.

"Mcilwain," he said and paused to listen. The only voices that could be heard in the office besides Cannon's on the phone were those of a couple of agents down the hall. As with many tech guys, it was taking Cannon ten sentences to say what he could have easily said in one.

"Hang on," Mcilwain said. "Strickland said you found absolutely nothing at all on the flash drive. She said that *you* said it had never been written on." Mcilwain waited through Cannon's reply and said. "OK, that's what she said. So I don't understand what you're getting at."

Mcilwain wedged the receiver between his cheek and shoulder, grabbed his cell phone, and pulled up the calendar. "Yeah, that's the date. I stayed behind to watch security video while Strickland—" Mcilwain was cut off. He listened as he looked at the calendar date. He said, "That can't be right," and then fell silent again, listening to something that was beyond belief. He finally dropped his forehead into his right palm.

"That. Is. Absolutely. Impossible."

Chapter Ten

Ten miles south of Quito, Ecuador, the town of Tambillo was situated just a mile west of Highway 35. Five miles to the east of Tambillo railroad tracks ran north and south in a parallel line with Highway 35. An abandoned building the approximate size of an American fast food restaurant stood near the tracks. Once used in the '50s as a stop for travelers, the old station had fallen into a dilapidated state. Hunks of cream-colored stucco lay at its foundation from years of water damage where the roof had been neglected. The interior furnishings had been pilfered long ago. Even the ticket counter had been dismantled and hauled away, leaving only a faint outline on the dirty cobblestone floor.

Behind the abandoned station and running west to east was a mostly dirt-packed road with shallow, smoothed-over ruts where old pickup trucks had hauled coal to refuel passenger trains. The unnamed road wound out of sight around the lush green hillsides and small mountains beyond. Three bumpy miles to the west, the hilly terrain flattened and opened to a narrow clearing the length of ten football fields. It was near sea level and just long enough for a Cessna Citation to perform a short field landing and takeoff.

Colson opened the maps app on his phone and typed in the coordinates the pilot had given him for the landing strip and Quito Prison. A third set of numbers was entered and saved. It was nothing like landing in Atlanta or Orlando or even Daytona. The landscape was totally blacked out at 01:00 hours. There were a few scattered lights in the sea of darkness to give Colson a better perspective of their decent, but very few. The small jet banked left on final approach and extended its flaps. They touched down a little rough, but Colson gave McCollum the benefit of the doubt since it was a grass-and-dirt strip. The engines roared in reverse thrust, and the Cessna came to a complete stop. There was no turning or taxiing as was normal at a commercial airport. Colson assumed all McCollum would have to do on departure was spin around and take off in the opposite direction, depending on wind direction. Hopefully, with two passengers instead of one.

McCollum stepped from the cockpit, popped the hatch, and lowered a set of stairs. Colson stood and felt static pull the hairs of his head to the ceiling of the fuselage.

McCollum said, "I'm gonna stretch my legs. Are you going to sleep in here?"

Colson said, "No, you guys didn't give me enough time. I need to get moving."

"At one in the morning?"

"Unless you will stay later and give me more time."

McCollum shook his head. "Can't. Remember, wheels up at nineteen hundred hours," he said, checking his watch, "that being *today*." McCollum gestured ahead to where a metal shed stood, hauntingly illuminated by the alternating red and green wing strobes. A squat car sat in front of the shed. "Keys should be sitting on top of the front driver's side tire."

"I'm surprised it has four wheels," Colson said sarcastically. He lifted the box and followed McCollum down the stairs. He found the keys where McCollum said they would be, folded himself into the Fiat, and then dropped the box on the passenger seat. He slammed the flimsy door shut and started the sewing machine–sounding contraption. He checked his phone before dropping the gear into first. It wouldn't be until business hours in the morning before Augustine responded to his question. He would have seven hours to scout out his destinations and prepare himself for a day there was no preparation for. He retrieved the first set of coordinates, sat the phone on the tiny console between the seats, and drove the Fiat away into the darkness.

As a GS-13, Mcilwain was an assistant group supervisor. Strickland was a GS-12, and the remaining agents in the group were either new guys starting out as GS-9s or GS-11s. Mcilwain didn't often exercise his limited authority, but he and Strickland were given a new case and were prohibited from deviating from the assignment unless directed otherwise by the SAC or group supervisor.

Mcilwain heard the voice of a young man down the hall and the copying machine spitting out paper. His name was Ted, and he had been an intern before finishing his degree and going to training at Quantico. He knew what the young agent had been working on since joining the group five months ago: summary cases, the tedious task of reviewing cases from local agencies that may have the potential for a federal investigation or may have ties to active FBI cases. Mcilwain jotted information down on a post-it note and called Ted's name.

Ted appeared at Mcilwain's door holding a stack of photocopies. Mcilwain waved the young agent inside and said, "Aren't you reviewing a state fraud case?"

Ted hefted the stack of papers slightly to prove he hadn't been goofing off. "Yeah," he said. "I mean, yes. Two actually. One in Melbourne and another in Tampa."

"Do you think they are related?" Mcilwain asked in a curious tone as if he believed Ted might have unearthed evidence to solve the crime of the century.

"It's a very good possibility, but I'm just getting started."

Mcilwain held up the post-it note. "I took a call from an informant yesterday. Take it."

Ted shifted his papers to one arm and took the paper from Mcilwain. "What's this?"

"Here's what I want you to do," Mcilwain said without answering Ted's query. "This may be the link you are looking for. I need you to prepare an administrative subpoena for the business at that location and get all the video and financial transactions they have for that specific date."

"The whole day?" Ted asked.

Mcilwain nodded.

Ted smiled. Mcilwain knew the young agent would love nothing better than to get out of the office and do real FBI work. There's hardly anything more exciting than approaching Joe Citizen for the first time, flashing your credentials, and saying, "I'm Agent Ted with the FBI." Mcilwain couldn't remember the boy's last name.

Ted turned immediately, stopped short, and turned back to Mcilwain. He said, "Ah, do I record my case number on the subpoena or did you cut a new one?"

"Of course not. This case is *all* yours. Besides, I'm busy with Strickland on something else. But we're a team, and as such, we help each other and cover each other's backs. I'd be a shit if I didn't pass the information on to you, but there's just one other thing I need you to do and then you can run with it."

"What's that?"

Mcilwain pointed his finger at his own chest. "*I* will review the security footage first. It's *my* informant, and if he's steering me wrong again, I want to know first thing. Understand?"

"Yes, sir," Ted said and scurried out the door.

Colson took advantage of the dark countryside. He drove to the first location he had saved in his map app. It was a totally deserted area and totally dark with the exception of the Fiat's two headlight beams bouncing up and down on the uneven road. He ran out of road at the crest of a plateau. Now he could see faint lights to his northwest, which, according to the map app, should be the capital city of Quito. Colson was surprised by the coolness of the night. He had never been to South America and expected the heat and clamminess of Florida. He rolled his driver's window down and listened. A breeze made the hip-high grasses in the rolling field whisper, but otherwise there was nothing. There were no buildings, no abandoned vehicles, and no voices. He cut off the headlights and changed into the BDUs and a fresh pullover shirt.

Colson had found it impossible to sleep on the plane, but the adrenaline he felt during the planning stage was beginning to wane, and the need to sleep was winning the battle. He set the alarm on his phone for 7:00 a.m., crossed his arms, and mostly dozed for the next four hours, checking his phone every half hour. He recalled checking his phone for the last time at 4:10 a.m. Then the hideous alarm went off at seven, making him jerk in his seat. He felt like his neck was broken. He stepped out of the Fiat into the cool morning air, stretched, and walked in circles for five minutes before feeling somewhat normal again. He had been wrong about there being no buildings. What he hadn't seen during his dark drive was a squat cinder block structure close to a wooden power poll. It looked to be maybe ten-by-ten feet square with no roof. He took note of the pile of gravel against the front wall and around the power poll and then made a slow 360-degree spin to survey the land around him.

The view of the countryside was beautiful in its own way. The rolling hills reminded Colson of his childhood in Ohio, except the high grass would be replaced with stalks of corn. He could clearly see Quito in the distance against a backdrop of a rolling mountainous region. The capital city consumed the majority of the valley. But it didn't remind Colson of any capital city he had ever seen. There were no high rises, just a flat city of buildings set in clumps. He walked to the passenger side and dug around in his box for a roll of wide masking tape. He made the needed adjustment to his wardrobe and climbed behind the wheel for his journey to Quito Prison. Colson first lifted his phone, summoned the map app, and then saved his current location as a way point before coasting down the road. At the main road, he saw a sign he hadn't seen on the dark drive in. It had an arrow pointing upward from the direction he had come that read, "Pichincha." Colson figured it was the name of the road or the name of the crest where he had napped. It could have very well been the breed of a small dog for all he knew, but he committed it to memory before pulling out. He figured no self-respecting colonel would show up to work before nine o'clock, so he drove slowly to familiarize himself with the area in the daylight.

The Columbian city of Pasto was approximately two hundred miles northeast of Ecuador. It's roughly half a million of inhabitants were largely employed in the food, beverage, and furniture industries. Now a bustling city, it had once been isolated from the rest of Columbia due to its geographical location after the war of independence from Spain. But aside from the mostly law abiding and hardworking citizens of Pasto, the fact remained that the nation of Columbia was still the world's top producer of cocaine—not within the cities proper, but secreted in its desolate mountainous regions.

The Bancafe building was the tallest at six stories high, looking over the square at Pasto Narino Plaza. DEA Task Force Agent William "Bill" Fitzgerald grabbed an old phone book from the bookshelf, rolled it up like a log, and shoved it behind his back in the chair of his third-floor office. At 6' 3", he had been the tallest agent in the Atlanta field office before being tapped as one of a few liaisons assigned in Columbia to assist their federal officials with intelligence gathering and sharing. But of course he had been instructed as to what information he would and would not share. Fitzgerald had no doubt that the Columbians operated in the same fashion.

Fitzgerald leaned back against the rolled phone book and sighed. In his twenties and early thirties, his height had been an asset both in his career and love life. Until he'd passed the age of forty-five, female agents had always referred to him as the tall, dark, and Yankee office Casanova. Now, just over a year from retirement, Fitzgerald was tired and ready to move on. His six-three frame had become a lanky burden. He had to fight against the constant urge to hunch over his desk. The ensuing pain when he stood was unbearable.

The office faced the busy plaza square and provided a pleasant view. It was a simple office with an old desk and top-of-the-line computer. An antiquated push-button phone he'd never used rested to his left on the desk. There was a three-shelf bookcase against the wall to his right filled with paperbacks. He had read them all multiple times. They were all fiction—nothing official. The solid wooden door behind him had an official-looking placard stuck to the side facing the elevator that read, "Contador," meaning "Accountant," in English. No one ever knocked, and the old push-button phone never rang.

Fitzgerald, or "Fitz" as his buddies called him, had been stationed in Pasto, Columbia, for eleven months. It was typical for an agent to be assigned overseas prior to retirement. He had already been assigned to two field offices and suffered through his required stint at Quantico. With one year and one month left before hanging it up, he found Pasto a beautiful assignment with beautiful women. God knew he had been through any woman at the Buffalo and Atlanta offices who had entertained his advances. He supposed being divorced made him the perfect candidate for his current and final post. And it would make the husbands of many female agents feel much more at ease. As much as he liked the area, Fitz was convinced he could do the remaining thirteen months standing on his head, and in fact, he might never leave.

Fitz checked the computer file in front of him for the third and last time before making the call. He was a player and womanizer, but he was always thorough with his work when not distracted by the female of the species. He would double-check and triple check the information to know for certain that what he passed on was golden. The gospel according to Fitz. He had been gathering as much information as he could about an individual for his direct supervisor, but so far he had come up dry. He touched an icon on his satellite phone and waited for the connection. It took a full twenty seconds.

"Augustine," the voice said.

"It's Fitzgerald, sir."

"Fitz," Augustine replied. "Anything else you can tell me?"

"Ah," Fitzgerald began, checking the handwritten notes in front of him. "Not really, sir. Ramos Enrique Guerra, born 21 July 1961, fifty-five years old. Colonel with the Ecuador State Police since 1985. Specific date not verified. Currently, the commandant of Quito Prison. A dozen or so abuse inquiries and accusations of blackmail and general corruption, but tame by typical third-world standards. No complaints substantiated and no charges or discipline followed. Some indication of drug trafficking, but only from unreliable informants. Nothing credible."

"I see," Augustine said flatly. "Very well."

"I'm sorry nothing came up. I can go back and…"

"No, that's enough. Just be on standby until you hear back from me."

Fitzgerald squinted at the computer screen, seeing nothing of interest to the DEA. "Sir, ah, is there anything I should know about this guy? Like I said, I don't see anything—"

"You heard me, Fitz," Augustine interrupted. "I said just stand by. And that means *do not* be going out and getting drunk and chasing women until you hear back from me."

"Yes, sir, but can I ask one question?"

"What?"

"Is someone in trouble?"

Augustine chuckled. "You mean are *you* in trouble? The answer is no."

"Then who?"

There was a brief pause as if Augustine was considering his question. "You don't want to know," he finally said before the connection went dead.

Colson had contemplated multiple options two days ago under his canopy on Daytona Beach. Maybe not multiple, but at least a couple. There was always the old-fashioned jailbreak. He had worked in the jail off and on for over three decades. Each time his turn came up, a new jail extension had been added to accommodate the ever-growing inmate population. It was never the same design as the previous one due to the county switching to the lowest-bidding architect and contractor at the time. And each time it required a week of walking around the growing complex to find his way around without getting lost. Jailbreaks in Clay County were almost unheard of—that is, at least those reminiscent of the famous escape from Alcatraz. These days unscheduled cell searches were conducted on a constant basis and inmates were moved frequently to prevent such escape attempts. There was no way of knowing how Quito Prison was designed or operated, but chances were excellent that even Colonel Guerra had learned a thing or two about escape prevention. And even if Colson had devised an escape for Taylor and had figured a way inside, they both would be as lost as a ball in the high weeds on their way out. And most likely shot in the process.

Colson had dismissed an escape attempt the very moment it came to mind—at least in the traditional sense. So there had to be another way. If Taylor's arrest had been justified, which the arrest itself probably was, there would be no chance that the plan Colson had settled on would work. However, it wasn't the arrest that was unjust, but the demand for such a ridiculously high cash bail. An unreasonable amount not set by a judge, but a criminal in a police uniform. Any legitimate official would immediately deny Colson's proposal and identify it as a bribe; then follow up with a threat of prosecution. But Guerra was not operating in a legitimate capacity by any civil standards. His thoughts turned to his daughter, Nicole; his grandson, Jack; and his new love, Beverly. The reality that he might never see them again had set in, and it bothered him more than he'd expected.

He pushed the tiny brake pedal of the Fiat to the floor when a flatbed truck piled high with cantaloupes swerved in front of him from a side street. Black exhaust spewed from the tailpipe and was instantly distributed through the cabin of the small Italian car. Colson coughed and jerked the car into the right lane behind a blue transit bus with the name "COSIBO" stenciled on its rear. It stopped dead at the curb as a stream of pedestrians exited onto a wide sidewalk. A string of row houses painted burnt-orange, cream, tan, and off white lined both sides of the street. Colson guessed the different colors were chosen to denote the separation between each residence. They each had small wrought iron balconies. Hanging baskets with red and yellow flowers drooped over the balcony railings. It was the Avenue Pichincha. The same as the crest where he had snoozed overnight. Colson admired the quaint capital of Quito set in the foreground of a large mountain range and was somewhat surprised by its cleanliness. He had always pictured a third-world population living in squalor. Colson began to worry he may have underestimated the National Ecuador Police, or as they would pronounce it, the *Policía Nacional del Ecuador*.

As new passengers climbed into the bus, he took the opportunity to check his phone for a reply from Augustine. It appeared as a tiny envelope in the left corner of the screen. Colson took a deep breath and opened the message. He read the short reply quickly twice and then slowly the final time to affirm his worst fear. A bead of sweat ran down the side of his cheek and down his neck, causing him to shrug and absorb it with the fabric of his shirt. A cheesy-sounding horn from behind made him glare into his rearview mirror at a Hispanic man gesturing wildly with his hand. He glanced ahead and saw the bus had moved on. Colson slammed the Fiat in gear and swung it in a U-turn. He cursed at the small buzzing engine of the compact car as it pitifully begged for a supernatural force to propel it forward. Colson jerked and grinded the gears as he diverted to the small airstrip he had left hours before.

Max Rollins stood facing the large reinforced plate-glass window in the director's office while Danz stood holding a small computer tablet while bent slightly at the waist with one eye stuck to the lens of a short telescope mounted to a tripod. The Vehicle Assembly Building gleamed white in the midday sun and the sky was deep blue with just a few lonely clouds drifting out to sea. Danz pulled his face away from the telescope and touched the tablet. Claxons began to blow in the distance for the next ten seconds, but were muffled by the thick window glass. When the thunder came, it was deafening, even at a distance of three miles. The rumble grew in enormous intensity and the resulting vibrations overwhelmed their bodies to the point where both men would have felt as if an evil spirit was taking possession of their souls. Accompanying the sustained roar was a distant glow that morphed from orange to a blinding quasar of white light. Just as quickly as the explosion of sound and light grew, it ceased, and the office fell completely still and quiet. Danz and Rollins remained silent until their senses returned to normal.

"I hate those tests," Rollins said in a tone of disgust. "The first Tuesday we were here they didn't warn us. I was working on the data at my desk, and I thought we were under nuclear attack."

"This *is* NASA, Max," Danz said. "They test solid booster rocket engines here, midmorning, every other Tuesday. That particular one is the world's most powerful solid rocket booster in preparation for deep space travel if we can ever recover our budget. You should consider it an honor to watch."

Rollins lowered himself into a corner armchair. "Whatever."

Danz turned his gaze downward where a black limousine pulled around the circular entrance and disappeared under the front overhang several floors below. He opened his desk drawer, pulled out a sealed legal-size envelope, and dropped it dead center on his desk. Rollins was now slouched in the chair in the corner of the office. He hadn't been at work for four hours, but looked as if he had pulled a double shift doing hard labor on a chain gang.

Danz said, "You'd be well advised to tuck in your shirt and straighten your tie unless you want to run back to your office in the next sixty seconds. He's here."

"Who's here?"

"The committee chairman."

Rollins blurted, "Senator Bozich?" He jumped to his feet and fast walked to the small restroom at the rear of Danz's office. Danz could hear Rollins wrestling with his belt and the sound of clothing being adjusted. Rollins emerged from the restroom using his hand as a comb to flatten his disheveled and thinning hair. He walked to the office door while straightening the knot in his tie. "Shouldn't we be in the lobby to greet him?" he said in an urgent tone. Danz sat behind his desk and shook his head.

"No. It's supposed to be a surprise visit. I got a heads up call this morning, or I wouldn't have known. But by all means, help yourself if you think you can get down there in time. I'm not the politician here and have no need to kiss ass."

Rollins narrowed his eyes at Danz but remained silent. He pulled open the office door. A man stood on the other side with his hand extended for a handle that was no longer there. He was an older but fit looking man and wore a medium-gray suit and red power tie. The man looked up at Rollins, stone-faced.

Rollins extended his hand and said, "Senator Bozich. I'm Max Rollins, project supervisor."

The senator brushed past Rollins without a word. Danz stood and stepped around his desk to shake hands. Rollins silently closed the door and stood with his arms crossed.

Danz said, "This is a pleasant surprise, Mr. Chairman."

The man offered a quick nod and said, "I'm sure it is, Director. I have a much-needed few days off before returning to Washington. I want to report back to the committee that I've personally inspected the research facility to assure them we are achieving our goal."

"I understand," said Danz, offering the senator the large envelope. "I have reviewed the latest data. Since you are here, you may want to deliver it to the committee personally."

The senator nodded and took the envelope. "I hope this data is convincing."

Danz shrugged. "How convincing should it be?"

"*More* convincing. It should be more reflective of your computer models."

"With all due respect, Senator, a computer model is only as good as the data inputted. The adjustments will reflect a combination of what the computer models indicate and the actual data collected. Subtle adjustments can be more convincing at times than embellishments that can appear suspicious on their face."

The senator remained stone-faced and changed the subject. "Any other problems? I understand you still have one employee unaccounted for."

"No, sir. Everything is under control. Although the employee remains unaccounted for, he has been contained." Danz made a hand gesture toward the large window. "Our security force and local authorities have maintained an airtight perimeter of the entire facility and the surrounding federal lands. It is a virtual impossibility that anyone could have survived this length of exposure without food and clean drinking water."

"For your sake, I hope you are right, Danz." The senator pointed a bony finger at Danz. "I expect you to notify me immediately if any other problems arise. I'll be back in Washington on Monday, and don't forget we have an election in less than a month, so be sure to vote."

The chairman spun and walked toward the door. Rollins grabbed the handle and opened it. The senator didn't break stride as he walked past Rollins, but pointed the same bony finger at him as he had at Danz. "You too, slick," he said.

Rollins shut the door and plopped back down in the corner chair. "What an ass," he said.

Danz grinned. "He's a politician. Same thing."

"So he doesn't know about Colson?"

Danz shrugged. "No need. Colson's out of the picture. When or *if* he makes it home, it'll be far too late for him to find Parker and cause any damage. I mean, we've had the FBI and every local cop in North Florida looking for him with dogs, drones, and helicopters for two weeks. Hell, you had our entire security force out there and the only thing you found was an abandoned boat."

"But that doesn't mean he's not alive out there."

"What?" Danz scoffed. "This coming from the guy who's been trying to convince me that Parker's an alligator turd by now. Three weeks from now we'll be out of the woods and can get back to work without interference from Washington every other day."

"And if Colson makes it back?"

"What do you suggest?" Danz asked.

Rollins stared into space for a long moment as if he hadn't expected the question. "I may be middle aged and a little soft around the middle, but if Colson gets back and starts stirring up a bunch of shit, I'll take him out myself."

Danz leaned back in his chair and crossed his arms. "Good luck with that."

The time on Colson's watch was 8:45 a.m. He sat in the Fiat gripping the steering wheel hard. Had it been the neck of some small animal, it would have died from suffocation and a pulverized neck bone. He stared at the vacant landing strip. Half in disbelief and half expecting what he would find. The text from Augustine had revealed the jet's tail number was indeed registered to the federal government. Not the FBI but the National Aeronautics and Space Administration. Colson was seriously disappointed in Agent Mcilwain. He thought he had pegged him as a good guy—a snooty FBI agent, but good nevertheless. He said he had been military police but could have lied. The private flight was just too good to be true. He cursed himself for not being more careful.

Colson jerked his head in both directions. He was allowing paranoia to creep in. Would they have given him up? Was Colonel Guerra and his band of corrupt thugs lying in wait this very moment, ready to pounce on him? Not just yet. The airstrip, small building, and the open field appeared vacant. There were no vehicles and no human activity. The realization of his situation felt different now that he was actually there. He had considered being captured or killed, but pondering the thought thousands of miles away was far different from being in the reality of the moment. Even if he gave Guerra the money, he would be arrested for entering the country illegally, and then it would be his daughter's turn to receive a phone call. What would his ransom be? Two hundred thousand? A half million? He could not allow that to happen.

Colson jammed the tiny gearshift into first and aimed the Fiat back in the direction of Quito. The tunnel he had studied on Google maps before he left came into view directly ahead. The Avenida 24 de Mayo dropped under the city streets for a mile before emerging back into the bright morning light. Suddenly there it was, ahead about a tenth of a mile on the right: Quito Prison. Colson had no idea when the Internet photo he'd studied earlier had been taken, but there was no mistaking the facility with its decorative iron fencing separated by the off-white posts and dark-bronze light fixtures. Colson drove the tiny Fiat halfway up on the sidewalk, directly in front of the metal door in the retaining wall he had seen in the photo. There were no other vehicles parked out front, mainly because there were no legal parking spaces.

Colson knew jails and prisons maintained guard lines, providing an enforced buffer or safety zone between the public and the inmates. The nose of the Fiat was probably three inches from a metal post with thin metal signage riveted to the top that read, "Prohibido el Paso" in red lettering against a white background. Colson never became fluent in Spanish, but the message was clear enough. He was in a prohibited area. It shouldn't take long for the car to stand out like a turd in a punchbowl to whoever was monitoring the perimeter security cameras. That person was obviously not asleep at the wheel because the steel door in the block wall opened within thirty seconds.

It was a dark-skinned man with a moustache, wearing a tan military-style uniform shirt and dark-brown uniform pants. He wore a dark-brown beret and held an AK-47 slung over his shoulder at low ready. Colson leaned to his right and manually rolled down the passenger-side window as the man stopped and hunched over to speak.

"Moverse a lo largo no se puede aparcar aquí," he said, gesturing down the road.

Colson shrugged and said, "Do you speak English?"

"I said," the officer began in a thick accent, "move along. You cannot park here."

"I came to speak with Colonel Guerra."

The officer's eyes narrowed on Colson. "The colonel? I have not been told of any appointment with the commandant."

"I know he wants to speak with me," Colson said, handing a business card to the officer. "Please let him know that I'm here."

The officer took the card and studied it for a long minute. He squeezed a microphone on his lapel and spoke in Spanish. The only part Colson recognized was his name, which the man seemed to have difficulty pronouncing correctly. He heard a man's voice answer. His tone sounded bright and a little excited. The officer spoke again into the microphone and appeared to be more relaxed. He stuck his head back down to the window.

"The colonel said you have something for him, but you should have made an appointment. I am to escort you—"

Colson stopped the officer with an upheld hand. "Yes, I have something for him, but I do not need to meet with him. Just talk right now." Colson punched his phone screen and the call was answered on the first ring.

"Senor Colson," Guerra said. "How good of you to visit. I look forward to meeting you and taking care of our business. However, you could have saved yourself considerable time and expense by simply wiring the bail."

"Well," Colson said casually, "I needed to get out of the house for a while. I'm just calling to let you know I'm in town."

There was a pause as though what Colson had said didn't make sense. "But you are already here, Colson. If you will accompany my officer, I will have Taylor prepared for release and both you and he can be on your way with my blessing."

"Hold for a second, Colonel." Colson separated the flaps of the cardboard box on the passenger seat for the officer to see inside. The officer's eyes widened at the tight bundles of cash lining the box.

"You see," Colson said to the officer who only nodded silently.

Colson suddenly lifted his foot off the clutch, jerked the Fiat off the curb, and sped away, leaving the guard looking on in bewilderment.

"Colson?" Guerra's voice came over the phone speaker."

"I'm still here."

"What is going on?"

"I just flashed your officer the hundred grand. You ever made a dope deal, Colonel?"

"What?"

"A dope... forget it. Of course you have. So you should know the first rule about doing a deal with an unknown."

Guerra did not respond. Colson waited three seconds before finishing his own question. "So you *do* know, don't you, Colonel? You never have money and the product in the same place. Now you know I'm good on my end. We just need to be certain you'll do your part."

"Yes, I know," Guerra said, his voice turning serious. "And I can call fifty state police units to stop you, arrest you, and confiscate everything you have."

"I'm sure you can, but you won't."

"And why is that?"

Colson jerked the Fiat through a roundabout in the center of town. He felt like he was in a James Bond movie with Guerra's clichéd responses and tough-guy demeanor.

"I'll be happy to tell you why. You don't want fifty state police officers splitting the hundred grand up two grand apiece. They'll be drinking tequila, hiring prostitutes, and doing the Mexican hat dance all weekend with *your* money. That's why."

"So what do you propose?"

Colson checked his watch. "It's nine thirty. Clear your calendar, and I'll call you back at two o'clock."

Colson tried to stay in the immediate vicinity and counted his turns to keep from losing his bearings. After he put some distance between himself and Quito Prison, Colson pulled behind a building he had seen minutes ago and circled around to park. It was white and gray, and rounded in front to accommodate the curve in the narrow cobblestone street. Elegant lettering on the façade read, "*Café Restaurant Lena Quintena.*" It was just 10:15 a.m., and Colson was famished. He had noticed an open area on the roof under an arced tin covering with hanging baskets that he assumed was for open-air dining. He didn't particularly care whether he ate in the open or not, just as long as he got something decent in his stomach.

Colson had one last text to send. He thought again of Nichole, little Jack, and Beverly. After driving through the city with its quaint cobblestone streets, modest row homes, and mountainous view, he would have enjoyed being on vacation there with Beverly, but under very different circumstances. He seriously doubted he could ever return if he escaped from Colonel Guerra's jurisdiction. He grabbed his phone and typed in his final text message that ended with,

Wish you were here

He sent it to whichever overhead satellite would capture and deliver it.

At 11:00 a.m. Colson noticed a man approach the entrance and unlock the door. Moments later, several others, probably employees, began to trickle into the café. He stuck the cardboard box in the Fiat's small trunk and then popped the hood and disconnected the engine's battery. He slammed the hood, then closed and locked the door. He wouldn't dare carry that amount of money stuffed in his deep cargo pants pockets, and if anyone had designs on stealing the Fiat, they would give up when they found the battery was dead. At 11:20 a.m., Colson pushed through the café door and found his way to the rooftop dining area where he ordered what the young waitress recommended. Her English was quite clear with just a hint of local dialect. She said most tourists ordered their fresh fish or "langostinos" in garlic butter sauce. Colson gave her a grin and a nod. In ten minutes, the buttery dish lay before him. The benefit of being the first customer he guessed. And the food wasn't good. It was incredible.

Chapter Eleven

Agent Mcilwain sat at his dining room table with his personal laptop propped open. He had watched the store surveillance video so many times he had lost count. Special Agent Ted had wasted no time at all trying to impress his senior agent. It was ironic to Mcilwain that he had hated working the Parker case when he and Strickland were assigned to it and now he desperately wanted it back. He would have to tell Agent Ted there was nothing of value on the surveillance video and his informant had been mistaken. He couldn't use the video evidence in any prosecution, even if he were back on the case. He had directed a junior agent to obtain the video under false pretenses and under an unrelated case number. He couldn't report it to his supervisor or even Strickland. So much for satisfying a curiosity when there was nothing on earth he could do about it.

Mcilwain closed the laptop and paced in his modest living room. If he took any official action and the circumstances of how the evidence was obtained came to light, which it would, he would be crucified by the Office of Professional Standards for gross violations of their code of conduct. If only he was an independent operator, far from the clutches of the OPS. A whistle-blower. A civilian with the same information couldn't be touched. He or she would be protected at the very least. Someone like…

Mcilwain stopped pacing and slapped his forehead as he assumed Einstein had when he made his final calculations of $E = mc^2$. "Colson," he blurted to himself.

Colson was sick of dealing with the likes of Colonel Guerra. It reminded him too much of working undercover narcotics. People who thought they were such bad asses had an extreme arrogance about them. They thought they were smarter and slyer than their competition and the cops. The suspense of living on the edge and dodging the law contributed to their arrogance. When the bad guys *were* the law, with virtually nothing standing in their way, it made their attitudes even worse. Colson had enjoyed the undercover game for the first three years, but was more than ready to get out by the time he was reassigned.

He had made one more trip to Pichincha to hide the cash before calling Guerra. His intent was to be short and not sweet about it. Guerra had started with his amiable bull crap, as if they were old pals, but Colson was too tired and frustrated to abide any more of it.

"Knock it off, Guerra," Colson snapped into the phone. "You don't like me any more than I like you, so just listen. The crest of the hill at Pichincha. Seven o'clock tonight. You bring Taylor with you. No guns or you'll never get the money. When I see Taylor alive and well, you'll get your bail. It will be close by. If not, you might get me, but you'll never find the cash, Got it?"

"This is highly irregular," Guerra replied.

Colson had practiced the appropriate response and bluff before placing the call.

"I'll tell you what's highly irregular, Colonel. A country in decent standing with the US and a member of the League of Nations turning a blind eye to one of its highly decorated officials participating in kidnapping and bribery. I've already reported your activities to the FBI. We both know Taylor broke the law, so there was nothing they could do to make that go away, but they know where I am and what I'm doing. If I don't return with Taylor after posting this ridiculous bail, as you call it, they're going to make so much noise through your government channels that you will become an embarrassment. An expendable embarrassment."

"They would do no such thing," Guerra growled.

"Is that a fact?" mocked Colson. "You don't strike me as a very charitable guy, Colonel, and when your superiors find out you haven't been giving them a piece of the pie, they'll bury you under your own prison."

After Guerra reluctantly agreed to the meeting, Colson drove back to the small community of Tambillo at the foot of Pichincha, found a small road to park on in the shade, and prepared for the meet. He had laid his seat as far back as it would go, but he couldn't snooze. Seven o'clock was when he was to meet the jet, but of course there was no jet to meet. He suspected Guerra hadn't known about the jet, or he would have been happy to remind Colson that he'd been helplessly abandoned.

It was almost time. The day had turned a little cool, and the sun was easing its way toward the horizon. Colson had no idea what to expect, but he would at least try. Taylor would know he had tried. He drove back to the top of Pichincha at 6:40 p.m. and turned the Fiat around where the road ended. If Guerra had sent an advance team, they were well hidden. There was no one to be seen. But that wasn't surprising. This was Guerra's territory, and he had no reason to think Colson had the ability to do anything less than turn over the cash.

The headlights moving toward Colson didn't bounce up and down. The road was not quite that rough. What he thought had been a dirt road during the night turned out to be dirty cobblestone, so the headlights made more of a vibrating, side to side jerking motion like the eyes of a drunk driver when cops perform an eye test. It was a dark-colored Jeep with the ragtop pulled tight over the passengers beneath. Not an old dilapidated two-door Wrangler, but one of the new four-door models set high atop four fat tires and complete with two spotlights mounted on either side of the hood and a thin red LED police bar on top.

It was just turning dusk. The headlights were not yet necessary, but probably a good idea. The high beams of the Jeep made Colson raise his arm to block the light. Colonel Guerra would want a good look at him before stepping from the safety of the vehicle, and Colson was certain he would make a personal appearance to ensure he alone touched the cash.

"Turn around slowly with your hands up," said a thick Latino voice over a public address system in the Jeep.

Colson turned 360 degrees and stood with his hands extended to his sides, squinting at the high beams. The lights blinked off, leaving Colson night-blind for ten seconds. The front Jeep doors were pushed open by two uniformed prison guards, both over 6' tall and probably close to 250 pounds. That was pretty tall for the normal Latino male, but big men were needed in prison settings, or they wouldn't last a week. They had to be men trusted by the Colonel and probably had years of seniority. But would they be as complacent as he hoped? Colson wasn't quite 6′ tall, but regardless of his height, it would mean the guards would have to bend way down to conduct a thorough pat down. Colson turned and placed his hands on the hood of the Fiat and tried to relax when they came within two feet. Colson didn't see any exposed guns, but was certain they were concealing at least one apiece.

He could feel the guard to his left gazing at him while the one to his right started the pat down at his neckline, then down the center of his back, and around his waist. He squatted to search down the outside of his pants and around his ankles before standing and patting the outside of his pockets. Satisfied, they turned back to the Jeep but kept their position to Colson's right and left, gripping his biceps. He recognized the guard to his right as the one he'd flashed the cash at earlier.

"Senor Colson," Guerra said, dropping from the back seat. Colson's eyes had adjusted, and he quickly recognized the silver oak leaves of a Colonel in the center of his shoulder boards. He had worn a pair of shoulder boards himself as a major, but not with the ridiculous fringe hanging from the edges. But where was Taylor? Guerra stood at parade rest with his hands clasped behind his back, apparently showing Colson he was unarmed.

"Where's Taylor?" Colson said.

Guerra nodded to the interior of the Jeep. "He is here. And the dinero?"

"Close by. I need to see Taylor."

"You know it's curious," Guerra said. "There is no record of your flight into my country, Senor Colson."

"What difference does it make?"

Guerra straightened his stance as if shocked by the question. "Oh, it makes quite the difference if you have illegally entered a sovereign nation without going through the proper channels and providing valid identification to immigration officials. Does America not take exception to such activity?"

Colson narrowed his gaze at Guerra. "Not nearly enough. If I had come through customs with that amount of money, you know as well as I do that some immigration official would be counting it tonight, not you. Now let me see Taylor."

Guerra nodded to the door, and Taylor or what would be better described as a resemblance of Taylor poured out of the seat and clung to the doorframe to stand. Colson took a half step toward the Jeep, but the guards grabbed him by both arms. Taylor looked like he hadn't eaten for weeks. His overgrown beard framed a sunken face and thinning neck. His dark skin, normally gleaming with sweat from the humidity of Daytona had turned a dry, grayish color. Colson felt rage rise from the bottom of his feet to the top of his head. He had worked in American jails for half his career, and inmates would leave tens of pounds heavier than when they arrived. There was simply no excuse for such treatment.

Guerra had no reason to fear Taylor's lack of restraints or close proximity. It was everything the former UFC fighter could do to stand erect. Guerra walked toward Colson slowly, looking from side to side. Colson deliberately controlled his breathing and tried to relax. It worked because the guards released their grip and took a step back for the Colonel to take charge. Guerra spit on the ground and stopped five feet in front of Colson.

"I'm a reasonable man," Guerra said. "I am willing to overlook your crime if you will produce the money. Otherwise, I will take you into custody and find it myself. You would not have hidden it very far."

"Fine," said Colson. It was almost fully dark, and he let his arms hang straight to his side and cupped his hands together just below his belt line as if making a respectful plea before a judge. "All I ask is that Taylor is helped to the car. Then I'll get it for you and we both can be on our way."

"I don't think so," Guerra said while momentarily cutting his eyes to the guard on Colson's right. "I conduct business *my* way in this country."

Colson didn't miss Guerra's eye movement and had been waiting for it. In his peripheral vision, the guard to his right shoved his hand into his uniform shirt. Like many uniform shirts, the top and bottom buttons were the only functional ones with a zipper closing the middle portion. His had been left unzipped just enough for a hand to reach in for a gun. There was no reason for him to be in a hurry because they had already patted Colson down for a weapon. Or had they been a little complacent? Colson was not as slow as the guard. Keeping his eyes leveled on Guerra, he shot his right hand down to the seam he had cut on the inside of his left leg and grabbed the hard rubber handle of the Shrike and jerked it out, ripping the masking tape that held it in place.

Colson had not been familiar with the Shrike Tactical Tomahawk until he first bought it from Paul, the owner of Code 7 Police Supply. But in the intervening days, he'd researched its uses and was very impressed. First used by the military, the fifteen-and-a-half-inch, twenty-three-ounce tool was used for everything from cutting through wooden and steel doors to chopping firewood and hacking holes in concrete walls. Firefighters adopted the tool to free people trapped in motor vehicles, and police made use of them to make forced entry into homes, shatter auto glass, obliterate padlocks, and slice heavy chains like bread. The Shrike had an appealing balance and weight, and it was hammer forged from all chrome-moly 4140 steel construction with the leading edge as sharp as a razor and a piercing talon at the tail end.

Colson swung the Shrike up across his body at chest height and buried the rear talon in the general area of where the guard had stuck his hand into his shirt, and it stuck there. It was followed by a scream that sounded like that of pig being butchered. Colson could not see where the talon had struck but would have been proud to have known his aim had landed dead center on top of the guards hand, pierced through his palm, and stuck a quarter inch into his chest.

Colson jerked once, making the guard scream again. He side kicked Guerra in the stomach as he jerked a second time to free the Shrike and used the momentum to slice it back across his body and then caught the guard to his left across the chest with the tomahawk's head as he reached for his own weapon. The new blade easily sliced off the guards right index, middle, and ring fingers. The second guard's response was a look of shock at Colson before grabbing his right hand and looking down at his feet for his fingers, not realizing they had fallen inside his tucked uniform shirt. Colson shot his hand under the guard's shirt and pulled his handgun from an interior holster as the man went to his knees and began rocking back and forth.

Colson swung the pistol at Guerra who had gotten to his feet and was running back toward the Jeep. Colson aimed but it had become too dark. Not being able to see where Taylor was standing, he didn't fire in his direction. Instead, he aimed at his feet and fired. Guerra scurried at the sound of the gunshot and jumped in the driver's seat. Colson ran toward the Jeep and pulled the staggering Taylor away by the arm as

Guerra sped off, leaving his guards whining and thrashing around in front of the Fiat. Colson threw Taylor's arm around his neck while grabbing him around the waist and fast walked him to the Fiat with the pistol leveled on the guards. Neither were capable of firing a weapon, but Colson kept the pistol at the ready in case they made any attempt to stop him. Colson supported Taylor on his feet while snatching open the passenger door. That's when he heard the heavy thumping sound.

Detective Lieutenant Cantrell walked through the automatic glass door in the ICU Unit of Florida Hospital Oceanside and up to the nurse's station. A young twentysomething nurse glanced up from her computer and said, "Can I help you, sir?"

Cantrell lifted his badge case high enough for her to see his star and credentials and then said, "Has there been any progress with Mr. Bankston?"

"Well, he's conscious now but his jaw is wired shut and he can't speak."

"But he can hear me, correct?"

The nurse nodded silently. Cantrell thanked her and stepped into ICU Room 3 with his pad in hand. The figure on the bed looked miserably uncomfortable with both legs in traction and one arm in a cast up to his shoulder. Bankston's head was turned toward the far wall, and the hiss of an oxygen concentrator was making an artificial inhale and exhale noise. Cantrell rounded the foot of the bed and looked at Bankston's face. It looked surprisingly better. It had regained more of a normal color as opposed to the milky near-death shade from a week ago.

"Mr. Bankston," Cantrell said softly but firmly. "I'm Lieutenant Cantrell with the Volusia County Sheriff's Office. Can you hear me?"

Bankston's eyes fluttered and then opened. He gave Cantrell a long look and then nodded.

Cantrell said, "Is there anyone we can call? Family, children, employer?"

Cantrell shook his head slowly.

"Well," Cantrell continued. "We have several witnesses that said you had the green light. I know it doesn't mean much right now, but fault is at least something else you don't have to worry about. Of course, had that not been the case, maybe the semi driver would have bothered to stop and render aid and waited for the police. Unfortunately, we still don't have anything on the driver's identity, but I'm confident we will. In the meantime, concentrate on getting better. I'll check in on you every few days. If you think of anyone you'd like me to contact, try to let the nurse know. Can you write with your left hand?"

Bankston nodded.

"Great. I'll see you in a few days."

Cantrell flipped his pad closed and turned toward the door. After the first step, he was stopped by a loud groan. He turned back to the bed and saw Bankston pointing. Cantrell shrugged and then noticed he was pointing at the notepad. He stepped back to the bed and gave Bankston a pen, flipped the pad open to a clean page, and laid it on the bed. Bankston seemed to struggle over the formation of the letters. When finished, Cantrell picked it up. It looked like a first grader's writing.

It read, *Who else hurt in the wreck?*

Cantrell said, "It's a miracle, but no one else was seriously injured."

Cantrell laid the pad back down at Bankston's beckoning hand gesture and picked it back up when he was finished. It took him a moment to process the man's question. There was only one spelling of that particular name in the area. He looked from the pad to Bankston and back to the pad to be certain.

Where is Colson?

"What?" Cantrell said. "You mean *Grey* Colson? What in hell does he have to do with the accident... or *you* for that matter?"

Bankston wrote one last note and passed it to Cantrell.

Bring him to me!

The thumping noise became more pronounced as the taillights of Colonel Guerra's Jeep grew smaller in the distance. Guerra was no doubt calling for backup, but he was not willing to hang around with his injured men in the meantime. Colson slid Taylor's slumped form into the front seat of the Fiat and rejoined the injured prison guards, both still clutching their injuries. Colson had no intention of killing the men, but would have if that became the only option. Instead, he gave both a solid punch to their temples, knocking them out cold. He scrambled to the gravel pile, kicked off the thin layer covering the cardboard box, and hustled back to the Fiat.

One moment it was pitch black, and the next moment the Jeep was backlit by blinding duel spotlights. Colson could clearly see the outline of the Jeep as it tipped onto the driver's side from the sudden rotor wash of a Huey helicopter that crested the hill from seemingly nowhere. The spotlights hovered a moment over the overturned Jeep and then moved in Colson's direction. The beams now aimed low as the Huey shot forward with its nose pitched downward, no more than a dozen feet off the ground.

Colson covered his eyes with his forearm but the lights vanished. The Huey was still out there, moving closer. Colson squatted next to Taylor who remained silent and slumped in the Fiat's passenger seat. It was pitch black with the exception a million brilliant stars in the night sky. The outline of the helicopter against the starry backdrop made a black hole in the sky. It descended and settled to the ground fifty feet away. Colson stuck the box under one arm and threw Taylor's arm around his neck. He jerked Taylor from the seat and turned away from the rotors wash, furiously pushing Taylor to walk alongside him. There would be no way to escape. Colson turned around and held the Shrike high in defiance as the beam of a flashlight illuminated him from behind him.

"Colson," the man's voice shouted, but not in the Latino dialect he had expected. "Let's go you crazy bastard," the shout came again. Not Latino at all. It was the voice of a Yankee. A thick New Yorker's dialect. One he hadn't heard in years, but never forgot.

"Fitz?" Colson shouted at the approaching figure. Two additional dark figures flanked Fitzgerald and rushed to take Taylor's weight from Colson's shoulders.

One of them shouted in Colson's ear, "We have to move *now*."

The two men hefted Taylor into the Huey's side door and buckled him in. Colson followed Fitzgerald and buckled up in a rear-facing seat. He felt a slight g-force as the helicopter lifted off but it didn't climb as much as it tilted and sped forward. The tinny sound of the pilot's voice came over an overhead speaker. "Twenty minutes to the border. Low and fast until then."

Fitzgerald slid the side door of the Huey shut and dropped back into the seat next to Colson. The noise of the Huey dropped to more of a tolerable level, but being constructed as a military craft, it didn't afford the quieter comfort of a civilian craft. At least they no longer had to shout at each other.

Fitzgerald patted Colson on the shoulder and said, "Thanks for the message, but the very *last* place I wish I was is here." He gestured to Taylor sitting upright, supported only by the five-point restraints strapped around him. "Your friend needs a hospital."

"No question," said Colson. "Where are we going?"

"Antonio Narino Airport in Pasto."

"Pasto?"

"Columbia."

"Any good hospitals there?"

Fitzgerald shook his head. "None that I would take my dog to."

"He needs fluids at least. He's dehydrated."

"I'll have a medic meet us at the airport. There's a twin turbo prop fueling to get you back to the States. They can hook him up to an IV for the trip. Without the coordinates you sent, we would have never found you. By the looks of your friend, he'd be dead by tomorrow."

Colson looked around the fuselage. One of the men who had helped with Taylor sat silent in the seat next to his half-dead, one-eyed friend. The other sat on the floor with his knees pulled up to his chest. Both wore military-style coveralls and olive drab ball caps with no insignia.

Colson turned back to Fitzgerald and said, "Operation Snowcap?"

Fitzgerald laughed out loud and slapped Colson on the knee.

"Seriously? They pulled the plug on Operation Snowcap in 1994, but you wouldn't know because you had already been sent back to the sheriff's office by then." Fitzgerald gestured around the fuselage with his hand. "This Huey is a relic of Snowcap though."

Colson shrugged. "So what's the operation called now?"

"Well," Fitzgerald said, "Let's just say it's called the 'We Need to Fix the Shit We Caused in Operation Snowcap' Operation."

"Either way, I owe you and Augustine more than I can ever repay," Colson said.

Fitzgerald released a snort of disgust. "Owe Augustine? Seriously? I'm the one who's had to go without liquor and women for the last twelve hours."

Agent Mcilwain and Strickland waited in the lobby of the Volusia County Sheriff's Office Operations and Investigations office for five long minutes before being escorted to Lieutenant Cantrell's office. The three shook hands and exchanged the usual professional introductions before settling into their chairs.

"Lieutenant Cantrell," Mcilwain began. "We understand you were able to communicate with Robert Bankston yesterday."

Cantrell sat silent for a long moment before answering. "We are conducting a hit-and-run investigation. We fully expected it to turn into a vehicular-homicide case until he regained consciousness."

"Of course," Strickland injected. "We've been waiting on word from the hospital that he had come out of the induced coma. They said someone from county had been in to see him shortly after he woke up. But they also said he couldn't speak due to his jaw being wired."

Cantrell nodded. "That's correct. He can't speak. You'll have to forgive me, but why is this an FBI matter? Do you have any information about the semi or the driver?"

"No," Mcilwain said. "We are or rather we *were* working another case that Mr. Bankston may have information about. The nurse said he wrote notes to you. Would you please tell us what he said?"

"This has to do with your missing scientist, doesn't it?" Cantrell said without answering the question. Mcilwain and Strickland exchanged a glance.

Strickland said, "Look, Lieutenant, if you're withholding any information—"

"No, *you* look," Cantrell snapped. "We're not in the federal building, and you don't come in here suggesting that I'm withholding anything. I couldn't care less about your mysterious scientist, and I have more important things to do than play federal agent. What I *do* have jurisdiction over is my county and the safety of its citizens. And I have a lunatic driver in an unidentified semi who almost destroyed the intersection of Dunlawton and A1A. It's still impossible to believe no one was killed."

Mcilwain raised a hand in surrender and shot Strickland a look she could only have interpreted as "Shut up." He kept his eyes on Strickland as he spoke. "No one is suggesting that, Lieutenant." He turned back to Cantrell. "I'll tell you anything we know about the accident, but unfortunately we haven't been investigating the accident. It's not our expertise. But any information Mr. Bankston provided to you may be extremely valuable in the Parker investigation."

"I thought you said it was a case you *were* working," Cantrell said.

"Technically, that's correct, but certain things have come to light that could change the trajectory of the case."

Cantrell looked over his reading glasses at Mcilwain. "So you're freelancing?"

Mcilwain shrugged. "It's our lunch hour. The boss doesn't typically care how we spend it."

Cantrell leaned forward on his elbows. "OK, off the record, how is Bankston involved?"

"We know how, but not why," Strickland said. "He is on hiatus from the Justice Department but we haven't established his involvement with Grant Parker. We *do* know he was in Parker's apartment on the same day Grey Colson and Parker's half-sister were there. It appears on video surveillance that Bankston followed Colson and the half-sister when they left."

Cantrell nodded in understanding. "So that's why."

"That's why, what?" Mcilwain said.

Cantrell reached in his desk drawer and sat two pieces of notepaper in front of the agents.

"This is what Bankston communicated to me. He first wanted to know if anyone else was injured in the accident, and I say accident with a grain of salt. Then he insisted I deliver Grey Colson to him."

"So, they were working together," Strickland said.

"No," Mcilwain said. "I doubt they were at first. Otherwise, he would have greeted the half-sister and Colson in the parking garage. I don't believe Bankston wanted to approach Colson."

Cantrell chuckled.

"What?" asked Strickland.

"You don't know Colson like I do. If someone was following him around, Colson would make the introduction himself, and it would be a lot more interesting than a 'Hey, how ya' doin' moment."

Strickland rolled her eyes. "I'm not surprised."

Mcilwain said, "Have you notified Colson?"

"I tried calling and going by his condo. He wasn't there and none of his neighbors have seen him since yesterday morning."

Mcilwain sat silent. Strickland continued studying the notes. Several seconds passed before Cantrell spoke. "Is there something about Colson you're not telling me?"

Mcilwain said. "When did you go to his condo?"

"This morning on my way in. Why?"

"Just curious. I thought he was retired."

"So he says, but I swear he doesn't know the meaning of the word."

Bill Fitzgerald was as good as his word. The Huey flight to Pasto was uneventful, and even though Taylor had taken only a few sips from a water bottle, he looked better. Simply knowing he was heading home had had a positive effect on his physical well-being. He muttered a few words but remained silent for the most part. The Huey touched down next to a Beechcraft A36 Bonanza Turboprop. It wasn't the same luxurious ride NASA had provided for the trip south, but to Colson it was a beautiful sight, and it belonged to people he trusted. The medic aboard the Bonanza went to work immediately on Taylor, recording vital signs, taking his blood pressure, and inserting an IV.

Fitzgerald accompanied Colson to his seat and spouted the lines he had apparently been ordered to repeat about confidentiality, the public and political repercussions if the agreement was broken, and how delicate international relations would be affected. Colson agreed without hesitation. He and Fitzgerald had worked for Donnie Augustine as task force agents in the early '90s, and they knew he was perfectly capable of keeping his mouth shut. There would not be a word spoken about their short incursion into sovereign territory or assistance in the rescue of Taylor. He had earned their trust. Otherwise, there would have never been an incursion or rescue.

Colson and Fitzgerald caught up with the past twenty years as the pilot finished his preflight check. There was only time for the Reader's Digest version, but it was better than nothing. Colson shook Fitzgerald's hand and told him to go have a drink. He assured Colson that would be the case as soon as humanly possible.

At a cruising speed of a little over two hundred knots, the trip to Daytona took an extra hour. The Bonanza touched down in Daytona just fifteen minutes after Colson replaced Taylor's IV bag. They taxied to a waiting ambulance where two paramedics once again checked Taylor's vitals and loaded him onto a gurney. Colson wasn't permitted to ride along. He almost expected a DEA agent from the Orlando field office to be standing by in a dark sedan to drive him, but what more could he expect. Augustine and Fitzgerald had already stuck their necks out farther than they should have to help him and Taylor—even at the risk their pensions being imperiled. Involving yet another agent in the mix wouldn't be wise. It would be another unnecessary person to swear to secrecy. Colson carried his cardboard box around the perimeter of the airport and hailed a cab.

Chapter Twelve

Mcilwain and Strickland walked to the elevator in silence. Mcilwain pressed the button for the top floor and glared at Strickland.

"We're partners, Myra" Mcilwain began. "Why didn't you tell me about Colson's flight?"

Strickland shrugged. "Because I didn't think it mattered. The man got what he wanted."

"I should have known. The SAC would have never approved it. You *still* should have told me."

The elevator door slid open in front of the director's executive suite. Mcilwain pushed through the door followed by Strickland. He walked straight to Danz's interior office door without checking in with Mrs. Blackwell with the hair bun.

"Agent Mcilwain," she called to him as he disappeared behind the door. Danz looked up from his computer and slid the reading glasses off his nose. Mcilwain and Strickland stopped behind the two chairs facing his desk.

Danz folded his glasses and laid them gently on his desk pad.

"What can I do for you, Agent Mcilwain? Is there a new development in the search for Parker?"

Mcilwain crossed his arms. "You know damn well we were taken off the case. Don't try and tell me you weren't the reason either. This whole thing stinks. First, you were all hot and heavy for us to find your traitor scientist, and then you suddenly decide you don't need our help. You mind telling me what the hell is going on?"

Danz casually leaned back in his chair and swiveled from side to side. Strickland stood in silence just off to the side of Mcilwain.

Danz said, "I appreciate your dedication, Agent Mcilwain, but these are sensitive issues we are dealing with, and the situation is fluid. Now, I know you hold a high opinion of yourself and your capabilities and the law, but there are simply things that rise above your paygrade. I suggest that you watch your tone, and I'll try to forget this incident ever occurred. Now please excuse me. I am very busy trying to run—"

"Where's Colson?" Mcilwain interrupted.

Danz shot Strickland a look and said, "Ask your partner. It's not my day to babysit him."

"I'm asking *you*, Director."

"You know, you and your partner should talk more. It was my understanding from Agent Strickland here that Mr. Colson needed assistance with a flight and that it was his condition to cease his interference in our affairs. It sounded like a reasonable settlement, so I agreed. And now, after being gracious enough to assist, I get the third degree from you, Agent Mcilwain. My patience is wearing thin."

"Go on," said Mcilwain.

Danz drew a deep breath and blew it out. He slid his reading glasses back on, touched his computer keyboard, and studied the screen.

"Agent Strickland informed me that Colson needed to expedite the release of an acquaintance from custody." He looked from the screen to Mcilwain. "That is far beyond the scope of NASA, but I agreed to provide transportation under the circumstances. Colson was given a time frame of twenty-four hours because I cannot justify our resources being tied up for endeavors completely unrelated to our mission. I have a strict budget, and I am held personally accountable by the taxpayers. I risked incredible scrutiny by arranging the flight, but I will not stand by and allow myself or this agency to be found culpable in any of Colson's shady activities."

"You didn't answer my question."

"The answer to your question is I don't have the foggiest idea. Colson didn't show up at the appointed time and our pilot was forced to return without him. I'm sure he can or already has found suitable commercial transportation back to the States. Have you bothered to call or visit him? I mean, you *are* the FBI, correct?"

Mcilwain stood silent and nodded slowly, boring a hole through Danz with his eyes. Danz returned his glare with a satisfied smirk.

Mcilwain said, "You're absolutely correct, Director Danz. I believe we both have a lot of work to do, and I can assure you I am motivated to do my job extremely well."

Mcilwain turned, walked to the door, and pulled it open. He glanced over his shoulder and said to Strickland's back, "You coming with me?"

The young Latino man had been cruising his 1989 Impala up and down East Sunrise Boulevard for the past hour. His hair was close cropped, and he wore a white tank-top undershirt and baggy black jeans. The Impala was only a suggestion of its former self. Totally rebuilt from the ground up, it boasted an electric-blue coat of metallic paint, sheared off suspension, and chrome deep-dish mag wheels. Those in the car restoration business would call the makeover a rotisserie restoration and some would refer to it as a frame off restomod.

Recently transplanted from Chicago, Carlos Augusto was extremely proud of his recent promotion to "Inca." It was his first true promotion in the Latin Kings organization, the largest and most dangerous Latino gang in the Americas. When he heard of a chapter being formed in Fort Lauderdale, he jumped at the opportunity. The women were beautiful and scantily dressed, and it was summer year round.

The tattoo on his left arm was a black and gold crown with a three-pronged, pitchfork-type symbol protruding from below. Carlos was proud to cruise with his arm lazily slung out the window, displaying the Latin King's symbol. They were the only family he had ever known or cared about. But he quickly withdrew his arm when meeting patrol cars because the police were quick to identify the tattoo and find a reason to stop and harass him. There were other gangs who were comrades and some were enemies. The cops were the enemy of all.

The three other young Latino men in the Impala had yet to receive a promotion of any significance. They had not been transplanted from the Chicago tribe, but had been recruited by Carlos to grow the Fort Lauderdale chapter. They had a long way to go to be as accepted and trusted as Carlos. To the three new recruits, Carlos embodied everything they wanted to be. They were eager to learn and more eager to please.

Ghetto rap filled the interior of the Impala and could be heard by any pedestrian or driver for over two hundred feet. The bass amp thumped in the trunk, causing the entire car frame to vibrate. A cell phone was stuck to the front of the dash with a strip of Velcro fighting to hold it in place. The only way Carlos knew a call was coming in was when the screen came to life, displaying a phone number beginning with area code, 872—the area code for Chicago.

Carlos quickly silenced the ghetto rap. His three passengers continued mimicking the song as if it was still playing until Carlos shouted for them to shut up.

"Cállate!" He tore the phone form the Velcro and held it to his ear, "Sí."

Carlos sat up straight from his slouch and jerked the Impala into the next parking lot. The three newcomers remained silent and riveted to the one-sided conversation.

"Sí, Coronas," Carlos said and snapped his finger and pointed to the glove box. The newbie gangbanger in the passenger seat flipped open the glove box and then pulled out the only items inside: a black notebook and pen.

"Escribe esto," Carlos said, ordering the man to write.

"Thirteen zero three South Atlantic Avenue, Daytona Beach."

The passenger furiously wrote as instructed.

"Blue Corvette. Grey Colson. White boy. Sí que se hará."

The newbie gangbanger stopped writing when Carlos stuck the phone back on the dash.

"What will be done?" he asked in a respectful tone. Carlos rubbed the thin whiskers on his chin and patted the shoulder of the new gangbanger.

"Yo, vato. This Colson has done a great crime against our family and must pay." He looked to all three who were nodding agreement. They knew better than to ask when, where, or why they were expected to act. They were at the literal bottom rung of the ladder and to question anything was considered blatant disrespect. Carlos dropped the Impala into drive and pulled back onto East Sunrise Boulevard in the direction of A1A.

"It is time to test your loyalty."

Colson woke at 6:00 a.m., got a shower, and walked into the hospital main entrance at 6:40 a.m. with coffee in hand. He had to kill twenty minutes in the lobby since visiting hours in ICU didn't start until seven. He used the time to call and thank Donnie Augustine for the rescue operation, although he didn't use those words. He knew Augustine had taken a huge risk, so Colson chose his words carefully and was so vague that only he and Augustine knew what he was referring to. The conversation was short, but conveyed what Colson wanted to say. Augustine's short replies did the same.

At 7:01 a.m., Colson was standing at the nurses' station and then at the foot of Jay Taylor's bed twenty seconds later. It amazed Colson that just a few short hours of rehydration and decent rest had restored Taylor's color. He was out cold and wired up like a home theater sound system. His lifeless eye was about half open as he slept. Colson walked to Taylor's side and placed his hand on his shoulder as a nurse walked in pushing a rolling cart with a flat-screen monitor bolted on top. Colson spent the next ten minutes giving her Taylor's information and the most important item of course: his company insurance card. Taylor was covered as his sole employee.

After signing Taylor's admittance paperwork, the nurse gave Colson a smile and told him the doctor would be checking in soon. When he turned back to Taylor, his good eye was open. Colson gave him a grin and said, "Well, I see you're awake, Dead Eye." Taylor reached out and shook hands with Colson.

"Thank you."

Colson shrugged. "It's the least I could do. I can't afford a new bodyguard at the rates they charge these days."

"What is Operation Snowcap?"

"I see," Colson began. "So you weren't passed out on the chopper after all."

"Not totally. My ears were working."

"Snowcap was an operation run by the DEA back in the late '80s. Mostly a search and destroy counternarcotics mission to cripple Columbia's drug trade, but that's not important right now, and you and I weren't part of it. Just the Huey."

"Was I hallucinating or were you swinging a tomahawk around?"

"Oh, that's one of my new toys. It's called a Shrike."

Taylor shook his head and winced as if he had pinched a nerve in his neck.

"Only you, Colson."

"You just need to go back to sleep," Colson said and shook a finger at Taylor. "You're going to burn up all your paid sick days. You've already burned up all your vacation days for the next three years gallivanting around Ecuador."

"Thank God we're out of there."

Colson moved closer to the bed and lowered his voice. "I wouldn't count your Colonel Guerra out just yet. I get the feeling he's pretty embarrassed and ticked off about now. Get better soon my one-eyed friend. You never know when I might need your services."

"Mr. Colson," a young woman said from the door. It was the nurse from the ICU desk. "There's another patient that has requested to see you." Colson gave her a bewildered glance. The nurse seemed to read his expression. "A Mr. Bankston," she said and pointed past the ICU desk to a glass room on the opposite side. "In ICU 3. He must have seen you walk in." Colson looked past the nurse and saw an unfamiliar figure wrapped up like a mummy from head to toe.

He said, "I'm sorry, but I don't know anyone else here."

"I'm sorry. He's very insistent. If you'd like, I'll tell him—"

"Wait. What's his first name?"

The nurse referred to a chart in her hand. "Robert. Robert Bankston."

Colson searched his memory, repeating the name silently in his head. "Thanks," he told the nurse and walked to the room.

The nurse caught up to him before he stepped inside. "He can't speak. His jaw is wired." Colson gave her a nod and went to the foot of Rob's bed. He had been convinced the man was dead after the horrific accident and was so caught up in his plans to free Taylor that he hadn't given it another thought.

He felt a little embarrassed that he hadn't at least inquired about him, but then again, he didn't really know the man.

"So Rob is your real name?" Colson said.

Rob nodded and tried to speak from behind his clinched teeth. Colson had no idea what he was saying.

"You don't have to speak," Colson said. "My guess is the locals haven't tracked down the semi or the driver, right?"

Rob shook his head.

"I figured as much. I thought I had a pretty good idea who was behind it, but now I'm at least ninety-nine percent certain. They were gunning for both of us. I had a few pressing things to take care of, but I'm back now, and I'm pissed."

Rob widened his eyes, but didn't attempt to speak. Instead, he pointed to a notepad sitting on a bed tray next to a plastic pitcher of ice water with a long straw sticking out of the top. Colson picked up the pad and handed it to Rob. He flipped to the back page then backed up three pages and handed it back to Colson. The writing was in clumsy block letters, but readable. Rob had apparently written with his left hand and taken a considerable amount of time doing so. Colson backed into an armchair and began reading. At the bottom of the first page, Colson looked up. Rob's eyes were wide and his quick, excited breaths made a sucking sound through his clamped teeth. Colson wished Rob would have been as excited about revealing his secret that day at Giuseppe's. It would have been much easier. Revealing it now pretty much proved Rob was working alone... and unprotected.

"What does this have to do with NASA?" Colson asked. Rob just pointed at the pad again and shook his finger, prompting Colson to read on. When he finished the last two pages, he read them again—and then a third time to take it in. He flipped the pad closed and stared at Rob.

"So now we know for sure about the black semi. So much for being ninety-nine percent certain. This is the most unbelievable crap I've ever heard of. Are you certain about this?"

Rob nodded slowly.

"The cost to pull this off would have to be in the billions every year."

Rob motioned Colson back over to the bed and grabbed a pen. Colson opened the notepad to the back cardboard flap and held it steady while Rob slowly wrote out an e-mail address. He dropped below the e-mail address and began to write PASS...Colson stopped him.

"Password?"

Rob wrote off to the side 2PETER37.

Colson flapped the notepad against his palm and eyed Rob.

"Why trust me with this? You don't even know me."

Rob wrote on the palm of his hand. *No one else.*

Colson shook Rob's left hand. "It looks like I have a scientist to find, doesn't it?"

Agent Strickland stood with her hands on her hips watching Agent Mcilwain empty his desk. He had very few personal items, and they all fit in his slender briefcase. A personal computer tablet, four Cross ink pens, the *FBI Legal Handbook*, and a framed photo of his dog—a miniature pincher named Charlotte. Mcilwain pressed the lid down with a click and looked up at Strickland.

"It was fun while it lasted," he said.

"What the hell happened in the hearing?"

Mcilwain shrugged. "You know those OPS guys. All righteously indignant and smug."

"Not all of them," Strickland corrected. "I came from an assignment in the Office of Professional Standards, and I never acted that way. What were you thinking going off the reservation and grilling Danz? We were ordered off the assignment, and you should have known he would complain. I'm surprised they didn't serve me with disciplinary notice for simply going with you. Don't tell me they fired you."

Mcilwain chuckled. "Fire me? If you worked OPS you know how difficult it is to fire a federal agent. You pretty much have to commit a forcible felony."

"Suspension?"

Mcilwain nodded. "Thirty days and reassignment to the Atlanta field office."

"What was the charge? Code of conduct violation?"

Mcilwain snatched up his briefcase and stuck out his hand. "It's been good knowing you."

Strickland shook his hand and said, "What are you going to do for thirty days?"

"Besides packing you mean? I think I'll be a beach bum. I might even hang out with Colson under his canopy a few days. It looked restful, and it would be nice to see how it feels without this ridiculous suit and tie."

"You have to be joking."

"Watch me," Mcilwain said and strutted to the office door swinging his briefcase.

Grant Parker scratched his thickening beard while looking out the rectangular window on the north side of the tree house. It had been two days since the last activity, but it was close. He had heard the buzz of the outboard motor growing louder and then cut off abruptly. It had landed on the opposite side of Gaines Island. It was just the night before when he had covered the pit beneath the tree house. It had taken him two full days to dig with a small folding shovel and distribute the dirt evenly around the perimeter. He'd strung vines he had cut from trees and pulled from the undergrowth across the top of the pit in a checkerboard pattern and then covered the opening with Spanish moss, dead limbs, and leaves. If someone was chasing him, the hidden pit might come in handy. He would have to remember to swing to the far side of the pit when climbing down or the fall would cripple or kill him. In that case, being crippled would be worse than being killed outright by the fall.

Parker second-guessed his decision to dig the trap when he heard two sets of footsteps moving toward his position through the undergrowth. He watched them coming through the small window facing south. They walked about ten feet apart and scanned the ground. Both carried shotguns pointed downward at forty-five degree angles. Parker wondered if they were watching their step to avoid snakes or if they were looking for tracks or other signs of human activity. They were moving quick and sloppy, not like commandos Parker had watched in the movies. And they were talking loudly. Something about football, but he couldn't understand the entire conversation. They both wore the same white NASA security shirts and dark pants he had removed from the dead officer several days ago. He had lost count. Why count the days when you can't leave?

The two security men passed less than a dozen feet from the edge of the pit, still chatting and occasionally chuckling. If one had fallen in, the other would certainly have investigated further and noticed the moss-camouflaged structure just above their heads. But then again, given the sloppy way they were searching, Parker could have been sitting beneath the tree on a lawn chair with a glass of ice tea and they probably wouldn't have seen him. Ten minutes passed before he heard the outboard motor crank and throttle up. The sound of the boat slowly diminished until the only sounds left were the birds, the bugs, the breeze, and the leaves scratching against each other in the wind.

Parker backed away from the tiny window and scooted across the floor. He set his elbows on his knees and dropped his head in his hands. He thought of his mother and half-sister. He hated worrying them, but he didn't have another option. Would his mother die while he was in hiding? Her health was deteriorating, and his disappearance would only make things worse. And for what? Parker banged his first on the floor once to relieve his building frustration, but quickly calmed himself down. With his luck, another security officer would be drifting offshore and hear his childish tantrum.

Parker's dream had been to work for an agency like NASA. The pay was generous, the work was interesting, and job security with the federal government was practically guaranteed. But just as many other things in life, outside appearances are often illusions and reality can be a disappointment. He never had much of an interest in the political world, but he found that even in the world of science one could not escape its grasp. At first, he had no idea that the project he was assigned to was anything other than a theoretical exercise—a means of testing data against computer analysis and scientific calculations. That is, until he met Robert Bankston and the veil was lifted. It was then so obvious that Parker couldn't believe he had missed it.

He had met Bankston at the wedding of a couple he had never met before, but his girlfriend at the time was a bridesmaid and he felt obligated to attend. Bankston was a friend of the groom's family and happened to be in town on other business. In casual conversation at the reception, Parker had joked about not knowing anyone and being bored out of his mind. Bankston had laughed and said he was in the same boat. He had introduced himself and told Parker that he was an investigator with the Department of Justice. Parker was intrigued, and when he mentioned his work with NASA, Bankston appeared suddenly intrigued also. Parker was bound by a confidentiality agreement and knew better than to mention the "Group with No Name." He only revealed that he worked as a theoretical statistician.

What would have normally been a short, polite conversation had turned into a lengthy discussion with Parker asking a thousand questions. He realized after an hour of Bankston's commonsense explanations and answers to his questions that he had been so focused on the task at hand, he was blind to the big picture. His heart sank with the realization of the wide-ranging implications resulting from his involvement. He felt he had been used like a prostitute and all of his education and hard work were being misused for a manipulative and deceitful purpose—like a powerful handgun in the hands of a criminal instead of in the hands of a policeman.

In the following weeks, Parker never felt the same walking into his office. He could now understand the vague innuendos spouted by Max Rollins and his "wink-and-nod" attitude toward the project. With each passing day, Parker became more determined to be the handgun in the hands of the cops instead of the criminals. The next month, Bankston returned to Daytona, but not for a wedding. He and Parker had decided on the course of action that ultimately resulted in him sitting alone in the tree house on Gaines Island. He didn't regret his decision, but wished he had realized that one solitary scientist had no chance taking on not only the majority of the scientific world, but the political world as well.

Parker leaned back against the wall and wondered what was happening in the world away from Gaines Island. Had Bankston received his last e-mail or had it been blocked, as Max Rollins said? Had Bankston found the flash drive or had he abandoned Parker since he had vanished? Parker found himself staring at the sticks propped against the far wall. Each one was cut to the length of a yard stick and whittled down to spear heads on both ends. He was not a violent person, but he would absolutely defend himself if necessary. If he stabbed an animal or human aggressor with one end and it didn't do the job, he would flip it and stab it with the other end. But he had decided that it wasn't going to come to that. He had to let his family know he was alive no matter what happened to him later.

No more than two days, he told himself, *and I'm going home no matter what.*

Ten Broward County Harley Davidson motor units formed an inverted "V" formation ahead of the presidential motorcade on a totally deserted Port Everglades Expressway on its route to Fort Lauderdale-Hollywood International Airport. The expressway had been closed to midafternoon traffic fifteen minutes earlier by a swarm of Broward County

Sheriff marked units, causing a traffic juggernaut for five miles in each direction. In an effort to keep the commander in chief on his reelection campaign schedule, the Secret Service limo driver had been instructed not to waste any time getting to the tarmac, so he pushed the 20,000-pound, armor-plated beast to its best speed of sixty miles per hour.

The president glanced out of the five-inch-thick bulletproof glass and swirled two fingers of bourbon around two ice cubes in a short glass. The man seated across from the president was the senator and recently appointed chairman of a revived Senate Select Committee formed immediately after the last State of the Union address. Senator Bozich was revered by the Washington elite and had chaired almost all committees on the hill at least once in his forty-four-year career. At the age of seventy-one, he showed no hint of deteriorating health or signs of slowing down. The senator's colleagues and the mainstream media endeared him with the title of, "The Silver Stallion," while his political opponents and the talking heads on the radio referred to him as, "The Slithering Socialist."

The senator offered the president a grin of satisfaction and said, "Excellent speech, Mr. President." The president took a short sip from his glass and nodded.

"In large part, thanks to you, Senator Bozich. The cumulative facts of your research are inarguably the best that have been documented since I reappointed the committee. Anyone disputing your findings will look like a fool. Especially that right-wing idiot the Republicans nominated."

The senator sighed and said, "In all fairness, the group never totally abandoned their work."

The president gave the senator a blank look and paused a beat. "And how did you accomplish that under the nose of a Republican administration for four years?"

The senator shrugged. "The money had to be allocated, and although the rate of growth had been capped, the funds continued. I consider you an extremely wise man, Mr. President, but you have to admit that the budget is such a goliath that even *you* have no way of knowing where every penny is spent."

The president took a sip of bourbon and sat the tumbler in a cup holder. "I'm sure you're right, senator. I'm going to announce the summit of nations tomorrow at the afternoon press conference, and I would like for you to be there in case I need your input."

"When do you plan on conducting the summit?"

"Late January. I know I'm being optimistic. If I'm beaten, there will clearly be no summit. Hopefully, this last push through Ohio and Florida will wrap it up. Of all the states, those two are pivotal if I'm to win a second term."

The senator leaned forward and placed his hand on the president's shoulder. "You *will* win Ohio and Florida, and you *will* most certainly have your summit."

"Not if your counterpart, Franco LiVigni, has his way."

"Franco Livigni," the senator said mockingly. "Ever since he began vying for the GOP chairmanship he's been rattling the same sword and feeding Senator Greathouse with all the false information he's been spouting. The average Joe and Jane on the street doesn't care about his agenda. They're only interested in free health care, free childcare, free college, free food stamps, and free unemployment benefits."

"That's never stopped him before. What makes you think he won't continue?" the president asked.

"He suffered a little setback with one of the minions he sent to interfere with our project."

"And did he interfere?"

"Thankfully not. He was involved in a vehicle accident."

"Pity."

Senator Bozich nodded, and they road in silence until the motorcade made a wide arc into the airport entrance. A swell of onlookers and supporters lined Aviation Boulevard where the limo slowed near the rear gate on its way to the tarmac. Men, women, and children of every conceivable age were waving and holding homemade signs, either in support of or in condemnation of the president's policies over the past four years. The shouts of the crowd were nothing more than muffled mumbles through the thick bulletproof glass. Once past the gate, the crowd disappeared, and the only sound was the constant hiss of the air conditioning vents.

"Speaking of your project," the president said, breaking the silence, "I heard rumblings of some type of problem you were having at NASA. Something I need to be concerned about?"

The senator shook his head.

"No, sir. There are always problems in a bureaucracy, and I would immediately make you aware of any problem that rose to your level of attention. There are simply not enough minutes in the day for me to interrupt you with every problem we encounter."

"So everything is under control?"

"Mr. President, I have been in this business for the better part of my adult life. There are issues brought to your attention every hour from some quarter in the government.

Some require your attention. Some are addressed by those you trust and have given delegated authority."

"And others are?" said the president.

"Well," said the senator, "other problems are not brought to your attention for the sole purpose of protecting you from scrutiny and, more importantly, to protect the common goals that we share with the world."

The president chuckled, lifted his bourbon, and held it up in salute. He gulped the last of the drink and dropped the tumbler back in the cup holder.

"I have to hand it to you, Richard. You're the Rembrandt of bullshit if there ever was one."

Chapter Thirteen

olson touched the TV remote and silenced the annoying political ad. He had visited a much better looking Taylor earlier, if that was possible. He had been moved to a regular room and was recovering well. It was easy to gauge Taylor's well-being by how often he bragged about his UFC fighting victories to the female nurses and how frequently he threatened male attendants with a slow death if they continued to stick him to draw another vile of blood.

Colson stopped at the kitchen counter and grabbed the napkin-wrapped sandwich he had made and a bottle of water from the fridge. Although the political ads were annoying, Colson recognized the importance of staying informed of the issues. They directly affected people's lives, specifically those closest to him, including his grandson, daughter, and current soul mate. He had come to realize over the years that politics was not just a game played in Washington by a bunch of elites smoking cigars in a gentleman's club, but a potentially dangerous organization of power grabbers who care nothing about how their actions affect people outside of the beltway. He suspected there were a few with good intentions, but far too many were only in it to benefit themselves.

Colson rode the elevator to the ground floor and crossed the hot asphalt parking lot to the gate at the sea wall. The local economy was recovering, albeit slowly. He could only gauge it by the number of cars he watched on the beach roadway over the summer. It was clear things had at least improved, and he was convinced it was not because of Washington, but in spite of it. He passed by the spot where Mr. and Mrs. Hammond routinely sat in the shade of their rented umbrella, but they were absent that day. He waved to Thomas Chapman who returned a slight smile and lazy salute. He sat reading a book beneath the shade of a nearby canopy, roughly the size of Colson's. He had been the pastor of a church in Colson's old Georgia stomping grounds and insisted on being called Pastor Tommy because that's what his congregation had called him.

Colson got comfortable in his reclining beach chair and devoured the sandwich in five bites. The sound of slow-moving cars, trucks, and jeeps behind him and the sound of the waves before him was his favorite therapy. When last he sat in that very spot, he expected he might never return. He was confounded by the fact that Colonel Guerra hadn't been blowing up his cell phone with demands and threats. But he was back in America, Taylor was safe, and he was satisfied. *Almost.* There were too many things on his mind, including Bankston's revelation of what was going on at NASA. He had checked Bankston's private e-mail. There were only five messages, all presumably from Grant Parker with the ambiguous title of NewBlueSky10 and only a date and time in the subject line. The dates were for each month leading up to the week when Parker became a fugitive.

The e-mail attachments contained nothing but two sets of figures and locations that were totally meaningless to Colson. Bankston's conspiracy theory gave Colson an idea of what the data referred to, but he was no statistical scientist like Parker and couldn't make heads or tails of its relevance or how it could prove Bankston's claim. It seemed too outrageous on its face, but how could a person know the truth?

Colson thought of his late mother. She had no high school diploma and certainly no college degree, but she was as confident as anyone he had ever met when it came to identifying the truth of a matter. She described it to Grey as spiritual discernment. He had no idea how often she was right about the motives or honesty of people, but she had remained confident in any case and governed her life accordingly. Colson concluded that at times when there is no clear answer, no physical proof, no reliable witnesses, and no convincing evidence the only thing to go on were what cops call gut feelings, or, as his mother had termed it, *an inner voice.*

A small sandpiper landed just outside of Colson's canopy and walked within two feet of his recliner in search of a morsel of the sandwich he may have dropped. Colson wadded a small piece of sandwich crust into a tiny ball and dropped it at his feet. The sandpiper took two quick steps on its fragile legs and eagerly plucked it up. A bird wouldn't dare come that close to a person in Clay County Georgia, but shorebirds were accustomed to humans and not easily frightened away. It occurred to Colson that humans were not unlike a sandpiper when it comes to growing too comfortable in thinking or believing almost anything if told by enough people. Given sufficient time, it was similar to brainwashing. People could be conditioned to accept almost anything.

Colson stood and walked to the edge of the canopy next door. Pastor Tommy closed his book, peered at Colson over his reading glasses, and said, "Afternoon, Grey. How's things on your side of the beach?"

Grey ducked under the canopy and said, "May I pick your brain for a few minutes, Pastor? It's a pretty deep subject."

Pastor Tommy slid off his glasses and dropped them on top of the book in his lap. "Of course. I'm sure it's not as deep as the ocean out there."

Colson looked over his shoulder at the shore and then back to Pastor Tommy.

"I wouldn't be so sure of that."

Agent Mcilwain pulled his personal Ford pickup into the plaza parking deck at 201 South Orange Avenue and rode the elevator to the third floor. The Orlando office of US Senator Edward Greathouse was just two blocks from the FBI field office. He had visited the building several times and hoped he wouldn't bump into anyone he knew. He wore blue jeans, a dark-blue golf shirt, and sunglasses. He didn't have access to his issued Dodge Charger during his suspension, and it was probably for the best, although he missed the horsepower of the hemi engine.

He walked to a pair of frosted glass doors and through a modest lobby where a young man dressed in a white shirt and red tie sat typing at a computer. Mcilwain walked to the desk and slid off his sunglasses.

The young man gave Mcilwain a blank look and said, "May I help... oh, Agent Mcilwain. I didn't recognize you at first."

Mcilwain grinned. "No problem. Is the senator in?"

"Are you working undercover or something?"

Mcilwain initially didn't understand the assistant's question. He looked down at his shirt and chuckled. "Oh, I didn't think about that. It's my day off, and I thought I'd give myself a break from the suit."

The young assistant shrugged and then stood and walked toward a door down a short hallway. "It's no problem. It's a good thing you called first. I have to tell everyone else he's in Washington. This election is driving everybody crazy, including the senator."

The assistant led Mcilwain into the office and quickly departed, pulling the door closed behind him. Senator Greathouse sat sideways in a chair behind his desk watching a flat-screen television on the wall. The volume was muted, but Mcilwain could see the president conducting a press briefing. Mcilwain wasn't so certain his decision to meet the senator was a good idea. He was already in enough hot water, and this move could be a career ender. But Greathouse had been cordial and friendly during their previous encounters, even though it was always on a professional level.

Greathouse was a former federal prosecutor. He was about Mcilwain's age, which made him a relatively young man as a freshman senator in his first term in office. Mcilwain hoped he might be someone who would take him seriously and not dismiss him as a conspiracy theorist.

Greathouse stood and shook hands with Mcilwain. He said, "Good to see you, Mike. You still making those big fraud cases?"

Mcilwain offered a weak grin. "Not at the moment."

"Well," Greathouse said, "you're cases were always a prosecutor's dream. Not many agents are as thorough as you are. I wish we had more time, but I'm headed to Jacksonville in an hour to meet with Governor Bagwell at his final campaign sweep before the election. This one is gonna be a nail-biter. I've never seen the polls as close as they are this time around."

Mcilwain remained standing and said, "I don't want to take up too much of your time."

Greathouse gave him a dismissive wave and sat. "Sit down, Mike, and tell me what's going on."

Mcilwain gave Greathouse a brief summary of recent events including his and Strickland's assignment to find Grant Parker without the support of the US Marshals or additional FBI agents, Director Danz assuming control of the investigation and providing documentary evidence he'd collected without follow-up investigation by law enforcement, the speedy issuance of the espionage warrant for Parker without question by the federal judge, the involvement of Grey Colson and Robert Bankston, the blank flash drive recovered from Parker's condo, and Colson being summarily removed from the case, suspended, and reassigned because—as he believed—he had gotten too close to the truth.

Greathouse listened politely, occasionally nodding and sometimes squinting as if trying to arrange the facts in his head.

He said, "I think I know you pretty well, Mike. You're smart and analytical, and I can't recall a case you brought to the US attorney's office that wasn't air tight." He opened his hands on the desk, palms up. "But what do we know that we can prove?"

Mcilwain looked at his feet. "That's the thing. I don't know what all this means. I don't know what they're hiding or what motivation they have to hide it."

"Then where do I start and what about Parker? It's been weeks since he went missing and chances are fifty-fifty that he either fled the jurisdiction or is dead. We need him if there's a chance of exposing a conspiracy with NASA, and we have to know what it is."

Mcilwain nodded. "Believe me, I understand, and I shouldn't have wasted your time with something that's probably nothing more than paranoia on my part."

Greathouse checked his watch and said, "I'm not blowing you off, Mike, but I have to get going."

"Thanks just the same," Mcilwain said as he stood and moved toward the door.

"Look," said Greathouse. "You have a couple of weeks. See what you can find out and make another appointment if you come up with anything. You'll survive this setback. Damn shame the flash drive you found was blank. It could have shed a lot of light on what's going on... if anything."

Mcilwain hesitated at the door for a long moment as he wondered if the last bit of information was worth telling to Greathouse. What if he was wrong? As Greathouse had told him, he had never presented a case that he wasn't 100 percent certain about. Suspension or no suspension, he had a reputation to think about. Mike could walk out now, lick his wounds, and take the Atlanta field office by storm. It was a larger group with more room for advancement than Orlando. There was more potential for being assigned high-profile cases and further solidifying his career. But Mike knew there was a reason for his hesitation. He *had* to tell someone.

Mcilwain turned back around where Greathouse stood two feet away, waiting for him to open the door.

He said, "The flash drive wasn't blank."

Greathouse's expression became one of puzzlement. "But I thought you said—"

"Yes, I know what I said, and it *is* blank now, but it wasn't when we found it. That I *can* prove."

The low-slung blue Impala driven by Carlos Augusto made a slow right turn into the Sundowner parking lot at 2:15 p.m. Ramone sat to the right of Carlos. Paco and Miguel rode silently in the back as the *thump-thump* of the subwoofer in the trunk vibrated their seat. They'd spent the drive from Fort Lauderdale planning the hit, but it had all been speculation since they didn't know the layout of the complex, which condo their target lived in, or what Colson looked like. Today would be their reconnaissance day unless an opportunity presented itself that they couldn't pass up.

"Back there," Ramone said, pointing to the drive-under opening in the building.

Carlos muted the thumping gangster rap and eased the low-slung Impala slowly over the two yellow speed bumps; then he emerged in the guest parking lot. He made a slow circle around the parked cars and ended up where they started.

Carlos said, "I don't see no blue Corvette." He waited until an SUV backed out of a space and then parked the Impala in its place.

"Stay here amigos," Carlos said to the three junior gangbangers and stepped out onto the hot asphalt. He cringed at the sound of a female singing karaoke under a canopy at the pool. Dozens of tourists were gathered around the pool with their beach towels, bottled water, and coolers. Two men were grilling something that smelled like hamburgers under a structure at the far end of the pool, and children and teenagers were splashing in the water and throwing beach balls. Then he saw a Hispanic-looking girl with her dark hair pulled back into a ponytail pushing a blue laundry cart through the drive-under and down an interior hallway. He half jogged to catch up to her and rounded the corner behind her.

The walkway was narrow and paved with a mixture of small round pebbles, amplifying the irritating sound of the cart's hard plastic wheels. She pushed the cart past a door on her left and pulled it open. She struggled with the cart in the tight passage, trying to make the ninety-degree turn and fighting against the weight of the heavy door. Carlos trotted to the door and held it while she maneuvered the cart inside. She awarded him with a smile.

"Gracias," she said.

"It is my pleasure," Carlos replied. "Maybe you could help me."

"I am just a maid," she said while dumping bath towels and washrags in a washing machine.

"I'm looking for a man about a job. His name is Grey Colson."

The girl finished filling one machine and pushed a button. The sound of water spraying inside the machine filled the room as she started filling the next one.

"Did you go to his condo?" she asked.

Carlos made a sucking sound through his teeth and shook his head. "The problem is I had the number written down but lost it."

"I'm sorry, but we are not allowed to give out information about the residents."

Carlos stepped inside the small laundry room and let the door close behind him with a click. He slid one hand in his pocket and then crossed his arms. With her back to him, the girl continued loading the washing machine. Obviously sensing his presence, she slowed her work and glanced behind her. Carlos leaned his right shoulder against the door, revealing his colorful tattoo. He looked down at the inked crown and back to the girl.

He said, "You know this, don't you, Chula?"

The girl backed against the machine behind her and braced herself on either side with her hands. Carlos saw recognition in her eyes and grinned.

"You *do* know."

Carlos watched the girl's chest move rapidly as her breaths came quick and short. She had olive skin and beautiful black hair held back with a blue bow. He suspected she may have escaped a Latino neighborhood for a lowly legitimate job working for gringos. She would make a fine companion for a newly promoted Inca, but her reaction told him her friends had probably been members of a rival gang.

"Please," she said, "I don't know…"

Carlos closed the small space between them in an instant. He put his left hand over her mouth and the needle-sharp point of a switchblade under her chin. Carlos felt the quick breaths from the girl's nose on the back of his hand and the vibration of her muffled plea. He pressed the tip against her skin.

"I warn you," he said softly, moving his face close to be heard over the churning washing machine, "I will cut you if you scream or don't tell me what I want to know. You know I will, don't you, chula?"

The girl nodded. Carlos moved his hand to her cheek and patted it lightly as a single tear ran down and through his fingers.

"Now, you were saying?"

"I don't want no trouble. Please. He lives in number five-ten, but he's not there."

"And how do you know that?"

"Because I saw him go out to the beach. He is just down the steps and across the beach road under a black canopy."

Carlos lowered the switchblade, smiled, and patted the girl on the cheek.

"Very good, chula. You know what happens to women who cross the Latin Kings?"

The girl silently nodded.

"Good," said Carlos as he opened the door and stepped into the hall.

"Hey," the girl called behind him. "He used to be a cop."

"Even better," said Carlos as the door clicked shut behind him.

Colson's talk with Pastor Tommy gave him a fresh perspective. He told him nothing about Grant Parker, the FBI, or Robert Bankston in the hospital, or the unbelievable allegations against NASA, although he did sneak it in the conversation as a theoretical question. It was just a normal conversation about the way things were through the eyes of a man of faith. Colson half expected what Pastor Tommy would say, and he wasn't disappointed. It was the perceived battle between science and faith. Had science proven that God does not exist? Quite the opposite, as Pastor Tommy had said. The more discoveries man made, the more they should be convinced of the existence of a Creator. But unbelievers resist it at every turn and continue their search until they back into yet another discovery that only the existence of God can explain.

"For instance," Tommy had said, "recently discovered 'dark matter,' which is the most predominant substance in the universe and holds everything together like glue. It is something that can't be seen, touched, or heard and has no aroma, yet it is there. The literal hand of God keeping every living thing and nonliving thing from flying apart into particles smaller than atoms."

Colson stepped out from under Tommy's canopy with the assurance that Tommy didn't only study the Bible in his free time. The good pastor had admitted to being secretly obsessed with science, having his nose stuck in every available book on the subject, and watching the Science Channel whenever possible.

Colson settled back in his chair and concentrated on everything he knew about Grant Parker, beginning with his half-sister. Grant Parker's condo had looked like it had been cleaned by a brigade of maids. Then his abandoned black Challenger had been parked the wrong direction according to Lisa. And there was the empty flash drive case, the tent shoved under the bed, and the photo Lisa had given him of Grant in hiking apparel. But there was something else. Some small piece of information hiding in the recesses of his mind, but he couldn't find it.

The *thump-thump-thump* of the bass amplifier distracted Colson from his thoughts. It was normal to hear all genres of music spilling from the windows of passing vehicles on the beach road, including, but not limited to, rap music; however, in most cases, people kept the volume at a respectable level. Even so, it would pass in a matter of seconds, drowned out by the constant breeze and crashing waves.

Colson closed his eyes and replayed the search of Parker's residence in his mind. He and Lisa had initially split up and searched separate ends of the condo. He could see the bedroom as if he still stood there: the boat paddles above the headboard that hung in the form of an X, the well-made bed with the couch at the foot, the tidy closet with dress clothes on one side and casual on the opposite side, the dress shoes and hiking boots and tennis shoes, the tent under the bed, and the Atlanta Braves cap. And then there was another hat with awkward lettering. He strained to focus and recall what those letters were.

The thumping hadn't gone away. Colson looked back at the low-slung Impala that had nosed into a spot in the thick sand. The dark tinted windows prevented him from seeing inside, but he noticed the side mirror vibrating from the obnoxious bass pulsating in the trunk. The driver's window slid down, allowing the gangster rap to be heard loud and clear. The sunglasses in the side mirror were aimed directly at him. Colson flipped up the lid of his cooler, removed the ASP expandable baton, and laid it in his lap. He faced front and lifted his cell phone. Pulling up the camera app, he reversed the screen as if taking a selfie, zoomed in the view, and held it so that the blue low-rider filled the screen behind him.

The thumping finally ceased, and the Impala's four doors opened simultaneously. Four skinny Latino-looking types spilled out. They each stretched in their own fashion and looked up and down the beach, with the exception of one: the driver. He just stood, glaring at Colson's back. Colson took the opportunity to snap two photos. All four wore white, wife-beater tank tops and baggy pants hung low enough for the public to be blessed with a view of their undershorts. Colson glanced over to Pastor Tommy's canopy. He had probably been irritated by the obnoxious rap, but had chosen to ignore it and returned to reading his book.

If the four Latinos wanted to be obvious, they had met their objective. Colson had attended monthly gang intelligence meetings during his final years at the sheriff's office and immediately recognized the guys as gangbangers. If that was not the case, they were excellent actors, but there wasn't a movie crew in sight. The group of four huddled for a moment and then three of them broke away and walked to the shore, leaving the driver milling around in the sand and leaning against the trunk. Colson had never seen dyed-in-the-wool gang members at the beach in all the years he'd spent there. At least none that advertised it. It was precisely the reason he asked friends to keep an eye on his canopy setup when he made lunch. You could never be sure when the wind would blow some trash in. Colson lowered his phone and waited.

A minute later, the driver appeared to his left, making a show of surveying the beach both north and south. No, he wasn't a good actor at all, which explained why there was no film crew. It was when the driver turned around to make a show of looking at the condos that Colson saw the Latin Kings tattoo, thus removing any doubt in his mind who he would be dealing with. Distributing photos of gang tattoos was one of the main reasons for officers to attend gang intelligence meetings. After spending a short time making his architectural observations of the condos, the driver turned and stared at the black canopy with "Corvette" written along the edge in bold white lettering. He strolled to the edge of the canopy and stared down at Colson through his tiny sunglasses.

He grabbed one leg of the canopy so the wind wouldn't blow his tiny frame away like a kite and said, "Nice tent, Holmes."

"Glad to hear that," Colson said flatly.

"So you have a Corvette, Holmes?"

"You're not from around here, are you?" Colson said, ignoring the question.

"Don't worry where I'm from, Holmes, but I have family in Ecuador. Have you ever been there?"

Colson kept his sunglasses on the driver, but cut his eyes to the shore where the other three gangbangers were standing twenty feet away from the shoreline, watching bikini-clad women and young girls strolling down the beach. They looked back at their apparent leader every five to ten seconds. Colson decided evasion was the best tactic, so he would be as artful as a politician on television and not answer any of the driver's direct questions.

"You must have mistaken me for Sherlock Holmes since you keep calling me that, but I'll take it as a compliment. Tell you what. If I see a guy wearing an 1870s trench coat with a deerstalker hat and pipe, I'll let him know you're looking for him."

Carlos shook his head and made a sucking sound through his teeth. He said, "No, vato, I know very well who you are, Grey Colson."

"Then what's this *vato* business? What happened to Holmes?"

"Cabron."

"Now you've totally lost me with the Español, but I know who, or rather *what*, you are too."

"You know nothing, cabron," said Carlos.

"You just can't decide what to call me, can you? You're a gangbanger with the so-called Latin Kings." Colson pointed straight ahead to the shore with the collapsed shaft of the ASP where the other three now stood looking directly at the canopy. "And I suppose those three are your Latin Queens."

Colson stood and jerked the ASP downward a quarter second after Carlos took a long step under the canopy. With the passing vehicles just feet behind the canopy and the buffering of wind and surf, the attention-getting snap of the ASP was almost silent, but the sudden appearance of the metal baton from nowhere froze Carlos in place. The other three gangbangers had taken two steps toward the canopy but were halted by Carlo's raised hand.

Carlos took a slow step back from under the canopy and gave Colson a smirk.

He said, "Not now, Holmes. Not now. This was just an introduction."

Colson took one step forward, holding the ASP down and parallel to his right leg. He towered easily over Carlos by a head.

"Now it's just time for you to get lost."

"What," Carlos mocked, gesturing to the ASP with a nod. "You couldn't kill a mosquito with that stick."

"There aren't any mosquitoes at the beach, you idiot, but you should see how it works with other vermin who invade my space."

"We'll see," Carlos said and turned his attention to Ramone, Paco, and Miguel. "Vámonos."

The three gangbangers walked behind Carlos and back to the Impala. Carlos resumed his stare down with Colson, who stood still and defiant.

Colson followed the other three with his eyes and said, "I finally figured out why you guys lower all your cars to three inches off the ground. Latin Kings are too short to crawl into a normal car."

Carlos stood still and silent with his hands balled into fists, flexing the muscles in his skinny arms and clinching his jaw in a steady rhythm. Colson knew the thug standing before him was using every ounce of self-control he had to keep from pouncing. There wasn't a doubt that this was the call he had been expecting from Colonel Guerra, and he had gotten the message. The game wasn't over yet. He would rather end it here and now as opposed to when those cowards came back in the middle of the night. But instead of pouncing, Carlos made some ridiculous gang gesture with his hands and stomped off to the Impala and drove away with the gangster rap music thumping until the noise was mercifully swallowed by the surf and wind.

Colson looked over to Pastor Tommy who sat looking in his direction with his book in his lap. He shook his head at Colson in disgust. Colson gave him a thumbs up and returned to his lounge chair.

Little Man Syndrome, Colson thought. Some of the worst fights he had were with small guys who tried to make up for their size by playing the tough guy. The wind rushing inland from the Atlantic had nearly blown the gangbanger away like a mosquito. That's why there were none at the beach. Suddenly the pictures in his mind replaced the ocean view with the image of Parker's bedroom—specifically the closet. What he had been trying to remember came into view: the ball cap with the haphazard lettering on a background of weathered boards.

Mosquito Lagoon.

⚜Chapter Fourteen⚜

C olson sat his drink on the side table, pressed his feet against the heavy aluminum balcony railing, and tilted his deck chair back against the sliding glass door. At four o'clock, the sun was on the front of the building, leaving him in comfortable shade. Half of the visitor parking lot and the community swimming pool were being consumed by the afternoon shadow. Most of the older beach goers had vanished at three o'clock to get cleaned up for early bird specials. High tide was in the process of claiming the beach, and the surf had crossed the beach road, leaving a few drivers with the task of trekking through the thick sand near the sea wall to the public access road. One motor home was almost swept into the ocean as the driver repeatedly spun his tires in drive and reverse until they rested in self-made trenches. Colson briefly thought about riding the elevator down to assist, but six other men chipped in and helped push it to safety. The umbrella rental guy was making his afternoon pickup of umbrellas and chairs, stacking them neatly on a trailer and moving on.

Colson paid little attention to the pickup circling around the public parking lot. There were different cars, trucks, and motorcycles in the parking lot every week as vacationers came and went. The pickup slipped into a spot. A lone man exited the driver's side and arched his back as if he had been on the road for hours. He was a clean-cut young man wearing tan slacks and a rose-colored polo shirt. Real preppy. The man turned to face the condo and held one hand against his brow to block the glare. And he was looking directly in Colson's direction. Colson lifted the binoculars from the side table and focused in. It was Agent Mcilwain.

Mcilwain gave Colson a lazy wave, walked toward the building, and disappeared into the drive-under. He would be coming up the elevator. Colson stood, dropped the binoculars in his chair, and then stepped up to the railing. He scanned the rear lot for other agents and unfamiliar vehicles, but nothing else was suspicious. He fast walked through the balcony door, snatched the ASP off the kitchen counter, and stuck it in the pocket of his shorts. He was out the front door in less than five seconds, scanning the front lot for other agents in black government cars. He didn't see anything strange or out of place. There were no snipers lying in wait on the flat roof of the abandoned Sunsations Gift Shop across A1A, only normal traffic slipping by.

If Mcilwain was coming to finish the job they had failed at twice, he had no tactical training whatsoever. Colson stepped into the stairwell across from his unit's front door and watched through the narrow window above the knob. Mcilwain casually walked to the door, knocked and waited. Colson stepped out barefoot and silent behind him and jerked the ASP downward with a loud metallic snap. Suddenly, Mcilwain froze and raised both hands without turning around.

"Colson," he said in an even tone.

Colson said, "You're either awfully stupid or awfully brave to show up here, Mcilwain."

Mcilwain turned slowly with his hands at shoulder height. "I'm just here to talk."

"I hope you're better at talking than you and your NASA friends are at assassinations."

Mcilwain looked genuinely confused. "What are you talking about? Assassinations? Can we just go inside and talk?"

"I can hear you fine right here," said Colson. "I'm talking about the semi that mowed down Rob Bankston and missed me by an inch and then your co-conspirators abandoning me in Ecuador at the whim of Colonel Guerra. None of that rings a bell?"

"I'm sorry, Colson. I had nothing at all to do with any of that. I did find out about the NASA jet, but only after the fact. I had no reason to suspect differently. Hell, the FBI has never even sent *me* anywhere on a private jet. Look, I'm on suspension right now for getting in Danz's face and accusing him of covering up God knows what, and I'm being transferred to Atlanta at the end of the month."

"And I'm supposed to believe you now?" Colson asked.

"You don't have to, but please listen. You're right about Danz, but I only have a small piece of the puzzle. I can't prove anyone is guilty of anything when I don't know what the crime is. You know that as well as I do. If you know anything… anything at all, you need to tell me."

Colson turned toward the street. Mcilwain stepped up and rested his hands on the railing. Colson tapped the tip of the ASP against one of the aluminum pickets. It made a tinny, hollow sound. He turned to Mcilwain.

"How am I supposed to trust you, Agent Mcilwain? Who even suggested I had information?"

"No one, but before you left for Ecuador, you said you had met with Robert Bankston. I know he worked for the Justice Department and was working to find Parker without their knowledge or approval. He wasn't going rogue to arrest Parker and be knighted a hero. My gut says they were working together on something they felt very strongly about."

"Then why don't you ask Bankston?"

"He refused to talk... or I should say communicate. His jaw is wired shut."

Colson shrugged. "Has anyone from the Justice Department questioned him? I mean, if he works for them you'd think they would be concerned... or a least curious."

"They never responded. We informed them about the accident and—"

"It was attempted murder," Colson corrected.

"OK, the attempted murder... although we didn't know it at the time. They just thanked us for the info and that's the last we heard. As far as they're concerned, he was AWOL, and they have apparently disavowed him."

Colson stood silently and turned back to watch the traffic on A1A. Mcilwain had showed up in a pickup and it didn't appear anyone was covering him. He had dumped the FBI suit for slacks and a polo shirt, but Colson wasn't buying the story. He had worked undercover long enough to know the whole thing could be a ploy to find out what he knows, making him as dangerous as Parker was to them. If he told Mcilwain anything, he could end up like Parker and vanish from the face of the earth.

"Why the sudden change of heart?" said Colson.

"What do you mean?"

"At some point you realized something or found out something significant to make you suspect Danz and NASA were the criminals, not Parker, right?"

It was Mcilwain's turn to pause and study the lazy A1A traffic. Colson knew from the man's silence that he'd hit the nail on the head, so he didn't press the issue. He might confide in Mcilwain if the agent revealed something that tied together what he knew and what Mcilwain now knew. But as it stood, both had important information, and both were hesitant to be the first to reveal it. Two puzzle pieces in the possession of two different people and neither willing to fit them together for a clear picture. Trust requires more than two or three brief conversations with another person, whether they are fellow law enforcement officer or not. And Mcilwain had not pegged out Colson's trust meter.

Mcilwain finally nodded. "Yes I did, but I don't know *how* significant it is. Are you still going to look for Parker?"

"Yes, and I intend to find him, dead or alive."

"Then you *do* know something."

"I didn't say that."

"You didn't have to," Mcilwain said. He pulled a card from his pocket and handed it to Colson. He said, "I can understand you not trusting me yet. I don't even know if I can trust you either, but it's vital that you contact this man as soon as possible."

Colson read the plain white business card with the gold eagle emblem on the top-left corner. The wording, "State of Florida" was on the top-right corner and "Edward Greathouse—United States Senator" was in the middle. An Orlando address and three sets of phone numbers filled in the bottom.

Mcilwain said, "The senator's cell number is written on the back."

Colson chuckled. "Seriously? Even if I had information, you expect me to trust a politician?"

"He's a good man. I've known him since he was a federal prosecutor. He'll be back in town in three days."

"Well, I assure you if I locate the remains of Jimmy Hoffa or the Arc of the Covenant, he'll be the first to know."

"You don't understand. This has nothing to do with Parker or NASA."

"Then what's this about?" Colson asked.

"I met with Senator Greathouse yesterday and told him everything about Danz and NASA and Robert Bankston and, ah... you. He said your name came up recently."

"Well, aren't you just a pal? So what does he want to talk to me about?"

"Do you know the name, Rafael Correa?"

"Never heard of him."

"He's the current president of Ecuador. Apparently, his administration has petitioned the US government for the immediate extradition of you and Jay Taylor for escape and aggravated battery of government officials."

Director Danz stepped into Max Rollins's office and closed the door. Rollins sat at his desk, studying his computer monitor through a pair of reading glasses. Their discussions in the past week had been few since the search for Grant Parker had all but petered out. The twenty-four-hour shifts had ceased after the second week. On the third week, half the security force was assigned to perform daily searches and the other half was returned to normal duties. Now the entire force was back to their routine of manning the gatehouses, locking doors, and patrolling the complex. Danz and Rollins had convinced each other that Parker was a man-sized pile of alligator excrement at the bottom of the marsh, and it was becoming a moot issue anyway. The election was in two weeks.

"What is it?" asked Danz, falling in behind Rollins and looking down at the scene on his monitor. The satellite image was zoomed in on the top of a building on the corner of a city street with a triangle-shaped water fountain on the west side. From above, the building looked like a slanted rectangle. A line of trees, spaced perfectly to follow the shape of the fountain, sprouted from openings in the concrete. The area looked somewhat familiar, but Danz didn't recognize it from the aerial view. The vehicles on the streets were stationary, so Rollins must have taken a screen shot.

Rollins pointed at the screen with the tip of an ink pen. "Right there. You see it?"

Danz bent forward to get a closer look where two traffic lanes from a side street disappeared under the building. Rollin's pen was touching the top of a pickup truck.

Danz said, "What am I supposed to be seeing?"

"Mcilwain's truck. I've been tracking him like you said."

Danz said, "What's that building?"

"Seaside Plaza on South Orange in Orlando."

Danz nodded. "OK. I know where you're talking about. When was this?"

"Yesterday."

Danz shrugged. "It's not a federal building. He's on suspension until next month, and then he'll be gone. What's the significance?"

"Maybe nothing, but—"

"But what?"

Rollins referred to notes on his desk pad. "The Seaside Plaza, 201 South Orange Avenue, has eight vacant suits, one real estate conglomerate named Highwood Properties, the Orange County Clerk of Court's Office, the corporate offices of Seaside National Bank and the Orlando Office of Senator Edward Greathouse."

"You're not suggesting he went to see Greathouse are you?"

"Maybe."

"That's ridiculous. He's just an agent—a dishonored agent on suspension nonetheless. Greathouse wouldn't give Mcilwain the time of day. Even if he did, there's nothing to tell him or show him for that matter. You said this was yesterday?"

Rollins nodded.

"Well, there you go. I happened to see Greathouse on live television last night at a campaign rally in Jacksonville for Governor Bagwell. Is this really what you drug me down here for?"

"You said to keep you in the loop, so that's what I'm doing," said Rollins in a mildly frustrated tone. "But that's not the only place Mcilwain went that might interest you. It sure as hell interests me."

Rollins selected a drop-down menu on the screen and scrolled down to a saved file. The previous scene vanished and was replaced with another zoomed-in photo that was clearly an oceanfront complex on A1A. The photo was so clear, it was as if it had been taken from a helicopter a hundred feet in the air. Even individual breakers at the shore were identifiable. Rollins pointed again with his pen. An identical pickup truck was in a parking space between the building and the ocean.

"Do I have to ask?" Danz said impatiently.

Rollins dropped his pen and reading glasses on the desk and then turned to face Danz. "I tracked him from downtown Orlando to this location."

Danz shrugged. "So he went snooping around Parker's condo again. There's nothing to find."

"This is miles north of Parker's condo. It's the Sundowner. Grey Colson's complex."

Danz stood silent for a long moment, looking at the screen. "Any sign of Colson or his car?"

Rollins shook his head. "Not that I've seen. But then again, I haven't been looking for Colson, just tracking Mcilwain. Who do you consider to be the biggest threat?"

"Honestly, with only two weeks left before the election, I doubt either of them are a threat. We're too close."

Rollins stood and ran his hand through his hair. "You need to let me start searching for Colson in case he made it back in one piece. If Mcilwain is looking for him, he may know something, or at least Mcilwain has a reason to think he does."

"And do what if you find him?"

Rollins stared at Danz but didn't respond. Danz crossed his arms, understanding Rollins's silence and said, "I don't understand why you want to get your hands dirty with this. You were in the same room with Colson not three weeks ago and wouldn't take him on. You tried to mow him down with a semi and missed. What makes you think you can handle him now? Do you have another brilliant plan up your sleeve?"

Rollins didn't answer the question, but said, "Let me ask you a question. How pissed off would you be if you were deliberately stranded in a third-world country and left for dead?"

Two hours and ten minutes after takeoff from Orlando International Airport, the Jet Blue Airbus A320 went wheels down at Reagan International Airport. The short 5.4 miles from the airport to the Hart Senate Building required an additional forty minutes of stopping, changing lanes, and creeping along the George Washington Memorial Parkway through horrendous Washington, DC, traffic.

Max Rollins felt anxious in the back of the limousine but reveled in the luxury of the moment. At forty-eight years old, he knew it would be impossible to climb the Washington political ladder any higher than maybe campaign manager or lobbyist, but he was determined to be a full-blown, beltway insider. His first taste of the political world became an addiction after his time on staff with former Congressman Ken Cooper. Never before had he been exposed to black tie events, cocktail parties, and powerful people until then. But just as quickly as his political ambitions had been given birth, the rug was snatched out from under his feet when the Republicans recaptured the House of Representatives and the congressman was defeated by a Tea Party right-winger. It took three months of phone calls, e-mails, and cashing in the few favors he had left to land the political liaison position at NASA.

Rollins shifted nervously in his seat. He was worried and wondered what would happen after the election. Would there be a need for a political overseer on the project after the president's summit? The president would be a lame duck in his last two months if he lost to Bagwell. He would have failed to accomplish what he and many others before him had failed to do, and his miserable legacy would be set in stone. What was never set in stone were jobs within the Washington beltway. Would Rollins lose his position once again and be left to grovel and plead to every politician and staffer on Capitol Hill? No, he had to secure his future now before it was too late.

The limousine turned off of Constitution Avenue onto First Street and immediately stopped at a barricade. Beyond was a closed off two-lane street with angled parking on either side between the Hart and Russell Senate Office Buildings. Small traffic lights were affixed to four posts with red-and-white striped arms. All the lights were red. The limo paused for only a moment before the arm in front lifted and the light switched to green. Rollins couldn't see through the tented windows of the guardhouse off to the right, but whoever was inside must have recognized the senator's car and driver.

Rollins was escorted through a marble-tiled lobby to a security checkpoint. After dumping his pockets and walking through a body scanner, the driver led him to the third floor, where he was deposited in a conference room. He chose one of the swivel chairs in the middle of a long oval table and sat his satchel on the floor. The view from the large window was of an old stone-and-brick building he guessed must be over a hundred and fifty years old. Chiseled in stone above the old entrance was Thompson-Markward Hall. Rollins had no idea of the name's significance. The only thing he knew for certain was if he failed at the day's endeavor, the only stone his name would ever be chiseled into would be above his grave.

The door opened behind him and Senator Bozich appeared quickly to his right at the end of the table. For a seventy-plus-year old man, the senator was as quick on his feet as a college athlete.

Rollins stood out of respect and said, "Mr. Chairman, ah... Senator." The senator waved for Rollins to sit while he remained standing with his arms crossed.

"I remember you from Danz's office," the senator said dryly. "What happened to the regular courier?"

"Ah, I felt it vitally important that I personally deliver the final data in person and make you aware of a situation that could potentially be damaging to the program, not to mention the election."

The senator stood stone-faced. His arms remained crossed. The old man was closed off and untrusting. Rollins suspected a few decades in Washington had that effect on everyone. Being the seasoned politician that he was, the senator never spoke or reacted quickly. He would process information methodically and choose his words carefully, even with a flunky like Rollins.

"Why didn't Danz come?" the senator asked.

Rollins didn't answer. The senator formed a sly grin and said, "He doesn't know you're here, does he?"

Rollins shook his head.

The senator eased into the chair at the head of the table and laced his fingers together on the polished oak surface. He said, "You have my attention."

Rollins rehashed the circumstances involving Grant Parker and their extensive search. The senator made a show of checking his watch for the first three minutes but otherwise remained silent. Rollins continued by relating the brief involvement of FBI Agents Mcilwain and Strickland. The senator was clearly familiar with the story due to a look of boredom creeping across his face. Rollins had no idea exactly how much the senator knew, but believed he hit the sweet spot at the mention of Robert Bankston, Grey Colson, and their attempt to locate Parker before he was locked up and silenced in a federal prison. The senator was enough of a professional politician to contain his emotion or surprise, but he had stopped checking his watch, and Rollins took that as permission to continue.

Rollins explained their attempt to remove Bankston and Colson from the equation—lying when he said that it was at the direction of Director Danz—and that it had been halfway successful. He continued with Colson's trip to Ecuador and suspected return. That he didn't embellish because Danz had directly approved the use of the NASA jet, which in Rollins's haughty opinion was a foolish risk and an unreasonable expenditure.

The senator broke his silence. "Are you certain this Colson is back in the States?"

"Ninety-nine point nine percent, sir."

The senator stood. "I appreciate your candor, but we are mere days away from the election. Why would this Colson even bother to search for Parker under the circumstances?"

"Three reasons. We don't know how much Bankston learned from Parker, but we know they were communicating, and he most likely knows enough. And we know Bankston and Colson got together at least once, so we have to assume Colson knows just as much."

"What's the third reason?" the senator asked.

"He stalked Director Danz and insinuated that the semi accident was orchestrated, and then Danz dropped him off in Ecuador and abandoned him. He's not a stupid man, Senator, just a smartass with a real big chip on his shoulder. And he's just smart enough to be dangerous. I also know Agent Mcilwain went to Colson's condo yesterday and stayed for an hour. It's obvious they made contact."

"Have you been following them both?"

"I will be with your approval. A satellite was retasked before the semi accident. Senator, the threat of either Colson or Mcilwain sabotaging our project is very real—a literal threat to national security."

The senator sat back in his seat and leveled his gaze on Rollins. "That's a bit dramatic, don't you think? You didn't fly all the way to Washington because you're truly concerned about national security. What is it you *really* came to me for?"

Rollins looked down at his hands and then back to the senator. "Ah, sir, after the election I don't suppose the party will need a permanent political liaison at NASA. Especially not after the summit the president is planning."

The senator leaned back and crossed his arms—once again closed off and untrusting. "You came to me for another job. I should have known."

Rollins's breathing became shallow. He paused while processing whether he had done himself a favor or cut his own political throat. But this was how the political game was played. Surely there was a time when the senator had done the exact same thing.

"Senator," Rollins said. "It's true that I'm looking out for myself but who the hell doesn't? I didn't fabricate Colson, Bankston, or Mcilwain. They're very much real and can do damage. That's the very reason I was sent to NASA—to look out for your interest and the interest of the party. I assure you I can make this all go away if you'll allow me to."

The senator appeared to be considering Rollin's words and coming to a decision. He pointed a bony finger at Rollins and said, "Involve no one else, and I don't want to know anything about it, you understand?"

Rollins nodded, stood, and extended his hand. The senator stood and dropped his arms to his side.

"No one is making a deal here, but there will be a position waiting for you after the election."

"Thank you, Senator," Rollins said and turned to the door. After opening it, he looked back and said, "Sir, you didn't ask my name."

Without looking at Rollins, the senator replied, "I don't want to know it. I'll remember your face... believe me."

Canal Avenue runs east off South Ridgewood Avenue just a few miles south of New Smyrna Beach. Colson moved at the posted speed of twenty-five miles per hour down the narrow two-lane road through a sharp right-hand curve. A small green signpost notified him that the name of the road had been changed to River Road. He immediately saw the large community of single and double-wide trailers and fifth-wheel trailers parked in neat rows. About midway through the group of trailers, a wide sandy road intersected them and disappeared eastward to the coast. Colson made a slow turn on the sandy road. To his right sat a sign in a red brick frame with large white letters: Mosquito Lagoon Fish Camp. A red arrow pointed straight ahead.

The trailers gave way to tents and pop-up campers further down the road. Colson passed a roadside shack on his right with a cabin-style porch at ground level and a sign above the door that read, "Live Wire Bait & Supply." Two pickup trucks were parked out front where two older men wearing overalls and holding fishing poles stood chatting. Colson slowed the car and rolled down the passenger-side window. The blue Corvette immediately got the old gentlemen's attention. Colson knew the sleek sports car was not the normal vehicle of a fisherman, complete with poles and a tackle box.

"Is the fish camp close?" Colson said, leaning over the middle console. One of the older men just pointed further east. Colson gave him a wave of thanks and continued toward the inland waterway. Five hundred feet later, a moss-green-colored building came into view, situated a hundred feet or so back from the open water. Another moss-green-colored building stood at the water's edge with a long pier and boat slips extending from both sides. The building looked like a larger version of what old church congregations used for camp meetings and all-day singing and dinner on the grounds, except it was totally screened in. He suspected they hadn't named the place Mosquito Lagoon for nothing.

Colson carried the photo he had taken from Parker's condo as he pushed through the screen door of the pavilion. There were three rows of picnic tables sitting on the concrete floor and three deep fryers or boilers sitting against the far wall. At two o'clock in the afternoon, it was too late for lunch and too early for dinner. A lone motorboat sat in the nearest pier slip, but the place was otherwise deserted. A male voice called from behind him.

"Can I help you, sir?" The young man was in his mid-twenties, wearing blue jeans and a moss-green-colored shirt that matched the surrounding buildings. Above his left breast was the Mosquito Lagoon logo, exactly as it had appeared on Parker's ball cap. The young man had a high and tight haircut and a three-day growth of beard. He stepped through the screen door and let it close behind him with a *clack*.

Colson decided there wasn't time to explain the entire situation, not that the young man would've believed him anyway. He pulled his Volusia County major's badge out and flipped it open. He held the photograph in front of the young man and said, "Yes, do you recognize the man in this picture?"

The young man squinted at the photo. "I don't have my glasses, but if he is a regular here, Momma Ball will probably know him."

"Momma Ball?"

"Yeah, she runs the camp," he said and pointed at the main moss-green-colored building.

Colson followed the young man across the sandy road and into the main building. They walked into the aroma of fresh soil and kerosene, with a touch of earthworms on the side. The wide plank floors were clean and swept, but creaked with every step. The wall behind the counter was lined with fishing poles with little white tags dangling from their reels. A refrigerator sat off to the right behind the counter with a glass door and stacks of short Styrofoam cups, probably filled with the earthworms. A slender woman in her late forties or early fifties stood jotting something on a calendar that hung on the side of the refrigerator. The woman's hair was blond with a touch of gray and tied in a long ponytail. She turned when Colson and the young man arrived at the counter.

The woman smiled and said, "What can I do for ya?"

The young man said, "This policeman is looking for someone."

The woman looked from the boy to Colson. "Policeman huh?"

Colson showed her the badge and handed her the photo. "Sheriff's Office actually. You must be Momma Ball."

She took the photo and studied it. "Ah, that's just what the boys here call me. You can call me Judi. Who's this supposed to be?"

"He's wanted," said Colson. "He used to be a NASA scientist.

"That's right," said Judi. "I saw it on television."

"But you don't recognize him as a customer?"

Judi shook her head. "Not really, but I'm certain this is Mosquito Lagoon in the photo."

"Really? How?"

"That huge drift wood formation behind him. It's the biggest one on the lagoon called the Devil's Claw."

The young man said, "Can I see it again?"

"I thought you didn't have your glasses," said Colson.

Judi handed the young man her reading glasses from around her neck. "Use these, Roper." She turned to Colson. "If he's been here, Roper would have had more of a chance seeing him since he does our fishing tours."

Roper looked at the photo for what seemed like over a minute and nodded. "OK, I had only been out of the navy and working here three months. This would have been a couple of years ago on Gaines Island." Roper pointed at the photo. "That drift wood is the only one in the lagoon that large. He asked about camping there."

"On Gaines Island?" asked Judi. "Camping's not permitted there."

Roper handed the photo back to Colson and said, "That's what I told him. Seemed strange too. He was the only person I had taken out by himself. Usually people go out with their family or fishing buddies."

"Great. Thanks," said Colson. "Can I rent a boat, and do you have a map marked with the islands?"

Judi reached under the counter and laid a crude drawing of the lagoon on the counter. She turned the map around, put her finger on a spot, and said, "Gaines Island is a good seven miles upriver, but it's the weekend and all the rentals are out." She turned and referred to the calendar on the refrigerator. "Next available boat won't be until Monday, second half of the day."

Colson realized he was being too hasty. He wasn't prepared or dressed for an immediate expedition. There was also the need to pass on the data to someone before traipsing into the unknown.

"Sounds good," he said. "Put me on the calendar."

Colson gave Judi a credit card deposit and said to Roper, "How far would you estimate Gaines Island is from the Kennedy Space Center?"

Roper shrugged. "Why? There ain't no roads from there to the Space Coast."

"I mean as the crow flies. If you had to walk it."

"If I had to guess, I'd say eight to twelve miles. We've watched the launches from here, but why would anyone want to walk through the marsh?"

"Just curious," said Colson. He walked out and climbed back in the Corvette. He cranked the engine and set the temperature to sixty-five degrees. It was late October and still in the mid-eighties with a heat index of ninety degrees. The air blowing on high quickly cooled the small cabin. Colson took a moment to study the map. There were literally dozens of tiny, medium, and large Islands in Mosquito Lagoon. Fortunately, Judi had been kind enough to highlight the fish camp and Gaines Island with a yellow marker.

Colson drove back down the sandy road and past the Live Wire Bait & Supply shack, which appeared to be Momma Ball's only competition. The two pickups and the old men in overalls were gone. He rolled past the campers and tents and then past the larger trailers. River Road was just in sight about fifty feet ahead. He glimpsed in his rearview mirror as he neared the intersection. The low-slung blue Impala moving in behind him was unmistakable.

Chapter Fifteen

G rant Parker's sister hugged him and cried tears of relief on his shoulder. She seemed so happy that he was home safe and assured him no one would come after him again. Relief swept over him when his mother smiled and kissed his cheek. He had been terrified that his disappearance would have drained the remaining life from her already frail body. She said she had prayed every day that God would protect him and bring him home safe. Tears welled in his eyes when he realized how much she had worried. The next moment he was at home taking a hot shower and sitting on his balcony, watching early morning waves lap onto Daytona Beach and slip back into the shallow surf. With the ordeal over, he was ready to get on with his life. He reached for his coffee mug and a sharp pain ran from his elbow to the back of his neck. The stabbing sensation at the base of his skull brought a moment of clarity and swept away his delusions.

Parker rolled to his side and coiled into a fetal position. He was hot and cold at the same time. His weak, undernourished body was clammy with sweat and shivered uncontrollably. Parker was unable to sleep and had nearly depleted his food supply. He would be foraging and hunting if his bones and muscles didn't ache and make him wince every time he attempted to stand. He had used the last of the bug repellent days ago, and now the mosquitoes were devouring him. The plan was to go back home and either face the music or leave the country, but neither option was possible in his current state. He had fanaticized about moving his small family to Belize. A friendly, warm, and simple place not as burdened with politics and power-hungry tyrants. But his mother was too frail and couldn't get out of the house to go grocery shopping, let alone survive a move to Central America.

Guilt consumed Parker. He would die there without saying good-bye to his mother and sister. They would forever wonder if he had abandoned them and started a new life or if he had died. He hoped they would believe the latter and not think he had been so selfish as to value his freedom at the expense of their heartache. He prayed that God would somehow convince them of that. He made another attempt to push himself up but every muscle in his upper body screamed in agony. He coiled back into a ball and said one more prayer. He opened his eyes and could see branches swaying slowly in the wind through the small window of his elevated hideout.

"I love you, Mom," Parker said and then closed his eyes.

Colson slowed the Vette and stopped. The midget Latino Kings from the beach were in the car behind him. The chopped-down Impala was as out of place at the fish camp as his Corvette was.

The Impala moved to within twenty feet and stopped. Colson watched in his mirror until the front doors of the Impala opened. When the main thug and his sidekick stepped out, Colson drove ahead fifty feet to the turn on River Road and stopped again. The two thugs jumped back in the Impala. It moved forward again, but they hesitated getting back out.

The driver laid on the horn, but Colson remained motionless. The thugs jumped out more quickly this time. Colson shoved the brake pedal down with his left foot and floored the accelerator with the other. The Impala disappeared from his rearview mirror in a cloud as the rear tires spun under the torque of 460 horsepower, propelling gravel, sand, and crushed seashells to the rear. The Corvette shimmied from side to side as the traction control tried to compensate for the tires' lack of grip on the road, giving the flying debris a wide angle of distribution. Colson heard the ticking sounds of projectiles bouncing off the hood, grill, and windshield of the thugs' Impala. He grinned at the thought of the body repair and paint costs the thug leader would have to dish out.

Colson gunned the 'Vette onto River Road and veered around the curve on Canal Avenue with the Impala in pursuit. The heavy four-door Impala with its passengers was no match for Colson's lightweight fiberglass rocket. He wondered what they were trying to accomplish. Another attempt at intimidation maybe? On the other hand, how did they know he was at the fish camp? He would have seen the Impala a mile away. He found out when he took the sharp right turn onto South Ridgewood Avenue. A Honda with a high-pitched, screaming exhaust system pulled alongside him. He had noticed the bright-yellow Honda coupe earlier but had no reason to associate it with the beach thugs at the time.

There had been four gang members at the beach, but only two had jumped from the Impala at the fish camp. There was one driving the yellow Honda, leaving one unaccounted for. Colson checked his rearview mirror. He had left the blue Impala far behind, and it was nowhere in sight, but thug number four was on his way driving another small white car similar to the Honda. Colson silently gave the Latin Kings credit for understanding the Impala would never catch him, and they obviously knew he would have spotted them immediately. They were coordinated to a degree and were probably communicating by cell phone or walkie-talkie. But they had seen too many *Fast and Furious* movies and didn't appreciate the capabilities of America's fastest sports car.

Colson slammed the clutch, dropping the Corvette out of gear for a fraction of a second. As soon as he lifted his foot from the clutch, the 'Vette would rocket forward, but that fraction of a second was long enough for the thug behind the wheel of the yellow car to raise a handgun and pull the trigger.

Rollins watched the surreal car chase play out in the comfort of the swivel chair at his desk. The newest satellite images on the monitor were as clear as his high-definition television at home. It was an unexpected turn of events and had momentarily distracted him from being curios about why Colson had gone to Mosquito Lagoon. It was dangerously close to the coordinates where Parker was last detected. He knew it was more than just a coincidence. Colson hadn't rented a boat or taken a guest, nor had he remained long enough for a fish fry. He hadn't stayed longer than fifteen minutes. And now out of nowhere he was under attack. Who were these people chasing Colson? Whoever they were, he could only wish them success. He seriously doubted it was a sanctioned government operation, but he intended to find out.

The office door pushed inward with enough force that Rollins felt a rush of air on his face. Danz locked eyes with Rollins and stormed in. The look on his face was of total disdain. Rollins could not prevent the corners of his mouth from forming a small grin. He realized in the short amount of time it took Danz to cross the room that conversations had taken place and decisions had been made.

Danz glared at Rollins and said, "What have you done?"

Rollins shrugged, "Why? What's the problem?"

Danz took a step closer and slammed his fist on Rollins desktop.

"You know damn well what the problem is. I've been separated from the project."

"You mean the chairman—"

"No," Danz snapped. "One of his flunkies came to pay me a visit. Don't act like you don't know anything, Rollins. What the hell did you do?"

Rollins stood and rounded his desk. The time for games was over, and he was sick of taking orders from a rocket scientist. He leaned into Danz and said, "I'll tell you what I've been doing. My *job* and *your job* too. You should have informed the chairman about Colson. He's dangerous."

Danz sighed and a smirk crossed his face. "It's clear to me now, Rollins. This has nothing to do with the project at all. The only thing you care about is your political career. Well, the truth is bigger than you, Max, *or* your political career."

Rollins scoffed. "The truth? You're so full of shit. You should have been a politician yourself."

"Fine," Danz snapped and pointed his finger in Rollins's face. "You and your political deadbeats can just run the project into the ground for all I care. Everything the federal government touches turns to crap. Why stop with some of mankind's most important research? And I fail to see how you are taking care of Colson sitting here on your ass."

Rollins cut his eyes to the computer screen and back to Danz. "It looks like I won't have to lift a finger."

"What are you talking about?"

Rollins moved back behind his desk and took a seat. "I believe you are no longer associated with the project, Director, so that information is now classified."

Danz stood silent. Rollins noticed him breathing hard through his nose. He seemed to be at a loss for words, so he offered a suggestion.

"Look, Director. You have plenty to do without worrying about a data collection project. Besides, isn't it rocket test day?"

Danz marched to the door and jerked it open. He turned and said, "No, and they're called main stage boosters, you imbecile."

Police officers qualify at least twice per year with various weapons including handguns and patrol rifles. There are not many things that can motivate cops to practice with their firearms more than the prospect of losing their jobs if they fail to qualify with a score of 80 percent or better. Many are enamored with firearms and practice every time the range is open. Others don't consider themselves gun aficionados, but understand that not practicing can have deadly ramifications in a devolving society whose hatred for law enforcement officers is growing at an exponential rate. Not every cop can be an expert marksman. Marksmanship is a perishable skill and even those who shoot very well early in their careers can watch their skill diminish without routine practice.

Most cops want to be the top shot in their agency, but shooting at paper targets in a climate-controlled gun range is a far cry from real-life gun battles. More often than not, there will be no time to line the front and back sights up perfectly, take a deep breath and pull the trigger back slow and smooth. Chances are greater that the officer will have to act in an instant at close range to stop the threat and stay alive. Those instances are taken into account in firearms training. The term often used is obtaining a "flash sight picture" of your target. The officer focuses on placing the front site on the target's center mass and pulling the trigger. Perfect it is not, but even if the rear sights are a fraction of an inch too high, too low, or too far left or right, one will still put a hole in the target.

The problem with street thugs is the lack of knowledge and practice. There is no required training, no minimum scores, and no battle strategies taught based on years of experience. The common street thug wrongly assumes that he is a badass just because he has a gun. Too many wrongfully assume they'll hit what they're shooting at. If they were smart, they would know better. Then again, if they were smart they would get a real job and stop playing thug.

Colson didn't hear a sound with the wind buffeting around his head at seventy miles per hour. He only saw a millisecond flash from the muzzle. What he did hear was the sharp crunch of glass. He saw spider web cracks covering his entire windshield. He punched the accelerator and concentrated to see the road ahead as he bolted past the Honda. He lifted his Glock from the middle console. He raised the .45 caliber to eye level and eased up on the accelerator enough for the Honda to come into view. It appeared a second later. The driver was in the process of raising his gun, but Colson already had his in position. As soon as the front sights of the Glock swept across the driver's chest, Colson pulled the trigger twice and punched the accelerator without waiting to see the result.

The yellow Honda began jerking from side to side in his rearview mirror. About a quarter mile ahead, a line of vehicles were approaching, including what appeared to be the top of a school bus. The Honda continued to swerve like a drunk was behind the wheel. Colson slowed and evaded the swerving Honda until he was behind it. As it passed, he saw the driver jerking from side to side in unison with the car; his white shirt was splattered with blood. Colson shot forward to the passenger side of the Honda and performed a pit maneuver by ramming the front left corner of the Corvette into the rear quarter panel of the Honda. The nose of the Honda pivoted away from oncoming traffic and followed an off-road trajectory.

Colson floored the accelerator and eyed the rearview mirror. Burning rubber created a thick cloud of noxious smoke as the Honda went sideways and rolled a half-dozen times, ejecting the driver on the second roll. It took three more seconds for the limp form of the thug to bounce and disappear into the thick grass. Colson kept his eye on the mirror as he waited for the white car to emerge from the clouds, but it didn't materialize.

Colson slowed to the speed limit and strained to see through the spider-webbed windshield. He touched a button on his steering wheel, spoke a command, and then waited. The sound of a phone ringing came through the speakers and was picked up on the second ring.

"Sherriff's Office CID, Lieutenant Cantrell," the male voice announced.

"It's Colson."

"Grey? Where've you been, I—"

"I'll fill you in later. Your guys are going to get a call about an accident on South Ridgewood involving a yellow Honda."

"Are you OK?"

"Yeah, fine. I'm just letting you know in case someone reports my tag as a hit-and-run perp."

"Are you?"

"Yeah, but that's what happens when Hondas pick fights with Corvettes."

"Oh, really?" Cantrell said and released a loud sigh. "Here we go again."

"Listen," said Colson, "do you know anything about Senator Greathouse? Is he trustworthy?"

"Senator Greathouse? How would I know? I mean, I voted for him and Sheriff Langston knows and likes him pretty well. When are you gonna fill me in?"

"Soon, I hope. I'm just going to have to go with my gut on this one I guess."

"I guess that accident is tied to whatever you're doing. What's the cross street off of Ridgewood?"

Colson had to move his head from side to side to see through a clear spot in the windshield. "I just passed Indian Creek Road. It's approximately two miles south."

"How bad? Does anyone need an ambulance?"

Colson paused a beat. "No, just send the meat wagon."

Agent Strickland drove the forty-five minutes from the Orlando office to Titusville and parked behind the Dixie Crossroads seafood restaurant. Her instructions had been vague as usual, and it frustrated her. What was the purpose of being so vague when she was going to know all the details eventually? She suspected the cloak-and-dagger thing was more important to men than women. She found the whole process petty and juvenile. Strickland had been given a credit card for gas and a motel until whatever she would be instructed to do was completed.

Dixie Crossroads sat just steps off of State Route 406. It was not a fancy restaurant, but a quaint, one-story seafood establishment with a long wraparound deck for outdoor dining. Hurricane shutters hung outward at the bottom to allow for a breeze while providing a measure of privacy from the passing traffic just a dozen feet away.

Strickland made her way to the front deck as instructed and scanned the length of tables until she saw the man at the very end. She had seen him before, but they had never spoken. He had always sat or stood silently and always acted uncomfortable. He shifted in his seat as she approached and then took a big swig of his ice tea before standing and shaking her hand.

"Why all the subterfuge?" Strickland asked. "Why aren't we just meeting at NASA?"

Max Rollins sat and said, "It's for the best. Director Danz has been separated from our project."

Strickland sat across from Rollins. "You're project? You call looking for Parker a *project*?"

Rollins shifted in his seat again and took another sip of tea. "Would you like something to drink?"

"No, thanks. Can you tell me why I'm here so we can get this over with?"

"It's about your former partner, Michael Mcilwain. It seems as though he's not going quietly into the night."

"What are you talking about? You had him disgraced and transferred. What the hell is he supposed to do?" Strickland said, raising her voice with each word.

Rollins raised his hand as if to calm her tone. "What's done is done. I need for you to keep an eye on Mcilwain… for his own good, mind you. You need to make contact with him and find out what he and Colson have been discussing and what they know if anything about the whereabouts of Grant Parker."

Strickland narrowed her eyes. "He's been in contact with Colson?"

Rollins nodded. "Yes. There may not be anything to it, but we have to know. You see, it's a simple assignment. Keep me informed about what he's doing, where he's going, and who he meets with, then find out what he knows. And be friendly about it."

"Why wouldn't I be?" Strickland said.

Rollins rolled his eyes and sat in silence as Strickland stood. The wooden legs of the chair made the sound of fingernails on a chalkboard as they scraped across the tile floor.

She said, "Anything else?"

Rollins pulled his wallet and slid out a card. "Here," he said, handing it to Strickland. "Put my number in your phone. I'll expect to hear from you daily unless something happens I need to know about immediately."

Strickland snatched the card and marched out to the black Charger previously driven by Agent Mcilwain. She took a phone from her purse and typed in Rollins's number. After pressing "save," Strickland retrieved a second number and pressed "call" then waited through a short voice-mail greeting. She impatiently waited for the beep and said, "Nick, it's me. You mind telling me what the hell is going on?"

ᑲᔅ⌁Chapter Sixteen⌁ᔆᕲ

olson turned his injured Corvette into the parking lot of the Cloverleaf Condos and stopped at the parking deck gate. He closed his eyes momentarily and replayed in his mind the day he and Lisa Riley met to check on Parker. They had exchanged brief introductions and both had driven to the top of the parking deck. He rewound his memory back to when they arrived at the gate. The numbers finally came to him: 0-1-0-1. A young security guard stepped from the main entrance and looked in his direction as the gate rose. The look on his face was a combination of curiosity and remorse at the damage to the gleaming blue sports car. Colson looked over at the security boy and shrugged as he pulled through the gate and disappeared from sight.

Colson pulled next to Parker's Challenger and parked against the concrete half wall. He grabbed Parker's key fob from his center console as he stepped out. Hot wind gusted around him. Being seven floors up seemed to amplify its velocity. He squatted next to the front tire and craned his neck downward. The toothpick was there. The car had not been moved. He entered the inner hall and walked past the scenic paintings to the end condo on the left. This time there was no need to rewind his memory. He had checked out his theory the evening he had first searched Parker's condo, but he didn't know its significance until later. He had watched Parker's half-sister punch five numbers into the door lock the day they searched his condo and committed them to memory... just in case. Colson had spent an entire afternoon figuring out why Parker used the numbers, 3-7-2-8-3. It could have been a subtle reminder to Parker every time he came home. Maybe he did it to torture himself for being involved in the project or maybe it was a constant reminder that he was doing the right thing.

Knocking might alert a nosey neighbor, so Colson pressed his ear against the door. He knew Parker wouldn't be inside, but wasn't so sure if the Latin Kings or even worse, government agents were. There was no sound except the hum of an air handler. He punched in the code, stepped inside, and eased the door closed behind him. He made another quick search of the condo. Someone else had been inside because the toilet tank was missing. Colson stepped out on the balcony and sat in one of the comfortable lounge chairs. It was made of teakwood slats with a thick weather-resistant fabric cushion. He pulled up the cushion at the bottom to admire the design. The frame had been expertly routed to accommodate each slat, creating a smooth surface for the cushion. It was far nicer than the PVC-framed, twenty-dollar chairs on his balcony. Probably only five bucks if he'd bought the PVC at Home Depot and made them from scratch.

The thought bothered Colson, but he couldn't understand why. Was it something about the lounge chair here or the PVC chairs on his balcony? Was it because the balcony was larger and didn't seem as cluttered as his? No. It was the thought of Home Depot. But why? It had nothing to do with...

Colson stood and marched to Parker's bedroom and pulled open the bedside table where he'd seen receipts and dismissed them as nothing. He raffled through them and found the Home Depot receipt dated over a year earlier. Colson instantly knew why Parker had kept some of the old receipts, especially from a place like Home Depot. People buy numerous items and don't use them all, or they buy tools and they don't work. Parker was a smart guy—a scientist for heaven's sake. He kept the receipt for returns, if necessary. Colson sat on the bed and read the receipt. A set of pulleys, forty two-by-fours, twelve four-by-eight sheets of ply wood, a hundred-foot length of rope, one large box of galvanized nails, one box of galvanized screws, a DeWalt cordless drill and circular saw with two additional lithium rechargeable batteries, and a $150 truck rental fee deposit. The total purchase price at the bottom was $1,057.30 with tax.

Colson didn't have to conduct another search of the condo to know for a fact that there was no cordless drill, circular saw, plywood, or two-by-fours they hadn't noticed before. He dropped the receipt back in the drawer and returned to the comfortable lounge chair on the balcony. He would think nothing of finding such a receipt if Parker was married with kids and living in a subdivision. He would be building a playhouse for the children or a shed to store a lawnmower. And why not have that much material delivered? The cost would be less than renting a truck. Not to mention the pain of unloading it piece by piece. Colson saw no homemade upgrades to the condo and certainly nothing inside that required the use of galvanized screws and nails. They were more expensive and made for exterior use to resist rust.

Colson stood and looked over the railing at the beach seven floors below. He was certain Parker hadn't built anything around the condo. That was a ridiculous notion. There was only one possible explanation remaining. He left the condo and returned to the parking deck. The doors to the Challenger unlocked when Colson got within three feet of it, and he slid behind the wheel. The engine came to life at the touch of a button, and he made the circular drive down to the gate. It automatically lifted when the pressure plate sensed the car's weight, and Colson pulled out into the sun, but stopped short when the young security guard stepped in front of the grill. Colson rolled down the window and said. "That's not the best place to stand, young man."

The young security guard stood his ground, but his entire frame quivered as if he had never experienced a physical challenge. Colson put the car in park, stepped out, and walked to within a few feet of the boy. He slid out his wallet to expose his badge.

"It's OK," said Colson.

The boy appeared to check his quivering and said, "That's Mr. Parker's car."

Colson nodded. "Yes, I know. I'm taking it in for forensic analysis. What's your name?"

"Err, Johnny."

"Do you know what forensic analysis is?"

"Ah, yeah. Of course I know."

"That's good, Johnny, but can I give you some advice?"

Johnny nodded silently.

"It's never a good idea to try to block a car with your body. If I had really been a bad guy, you would be roadkill."

Johnny nodded again. Colson patted him on the shoulder and got back behind the wheel.

"Hey," said Johnny. "Was that your Corvette earlier?"

"Yes. I'm leaving it here while we're working on this one. Keep an eye on it for me, and don't let anyone scratch it."

The rear tires of the Challenger barked when Colson stomped on the accelerator and shot out of the parking lot, leaving a perplexed Johnny in his wake.

Max Rollins couldn't believe Colson had evaded death once again. First the speeding semi, then the certain imprisonment or execution at the hands of Colonel Guerra, and now the new assassination attempt. The crash and death roll of the small yellow car was as spectacular as watching an episode of *Amazing Police Chases*, except it was in real time. The crash had no doubt killed the driver. The small white car had slowed and stopped at the carnage of thick cloud of smoke, steam, scattered sheet metal, and what appeared to be a body lying dead still in the grass. Rollins kept the satellite lens trained on the white car until the medium-size blue car caught up and tailed it back to an oceanside hotel just north of the Port Orange Bridge. He jotted down the coordinates and redirected the camera's view north to scan for Colson's car, but it was nowhere to be seen. He panned south and north again. He had lost Colson. He had to have ducked down a side street, but Rollins figured he would locate the 'Vette back at the Sundowner Condos later.

Rollins tried to piece the puzzle pieces together to make sense of the incident. Who else wanted Colson dead? Some disgruntled employee he had arrested for stealing money from a cash register? All Colson worked on were small-time employee theft cases. This latest assassination attempt had to be connected to something he knows about Parker and the group project. Most likely something he learned from Robert Bankston or something Bankston had given him. But who else would know and want him dead? Why do these new actors in the game want to silence Colson? What could they know that he didn't? There were too many moving pieces to the puzzle, but if Rollins wanted to move up the political ladder, he had to impress the senator by tying everything up in a nice little bow and handing it to him like a Christmas present. And it had to be quick. The election was fast approaching, and if he couldn't do something to demonstrate his value, the senator would leave him to drown in the great ocean of the unemployed. Or worse, if the election went off the rails because of something he *could* have prevented and failed to do so, Rollins would be in worse shape than whoever was ejected from that speeding yellow car.

Rollins decided Colson had to be confronted alive to find out what he knew and who else he may have told. A good few days in the gas chamber he had constructed for Grant Parker would do the trick, but the difficult part would be getting Colson there. Rollins couldn't use NASA security because they worked for Danz and legitimate law enforcement officials were out of the question. Rollins leaned back in his chair and tapped his chin with his right index finger.

Rollins grabbed his personal computer pad and accessed a secure government website with a fourteen-digit password. He found SB 2015–G in a pull-down menu under Senate Bill Grant Access and opened it to the Allocation program. He entered an account number in the open field, typed in an amount, and then an authorization code. He pressed, "enter," and it was done. Rollins knew making deals was not limited to the world of politics and money was the lubricant that greased the wheels of all negotiations.

He swiveled around to the main computer and played back the chase and subsequent crash of the yellow sports car. He paused the recording three times to print photos. They would be more than sufficient for his purpose.

It was time to introduce himself to his new friends.

Colson tapped his knuckle on the heavy wooden door. A small placard stuck to the wall on the right doorframe read, "301."

A muffled voice from behind the door said, "Yes?"

Colson responded by pushing his way inside. To his astonishment, Jay Taylor sat on the edge of the bed dressed in the new parachute pants and shirt Colson had brought to him the previous week. The new Ray-Bans he'd bought sat on the bed next to Taylor. The only reason he wasn't wearing them was because of the young doctor standing before him, shining a light down Taylor's throat. Taylor's color was back to normal, but he had not regained his former muscle mass.

He cut his good eye over to Colson. "Ah," was the only sound he could utter until the doctor clicked off his light and turned around.

The doctor said, "He's looking much better, don't you think?"

"Better than what?" Colson said

Taylor stood and flexed what was left of his biceps and pectorals.

"Funny man," he snarled.

The doctor flipped his chart closed. "Good timing, Mr. Colson. I'm releasing him today."

Colson rubbed his chin. "Are you sure about that, Doc? He still looks pretty peaked to me."

"Knock it off, Colson," Taylor said while reaching down and snapping the plastic ID bracelet off his wrist. He tossed it on the bed and stuck the Ray-Bans on his nose. "I'm outta here."

Two sets of automatic glass doors swooshed open, allowing Colson and Taylor to step out into the late October sun. Taylor followed Colson through two lines of cars and stopped short as Colson opened the door of the black Challenger. Taylor gestured to the car with his hand.

"Whose car?"

"Oh," said Colson. "It belongs to our elusive mad scientist, Grant Parker."

Taylor gave Colson a long gaze and shook his head. "You know, I'm not even gonna ask."

Colson filled Taylor in on the Latin Kings, Agent Mcilwain's visit, his conversation with Pastor Tommy, his second search of Grant Parker's apartment, and his visit to Mosquito Lagoon. Taylor sat in respectful silence for the fifteen-minute ride back to the Sundowner Condos. There was not a word of sarcasm, criticism, or second-guessing from Taylor. Colson suspected it was due to him saving Taylor's life and risking his own to do so. But he owed Taylor as much—twice over.

Finally, Taylor said, "Just tell me what you need done, and I'm on it."

Colson handed over a flash drive and said, "Get this to Senator Greathouse and tell him what I told you."

"How?"

"You'll think of something," Colson said and grabbed Taylor's shoulder with his hand and squeezed. "Remember, you're a detective now."

"Right. And what are you going to do?"

Colson steered the Challenger into the Sundowner parking lot. He turned to Taylor and smiled. "What do you think, you one-eyed Sherlock? I'm going to find Grant Parker."

Carlos stood facing the large window out into the parking lot of the low-rent Dolphin Inn Motel. The air conditioning unit blew cold air against the clammy undershirt sticking to his chest. The blue Impala and white Honda sat next to each other in the spaces directly in front of him. Carlos had seen the crumpled mess of the yellow Honda. It reminded him of a wadded-up piece of aluminum foil. The lifeless form of Miguel dozens of feet from the wreckage had enraged him. He'd wanted to stop at the scene, but the distant wail of sirens made him drive on. He had pushed the low Impala to its limit to catch up with Colson, but he had vanished. In his rage, the plan had been to go straight to the Sundowner Condos, but he doubted Colson had been stupid enough to go there. He decided it was more important to regroup and prepare an infallible plan. Ramone and Paco sat on the bed behind him with their backs against the headboard and their heads resting against the wall. Paco spoke.

"I'm sorry, Carlos. I stopped and tried to help Miguel, but he was gone, man."

Carlos pulled the switchblade from his pocket and clicked it open. He turned it over and over in his hand. The blade caught sunlight reflecting off the Impala's windshield and cast flickers of light against the ceiling. Carlos breathed hard through his nose, spun on his heels, and hurled the knife end over end into the Sheetrock wall six inches from Paco's head. Carlos took two steps and pointed his finger in Paco's face. He spewed a light mist of spittle as he screamed.

"You were *told* to run that puto Colson off the road and I would come finish him. You couldn't do that *one* thing."

Paco nodded and hung his head. He dared not wipe his face. Carlos reached for the knife and jerked it from the Sheetrock. He stuck the sharp tip under Paco's chin and raised it until they were eye to eye.

Carlos said, "You have not learned your place, chico, but you will. You will do what you are told, or I will cut you next time. Do you know how to speak to me now?"

"Yes, Inca. It will not happen again."

Carlos stared at Paco for a long moment and then lowered the switchblade. He gave Ramone a glance but he had looked away and remained silent for his own good. He had been riding with Carlos in the Impala and had done nothing wrong, but was clearly showing wisdom and respect by not adding a comment to the already volatile discussion. Carlos walked back to the window where he could receive the direct benefit of the cool air rushing from the vent below. There was nothing to see in the parking lot but random cars pulling in or backing out or cruising by, but he was not watching traffic. He was visualizing their next play and relishing the thought of drawing his switchblade across Colson's neck. They would lay low for a few hours and then find the damaged Corvette, thereby finding Colson in the process. Carlos broke the silence in the small hotel room.

"I should have killed the culo right there on the beach when I had him."

"What next, Inca?" asked Ramone.

Carlos turned to face the bed. "We find him tonight. Then we kill him and burn his Corvette with him in it."

Ramone stood and nodded toward the window. "What does that white boy think he's doing?"

Carlos looked over his shoulder and saw a large black sedan parked long ways behind the Impala and Honda. It would be nothing if someone was getting in or out of the car, but that was not the case. The sedan was parked so close to their cars, one would not be able to walk between them. The passenger-side window was lowered. The man seated behind the wheel wore a white dress shirt and loose tie. He had a cell phone to his ear and one arm resting on the back of the passenger seat. He stared directly at them through his sunglasses as if they were mannequins in a store window.

Agent Strickland adjusted the dial on her small binoculars and brought Mcilwain into focus. His pickup was backed in a space in the parking lot of Sunsations, directly across from the Sundowner Condos. She was parked in the lot of Timeshare Resale of Daytona, two buildings north. Spying on a fellow agent and former partner felt awkward. Mcilwain should be thinking about getting his affairs together and moving to Atlanta. Instead, he was there. Hoping to accomplish what? Did he think Colson could do anything to help him undo what had already been done? And nosing around bureau business would only make things worse for him when the group supervisor received her report. But unfortunately, she had to report to that creep Rollins first.

Strickland watched Mcilwain raise his own set of binoculars with every vehicle that entered and exited the condo parking lot. It continued for almost an hour with every SUV, minivan, truck, and car that came and went. Strickland had no idea how long Mcilwain had been there before she arrived.

Another ten minutes passed and then a black Challenger turned into the lot from the south. There was something familiar about it, but she couldn't put her finger on it. Mcilwain again raised his binoculars and Strickland followed suit. The Challenger bounced over the speed bumps and parked in a space at the seawall. A large black male wearing a tank top and sunglasses stepped from the passenger side and stretched. He slammed the car door and then walked to the seawall. He was apparently surveying the beach like a tourist when the driver's door swung open and a white male climbed out. She could only see the man's back as he walked over to join the black male. They both stood looking out over the ocean, and then the white male patted the black male on the back. They both turned and began walking toward the building, and that's when she saw the white man's face. It was Colson.

It didn't make sense. Where was his blue Corvette? It was then that it came to her. The car belonged to Grant Parker. But what was Colson doing with it? The forensics team had been instructed not to pick it up when they were removed from the case, but why Colson had it was baffling. She snapped her head to the right, expecting Mcilwain to be crossing the street, but he wasn't. He and his truck were gone.

"Damn it," Strickland snapped. She dropped the Charger into drive and turned south out of the parking lot. She should have caught a quick flash of Mcilwain's truck in her binoculars as he passed by if he had gone north, so he had to be headed south. She grabbed her phone and hit the speed dial. Rollins picked up immediately.

"Anything new?" he asked.

"I'm trying to catch back up with Mcilwain. He was staking out Colson's condo."

"What do you mean catch up. Did you lose him?"

"I'll catch up to him. Don't worry about it. He left when Colson and a black male arrived."

"A black male," Rollins said.

"That's what I said. I knew he had an employee, but I don't know if that's who it is."

"Where'd he park the 'Vette?"

"That's another thing. He's not driving the 'Vette."

"What's he driving?"

"That's actually the other thing. He's driving Grant Parker's Challenger."

The line went silent for five seconds. Rollins finally said, "That's bothersome."

"You think?" said Strickland.

Max Rollins ended the call, tucked his nine-millimeter Ruger under his left leg—just in case—and then laid the printed photos on the dash. He wasn't sure if the three young men in the hotel room were associated with the cars he was blocking in, but they were now staring a hole though him. Any doubt was removed when they exited the room. One came around the front of his car and the other two slipped in behind. Rollins didn't want to use the gun but would if necessary. The Latino-looking young men weren't exactly what he had expected. The one that had rounded the front of the car now stood glaring at him though the driver's side window. He lowered the window and waited for him to speak.

"Yo, Holmes," he began while making an odd jerking gesture with his hand, "you're blocking our cars. You got a problem or sumpin'?"

Rollins felt a bead of sweat run out of his hairline and down his neck. He said, "Not at all. I'm here to help you."

"Help us," he replied with a chuckle. The other two Latinos moved around to the driver's side and mimicked the first guy's chuckle. "You can help us by moving this piece of shit out of here."

"Look," Rollins said quickly and raised his hands, which had developed a slight quiver he hoped they wouldn't notice. He had never experienced a potentially dangerous encounter and was second-guessing his plan, but it was a little late for that. He decided to cut to the chase and take his chances. "I'm after Colson just like you guys, and I can help you find him."

Rollins heard a quick snap of metal on metal and felt a pinprick sensation on the side of his neck. He didn't know if it was a sewing needle or the very sharp tip of a knife. He suspected the latter. Another bead of sweat raced down his neck as he struggled for words he hoped would get him to the next portion of the negotiation alive.

"I'm not a cop, I'm not a cop," he blurted. The sting on the side of his neck didn't go away.

"Then who *are* you, white boy?"

Rollins pulled the photos off the dash and handed them over. The sting in his neck stopped as the main Latino shuffled through the photos. He took the opportunity to begin his negotiation. "We've been tracking Colson and want him as bad as you do. That's how I found you three. We can work together... for profit of course."

Carlos studied the photos. Rollins had taken still shots of the Impala behind the Corvette at the fish camp, then one of the Corvette pitting the yellow Honda, and one of the two remaining cars parked at the Dolphin Inn.

Carlos narrowed his eyes on Rollins and said, "How did you take these?"

Rollins pointed upward. "From a satellite in geosynchronous orbit." Rollins felt the prick against his neck again.

"You are a government agent," said Carlos.

"Yes, yes, but not law enforcement. I'm just offering you a reward for capturing Colson for interrogation."

"When I find Colson, there will be no need for interrogation. You have satellites. Why come to me when you can catch him yourself."

"Because it's not an official law enforcement matter. We can't be directly involved in his abduction. However, if he were delivered to us alive, we could do our interrogation and release him back to you to do with as you wish."

"Why would I do that?" Carlos asked.

"I'll give you fifty thousand dollars."

The prick in his neck intensified. Carlos said, "Why don't I take fifty thousand dollars from you now?"

"Because it's in an account that I can't access until Colson is delivered. You saw the photo of your cars here. The satellite is trained on this very location right now and recording in real time. If anything happens to me, you won't even make it out of the parking lot," Rollins lied.

Paco and Ramone turned their heads skyward as if they could actually see an object the size of a Volkswagen at the distance Daytona Beach is from Savannah, Georgia.

Rollins said, "It's two-hundred-miles high, guys. Believe me, you can't see it, but it sure as hell can see you right now."

Carlos said, "Colson owes my brothers a hundred thousand dollars, so that's what we'll take."

"Hang on," said Rollins. "I can understand that, but you are paying them back by killing Colson. The fifty thousand is for you and your... ah... friends, take it or leave it. I can locate Colson just as I located you and even track him wherever he goes. I'll pass his location on to you and even guide you to him." Rollins picked up an envelope from the center console and handed it to Carlos. "Here's five grand as a deposit—a gesture of good faith between men with a common goal."

Carlos closed the switchblade, dropped it in his pocket, and snatched the envelope from Rollins.

He said, "You need to know something, white boy, if you set me up or try to screw me over, there are hundreds of Latin Kings that will hunt you down. They will kill you and cut you up and use a meat grinder to make you into dog food."

Rollins nodded his understanding and said, "Give me your cell number and let me get back to work."

Taylor took State Route 44 to De Land and 441 through Leesburg on the hour-and-twenty-minute trek to the Villages. He had seen the advertisements on television, but was not prepared for how expansive the retirement community was. A literal city with more golf carts than cars. Taylor had never seen such elaborate golf carts. They were fashioned to resemble everything from Volkswagens to Mercedes. And parking for normal gas-powered vehicles was almost non-existent for an early Monday morning. He thought he had given himself a decent head start by leaving the condo at 6:00

a.m. since the event didn't begin until 11:00 a.m., but he hadn't anticipated the size of the complex or its population.

He drove through the main square at a crawl behind a line of cars inching toward what he hoped was a parking lot large enough to accommodate the growing traffic. The street was lined with palm trees, brightly colored shops, and open-air restaurants. The only things moving at or near the twenty-mile-per-hour speed limit were the golf carts of privileged residents on wide, private paths winding around the entire town. After fifteen minutes of inching forward, stopping, and inching forward again, Taylor arrived at the mouth of a large temporary lot where a flagger guided him toward a second flagger, who finally directed him into a parking space. He followed the crowd on foot back in the direction he had come to an opening in the community square where a large pavilion stood proudly in the center, decorated with red, white, and blue ribbons.

At 10:30 a.m. sharp, a Dixieland-type band began playing as the crowd continued to expand around and behind him. Mostly older retirees lived in the expansive community along with a sprinkling of middle-aged and young people. A color guard entered from behind, solemnly marched to the foot of the stage, and presented the colors. An old veteran in a Vietnam-era military uniform moved to the center of the stage and led the pledge of allegiance. He was followed by a children's choir singing the national anthem. After a sustained minute of cheering and round of applause, a man stepped behind the podium. It was Senator Edward Greathouse. Taylor had seen him walk from just left of the stage where two black sedans, one black limousine, and a gray Tahoe were parked. There were at least four men in dark suits with matching dark sunglasses standing near the limo, presumably Secret Service. Four to six additional agents were posted around the perimeter of the pavilion and at a rope line twenty or thirty feet from the stage itself.

Colson had told Taylor to think of something and he had. He had spent the previous evening studying photos and videos of speeches Greathouse had given. He had lived in Central Florida his entire life and knew many people, especially during his brief encounter with fame as an ultimate fighter in the UFC. It was a successful career, although cut short by his debilitating injury. Debilitating injury or not, a body can only stand so much abuse, no matter who you were. Without a formal education, retired fighters had a challenge finding satisfying and lucrative careers when their fighting days were over. Taylor considered himself fortunate to be working with Colson. It was either that or take on a job as a limo driver or bodyguard, such as the man standing next to the gray Tahoe.

Taylor knew he wouldn't get anywhere close to the Tahoe until the presidential candidate was announced and on stage. Once the Secret Service agents escorted Governor Bagwell to the pavilion, he could move in without drawing too much attention. He hoped. The introductions Taylor had seen Greathouse give on the videos averaged approximately three minutes, so he eased himself through the crowd in the direction of the vehicles. He caught some of what Greathouse was saying, but was not focused on the content.

"And the politicians in Washington have squandered your social security by spending it on social experiments, health care for illegal immigrants, and entitlement programs to buy votes. They call social security an entitlement. What they fail to admit is it is the only true entitlement program because you have spent a lifetime paying into it, only to have it stolen and allocated to pay for the frivolous spending in Washington."

Taylor reached the roped-off section near the parked vehicles and turned his attention to Greathouse, who was wrapping up his introduction.

"I've known Terry Bagwell for over twenty years. I've watched him build successful companies and employ thousands of Floridians from Pensacola to Key Largo. He is the only candidate in this race who knows how to balance a budget. He is the only person who will not permit the United Nations to drag our country into any agreement whose sole purpose is the worldwide redistribution of wealth. He knows how to cut spending, and he knows how to take care of his people. And in less than two weeks, he will not just be supporting and defending thousands of employees and their families in the great state of Florida, but will be supporting and defending all the citizens of the greatest nation on the face of the earth: the United States of America."

A roar of applause erupted as Taylor turned and saw the rear door of the limo open and Governor Bagwell step out. He was instantly surrounded by Secret Service agents as he walked to the stage and up the side steps. Greathouse made his final announcement.

"It's with great pleasure that I introduce the president and CEO of Bagwell International, the former governor of our great state and soon to be president of all Americans, the Republican nominee for president of the United States, Mr. Terry Bagwell."

The applause, whistles, and shouts of the supporters grew to a fever pitch as Bagwell took to the podium. Taylor craned his neck to see if anyone remained with the vehicles but saw no one. He had done his homework and was determined not to fail, but if his old acquaintance wasn't there, he would never get close to Greathouse without being shot. The sudden grip of the hand on his bicep felt like an alligator bite. Taylor instinctively balled his right fist and spun. The sight of his old acquaintance made him grin. He hadn't seen or spoken with the middleweight contender since he lost the eye.

"Danny Wade," Taylor said.

"I've asked you repeatedly *not* to call me Danny."

"Oh, so you still go by Dan "the Man" Wade? Were you able to get the good senator to call you that?"

"As a matter of fact, he does. It's good to see you, Jay. I didn't know you were interested in politics."

"I'm not. I came to find you."

Wade released his grip of Taylor's bicep and said, "You could have just called. I'm listed."

"I need a big favor, and you would have said no over the phone."

"So you thought you'd show up and intimidate me in person? Looks to me like you haven't worked out or lifted in six months."

"It's a long story, but I need that big favor and I need it right now."

It was seventy-seven degrees. The humidity was low and the sky was crystal clear. It was beautiful for a mid-Monday morning in Daytona. Colson stood on his balcony and sucked in a deep breath of sea air. One lone freighter moved slowly southward along the soft curve of the horizon, and the beach was abandoned with the exception of a man walking near the surf and swinging a metal detector from side to side at a steady beat. The late-year vacationers had retreated to their jobs, and their children had reluctantly returned to school.

Colson stepped into the kitchen and poured coffee into a large insulated travel mug. He carried it to the bedroom where he slipped on a pair of black BDUs, black Under Armor shirt, a Kevlar vest, and a black golf shirt. He slid a leather basket-weave belt through the BDU loops, threaded it through the holster for his Glock .45, and then pulled on a pair of black Hi-Tec boots. He strapped the sheath for the Shrike around his shoulder and adjusted it to a comfortable position under his left arm. The hard plastic sheath would hold the business end of the Shrike secure until a single jerk downward would remove it for whatever need arose.

Colson holstered his Glock and dropped two extra twelve round magazines in his lower right pocket. He placed his ASP in the left. A single drop of sweat ran down the side of his face. It brought back memories of the hundreds of times he had gone through the same laborious ritual of getting dressed for work. The gear would instantly make him weigh thirty pounds heavier for the next eight to twelve hours. After three hours into his shift, the anticipation of returning home to free himself from the bondage of the uniform would be at the forefront of his mind. But it was a necessity then, and it most certainly would be today.

He pulled a thin fisherman's vest he bought the day before from a bag labeled "Outdoor Adventures" but didn't slip it on. He was too hot and sweaty already, but it would conceal his modest arsenal at the appropriate time. Colson draped the jacket over his arm and took his coffee back in the kitchen where his phone was playing Steely Dan.

The photo on the screen was of Beverly. He touched the speaker option and said, "Hey, beautiful. I was just about to call you."

She replied in a snarky tone, "Sure you were. You must be awful busy. Too busy to call me."

"Never," said Colson. "Although it has been busy. I'll fill you in later."

"So why were you going to call me now?"

"Your friend Lisa Riley?"

"Yeah."

"With everything that's been going on, I've misplaced her number."

"You want me to get it for you?"

"Naw, just do me a favor and tell her something. Keep it confidential."

"Does it have anything to do with Grant? Did you find him? Is he alive?"

"Ah, yes… no… and I don't know."

"What is it then?" Beverly asked.

"Just tell her I'm ninety-nine percent certain of where he is, and I'm going to get him. Oh, and the most important thing: I love you."

"You love Lisa Riley?"

"Now who's the smartass?"

Dan "the Man" Wade held the rear door of the Tahoe open for Senator Greathouse. He was having a low-volume conversation on his cell phone as he climbed in. Taylor adjusted the rearview mirror as Greathouse plopped in the seat and continued his conversation, oblivious to the world around him. Dan climbed behind the wheel and maneuvered the Tahoe out of the roped-off area and down the main thoroughfare of the Villages instead of toward the exit to State

Route 441. Taylor eyed the senator through his Ray-Bans until he finished his call and finally looked forward. His face tensed for a moment. Taylor suspected the first thing Greathouse noticed was the tattoo of the three connecting "Ts" just below his neckline. But then his expression changed, and he appeared to relax.

Greathouse said, "Jay 'the Terrible' Taylor?" Taylor turned in his seat thinking it would be disrespectful to talk to the senator's reflection. He said, "You recognize me?"

"Sure. Where do you think I found Dan 'the Man'? I used to watch you fight."

"You act like you know why I'm here."

Greathouse shrugged. "I can only guess that it's about the Ecuador government demanding your extradition. They're being pretty loud about it."

"What are you telling them?" Taylor asked.

"I haven't been communicating with them. They're screaming at the State Department."

"What are *they* telling them?"

"I've encouraged them to delay. We're right on top of the general election and don't have time to fool around with them right now. Especially since they've made us jump through a hundred hoops to extradite criminals from their backwoods country. The treaty was signed in June of 1872 and is specifically limited in article two to murder, rape, arson, burglary, mutiny, forgery, embezzlement, and counterfeiting."

"Sounds like you read it."

"More than once. I might have missed a crime or two, but assault and battery wasn't one of the offenses agreed to. Technically, they don't have any standing, but we have to make a show of entertaining their request. I understand you work with Colson. Someone I trust likes him and vouched for him, so I figure we should trust you by association. And no one at state trusts the current regime in Ecuador."

"Really," said Taylor in a deliberately sarcastic tone. "I'm no fan of the whole damn bunch. But that's not why I'm here."

Taylor stretched his arm back over the seat and handed Greathouse a flash drive. Greathouse eyed the tiny device and said, "What's this?"

Taylor said, "Colson asked me to get it to you ASAP."

"Is this connected to—"

"Yes. Grant Parker and what NASA is doing."

Greathouse's eyes shot up from his examination of the flash drive. His expression turned serious, as if the tiny flash drive he held had morphed into a twenty-carat diamond or a lump of radioactive uranium. He leaned forward and said, "You need to give me the Reader's Digest version of what you know."

Taylor attempted to recite everything Colson had told him, from his initial involvement in looking for Parker, his interaction with Robert Bankston and the attempted assassinations. He even shared the counseling session Colson had with Pastor Tommy, although it was just thrown in for good measure. Perspective some might say.

Taylor pointed at the flash drive Greathouse was turning over in his fingers and said, "And all the data is right there in your hands."

"Sweet fancy Moses," said Greathouse. "If this is accurate and can be corroborated…"

Taylor shrugged. "I don't understand. Why would NASA bother with all this to begin with?"

"You might be surprised what some people will do for power and money, Jay. Other individuals have attempted the same and some have been successful, but never has a government agency funded by taxpayer's money collaborated in such a blatant effort." He held the flash drive up to eye level. "But without corroboration and testimony, this is as worthless as dirt."

Taylor said, "You'll have your witness and corroboration if Colson has anything to do with it."

"Does Colson know where Grant Parker is?"

"He thinks so. He's going after him tonight."

"Where?"

"He didn't tell me," Taylor lied. "He'd rather not risk assassination again."

"But what if he needs help?" asked Greathouse.

"He knows how to get in touch with me. Getting this data to you was very important to him. He couldn't risk it being taken away from him or destroyed. He's not in a position to trust anyone else."

"There's someone you *both* can trust, and I'm going to hook the two of you up in an hour."

Colson stood at the balcony railing and looked north and south. There was light beach traffic and no movement in the parking lot. He walked out the front door and patiently watched the traffic on A1A for another ten minutes before stepping back inside his condo. If anyone was doing surveillance on him, he or she was good, because he saw no telltale signs. Colson grabbed his coffee mug, draped the fisherman's jacket over his arm, and headed to the elevator.

The drive to the fish camp was basically a straight line, but recent events dictated he take a circuitous route. He climbed into the Challenger and cranked the air conditioner to its highest setting. He was still sweating under the Kevlar vest. The boat wouldn't be available until 2:00 p.m., so there was time to check for a tail. He turned north on A1A and tested the Challenger's performance. He stepped on the gas and held it until he hit sixty-five miles per hour. It wasn't quite as quick as his fiberglass rocket, but sufficiently impressive. He constantly checked the rearview mirror and changed lanes rapidly. Colson moved into the right lane and jerked back into the left turn lane. He turned left on Orange Avenue without signaling and then took a quick right on Nova Road to International Speedway Boulevard. He drove straight through the light and took a quick right into the Krispy Kreme parking lot, went behind the building, and back out to the traffic light. He waited through the red light, looking in all directions. There was no blue Impala in sight or anything that remotely resembled a gangbanger's ride.

Colson lowered the tinted windows and craned his neck to look skyward. No helicopters hovered ominously overhead or in the distance. Nothing and no one was following him. Years of conducting surveillance convinced him that anyone attempting to tail him would have been burned by his radical maneuvers. The light turned green. Six miles ahead was Interstate 95. Colson would head south and be at the fish camp in twenty-five minutes.

The young analyst was bored to tears and almost nodded off staring at the computer monitor. He had been stuck behind the desk since 9:00 a.m. when he relieved his fellow GWOAN coworker. Fortunately, they were rotating on four-hour shifts instead of eight. It would be helpful if they knew why and what they were doing. His normal day consisted of studying data, adjusting computer models, and writing summary results, not staring at the rooftops of beachfront condos and traffic. He had called Rollins twice already that morning when he had seen black vehicles leaving the location, only to be scolded both times because it wasn't the one he was looking for. If they weren't paying overtime, he would have already called the Federal Employees Union and filed a complaint.

The digital wall clock read 12:46 hours and he had only fourteen minutes left on his shift. He couldn't decide what he wanted for lunch before returning to his normal work activities and was considering his options when the black sedan moved to the condo exit and shot north on A1A. He grabbed his cell phone for the third time and hit the speed dial for Rollins.

"Mr. Rollins," he said cautiously. "I have a black sedan pulling out of the location and traveling north."

"Are you sure this time?" Rollins said.

"This should be the one, sir."

"Fine. Put a track on it, and I'll be right there."

The analyst slid the mouse, hovered the cursor over the black car, and clicked. A small red dot appeared on the top of the car and locked on. The view automatically adjusted so that the car and dot were centered on the screen, and the surrounding terrain moved slowly off screen. He sat back in his chair and hoped he had gotten it right this time. Then he revisited the lunch options in his head.

Rollins pushed through the door twenty seconds later. The analyst had no idea why the black car was so important, but it must have been a big deal because Rollins was acting like a kid on Christmas morning.

"Up," Rollins blurted. The analyst jumped from the chair and moved aside. Rollins bent over the desk and studied the monitor through his reading glasses.

The car was approaching the on-ramp for Interstate 95. Rollins formed a grin as he jerked his cell phone from his pocket and punched his finger on the screen. Rollins seemed mesmerized by the car and spoke urgently into his phone.

"Saddle your boys up. I've got him. It'll take you twenty minutes to catch up."

Rollins dropped in the chair and continued following the progress of the black car. He turned his head for an instant to the analyst and gave him a double take as though he had forgotten he was there.

"What are you still doing here," he barked. "Get out of here and close the door behind you."

Colson arrived at the fish camp fifteen minutes early and backed the Challenger into a gravel spot near the pier. Almost all of the slips were occupied with boats of various sizes, bobbing slightly in their spaces with the gentle ebb and flow of the lagoon. He slipped on his fisherman's jacket and walked through the screen-door entrance to the bait and tackle shop. It was deserted with the exception of the young man called Roper. He was sitting on a stool at the counter eating from a potato chip bag.

"Momma Ball," Roper called over his shoulder. The fiftyish woman emerged from a door behind the counter and eyed Colson. She slid on a pair of reading glasses and turned to the calendar behind her. She ran her finger across the calendar and turned around with a grin.

"Mr. Colson?"

"In the flesh."

Momma Ball spread her arms. "Well, you can have your pick. We have everything from sixteen-foot pontoon boats and twenty-six-foot bass boats to a forty-four-foot cabin cruiser."

"The sixteen-foot pontoon will do fine," Colson said.

"You need rods, tackle, or bait?"

"No thanks."

Momma Ball shrugged and spun a sheet of paper around on the counter with a list of rules and regulations, such as the number of passengers and weight permitted on board, the requirement to wear life preservers, the boat operator being prohibited from consuming alcohol, abiding by wake zone limits, and the liability of the operator for any damage. She sat a pen down and Colson signed at the bottom.

"You wanna keep the entire rental fee on the card?" she asked.

Colson nodded.

"Hey, mister," Roper said. "Do you need a guide? I'm not tied up."

Colson offered the boy a grin. "No. Thanks anyway."

Roper dropped back down on the stool with a dejected look on his face. Colson suspected he was bored sitting around the musty-smelling bait shop. Momma Ball reached behind her and set a key with a quarter-size plastic fob and the number "five" handwritten on it with permanent marker.

She said, "We close at seven. We charge for an extra half day if you're late."

"Sounds good," said Colson. He grabbed the key and walked out of the bait shop fully expecting to be charged the extra half day.

Chapter Seventeen

Jay Taylor pulled slowly through the Sundowner drive-under and saw the truck described by Senator Greathouse nosed in at the sea wall. He parked beside it, stepped out, and walked to the driver's window. The man seated behind the wheel rolled down the window and stuck out his hand. Taylor felt very much the same as Colson had felt about the man: wary, skeptical, and untrusting. He suspected that came from living with the retired cop for the last three years. But there were times when you had to make the decision to trust—at least in the short term. Taylor shook his hand.

"Michael Mcilwain," the man said. "You want to get in and talk?"

Taylor retraced his steps to the opposite side and climbed in the cab. He said, "So you're the FBI guy who stranded me and Colson in Ecuador."

Mcilwain shook his head. "I know you don't have a reason to believe me, but I had nothing to do with that. I knew the flight was arranged, but that was it."

"We'll see," said Taylor flatly.

"That's fine. Right now we have to get to Colson. Does he know where Grant Parker is?"

"He might."

"C'mon, Taylor. There are at least two government agencies trying to stop Colson from finding Parker. Either we do this together or you go by yourself, but it has to be done."

"Fine, let's go. Head south on A1A."

Mcilwain turned left out of the parking lot and pushed the truck twenty miles per hour over the posted limit without noticing the black Charger parked at the real estate office just north of the complex.

They rode in silence for three miles before Mcilwain said, "Do you have a firearm?"

Taylor turned and looked at Mcilwain through his dark Ray-Bans. "I can't."

"What do you mean you can't?"

"Because I'm a convicted felon," Taylor said.

Mcilwain jerked his head toward Taylor. "You're a what?"

Taylor turned his head and sat silently looking down the long road known as Atlantic 1 Alternate, or A1A. The souvenir shops, liquor stores, beauty shops, and fast food restaurants were zooming by as Mcilwain threaded the truck through the lazy traffic. Out of the corner of his good eye, Taylor could see Mcilwain shaking his head.

"Well, isn't that just wonderful," Mcilwain mumbled.

Agent Strickland had to punch the gas to keep Mcilwain's truck in sight, but held back just enough to remain unnoticed. She pushed the phone icon on the dash and gasped when she glanced up and saw an SUV at a dead stop at the curb. She jerked the Charger to the left and immediately back to the right to avoid two young girls on a moped. She hadn't realized Rollins had answered. Her heart was beating in her throat at the thought of killing someone… or herself.

Rollins's annoyed voice came over the speakers. "*Hello!* Is that you Myra? What's going on?"

"I'm trying to keep up with Mcilwain. We're south on A1A and he just turned onto the Port Orange Bridge. He left Colson's condo with a heavyset black male. It must be Jay Taylor."

"Fine. Call back when they get where they're going, but I have a feeling they're going to meet up with Colson."

"Colson? How would you know that?"

"Don't worry about it. Just stay on them, but watch your back."

Strickland paused, confused. "What do you mean watch my back?"

"On second thought, you should just back off. I have things handled," Rollins said.

"What? After all this cloak-and-dagger surveillance I've been doing for days, you couldn't stop me now with a Gatling gun."

"Look, Strickland, you take your orders from me and I'm telling you—"

Strickland pressed the "end call" icon on the dash and the interior fell silent.

"Asshole," Myra said to the dashboard.

She took the right at the foot of the Port Orange Bridge and stomped the accelerator. She topped the crest of the bridge at eighty miles per hour and finally saw Mcilwain's truck a quarter mile ahead. He had slowed considerably. She suddenly saw why and tapped her break. She slowed to the speed limit and passed the Volusia County Sheriff's car sitting at the foot of the bridge. They both picked up the pace once clear of the deputy's radar. In a way, she was thankful for the opportunity to settle down her heart rate.

Strickland followed the truck as it turned south on South Ridgewood through New Smyrna Beach. She felt she had done well with her discrete surveillance. Mcilwain was a good agent but was probably distracted by his recent bureau discipline and his delusional escapade to exonerate himself. Her concentration had been on the truck, but her training redirected her attention. The low-riding blue Impala in her rearview mirror had matched her turn for turn at a fixed distance since she topped the Port Orange Bridge.

Colson gave Roper a wave of thanks and steered the pontoon boat north with the map of the lagoon on his lap. The boat was probably larger than he required, but it felt more stable than a flat-bottomed johnboat. And it was shaded. A seating area wrapped around the bow, and Colson sat under a canopy behind the wheel at the starboard beam. It was not unlike the pontoon boats he had rented to cruise down the Saint John's River when Nicole was a teenager. There had to be a hundred small islands, and viewing them on a map was totally different from identifying them from his perspective in the boat. They all looked identical. That's what the young Roper had told him when he offered the use of a portable GPS unit. Colson was relieved he hadn't turned the offer down. He would have literally been fumbling around in a virtual corn maze without the device. It was not a state-of-the-art GPS, but it would get the job done. He leaned it on the fiberglass dash next to the wheel and compared his position to the crude map. Not all islands were named on the map, only Shipyard Island,

Orange Island, Plantation Island, Middle Island, and Gaines Island. According to the GPS, Colson was in the midst of a small island group about midpoint between Orange Island and Gaines Island. He had overshot the target by at least a half mile. He turned to starboard and entered a small canal between two of the unnamed islands on the map. He should emerge just north of Gaines Island if the map was accurate.

Roper had taken Parker on his first guided tour of the lagoon, so they would have left from the same fish camp. Hopefully, Parker would likely return to a familiar area to dock. The pontoon emerged from the canal forty minutes after Colson left the fish camp, where he had left the seriously bored Roper standing on the dock. It appeared no more remarkable than the other dozen islands he'd passed. There was very little beachfront if any. Some sandy areas at the shore but mostly abrupt drop-offs where century-old trees and thickets of wide-leaf foliage and moss hung out over the water.

Colson cut back on the throttle to reduce the engine noise and took thirty minutes to circle the island slowly. Colson listened and watched but saw nothing other than the undisturbed beauty of an otherwise deserted island. His passage would occasionally frighten pelicans and terns from their perch. He counted three alligators near the shore with their eyes and tops of their heads just breaking the surface of the water, only to instantly submerge when they felt threatened. But he hadn't seen what he was looking for. Was Roper mistaken? He decided he had missed the mark and started another circle around the island. Ten minutes into his second search, Colson saw the narrow inlet he had missed the first time. The GPS screen indicated his location as a small black dot on the west side of the island. Tall sea grass had grown from each bank and almost totally camouflaged the mouth of the inlet. Colson steered the pontoon through the opening. The tall sea grass made a scuffing sound as it brushed against both sides of the pontoon floats. The grass opened into what could be considered a lagoon within a lagoon and a small beachhead. That's when Colson saw it. Momma Ball had called it the Devil's Claw. The large mangled and twisted driftwood formation Parker used as a backdrop when Roper took his photo almost two years ago.

"There," Taylor said, pointing through the trucks windshield. "The black Challenger."

Mcilwain nodded and said, "Yeah, Parker's car. I have the tag memorized."

Mcilwain pulled up next to it, and they jumped out of the cab of the truck and stepped up to check inside. It was unoccupied.

Taylor scanned the camp for any sign of Colson and said, "He was going to rent a boat."

"C'mon," said Mcilwain and waved for Taylor to follow.

They stepped into the bait shop and were enveloped with the musty aroma of soil, kerosene, and earthworms. Taylor went right as Mcilwain went left until they arrived at the back counter. A young man sat on a stool at the end of the counter eating a candy bar. He looked at the mismatched men at the counter and said, "Can I help you?"

Mcilwain said, "We're looking for our friend, Grey Colson. Did he rent a boat earlier?"

Roper eyed Mcilwain and the silent Jay Taylor as if in thought. He said, "I don't think we're supposed to give out information about our customers."

"Look," Taylor spoke up. "That's his car outside, and we just missed him. I work for him, and this is Agent Mcilwain with the FBI. How long has he been gone?"

Roper looked back over his shoulder and called out, "Momma Ball."

Taylor and Mcilwain exchanged glances when the female voice yelled from the back, "What is it?"

"Customers," Roper yelled back.

Roper settled his eyes on Taylor. "Hey, aren't you one of the guys on American Gladiator?"

Taylor returned his gaze through his Ray-Bans. "You ever watch the UFC?"

"Naw," Roper said. "Just MTV."

Momma Ball appeared from a side door wearing an off-white apron smeared with dirt. "I'm sorry," she began. "I was just stocking the bait cooler. What can I do for you?"

Mcilwain said, "Our friend Grey Colson rented a boat earlier, and we need to catch up with him."

Roper looked at Momma Ball and said, "I didn't say anything."

"Well," she replied, "they obviously know him. What size boat do you need? We have everything from—"

"Just a standard fishing boat," Taylor interrupted. "And a map of the islands if you have one."

Momma Ball reached under the counter and handed Taylor a copy of the same crude map she had given Colson. He took it and gave her a credit card. She stuck the rules and regulations notice and waiver in front of Taylor, and he signed it while she scanned the card. Over her shoulder she said, "I marked Gaines Island for you. That's where he's headed. Did you gentlemen bring your own fishing equipment?"

"No," said Taylor.

"We have everything you need. Rods, line, bait, everything."

"No thanks."

Momma Ball spun around, handed the card back to Taylor with a key, and then cut her eyes over at Roper who shrugged and stood from the stool.

"Hey, you guys need a tour guide? I'm not busy."

"You could always help me," said a sarcastic Momma Ball.

"No thanks. We're good," said Taylor as he took a key with a white fob marked twelve in permanent marker from Momma Ball. Roper plopped back down on the stool with a bored and dejected expression on his face.

"Where you sending us, man," said Carlos into his phone.

"Just follow the directions I gave you," said Rollins. "You can't be but just a few minutes away. Once you get to the fish camp, you'll need a boat. Colson has pulled in on a medium-size island about five or six miles north of the camp, and as far as I can tell, he's alone. It'll be like shooting fish in a barrel, but don't shoot him. I need him alive."

Carlos said nothing. After a long pause, Rollins said, "You still there?"

Carlos held the phone away from his face and pressed "end call."

Carlos jerked the wheel of the Impala and pulled into a do-it-yourself carwash. He drove around the back and nosed into a stall facing the road. He said, "Get the guns out of the trunk and load them." Ramone and Paco jumped out and hustled around back. In two short minutes, they were back in the car, each with a handgun stuck in the waist of their pants.

"Was it good news, Inca?" Paco said from the back seat.

Carlos smiled. "Nunca falta una bestia muerta para un zopilote hambriento."

"The vulture, Inca?" asked Paco.

Carlos nodded. "Yes. You have much to learn, mi amigo. There'll always be a dead beast for a hungry vulture. An old saying that tells us that life doesn't fail to present us with opportunities. This will be an opportunity we will not pass up. Colson will die."

Ramone said, "So, we will not bring him back to the man? What about the rest of the dinero?"

"You too have much to learn," said Carlos. "No, we use the white boy for our purpose, and then we go home with the respect of our brothers. Do you not know that if we made this deal and brought Colson back there would be fifty federal gringos waiting to arrest or kill us?"

Ramone and Paco sat in silence and dared not dispute the Inca.

Strickland pulled the Charger over near the entrance of the fish camp and waited for Mcilwain's truck to disappear at the far end of the gavel road. The phone suddenly ringing over the speakers startled Strickland.

"Hello."

"It's me."

Strickland did not attempt to mask her frustration. "What the hell's going on, Nick? Why did you let me get screwed over and assigned to that slob, Rollins?"

"It wasn't my doing. He's a snake with his own personal agenda. He went behind my back."

"Well, I'm sick of it."

"I know. I know. He has essentially ruined me, and he'll ruin the program if he continues to employ his Neanderthal tactics."

"You people and your programs—no wonder the Russians are beating our ass in space."

Danz was silent on the line for a beat and then said, "What are you going to do now?"

"I told you I'm sick of this crap. I don't know what Colson and Mcilwain are doing, but I'm going to get them both in the same place and arrest them for obstruction before the wheels fall off of everything."

"Arrest them both?"

"What? You think I can't. Why do you think they give us a second pair of handcuffs? Or do you doubt me because I'm a woman?"

Danz's exaggerated sigh came over the speakers. "Not me. I'd rather fight a platoon of marines than tangle with you."

Strickland stopped the Charger when she rounded the curve at the fish camp. Parker's black Challenger and Mcilwain's truck sat side by side next to a covered pavilion near the pier, but they appeared unoccupied. She parked in the shade of a live oak tree. Spanish moss hung from its branches and swayed with the light October breeze just a few feet above her head when she stepped out. The boat slips were almost full, and the only sounds were of birds, bugs, and the occasional croaking frog.

Strickland walked through the screen door. No heads appeared above the isles of fishing lures, rods, floppy caps, and trinkets that she had no use for. In the back of the store, a young man sat on a stool behind the counter facing away from her making slurping sounds as he sucked the remaining drops of liquid from a straw. He spun on his stool with a Styrofoam cup in hand and eyed her.

He said, "Yes, ma'am?" She walked up to the young man and held her credentials at eye level.

"Agent Strickland, FBI."

Roper hesitated a moment and then called over his shoulder for the third time in two hours, "Momma Ball!"

"In the cooler," came the female voice from the back. "What is it now?"

"A busy Monday," Roper replied.

"Can you not handle anything on your own?" Momma Ball rebuked in a frustrated tone as she emerged from the back while wiping her hands on the dirty apron around her waist. She looked Agent Strickland up and down, from her black flat dress shoes to her dress slacks to her conservative blouse and business jacket. "Well, honey, you don't look dressed for a day of fishing on the lagoon."

"I'm not fishing," said Strickland, holding her credentials back up.

Momma Ball shook her head. "Apparently, no one's fishing today."

Strickland heard the screen door slap closed behind her but it only distracted her for a second. Her attention was on the woman behind the counter.

"I need information about the drivers of the two vehicles parked at the pier, as in where they said they were going, what type of craft they rented, and when you expect them to return. Your cooperation will be—"

"Momma caliente," came a male Hispanic voice from behind. She spun and saw a male in his late twenties standing just a few feet from her. Two others flanked him, six to eight feet on either side. The middleman wore a tank top, exposing tattoos on both shoulders and arms. He stood in a lazy pose with both hands shoved in his baggy pants pockets.

"You mean Momma Ball," Roper chimed in.

Carlos shot Roper a quick look and laughed. "Bola de momma? No, vato. I'm talking to *her*," he said, nodding to Strickland.

His smile vanished as he nodded to Ramone and Paco. As if they had practiced the move, both drew handguns from their waistbands. Ramone trained his on Strickland while Paco alternated his aim between Mamma Ball and Roper. Carlos produced a switchblade from his baggy pocket and released the blade with a dull click. He took a step toward Strickland and turned the blade over in his fingers.

He said, "You look like a federales to me." Carlos gave Ramone and Paco a quick glance and then narrowed his eyes on Strickland. "You see, amigos. The man already has federal agents on our backs. They use us like tracking dogs and then stab us in the back when they get what they want. And *this*," Carlos shouted, "is the law your parents and grandparents say we should follow while they call the Latin Kings criminals. You tell *me* who the liars and criminals are."

Carlos took a second step toward Strickland. "You don't do what I tell you and I will cut you. You know what I'm saying?"

Strickland stood still and silent.

"Turn around and put your hands on your head," Carlos ordered.

Strickland eyed Carlos and then turned slowly, lacing her fingers on top of her head. Carlos reached under Strickland's jacket and pulled out a Glock. He stuck the pistol in his baggy pocket and continued the search of Strickland's waistband, locating two sets of handcuffs, which he tossed to Ramone. He checked her neckline and ankles before standing and nodding to Ramone. "Take them to the back and make sure they stay quiet and locked up somewhere. Strickland reluctantly walked behind the counter at the point of Ramone's pistol and joined a silent and wide-eyed Momma Ball. The trio disappeared behind a swinging door. Carlos strolled to Roper who had stood from his stool with his back firmly pressed against the counter. His eyes had widened more than Momma Ball's, and the blood had drained from his face.

"And you, vato," Carlos said, "What do you do here?"

Roper shrugged nervously. "I'm just the river guide."

"Ah, I see. Then you know where Colson is going, don't you?"

Roper shook his head vigorously until Carlos stuck the tip of the blade under his chin.

"Yes, you do, don't you," he said more as a statement than a question.

Roper responded with a single silent nod.

Carlos said, "Get me a boat."

Roper shoved away from the counter and rounded it to the hanging keys.

"The boat *you* use," said Carlos.

Roper plucked a key with a white fob from the pegboard with the number "one" written in permanent marker and held it out to Carlos.

"No, vato. You are coming with us as our guide."

Ramone appeared from the back and joined Paco, Carlos, and Roper at the counter. They walked out through the screen door with Roper in the lead. The three Latin Kings could not see Roper's face, but his facial expression would best be described as dejected and *terrified*."

Chapter Eighteen

Colson checked the compartments under the long bench seat at the stern of the pontoon boat and found a chemical toilet. Under the front seats he located a flashlight and three flairs. He stuck the flairs in his side cargo pocket and held the flashlight as he climbed over the side onto the narrow sandy beachhead. The driftwood formation was almost as tall as he was and nearly as long as the pontoon boat. Colson thought it would make a marvelous conversation piece if he had a room large enough to display it. He tied the boat off on one of the larger limbs and examined the sand for any sign of human foot traffic. There was none, but Parker had been missing for weeks and any signs of his presence would have been eroded by rain, wind, and the shallow surf.

Colson's water-resistant watch read 16:40 hours, and it would be dark in a little over ninety minutes. He had checked the Internet for the time of sunset on October 24 and it would be at 6:53 p.m. or 18:53 hours. Gaines Island was far larger than it appeared on the crude map, and it would be a miracle to find Parker while it was still daylight. Colson fought his way up the steep bank and scanned the immediate area. There seemed to be no sign of human life or a man-made trail worn by hikers. Since the island was off limits to camping, it made sense that few would bother walking inland.

Every twenty to thirty feet Colson would stop and listen and make a 360-degree survey of his position. The compass app on his phone indicated that he had been walking directly north and cutting the island in half. He had been walking on a grade, and at 18:30 hours he caught a glimpse of the Indian River through the thick trees and undergrowth. Another fifty feet and the ground began a slight downhill grade, which meant he was at the approximate center of the island. What little sky he could see through the canopy of trees was becoming dim and gray. Fifteen or so minutes of light remained, but then something caught his eye. It stood out like an Easter egg in the brown and mossy green of the island floor: a small and completely out-of-place object a dozen feet ahead of him on the ground.

Taylor secured the boat to a half-rotted log that lay half submerged in the water. He climbed out, pulled himself to a relatively level ledge of rock, and pulled Mcilwain up to join him. They stood and turned in circles with their hands on their hips.

Mcilwain sighed and said, "It'll be like finding a needle in a haystack."

"Colson," Taylor yelled. The sound of his voice immediately fell dead, absorbed by the sounds of the surf, trees, and thick undergrowth.

"That's not going to work," said Mcilwain. "He wouldn't hear us anyway, and we can't assume he's found Parker yet. We could scare Parker off and never find him."

Taylor fixed his good eye on Mcilwain and said, "All right, Mr. FBI. What do you suggest?"

"We split up and go opposite directions. It'll double our chances. If you get lost or disoriented, just walk along the bank. We'll eventually find the boat or each other or both."

"Fine, but it's going to be dark soon. Then what?"

"Did you bring a flashlight?"

"Sure," said Taylor sarcastically, "But I left it in the boat with the microwave, big-screen TV and the cabin tent."

Mcilwain cocked his head and stared at Taylor. "You really have been hanging around Colson too long. Let's go."

Colson bent down and plucked the flimsy half-inch-wide-by-two-inch-long tab from the ground. One-half was a bright purple and the other was white. The white end of the tab had a bar code with the typical long list of random numbers at the bottom. On top of the bar code was 2 x 4 x 8. The purple left side had the outline of a pine tree and read, "Pressure Treated—Top-Choice Lumber Products—Georgia Pacific—Atlanta Ga.

Colson recognized the tab the moment he saw it. Every scrap of pressure-treated lumber he had ever purchased had one stapled to the end. He had torn off hundreds of them building decks on the house and a playhouse for Nichole. He felt a sense of relief knowing the tab had to have been from the lumber Parker had brought to the island. He doubted Parker had gathered the tabs up and sprinkled them randomly, so he had to be close.

Colson looked at the tab again and started to toss it to the ground, but froze and gave it another look. Above the bar code was the wording, "Above Ground." That didn't make sense. One of the reasons to use pressure-treated lumber other than normal weathering was to prevent rot from ground contact. Every piece of lumber he had ever bought indicated "Ground Contact." Parker was a scientist, so he had to be pretty smart. Why bother to go to the considerable trouble and expense to build a structure on a hot, humid island and not pay a little extra for lumber rated for ground contact. It didn't make sense... Unless...

Colson looked upward through the canopy of trees. The sky had gone from medium gray to a dark gray. The sun had dropped below the horizon, although he couldn't see it. He had been walking around like an idiot for almost two hours, looking for something he would never find. For all he knew, he could have passed underneath Parker a half-dozen times. Although the tree canopy was thick, small slits of remaining light could be seen with the gentle movement of the limbs and leaves. He needed to see a solid mass with no slits of light. Colson cursed under his breath. He had wasted two hours looking at the ground and the thicket of undergrowth. He would give the search another hour and then make his way back to the pontoon, and would start again in the morning.

At 19:20 hours, Colson could barely see his hand in front of his face. He checked the compass app on his phone. His eyes had adjusted to the dark, and he squinted when the app flashed on the screen. It was surprisingly bright. He turned it away from his face, allowing a moment for his eyes to readjust to the dark. His retinas continued to display an image of the bright screen when he closed his eyes as if it was burned into his cornea. Then there was a sharp sting on his right hip.

Colson jerked away from the sting and leaped backward from where he estimated the snake had been coiled. He had never been bitten, but had imagined what it would feel like. But then his brain registered a delayed sensation, and he knew then that it wasn't a snake at all. The crack of a gunshot had caught up to the stinging sensation in his hip a half-second later.

Ramone allowed himself a nervous smile for his accomplishment. Carlos and Paco would have certainly heard the shot and would be coming his way. He would be respected at the least or promoted within the gang at best. His first kill would make him into the man he always admired among the Latin Kings, even if it had been the product of a lucky shot. He had been hearing footfalls on the mossy ground and had listened intently and moved silently. Then, as if an answer to prayer, Colson had illuminated himself like a beam of sunlight from heaven.

Ramone squatted and listened. There was no cry for help and no sounds of movement. It was a clean one-shot kill. There were sounds of footfalls in the distance coming from another direction. It would be Paco and Carlos converging on his location, but they were still in the distance. He knew he needed to move carefully, but he wanted to be admiring and taking credit for his kill when they arrived. It would be an earlier night than he'd expected, and they would be back in the hotel room, celebrating with blunts, beer, and chicas, before midnight. There was still no sound other than distant running as he moved forward. Once he arrived at the point he estimated Colson had fallen, Ramone knelt and waved his arms in the air just above the ground. Nothing. Had Colson dropped several feet away or had he lived to run several yards from the spot? He stood and listened once again.

The bright light came from his right. Ramone spun, crouched, and covered his eyes with his left hand. He raised his gun and wrapped his finger around the trigger, but the brilliant flash and bark of a large-caliber gun exploded before he could get off the shot. His forearm erupted in pain and blood spattered across his face. He jumped to his feet and the adrenaline rush pushed him to run as hard as he ever had. The metallic taste of his own blood coated his lips. His numb arm flopped like a rope at his side as he pushed himself harder to escape the immediate area. He could see his own shadow ahead of him from the light trained at his back. His dimly illuminated path was a macabre, two-dimensional outline of reality. He ran in a chaotic zigzag pattern, stumbled over exposed roots, darted through razor-sharp briars, and slammed against the ghostly outline of trees until the world fell out from under him.

Agent Mcilwain jerked his pistol from his waistband and held it level as he turned 360 degrees.

"Where did that come from?" he said to the dark outline of Taylor against the moonlit waters.

"The shots sound inland, around the center of the island," Taylor replied. "Maybe splitting up isn't such a good idea. You know, strength in numbers."

"Colson must have found Parker or Parker found him."

Taylor jerked his sunglasses off and shoved them in his pocket. His paranoia of someone seeing his dead eye didn't matter much in the dark, and he could see absolutely zero with them on. There were two shots with very different sound signatures. He suspected the higher-pitched shot was a smaller caliber and the responding shot was a larger caliber with its deeper-sounding blast.

Taylor said, "Colson wouldn't fire first. His was the second shot, probably with his Glock forty-five."

"So much for getting Parker out of here alive."

"Maybe Parker isn't as innocent as Colson thinks. Maybe he needs a killin'."

"Or maybe," added Mcilwain, "he thinks we are the bad guys coming after him."

Crack, crack came another series of shots. The higher-pitched pistol shots were answered by a series of lower-pitched explosions. Taylor could almost feel the concussion of air pass him as the explosions forced a shock wave away from their respective muzzles.

"You need a gun," said Mcilwain.

"You have an extra?"

"No. Stay with me and let's go."

Taylor and Mcilwain sprinted through the thick undergrowth with no regard for being stealth. The shots continued to ring out, and a voice was yelling something ahead. It wasn't Colson's voice. It sounded younger and Hispanic. Names were being repeated over and over. They stopped to listen and adjust their direction. There was the sound of running just ahead of Taylor. He sprinted toward the sound with his hands ahead of him to keep from running full speed into a tree. But he hit something solid in spite of his precaution, and it bounced away from him. It was something at chest height.

A light hit him in the chest. It came from the ground. Taylor saw a small man holding a flashlight. The man raised the light to Taylor's face and then dropped it to the ground as he struggled to his feet. Taylor grabbed the flashlight and put the beam in the man's face. He was short. Maybe five-seven, and his eyes were wide with surprise. Maybe it was Taylor's size or the bulk of his recently replenished muscles. Or maybe his dead, milky eye had come in handy for a change because something had frozen the short man in shock. Taylor watched the man reach behind his back and swing a pistol in his direction. In one short movement, Taylor cocked his right arm and drove a punch straight into his nose. The follow through of the strike propelled the man back and off his feet as he pulled the trigger, launching a round straight up through the thick canopy above.

Taylor stomped on Paco's wrist, crushing bones and dislodging the pistol. He grabbed Paco around the neck with his meaty right hand and by the waist of his pants with his left. In one fluid jerk, he hefted Paco above his head and drove him straight down on his back. The impact instantly drove the air out of Paco's lungs and knocked him out cold. Taylor grabbed Paco's gun and flashlight.

"This place is crazy as hell," said Mcilwain from behind. "It's a damn war zone."

Taylor turned and could only see Mcilwain's dark silhouette. He said, "These must be the gangbangers Colson told me about."

"Gangbangers? When were you going to mention them?"

"It wasn't relevant. How could I know they would find Colson here? It doesn't make sense."

"Listen," said Mcilwain. "The gun fire has stopped."

Colson felt sticky blood oozing from the gunshot wound on his hip. He dropped to the ground and waited for another muzzle flash, but he didn't have to wait for long. *Pop, pop* came another double tap from about fifty feet away. The undergrowth was thick but not enough to hide the bright muzzle flashes. The gangbanger had to be in a prone position because the flashes were coming from ground level. Colson took careful aim and returned fire but realized it would be nothing but sheer luck scoring a hit through the trees and tropical growth.

Between each series of shots, the gangbanger yelled, "Carlos, Paco... Carlos, Paco." Colson inched forward on his belly and stopped each time there was a pause between the barrages of gunfire. The gangbanger wasn't moving and shooting. The muzzle flashes came from one stationary point at ground level and then they stopped completely. The gangbanger's shouting ceased and all fell silent. The noise of the gunfire had partially deafened Colson to the gentle sounds of the island's normal eco system. The rustling of tropical leaves, the buzzing of mosquitoes, and the chirping of crickets was replaced by a high-pitched ringing in Colson's ear. He shook his head vigorously, trying to shake the annoying sound. There were at least two others out there, and he had to be alert and ready. He dumped the Glock's magazine and combat reloaded another from his pocket. He racked a round into the chamber at the same moment a flashlight blinded him and a hand jerked him by the collar.

Colson tightened his grip on the Glock but stopped short of aiming and firing at the sound of Taylor's unmistakable voice.

"It's me, Grey, and Mcilwain's with me."

"Taylor? Glad you could join the party. There's at least two other gangbangers out there."

"At least *one* more," said Taylor.

"You met one already?"

"Yeah. He took a shot at me."

"And then what?"

"I may have broken his back."

"You *may* have?"

Mcilwain said, "You need to see something, Colson."

Max Rollins cursed the dark and slapped his laptop closed. He sat in his undershirt, and his back ached from hunching over his desk for the last four hours. His dress shirt and tie had been hanging on the back of his chair for the past two hours. Three boats had navigated to one of the central islands in the lagoon within a ninety-minute period. The trees covered each craft from view, and he could see no human movement whatsoever. Colson had been the first. Mcilwain and a black male, possibly Colson's employee, were in the second boat, and then the Latin King trio took out the third, except he counted four people, not three. Then there was Strickland who entered the fish camp, never to emerge again. The only explanation was that Colson thinks he has found Parker's hiding spot, but how could that be after weeks without decent food, shelter, or clean drinking water? The NASA security teams had searched the same island at least twice and came up with nothing,

He had watched as long as it was light and then for another hour. The only sign of life or activity were pinpoint flashes of light from two different points near the center of the island. He first suspected they were flashlights, but they were too intense and brief. There was gunfire in the middle of Mosquito Lagoon. If he was lucky, they would all kill each other on the godforsaken island, including Parker if he was still alive by some astronomical chance. It would have to wait until the next day. He needed to sleep. Rollins slipped on his shirt without bothering to button it up and left his tie where it fell to the floor.

He stepped into the cool air and arched his aching back. He walked toward the front parking row of the Operations Support Building and pulled his key fob from his pocket as a black SUV screeched to a stop behind his car. The driver stepped out. He was a man in his forties, wearing tan slacks and a black golf shirt.

He smiled and said, "Mr. Rollins?"

Rollins knew his car was blocked in, and the man didn't seem threatening at the moment. He decided to cooperate.

"Yes."

"I have an urgent call for you."

"For me?"

"It's on a secure line from the chairman."

"What do you mean, a call?"

"Please," the man said while gesturing to the driver's door. "The phone is on the console. If you'll please get in. It's OK. You can sit in the driver's seat and lock the door if you like. I'll stand by out here."

Rollins narrowed his eyes. He walked to the back window and peered inside. The man was alone. He walked back to the driver's door, slipped inside, and grabbed the phone.

"Hello."

"Rollins... Maxwell Rollins."

"Mr. Chairman ... ah ... Senator. I didn't think you wanted to know my name."

"I didn't, but the current situation has dictated otherwise."

"The current situation?"

"Did something go wrong down there, Rollins? You were supposed to keep me in the loop."

"No, sir. I mean, I'm still addressing the problem, but—"

"I'll cut to the chase, Rollins. I was served with a subpoena this evening to appear before a congressional hearing on Thursday."

"About our research?"

"What else would it be about? Now listen, you get your ass back in the office as quickly and quietly as possible. I want you to make all the data go away. I don't care how, but be thorough and clean with it. No smashed hard drives, no arson, nothing like that. Just do it. And then you tell that group of pencil-neck scientists that their services are no longer needed and they are to abide by their confidentiality agreements if they don't want to be sharing a cellblock in Leavenworth. Are you clear on all of that, or do I need to repeat myself?"

"I understand, Senator, but that might take all night."

"Then you better get started. I'm surprised the DOJ hasn't dispatched a brigade of FBI agents there already with a search warrant in hand."

Rollins rubbed his temple. A sharp headache had taken precedence over the pain in his back. He noticed the flashes of blue against the far buildings before the vehicles came into view. And there were at least a dozen spilling into the parking lot and headed to the front of the OSB building. Two black Tahoe's followed by a long line of black Chargers, all unmarked but with small blue strobes flashing in their grills, from behind their windshields, and on the decks above their back seats.

"Oh, shit," said Rollins, dropping the phone on the passenger seat. He could hear but not understand the chairman's muffled reply. He shoved the SUV in drive and eased away, leaving the man wearing the tan slacks and black golf shirt stranded with his hands held out to his side. He drove to the exit as the caravan of black vehicles and their flashing blue strobes circled the main entrance. They paid no attention to Rollins nor did they attempt to stop him, and he knew why. What they were looking for was imbedded in hard drives, not driving away in an SUV.

Colson followed Taylor and Mcilwain to the spot where the gangbanger had been firing.

"Hang on," said Taylor, stopping Colson in his tracks. "This is the edge of the pit."

"Pit?" asked Colson

"I almost fell in myself," Taylor said.

Mcilwain said, "Were you shooting anything other than your Glock?"

"No. I left my bazooka at home since it was a little too bulky for the occasion, why?"

Mcilwain clicked on his flashlight, aimed it downward, and said, "How would you explain this?" The pit, as Taylor called it, was a not the result of a natural occurrence but clearly man-made—an eight-by-ten-foot rectangle with a uniform depth of about six feet. Colson could see the markings left by a small shovel on the side walls, but the bottom of the pit was covered with moss, large palm fronds, and long limbs, which had apparently covered the opening until the gangbanger stepped in it. Now he lay slumped in one corner of the pit, silent and perfectly still. His left arm was soaked with blood from Colson's first shot but he failed to see what Mcilwain was talking about at first. The human brain anticipates certain information resulting from previous experience. If you show up at a suicide, you expect to see someone hanging by the neck or lying on the floor with a hole in his or her head and a gun nearby. The same thing goes for homicides and other types of crime scenes—different settings, different expectations. Certain circumstances dictate what images, smells, and other sensory information the brain expects to register.

Colson grabbed the flashlight from Mcilwain and walked around the pit until he was directly over the dead gangbanger. Protruding from the top of his head like the horn of a unicorn was the slender aluminum shaft of a hunter's arrow. Considering the short portion that was visible, he estimated the tip of the arrow had come to a stop in the area of the gangbanger's tonsils.

Colson clicked off the flashlight and said, "I have to admit, that's not something you see every day."

Taylor said, "How many more are out here?"

"Should be just one other," said Colson, "but this can't be related. The Latin Kings would be laughed out of town if they walked around with bows and arrows."

Mcilwain said, "Well, someone obviously is. I still don't know how anyone accomplished that shot unless this guy was face down in the dirt at the time."

Colson could see the dark outline of Taylor and Mcilwain across the pit. They stood silent for a long moment. He hadn't heard a second set of feet running through the foliage when he went after the gangbanger. There were no other voices other than the gangbanger calling for his two compadres, Carlos and Paco. And according to Taylor, one of them had been snapped in half. He rewound his memory further to the out-of-place lumber tag: Above Ground. Was it really possible?

"Look up," said Colson as he clicked on the flashlight and aimed it straight up.

The live oak tree was massive, maybe a hundred-plus years old. Undisturbed for a century, the clumps of Spanish moss that hung from its twisted branches were as long as a human body and as thick as a side of beef. Each branch was covered with smaller branches that were thick with leaves that had not yet begun to change to their autumn shade of brown and rust.

"What are we looking for?" asked Taylor.

"There," said Colson, pointing at a spot through the lower hanging limbs and moss. It was a foreign shape among the twisting limbs and abstract clumps of moss—a perfectly square void of total darkness. Colson moved to the other side of the pit and joined Taylor and Mcilwain for a better look. He aimed the flashlight back at the hole. This time the beam of light illuminated something even more out of place than the perfectly square hole: a partial palm and the thumb, index and middle fingers of a human hand.

Carlos crouched behind a tree and watched from a safe distance of fifty yards. He had seen terror in many eyes during his relationship with the Latin Kings. Young men who didn't size up to the gang's standards; rival gang members who trespassed in the gang's territory, which was wherever they deemed their own; and young girls who rejected his advances. But there were always others with him. The whole purpose of a gang was strength in numbers. He had never taken action on his own, with no one to back up his haughty attitude and terroristic threats. For the first time in his gangster career, Carlos felt the very real fear he had previously instilled in others.

He had heard Ramone's cries for him and Paco, but fear had frozen him mute. Paco had not called out or ran to help. Carlos accepted the very real possibility that they both were dead. The second white boy and large black man had come out of nowhere. If he started shooting, they would surely scatter and surround him as they had Ramone. A real street fight could not be waged in the open, but in a back alley or abandoned warehouse where there was nowhere to escape. Carlos tamped down his fear and decided he would emerge victorious and have more than enough to brag about. He would climb further up the Latin Kings' chain of command, but he would have to wait until he could back those men into a corner or against a wall. But an obvious obstacle remained: there were no walls and no dark corners on the island.

Mcilwain being the youngest and clearly the most agile among the three made the climb to Parker's nest. There was no way of swinging down to enter the floor hatch, but he was able to shimmy through one of the small side windows. At one point, Colson and Taylor heard moaning, coughing, and sounds of a short struggle emanating through the floor hatch.

Then Mcilwain's voice, "I'm here to help."

Colson recognized Parker from studying his photo, even with a full beard. First his legs slowly dangled from the hatch, then his thin torso, and finally his arms and upper body. The rope under his arms and across his chest hunched his shoulders in an uncomfortable pose as Mcilwain lowered him and began swinging him from side to side. Colson and Taylor stood on opposite sides of the pit, ready to grab Parker's limp body. He swung like a pendulum, and Taylor was the first to grab his arm and lower him to the ground while Mcilwain climbed down. Mcilwain and Taylor stood facing in opposite directions with guns in hand as Colson clicked on the light and shined it in Parker's face. It made him squint, which was an encouraging sign. He was alive and breathing but was quivering and clammy with sweat. He needed immediate medical attention.

"Grant," said Colson, patting him lightly on the cheek. "Grant Parker."

Parker's upper body jerked as if startled from a deep sleep. His eyes met Colson's. They were looking but not focusing.

"I don't care anymore," he said in a weak, raspy voice.

"Listen, Grant. Lisa sent us to find you and bring you home. We're not going to harm you."

"Lisa," Grant whispered. "I'm dreaming… Lisa."

"You weren't dreaming when you killed that gangbanger."

"What? So much noise… too much noise… couldn't sleep."

Colson chuckled at the notion that Parker was so delusional he would put an arrow though a man's head for disturbing his sleep. No, "Hey, can you keep it down buddy," or, "Hey, man, knock it off." He just shot him through the top of his head with an aluminum hunting arrow with no more thought than one might nonchalantly hit the snooze button on an alarm clock.

Colson said, "You're my kinda guy, Grant."

He helped him to his feet and slung Parker's arm over his shoulder. Taylor stuck the gun he had taken from Ramone in his pocket and grabbed Parker's other arm. There was a hint of twilight as they made their way downhill to the nearest shoreline. They followed the bank for the next thirty minutes until they could see the hazy outline of the pontoon boat. But there was more than one boat outline bobbing at the bank, and the form of a man was draped over the wheel of the second boat.

Mcilwain held his gun at low ready as he approached the second boat. A fraction of a second before Mcilwain could check the man's neck for a pulse, he jerked awake and looked in terror at Mcilwain.

"No," he cried.

"It's you," Mcilwain said. "What are you doing here?"

Roper appeared to recognize Mcilwain and his face relaxed. He raised his right hand six inches to show he was handcuffed to the boat's wheel. He said, "They made me bring them here. You gotta key?"

Mcilwain shook his head. "No."

"Aren't you an FBI guy?"

"Hang on," said Colson as he stepped into the boat and pulled the Shrike from the sheath under his arm with a quick jerk. Roper's eyes widened at the sight of the tactical tomahawk.

"Naw, man," he said with a nervous laugh, "you're not going to chop them off with that are you?"

Colson rotated the Shrike in his hand so the talon end faced forward. "Don't have to. I'll torque the other cuff off the wheel with this end. But I have one condition."

"What?"

"You don't charge me a late fee for the boat rental."

The gunshot rang from the shore, and Colson felt the sensation of a sledgehammer between his shoulder blades. As opposed to the first shot that he initially suspected was a snake, the close proximity of the gunfire was immediately unmistakable. He spun and saw Carlos at the shoreline, not twenty feet from the bow of the boat, and he was taking aim for a second shot. Colson's Glock weighed heavy in his side cargo pocket and there was no time to reach for it. And there was no time to hope that Mcilwain or Taylor would get their sights on Carlos in the next second and a half in the waning darkness. Colson instinctively threw the Shrike end over end in the gunman's direction. If nothing else, to distract him long enough for him to grab the Glock and return fire. But in the end it wasn't necessary. The Shrike took less than a half second to spin through the air and bury its talon in Carlos's neck, giving him a tracheotomy of forged steel. The razor-sharp tip of the talon had continued through the windpipe and severed his spinal cord. Carlos's eyes bulged, and his body stiffened before falling back and sprawling against the Devil's Claw.

Taylor and Mcilwain hustled to Colson as he dropped to the deck and rolled to his side grasping at the tail of his shirt.

Taylor yelled, "Colson."

Colson groaned as he pulled off his shirt and tore away the Velcro straps of the Kevlar vest. Taylor helped pull off the vest and tossed it on the deck. He whistled and said, "Damn, Grey. There's already a welt as big as a dinner plate."

Colson rolled up to his butt and said, "You think?"

"You're bleeding," Taylor said, pointing at Colson's hip.

"That's just a graze from earlier. Who would have thought? Thirty years of police work and I've never had anything more than a scratch. And within eight hours I get shot twice. Retirement sucks."

Colson looked to where Carlos had stood. His legs appeared to have locked in place with his upper body leaning lazily back against the driftwood. He slid his cell phone out of his pocket and handed it to Taylor. "Do something for me," he said and stepped into the shallow water. "I need you to take a photo."

"You serious?" asked Taylor.

"Just humor me and take it."

Max Rollins had been driving for two hours before he realized how far he had gone. He was technically in a stolen SUV, but he knew that was the least of his worries. He had to react quickly and that didn't include saying a kind good-bye to the man in the parking lot and casually walking to his car while the FBI or NSA or whoever they were swooped in on him. He realized dawn was fast approaching and once he snapped out of his self-imposed pity party, he looked up and found himself at the intersection of A1A and Solana Road in Pointe Vedra Beach.

By now the feds would have seized every piece of data they had collected and were likely sifting through it behind their desks at that very moment. He regretted not doing as the chairman had ordered and warned the other GWOAN members. Each would trickle into the OSB building that morning and be intercepted by agents who would escort them to private rooms for interrogation.

He convinced himself that there was no real crime to investigate. Just a bunch of political hacks doing everything in their power and using the force of the government to press their own agenda. The majority of the general public would still support their efforts because they had an unwavering belief that what they were being told was the undisputed gospel. No, this was serious business and a worldwide danger. Their project was vital to the future of humankind; it would be disastrous if their efforts were thwarted. The implications were devastating. If he was to prove himself valuable to the party and the movement, he could not shirk and hide. Rollins would stand strong and fight as any professional politician would and emerge unscathed. He turned left on Solana Road and aimed the SUV toward Interstate 95. At that point, there was nothing to lose.

The sun had not yet risen. A cool mist hung above the lagoon waters, but there was enough light to navigate. Mcilwain had ridden with Roper in the boat they rented while Taylor had steered the pontoon boat. Colson sat on the deck next to Parker who lay across the cool vinyl seats in front. Colson talked to Parker constantly to keep him conscious. Parker made little sense and was quite ill. Colson could only guess exposure was the reason the scientist was feverish and delusional. He didn't appear malnourished but was probably dehydrated. Colson fed him small sips from a water bottle until the two boats eased into their slots at the fish camp.

Colson had called Lieutenant Cantrell thirty minutes earlier, and he was standing on the dock in a dress shirt and tie with his hands on his hips when they climbed out of the boats. The blue strobes in Cantrell's unmarked car and the light bars of the two marked units illuminated the mist before they could even see the shape of the dock ahead. The distant *thump-*

thump of helicopter rotors grew with intensity as they docked. Two paramedics rushed down the length of the doc rolling a gurney with a bright-orange first aid kit strapped on top.

The paramedics climbed aboard the pontoon boat and hovered over Parker, taking blood pressure readings and shining a penlight in his eye. Colson backed off and stepped onto the dock with Cantrell.

"So this is Grant Parker," said Cantrell.

Colson nodded. "The very same."

"Well, he's in custody now. I'm putting two deputies on him until he's released from the hospital. One will be on the life flight with him and the other will chase the chopper to the emergency room."

Colson shrugged. "Good. At least two deputies and they need to be sharp because this isn't over yet. Not by a long shot."

"What's wrong with him anyway?" Cantrell asked.

"I guess three weeks in a jungle tree house will take its toll on a body."

"A tree house? How the hell did you find him?"

"Once a detective, always a detective."

Lieutenant Cantrell looked Colson over and knew it didn't take a detective to notice his bloodstained BDUs. "Looks like you got shot. What else happened out there?"

"Actually," corrected Colson, "shot once and grazed once."

"So do you now feel a little differently about Parker being innocent?"

"Oh, no. Parker didn't shoot me."

"All right, Colson. You need to start telling me what went on out there or—"

"Momma Ball... Momma Ball," Roper yelled while jumping off the boat and running toward the bait shop. He jerked open the screen door, making it slap against the plank siding as he disappeared inside. Mcilwain jogged in behind him.

"What's that all about?" Cantrell asked.

"I almost forgot about her," Colson said and fell in behind Mcilwain.

Cantrell held out his hands in bewilderment. "About who?"

They caught up with Roper in the room behind the counter. One wall was lined with shallow tanks of small feeder fish above shelves of white five-gallon buckets of dark soil. The scent of moss, dirt, and worms was twice as pungent in back as it was in the main shop. A room-size cooler stood in the back right corner of the room. Roper stood facing the door in silence. When the scuffing of their feet against the wood plank floor fell silent, Colson heard muffled shouts coming from within the cooler.

"Open the door," said Colson to Roper's back.

"I can't," Roper replied, stepping aside. The door latch was closed with one side of a pair of handcuffs locked through the hole where a padlock would normally be.

"I have a cuff key with my car keys," said Cantrell and turned to run back out.

"No," said Colson. "This will be quicker."

Colson snatched the Shrike from the sheath and stuck the talon end through the cuff opening. He quickly turned the handle in a circular motion like moving the hands of a clock from the twelve o'clock position all the way around until the cuff broke in two pieces and clacked to the floor. He snatched the door open to see a shivering Momma Ball and... Agent Strickland.

"Myra?" said Mcilwain.

Momma Ball skipped out of the door rubbing her shoulders followed by Strickland. Roper ran back out front and returned with two jackets with sales tags dangling from their sleeves. He draped them over the women.

Colson said, "I'm surprised you two are alive after being in there all night."

"It's just a cooler," said Momma Ball. "We keep it at fifty degrees but it still almost froze my ass off."

Mcilwain faced Strickland and put his hands on her shoulders. "Look at me, Myra. Why are you here?"

"Working," she said. "Doing what I'm told. You used to do the same."

Mcilwain dropped his hands and stepped back. "Does doing what you're told include tampering with evidence?" he said, his frustration clearly building with each question. "Does it mean hindering an investigation or deliberately stranding an American citizen in a hostile country?"

Strickland shook her head, "You're wrong, Mike. I never—"

"Don't insult me, Myra. Would you like to see the store surveillance video of you purchasing a duplicate blank flask drive and dropping it in evidence? Do you think I'm an idiot?" Mcilwain shouted. "We were supposed to be partners. I caught hell from Danz, and you stood by while he caused irreparable damage to my career. And then I find out you were in bed with him the entire time."

Strickland dropped her eyes to the ground without responding. Mcilwain's expression changed from one of anger to complete betrayal. "You mean, *literally,* Myra?"

Colson put his hand on Mcilwain's back as a silent message of support and to break into the heated conversation. He said, "I know what Danz was doing. Now people far more powerful and influential than us will know."

"It's not Danz," Strickland snapped. "He's a scientist, not a politician. He was originally in charge of the research, but he's nothing but a political puppet. He's been manipulated from the beginning."

"You're just covering for your lover," Mcilwain snapped back.

"Fine," said Colson. "Then who is responsible?"

Strickland glared silently at Colson for a long moment, still shivering beneath her jacket. Finally, she muttered, "Max Rollins. He's a snake and would set up his own mother if it meant gaining political capital."

Colson turned to Mcilwain. "Who the hell is Max Rollins?"

Chapter Nineteen

Max Rollins barged into the director's office at 8:15 a.m. and stood across from Danz who was typing on his computer. Rollins stood with his chest heaving as he caught his breath. He had fast walked through the lobby, past the elevators, up the stairwell, down the hall and through the office door without a glance at the office assistant.

"So who was it?" Rollins said in between breaths. "FBI, CIA, or the State Department? Did they question you? What did they take? Did they search the research lab?"

Danz continued typing without acknowledging Rollins's presence. He spun around, lifted a computer tablet, and began comparing information on it with information on his large desk monitor.

"Well?" Rollins demanded.

Danz offered Rollins a peek over his eyeglasses. "It's Tuesday and I'm busy. So if you don't mind," he said, nodding at the door. "Please excuse me."

"You're busy?" Rollins mocked. "The feds swarm down on NASA like a bunch of yellow jackets and you sit there and say you're busy like nothing's happened. What kind of fool are you?"

Danz placed his tablet on the desk in front of him. He leaned back in his chair and clasped his hands in his lap. "Listen, Rollins, because I'm only going to say this once. I'm a scientist and have been ever since I attained my doctorate. I admit I cooperated with the project because I believe in the science, whether or not it has to be tweaked at times to advance a worthwhile effort. But the dirty truth of the matter is that no matter what *I* believe, my hand was forced by you and people like you. The politicians hold the purse strings, and I don't want to waste my knowledge and career sending emissaries to the Muslim community to kiss their ass and tell them how much they contributed to the space program... which is zilch. Now, I plan to carry on with my career and rebuild this space program, but in your case... well, I have no idea what you're going to do, and I literally couldn't care less, you back-stabbing bastard."

Rollins stood dumbfounded for a long moment as he processed Danz's diatribe in his head. Then a smirk crossed his face. "No, no, no. That dog ain't gonna hunt, Danz. You're in this as much as anyone—actually more. If I go down, I'm dragging your ass with me."

Danz smiled. "Too late for that, Max. Maybe if you had stayed and cooperated like a good little politician instead of running off like a Chihuahua being chased by an alligator, you would have had a chance."

"What are you talking about?"

"I can't talk about anything specific because I'm under orders not to. I'm scheduled to testify before Congress on Thursday. You can catch it on CSPAN if you like."

Rollins's flipped Danz off and then stormed out the door.

Colson parked in the lot in front of the Operation Support Building. Movement caught his eye at the end of the row of cars in the back of the lot. He decided to sit for a moment and watch. People carried themselves in a unique fashion depending on their careers and lifestyles. It was no slight against anyone, just a reality. An executive would be dressed in an expensive suit, walking with his nose in the air and carrying an expensive briefcase. A scientist would probably be wearing a white smock over his suit and tie and wearing thick eyeglasses from years of study. The guys Colson noticed were wearing suits, dark sunglasses, and black dress shoes. They were gathered at the rear of three identical black Dodge Chargers like a coach meeting with his pitcher and catcher on the mound. Three cardboard boxes rested at their feet. They acted jovial but appeared somewhat weary as they loaded the boxes in their respective trunks and high-fived each other before sliding into their driver's seats.

They were not executives who had just been laid off due to the continuous gutting of the space program budget. They were too celebratory to be going home to tell their wives and children they were going to live off of unemployment checks. They were government agents without question. Taylor had told him he had passed the data to Senator Greathouse, but would he have acted *that* quickly? That would have to be a record if so. The three Chargers drove past him and out of the parking lot as he stepped out to watch them leave. Yep, government license plates.

Colson walked through the lobby and rode the elevator to the top floor. He pushed open the door to Director Danz's waiting room and maintained his stride past his assistant's desk and into the inner office.

"Sir," she insisted. "You can't go in—" The assistant's warning was cut short as the door clicked shut. Danz look over his glasses at Colson, who stood motionless just inside the door.

"Should I call security?" asked Danz in an even tone.

"No," said Colson. "I'm here for Max Rollins, not you."

"You just missed him."

"Where did he go?"

Danz shrugged and pressed a button on his phone. "His office I presume. I'll have you escorted there."

Danz's cooperation was coming too easily. Colson slipped his hand down his deep BDU pocket and got a good grip on his ASP. Danz stood from his chair, walked to the glass wall overlooking the expansive NASA complex, and turned his back to Colson.

He said, "You know, there was a day when NASA was the envy of the world. The most exciting and monumental events of mankind started right out there on those launchpads. It was my lifelong dream to be a part of it."

"Well," Colson said, "it looks like you got your wish."

Danz spun on his feet. "Everything looks better on the outside. It's not until you get inside that you see the politics involved and the ugly underbelly of an organization."

"Welcome to the real world, Director Danz."

Danz nodded slowly and took his seat back at his desk. A brief knock came at the door behind Colson, and a security officer stepped in and eyed Colson. He came to lazy attention and directed his attention to Danz.

"You needed me, Director?"

"Yes. Show Mr. Colson to Max Rollins's office, please."

"Just one question, Danz," said Colson. "Did you not realize that what you were doing here was wrong and that it undermines the people's trust of the scientific community, not to mention our very government, but that's not much of a stretch?"

"Absolutely," Danz replied. "But then again, what choice did I have?"

"The choice to do the right thing. It's always a choice."

Danz shrugged. Colson couldn't fathom Danz being so nonchalant about his deception of billions of people across the world. He said, "Hell, no wonder you guys never made it to Mars."

The security officer opened the door for Colson and took the lead out to the elevators. They rode to the lower level and stepped into a clean white reception area without a desk or receptionist.

"I thought you guys were finished and gone," the officer said over his shoulder.

"Finished?" Colson said. "I haven't even started yet."

They arrived in front of a black office door. The security officer knocked and tried the door lever.

"It's locked," he said.

"Open it," said Colson.

The officer pulled a ring of keys from his belt, fumbled for a particular key, and then opened the door. He stood aside as Colson entered and shut the door behind him. The medium-size office was vacant and disheveled. It was obvious a search warrant had been executed without regard for how the office was left. He walked to Rollins's desk. The computer was dark. Colson pushed the mouse around until it came to life.

Colson wasn't sure what he was seeing at first. It looked like a Google Earth view, but the longer he stared, he noticed something very different: a shadow crossing the ground and then a puffy cloud moving from the top to the bottom of the screen. He played with the zoom. It was of a tropical, marshy area, and he was able to move the view in all directions. It had to be real-time satellite imagery.

He jerked open the desk drawers. The contents appeared to have been rifled through with nothing but paper clips, pens, staples, and a few hanging folders left behind. He flipped through the folders and located one with several sheets of paper. They were still images printed from the satellite feed. Apparently, the feds had seen no value in the photos and left them alone. One zoomed-in image was of the same tropical landscape but late in the day. It was an island with two white boats visible on one side and a single white boat docked on the opposite shore. Gaines Island.

Colson quickly shuffled through the remaining photos. One of which appeared to be a cheap hotel with cars of various colors lining the side of the building, but the next was very familiar, even though taken from orbit. The surrounding landmarks made it unmistakable. The photo was zoomed in on the Sundowner Condos and the next was of Parker's complex with its "X" building pattern and connecting parking garage. The next was clearly a photo of his blue 'Vette battling the gangbanger's Honda after leaving the fish camp. The last photo held Colson's attention for a longer period of time, mostly because it was the most disturbing and caused his blood pressure to skyrocket: a photo of an intersection adjacent to the beach. It was A1A at Dunlawton Avenue, but that's not what made Colson's blood boil. It was a single moment in time captured a millisecond before the black tractor struck Rob Bankston. His Daytona Blue Corvette plainly stood out just ahead of impending obliteration of the Tahoe.

Colson snatched up the photo and barged out of the office door at a fast pace, leaving the security officer standing in the hallway with keys in hand. He stopped at the main desk where a young woman sat wearing a telephone headset.

"Did Max Rollins come through here?" he asked.

The woman nodded. "He just walked out to the parking lot," she said.

"What's he look like?"

"White guy. Mid to late forties. White untucked shirt and dark pants. Hair thinning on top. A little pudgy."

"Thanks," said Colson. He turned and jogged out then stopped under the entrance overhang. There was only one person fitting that description walking down a line of parked cars. It was the same man who was fidgeting behind him in Dan's office and at the elevator during his first visit to NASA. Colson jogged after him and called out, "Rollins."

Rollins glanced over his shoulder and slowed his pace. As Colson got closer, an expression of recognition crossed Rollins's face, and he bolted toward an SUV and jumped in. Colson sprinted toward the SUV but came to an abrupt halt when the front tires barked, pushing the front wheel drive in reverse. The SUV stopped within six inches of Colson's chest and jerked forward. Colson already had a firm grip on his ASP and extended it with an upward snap. He swung at the back window and obliterated it into a thousand pieces before Rollins could speed away.

Colson ran to the parked Challenger and was behind the wheel just as Rollins turned onto the roundabout and sped toward the parking-lot exit. Colson stomped the gas, fishtailed out of the roundabout, and was on the bumper of Rollins's SUV in seconds. He could see the shocked eyes of Rollins in the rearview mirror. Colson jerked the Challenger to the left and forced Rollins to turn right onto Saturn Causeway, keeping him inside the sprawling complex. But he still had not gotten used to the heavier weight of the Challenger and slid sideways as Rollins sped away.

Director Danz paced in his office before his attention was drawn to the window by the squealing of tires down at the parking entrance. Rollins's SUV was speeding east on Saturn Causeway and a bulky, black Challenger was after him. It seemed that Colson had found who he was looking for. A smile crept across Danz's face. He had been nervously preparing his responses to the barrage of questions he would be peppered with at the congressional hearing, expecting the absolute worst scenario.

Yes, he would tell the truth and yes his reputation would be tarnished, but the public had a very short memory, and he would be totally forgotten in a week when the next scandal hit the news. He had never been in the public eye before and would never be again after this setback. He was not running for office, and his cooperation would result in him maintaining a position at NASA. It wasn't as if he had dreamed up the project; the politicians who would ultimately take the brunt of the damage had thrust it upon him, but they would recover as most politicians do. The majority of the American public were on their side already. The Hollywood types would call it nothing more than a witch-hunt by the radical right, and anyone under fifty years old would agree and dismiss the hearings out of hand, if they even bothered to watch them.

Danz considered calling security, but decided to let the situation play itself out. Colson's and Rollins's vehicles grew smaller and smaller in the distance, and the heat rising from the pavement gave them the appearance of ghostly apparitions slowly disappearing into thin air. He stepped behind his telescope and found them about a mile away. Danz knew every turn and twist of the huge complex, but seriously doubted Rollins did. He had practically never left his office while stuffed behind his computer and pretending to supervise the GWOAN scientists... as if he had a clue about the significance of their research. The road was a dead end no matter which direction they went. He was relieved Colson hadn't blamed him for all his troubles and was curious what he would do when he caught up to Rollins. Like a dog chasing a car, would he know what to do if he caught it? Surely, Colson was not that foolish.

Danz watched Rollins speed on with Colson right on his rear bumper as they passed the observation gantry where friends, family, NASA staff, and VIPs had watched every NASA mission launch from the first Apollo rockets to the last space shuttle flight. If they continued straight, they would arrive at launchpad 39A, and if they swung left on Crawler Way, they would end up at pad 39B. Danz looked ahead where a small security shack sat on the right side of the road at the intersection with a white security vehicle parked alongside. Colson and Rollins blew past the shack and security vehicle, heading straight for pad 39A sitting another mile in the distance. The clunky old Crown Vic jerked out on the road behind them and gave chase as Danz's tablet beeped at him.

Danz turned and grabbed the tablet off his desk. A young man with dark-rimmed glasses gazed at Danz on the screen.

"We might have a problem, Director. There are trespassers in the restricted area."

"I'm aware," said Danz. "I'm observing from my office. There's a security vehicle after them. He'll take care of it. You are to proceed as scheduled."

There was hesitation on the man's face. "Sir, I understand, but—"

"Our time is extremely valuable," Danz said in a sterner tone, "and I am the one who has to explain when we delay our work and bleed tens of thousands of dollars from our already limited budget, not you, so you will proceed as scheduled. Do you copy?"

"Copy," replied the man just before his image vanished from the screen.

Colson was mulling over the situation, not knowing that Danz had pondered the same question: *What do I do with Rollins when I catch him?* Maybe tenderize him with his ASP just enough to ensure he would be sharing a semiprivate room in ICU with Rob Bankston? Or maybe just disable him to some extent and have him arrested for attempted murder? He would be doing neither if he couldn't get his hands on him. And now there was a marked security unit with flashing lights and siren gaining ground in his rearview mirror. The launch gantry just ahead looked like the skeleton of a transformer and was larger than Colson had expected. A tall water tower stood on the east side of the gantry and further in the distance was what appeared to be a huge cylinder laying on its side. Rollins drove erratically as if he couldn't decide what to do or where to go. He was quickly running out of real estate. He veered his SUV off the road and bounced across the uneven grass surface. The SUV lurched nose forward, and the rear raised slightly as if he had hit something, but it continued onward leaving a bent pipe that had been sticking up from the ground.

The security patrol vehicle caught up to Colson when he pulled into the grass and stopped. He shoved the gear in park at the command of the officer who had jumped out and was leveling a pistol in his direction. Colson stepped out and placed his hands on the hood of the Challenger as Rollins continued bouncing the SUV over the field of grass until he came to a long row of similar exhaust-type pipes protruding from the ground. The first pipe he hit must have punctured something vital under the SUV because it was spewing a cloudy mist from its undercarriage. The SUV slowed and came to an abrupt halt as it struck one of the larger pipes. The driver's door flung open, and Rollins jumped out and ran without looking back.

The security officer stopped a dozen feet from Colson, still holding his weapon at high ready. He said, "You can't be here, sir. You have to come with me right now. On your knees and hands behind your back." Colson complied as the microphone on the officers shoulder chirped. He heard the officer answer behind him. He had moved in behind to cuff him, but hesitated when a voice came back over his mic.

"Director says he's code four, but you both need to get out of there now. If he doesn't cooperate, cuff him and bring him back in your unit."

Colson heard the urgency in the radio operator's voice. He said, "I'll follow but what about Rollins? What's going on?"

The officer didn't respond directly but said. "There's no time. Let's go, *now*."

Colson got in the Challenger as the officer jogged back to the Crown Vic. Claxons began blowing loud enough to wake the dead, and a steady siren rose in intensity as if a tornado strike was eminent, but there wasn't a cloud in the sky. The officer led the way back down Crawler Way and then to Saturn Causeway, driving as fast as they had on the way in. Colson knew he would catch up to Rollins later and was somewhat thankful he had been prevented from confronting him in his heated mood. But what was going on that they had to evacuate the area? It felt surreal. Maybe some pissed-off aliens were arriving from another galaxy to attack their competition.

The cylinder ahead of Rollins was half the length of a football field. One end butted up against a concrete bunker, and it was nestled on huge yellow clamps. He dodged a series of large hoses, ten times larger than a fireman's hose, as he ran the length of the cylinder to the far end and around behind it before he bothered to look back. The sound of the siren and horns was deafening. He expected to see Colson running after him, but he wasn't there. He could see his SUV steaming in the field, but the black Challenger was gone. He suspected the security officer who was running a distant third in their car race had caught up to Colson and arrested him. Good job, but why hadn't they canceled the alarm and turned off the damn horns? Rollins tore off his sweat-soaked dress shirt and threw it on the long concrete slab behind the huge cylinder.

Rollins plopped down on his butt in the shade of what he considered nothing more than the world's largest paperweight. He dropped his head in his hands and tried to catch his breath. He cleared his throat and spit, wishing he had a bottle of water. He looked up at the huge round nozzle above his head. It was the size of an aboveground swimming pool.

"What a waste of good money," he scoffed and wiped sweat from his brow. "This place is nothing but a graveyard of old junk they don't even have the money to dispose of."

Rollins stood and decided to abandon his filthy shirt on the concrete. He had a long way to walk, and he needed water. He didn't hold out hope that Danz would send him a ride or they would have already done so when they caught up to Colson. Then he heard a curious noise that sounded like water running through pipes and a low reverberating hum. A pungent aroma of fuel filled the air around him, accompanied by loud ticking. His curiosity lingered for five seconds until horror enveloped his entire being, and his heart jumped into his throat. He was running before his brain had the time to send the flight signal to his legs, but he only covered ten feet. There was one last visual and audio memory that played in his mind before a blinding flash and a millisecond sensation of being thrown into a blast furnace. The memory was of Danz just weeks ago in his office.

They test solid booster rocket engines here, midmorning, every other Tuesday. That particular one is the world's most powerful solid rocket booster in preparation for deep space travel if we can ever recover our budget. You should consider it an honor to watch.

It was Tuesday, and Rollins had watched…up close.

Director Danz watched events unfold though his telescope with amazement. There was nothing he could do, and there was nothing he *had* done. Some may suggest he was negligent, but both Colson and Rollins were grown men and responsible for their own actions. To Colson's credit, he had heeded the warning of the officer and cleared the area.

In a morbid mood many years ago Danz mulled this particular scenario over in his head and wondered what the outcome would be. The solid rocket booster produced 3.6 million pounds of thrust at 22 million horsepower, resulting in a controlled explosion that burned a flame reaching 6,000 degrees Fahrenheit and was over a tenth of a mile in length. Compared to a human body burned in a crematory oven for four hours at an average temperature of 1,650 degrees, well... there really was no comparison. Even a nondirect hit would have vaporized Rollins out of existence faster than Scotty could have beamed him to the bridge of the USS Enterprise. He wondered what thought if any crossed Rollins's mind a millisecond before he turned to run.

Danz's tablet beeped at him from his desk. The same man appeared on the screen.

"Director," he said in an urgent tone. "We're not certain, but the first man may have been injured. We're calling EMS."

"For what?" Danz scoffed. "To bring a dustpan? Did any of you recognize the man?"

"Ah, no sir."

"They were trespassers, then. I'll handle everything from here and make the appropriate notifications. You just finish up your work. We're not going to be plastered all over the nightly news with a convoy of television news and cable trucks swooping down on us. You remind your people of their confidentiality agreements and keep your mouths shut. We'll all be on food stamps and living in the streets if the press finds out about another NASA screw-up."

Colson pushed the Challenger as hard as he could. The initial blast and thunderous roar was the most hellacious experience of his life. The concussion rippled the ground beneath him as if it was no more substantial than a pool of water. The frame of the car hummed and vibrated, and the steering wheel made short jerking motions in his hands. He dared not turn his head to look, but it felt like a Tyrannosaurus rex had caught up to him in a full stomping run directly behind him.

Colson passed the security vehicle and watched him drop behind. The old Crown Vic was being pushed to its limit but losing the race. He seriously doubted the security officer was concerned about where Colson was going. They both only wanted to escape Armageddon alive—likely deaf, but alive.

Colson's ears were ringing as he sped past the OSB building and turned north on Kennedy Parkway. Why had they not aborted the rocket firing? The security officer had been on their tail for over a minute and out at the field. He had been on his radio, so why wasn't a big red button pushed to stop the explosion? It all went back to why Danz had been so forthcoming and cooperative in his office. But why? The words of Agent Strickland played in his mind above the ringing in his ear...

Max Rollins. He's a snake and would set up his own mother if it meant gaining political capital.

"Danz," said Colson. The sound of his own voice sounded like someone was in the back seat, holding both their hands tightly over his ears. "You're a sly bastard, but it's starting to look like Houston's gonna have a big problem on their hands, old buddy."

ᯓChapter Twentyᯓ

The Carlton Shores Health and Rehabilitation Center on Nova Road was exactly two miles north of Giuseppe's Pizza where Robert Bankston first encountered Grey Colson face-to-face. The room was private, and the accommodations were decorated for more of a residential feel as opposed to the sterile environment of a hospital. Robert Bankston was moved to the facility over the weekend, and his body was feeling the first signs of real recovery. The wires clamping his jaw shut would remain for another three weeks, according to the doctor. He had lost thirty-five pounds from sucking down nothing but protein and vitamin shakes through a straw. His physical therapist's name was Brittany. She was a twenty-four-year-old graduate of Old Dominion University and an expectant mother—an extremely lovely girl. Robert looked forward to her daily visits, but not due to any sexual attraction. It was her pleasant demeanor, smile, and genuine concern that brightened his day. He knew her entire family history from their one-sided conversations. All he could do was offer a smile and grunt like a broken and mute old man.

Brittany had walked into Rob's room an hour ago with her expected smile and showed him a photo of her lab-mix, Maggie. She chatted through the entire session of exercising his legs and rotating his ankles. She helped him stand briefly at the foot of the bed and promised to have him walking down the hall by the end of the week. She was making notes of their progress in a notebook when the phone made a gurgling sound on the end table. It hadn't rung before, and he didn't know what it was at first. He figured the strange ring wouldn't disturb patients in adjoining rooms.

Brittany said, "Do you want me to answer?"

Robert tilted his head and shrugged.

Brittany lifted the cordless receiver. "Hello?" She listened for about ten seconds and then said, "It's a man named Grey Colson. He said he knows you can't talk but wants to know if you are watching cable news."

Robert and Brittany both looked up at the small flat television hanging on the far wall. A black-and-white episode of Gilligan's Island was on the screen, and the sound was muted. Robert pointed a finger at the TV and nodded.

"We'll find it," Brittany said into the phone. She grabbed the remote and handed it to Robert. She patted him on the shoulder and said, "See you tomorrow," and gave him a smile on her way out.

Robert surfed through the channels quickly and punched off the mute button. A male and female commentator flashed on the screen. In the middle of the screen was the still photo of Senator Richard Bozich. The commentator was speaking.

"Some have talked about an October surprise, but never expected one in November. This hearing wasn't even scheduled until two days ago when Senator Bozich and a top-ranking NASA official were subpoenaed to appear before Congress. If it is indeed a November surprise, the timing of this hearing may be too late since many states have concluded their early voting process. The White House press secretary and the chairman of the Democrat party held a joint press conference this morning in which the press secretary stated, and I quote. 'This hearing is a circus and a desperate act by the Republicans to smear the president and his commitment to clean energy.' Now let's go to Washington where Senator Greathouse is about to begin."

The camera switched to a setting similar to a courtroom with long rows of polished wood benches, nameplates, and skinny microphones. The scene switched to a different camera angle showing a wide view of the room filled with well-dressed people milling about and settling in their seats. A third camera shot filled the screen as Senator Bozich sat behind a microphone next to a man Bankston didn't recognize. The man leaned close to Senator Bozich, spoke, and then sat back straight with a poker face and placed his hands on the table. The camera finally settled on Senator Greathouse, who was looking down at a thin folder in front of him. Two large binders were stacked to his right. He removed his glasses and laid them on the folder as he began.

"Before my opening statement, I would like to thank the members of the House and Senate and the members of the press corps who are gathered here this afternoon. I would also like to thank Senator Richard Bozich for attending on such short notice. I'm certain you are curious as to the nature of this hearing, as are the great citizens of our nation."

Greathouse slipped his reading glasses over his nose and referred to the documents in front of him. "As some may know, but many do not, it was in 1895 when the American people were told by their government that the earth faced an inevitable ice age. It was termed, 'Global Cooling.' They were told that there was a consensus among the scientific community that a trend of cooler temperatures had been recorded across the globe, and it would only be decades before glaciers crept southward and the entire earth became a frozen tundra.

"Years later in 1918, when the climate conditions didn't demonstrate the predicted results, the title of the crisis was changed to 'Global Warming.' People were told it was settled science and it was mankind's fault for spewing carbon emission into the atmosphere, causing a greenhouse effect that would ultimately result in worldwide famine and desolation and death. One recent example of global alarmism was declared in the late 1990s when we were warned that by the year 2020, my state of Florida would be at the ocean floor. Just for the record, I live on the coast, and it hasn't moved during the past eight years I've been there."

A low chuckled rose from the crowd. The camera caught Senator Bozich sitting stoic and apparently bored. Senator Greathouse flipped the page and continued.

"And yet again, the accumulation of data over the following decades didn't demonstrate any accuracy in the forecast of a perpetually warming planet, so the crisis required a new title. ' Climate Change.' It was the safest term to use since there was no way to accurately predict what would happen decades in the future. And now anytime we experience a hurricane, snowstorm, Midwest drought, or forest fire it is attributed to climate change, even though the same activity has been occurring for hundreds of thousands of years. Now it has evolved to the point where climate change is credited for terrorism and unrest the world over.

"So according to climate change advocates, what is the answer? They say we need more and more federal regulations on the fossil fuel and auto industries to reduce carbon emissions. We subsidize the farming industry to grow more corn for ethanol, which results in farmers restricting the growth of wheat and other vital food products. The government subsidizes the production of electric vehicles that the majority of citizens do not want and cannot afford. Not to mention how impractical it is to purchase a vehicle with a limited range of fifty miles. The government subsidizes windmills and solar power companies such as Solaris and Green Gate Solutions that are now bankrupt due to high costs and lack of demand, again costing the taxpayers billions of dollars. The government demands higher and higher taxes on companies that produce CO_2 emissions and greenhouse gases, resulting in significant downsizing and costing American jobs. The government enters into what are called 'environmental agreements' with other nations. These agreements are in fact treaties and require congressional approval, but this administration has circumvented congressional approval and has unilaterally entered into these agreements unlawfully. And the administration knows the nations involved in these treaties have no regard for climate change and will flat out ignore their obligations. This administration has literally decimated the clean coal industry, resulting in thousands of workers joining the ranks of the unemployed. Senator Bozich," he said, looking up from his stack of papers, "I suspect you are aware by now that a team of federal agents raided the Earth and Science Division at NASA just days ago?"

A collective gasp spread across the crowd of politicians and press corps. An orchestra of camera clicks and flashes lit the entire chamber like strobe lights in a nightclub. A close-up of Senator Bozich filled the screen. His expression had not changed. He stared at Greathouse as if studying a child's painting: not impressed, not amused, and nonresponsive. Senator Greathouse waited for a beat and said, "Senator Bozich?"

"Is that a statement or a question?" Bozich asked.

"It was a question, Senator."

Bozich leaned to his right as the man seated next to him whispered in his ear. He nodded and leaned into the microphone. "At the advice of counsel, I decline to answer due to—"

"Ah, come on, Senator," Greathouse interrupted. "You being aware of a law enforcement activity is in no way incriminating. You being the appointed chairman of the House Select Committee on Energy Independence and Climate Change should have great interest in what is happening at NASA, the literal clearinghouse of global weather data related to climate change." Greathouse placed his hand on top of the two binders stacked to his right, "And you should also be greatly concerned about the data in these two binders. Well, Senator Bozich?"

"At the advice of counsel, I respectfully decline to answer."

Senator Greathouse sat silently staring down Senator Bozich as the low mumblings in the chamber began to grow in intensity. Three loud slaps of a gavel rang out from the opposite side of the chamber.

"Order. Order please," instructed the Senate president.

Greathouse slid the top binder in front of him and opened the cover. "Senator Bozich," he began. "It is clear that you are not willing to answer questions and that is your prerogative, but this is a serious matter, and we *are* going forward with this hearing, so you may respectfully sit and listen." Greathouse pointed down to the top page in the binder. "This is only the latest example of what was discovered by the agents. At this moment, over eighteen months of data has been collected and much more is expected in the coming days as this investigation continues." Greathouse lifted his finger and pointed in Bozich's direction. "This program is supervised and directed by the committee *you* chair and have oversight of at a cost to the taxpayers of over a hundred million dollars per year on this project alone."

Senator Bozich did not move or appear to blink as Senator Greathouse continued. "The data in this binder is what has been submitted for review and publication. It is the data this administration has used to instill fear in the entire population to support the president's position at the next climate change summit. It is entirely fabricated and a fraud. But *this* data," Greathouse said, placing his hand on the second binder, "is the *actual* data collected, and it reveals entirely different numbers as collected by ground temperature measurements, ocean temperature readings, and satellite imagery. I have reviewed previous quarterly submissions of data with the exact same results. Do you have nothing to say about this, Senator Bozich?"

Bozich leaned over to his attorney who shook his head but said nothing. Bozich leaned forward. "At the advice—"

"Please, sir," barked Greathouse. "Spare me the theatrics." He looked the room over and released a loud sigh. He gently closed the binder in front of him. "My friends, colleagues from both sides of the isle, and fellow citizens, the revelation of Climategate was widely ignored and dismissed in 2009 by climate change proponents when it was discovered that information was being fabricated by scientists in the United Kingdom to support the notion of man-made climate change, but this cannot and *will not* be ignored. It is criminal fraud that is being perpetrated, not only on the citizens of the United States, but the entire world population. It's a monster with its tentacles spread in multiple directions, and it was spawned by the United Nations. One such tentacle are subsidies dumped into green energy companies that are subsequently distributed to politicians who support and propagate the environmental movement, making it the largest money laundering operation known to mankind. Another tentacle is the growing carbon taxes leveled on American industry for the purpose of redistribution to other nations in order to level the worldwide playing field and diminish the United States standing in the world. And yet another tentacle is power. It has been said that controlling carbon is a bureaucrat's dream because when you control carbon, you control life, with the ultimate goal of global governance. In short, the manufactured hoax of man-made climate change is nothing but the communist movement by a politically correct name. The green environmental movement."

"Point of order," shouted a senator down the length of the table. "This is ridiculous. Will the honorable senator from Florida kindly yield sixty seconds for response and—"

"I will not yield my time, Senator," snapped Greathouse.

He turned his attention directly back to Senator Bozich. "Thank you once again for your cooperation, Senator. Your responses... or should I say lack of *any* response, is precisely what I expected. Your silence clearly demonstrates your complicity, but there's one more item I would like for you and millions across the nation to know before we call Director Nicholas Danz to testify. And I assure you *he* will not be pleading the fifth."

Senator Bozich began to squirm and adjusted his suit jacket when the camera turned to him, revealing the first signs of anxiety. An easel sat in the middle of the chamber holding a whiteboard. At Greathouse's nod, a young man stepped up and turned the whiteboard over, revealing a photo of a warehouse with black semi tractors parked side by side at an angle.

Greathouse walked to the easel and stood off to one side. He touched the top corner of the large photo and said, "This is a warehouse on Contractor Road within the NASA complex, and these Peterbuilt tractors were previously used to haul rocket fuel for liquid propellant engines and gasoline for routine vehicle and generator use at the facility. In addition, their original color was white with the proud NASA emblem plastered on both door panels. These vehicles represent one-third of Kennedy Space Center's available fleet, and they have been retasked over the past several years to transport something other than rocket fuel or gasoline, and they have been painted black with no identifying marks or emblems. These vehicles, which have been counted at over a hundred, have been transporting a mixture of nitromethane and propylene to fifty oil refineries across the United States."

The chamber again began to stir with low murmurings. Bankston watched with expectation but did not understand the relevance. He knew nothing about nitromethane or propylene, and suspected those attending the hearing didn't either. The murmurings trailed off as Senator Greathouse paced back and forth with his head lowered as if rehearsing what he would say next. At one point, he stopped and raised his head. The camera zoomed in on him and the large photo.

"Some of you might find what I'm about to say absurd, and I wish it were. First of all, there is no scientific proof of man-made climate change. And a consensus of scientific opinion *does not* create a fact of science. We know that gravity if a scientific fact, not because there was a vote among scientists, but because it can be demonstrated. The climate has changed from one extreme to the other since creation, even at times when there were no oil refineries, car exhaust, aerosol cans, or even humans walking the earth. Man-made climate change is based on computer models alone, and these models are only as accurate as those who input the data and later interpret it for public consumption. And they have been wrong time after time after time. Meteorologists can't even predict the weather accurately for a week, let alone decades or centuries in the future. The climate change alarmists are not concerned about their far-flung predictions being debunked because most will be long dead and unable to be held accountable when these supposed catastrophes are scheduled to occur. And in order to continue the propagation of their hoax long after their deaths, they have indoctrinated our children and grandchildren in the public school systems across our nation and on the weekends with animated shows such as *Captain Planet and the Planeteers* and *Bill Nye the Science Guy*. Just as the theory of evolution remains a theory, our school curriculums are written to teach the theory of evolution and the theory of man-made climate change as undisputed facts. The truly disturbing part is that most of those involved in the climate change hoax will never give up their agenda or admit their error. There is simply too much campaign money and power involved. They wouldn't admit the fraud of climate change if God himself were to descend from heaven and dispute it."

Senator Greathouse took a step toward the witness bench and looked directly into Senator Bozich's eyes as he spoke. "And then there are some who are so invested in the climate change hoax that they will deliberately try to artificially alter the environment for their own ambition of power and global influence. When the data continually failed to support their predications, they literally embarked on a crusade to create the very conditions they had predicted; the environment be damned. For lack of a better description, they have been spiking the nation's oil refineries with millions of gallons of super methane in hopes that given sufficient time, they could artificially create the very destructive conditions they have been predicting and warning the world about." Greathouse raised his arm and pointed in Bozich's face. "You, sir, are a disgrace and an enemy to mankind. It's not a rogue NASA scientist who should be tried for treason…it is *you*. I have already called on Governor Bagwell to appoint a special prosecutor to hold you personally accountable when he takes office."

The chamber erupted. The camera panned back to a wide shot. Lawmakers jumped to their feet and began shouting in the direction of Senator Bozich and at each other, with many waving their arms and pointing fingers. The loud claps of a gavel had no effect and only added to the rising volume. The camera zoomed back on Senator Bozich. The smirk he previously wore had vanished. A set of double doors flung open and four uniformed capital police officers shoved through the crowd, surrounded Bozich, and escorted him down the aisle amid catcalls and a swarm of reporters shouting questions.

Bankston found himself sitting straight up in bed. He held his hand up to his aching jaw and realized he had been smiling so hard that it hurt.

Colson stepped out of the post office in a good mood. The weatherman predicted an afternoon high of seventy-seven degrees, but the fall morning was bright and crisp. He had grown accustomed to the changing seasons in Daytona. Had he been vacationing, Colson would have been disappointed with the cooler temperatures. But this was home now, and he had no problem with the temperature change and the tourist population going away for the rest of the year. There were still a few die-hard snowbirds from Canada who stayed through the winter, but they were typically an older crowd who parked their Cadillacs and Mercedes at their vacation condos, only to come out of hibernation to shop or eat.

Colson paused to look over his Corvette, its Daytona Blue paint gleaming in the morning sun. He circled it to inspect the repairs. They were only cosmetic, and the boys at the body shop had done an excellent job matching the paint. He slipped in and lowered the windows as he pulled out on

A1A and headed north to Thames Avenue then swung into the RJ Longstreet Elementary School. A long line of people stood in a staggered line on the gymnasium floor of blue-and-lime-green spongy tiles, waiting their turn to vote in one of the booths lined along the walls. The line was longer than he'd expected, but Colson patiently moved with the progressing line for the next half hour until he was handed a voting card and stepped into one of the vacated booths.

Colson's final stop was the Florida Hospital Oceanside. He hadn't been to a hospital so frequently in his lifetime. He rode the elevator one floor and walked down a long hall to room 240. The door was slightly ajar, and he heard female voices from inside. A nurse stepped from the room just as he reached out to push the door open. She offered him a quick smile and brushed past him, leaving the door standing open. Lisa Riley turned as he stepped inside. She wore a concerned look, but smiled and stepped to the foot of the bed. The head of the bed was raised, and Grant Parker was eating a bland plate of hospital food.

"Grey," Lisa said. "Thank you for coming."

Grant sat his fork on his tray and gave Colson a look. He said, "Is this..." Lisa sat a hand on his arm and said, "Yes. This is Grey Colson."

Grant nodded. "Thanks, Mr. Colson. How in Heaven's name did you find me?"

"Just call me Grey or Colson. Mister makes me feel old. But to answer your question, I just followed the bread crumbs."

"Bread crumbs?"

"I'll explain when you feel better. How are you doing?"

"He contracted Lyme disease," Lisa said. "The doctor said he removed several blacklegged ticks from his body."

"Ticks?" said Colson. "You spend weeks in Mosquito Lagoon and it's not mosquitoes that get you, but ticks? Maybe they should change the name. Is he going to be all right?"

"They think so, but he'll be on antibiotics for several weeks."

The same nurse hustled back in the room and scurried back out with the food tray. Grant adjusted a control on the side of the bed and raised it higher. He pinched the bridge of his nose and yawned. "It's so crazy. I see images that don't make sense. It's like a strange dream. The sounds of shooting and shouting and the feeling of falling and floating."

"It makes more sense than you might realize, Grant," said Colson. He looked around the room and said, "Where are your babysitters?"

"The deputies?" said Lisa. "Oh, Lieutenant Cantrell came in last night and told them to be ten-eight, or something like that. He shook Grant's hand before he left and told him he was proud of him. I'm still trying to figure out what this is all about."

"There's my handsome man," came a voice from behind Colson. He turned to see Beverly standing in the doorway holding a container with three large Styrofoam cups. Her hair was perfectly cut with streaks of dirty blond highlights. She wore dark slacks and a blue-and-black blouse around her perfectly shaped figure. Colson walked to her and took the tray without a word. He held it to his side while wrapping his left arm around her waist. Her smile was wide and her bright green eyes were devastatingly gorgeous. Colson gave her a long kiss while squeezing her close.

"You brought coffee," he whispered. Beverly nodded and returned his whisper, "Of course. Cream... no sugar."

"Ah, Colson," said Grant from his bed. "Can I ask you something?"

"Sure. Shoot."

"I know I was sick and hallucinating some, but..."

"What is it, Grant?"

"Well, just my dream. There was an image of me shooting a crossbow and then you throwing a tomahawk at some guy. I thought I was in a cowboys and Indians movie."

Colson chuckled. "A tomahawk? Man, you really were out of it weren't you?"

ᑫᕼᑊᑊᕼChapter Twenty-One

ichael Mcilwain loaded the last box in the rear of the rental truck and pulled down the rolling door until the locking handle clicked in place. The light tap of a car horn drew his attention to a red Mustang parking in an adjacent parking spot. Myra Strickland stepped out. She was wearing jeans and a dark shirt under a light windbreaker. She walked up and stood silent for a long moment while eyeing him.

"I just wanted to apologize," she finally said.

Mcilwain shrugged and said, "It's OK."

"No, it's not, but I'm still sorry." Strickland stepped to the side of the truck and appeared to be reading the rental companies name on the side. She said, "What are you doing?"

"Leaving for Atlanta," Mcilwain answered.

"But I thought you'd be exonerated and reinstated at the Orlando office."

"Nope. Still on suspension and still being transferred. How did you make out with OPS?"

"Me?" Strickland said with a short laugh. "I'm lucky. They let me resign in lieu of prosecution. You know better than I do that tampering with evidence is a crime. Why didn't you report me when you found out?"

Mcilwain shrugged a second time. "We had been removed from the case by then, and I considered you a friend. You were my partner, and I hoped I was wrong and that there was another explanation."

"But you knew there wasn't, didn't you?" Strickland asked.

Mcilwain nodded and stuck out his hand. "I wish you the best."

Strickland took his hand and offered a conciliatory grin. "I still don't understand why you're still on suspension and being transferred."

"You already said it. I knew better and did nothing."

Beverly road with Colson to the Sundowner Condos. Even in November, it smelled of suntan oil and salty air. He kissed her again once they entered unit 510, and they made their way to the balcony after he dropped her suitcase in his room. A few cars and trucks moved slowly along the shore, and a handful of sun worshipers braved the mid-seventy-degree temperature to maintain their late-summer tans. Colson rocked his chair made of PVC pipe against the back wall and rested his feet high on the rail.

Beverly sipped her remaining coffee and crossed her legs, looking out over the Atlantic. She said, "Some on the news are saying that Grant Parker is a patriot, but there are just as many others who are still saying he is a traitor."

Colson nodded. "I guess it depends on which side of the political isle you sit on. Exposing the truth can sometimes be as dangerous as supporting a lie. I'm sure Parker is relieved. I believe knowing the truth was eating him from inside like a cancer."

"Why? Maybe he was just politically motivated."

"No," Colson said, shaking his head. "It must have been bothering him even before he met Bankston. He knew there was something deceitful happening early in his assignment and must not have known there was anything he could do about it. All of his education and talent was being used to promote a lie. It was his door code that told me, and it reminded him every time he came home."

"His door code?"

"Three-seven-two-eight-three. It has no significance to his birthday or social security number or anything else I could find, but on a phone keypad, the only word that combination spells is F-R-A-U-D."

"Obviously, there's something to what Greathouse is claiming since the president announced he would delay his participation in the climate change summit until the congressional investigation has concluded."

"*If*," Colson said with emphasis, "he is still the president in January. He's in damage control mode and denying any involvement. The leader of the free world actually said the first he heard of the NASA scam was on the evening news. The worst part is there are people who believe him. There is a big move for impeachment if the election goes in his favor tonight, but I still have faith that most sane voters don't appreciate being played the fool."

Beverly pulled her windbreaker tight after a sudden blast of cool wind blew in from the shore. She said, "I guess I've been so busy I never gave the subject much thought. I take it you are convinced now that what they're accusing NASA of is true." She gave Colson a look. "Did you believe in climate change before all of this came out?"

"Sure I did. It happens at four times a year around here, but I was convinced that the *man-made* climate change agenda was a hoax before the proof even came out," Colson said.

"Is that right? And how did my distinguished detective draw that conclusion?"

Colson waved down toward the beach. Pastor Tommy had climbed the stairs at the seawall with a book in his hand. He was not carrying his canopy or a folding chair. Colson guessed he must have just gone for an afternoon walk. He shielded his eyes from the afternoon sun and gave Colson a wave in return before making his way across the parking lot.

"He convinced me," said Colson, nodding in Pastor Tommy's direction. "We had a long talk."

"About climate change?" Beverly asked.

"Bigger than that. We talked about God."

"What do you mean?"

"He asked me if I had made plans before I left for Ecuador."

"What did that have to do with anything?"

"I told him that I did have a plan. More than one if needed. He then asked if I believed in God."

"I know you do."

"Right. And that's what I told him. He slapped a sand flee on his arm and asked me if there was anything a flea that small could have done to prevent me from getting Taylor out of Ecuador. Of course I told him no. He then asked a rhetorical question. How arrogant is man, who on the scale of the universe is far more powerless than a sand flea, to believe he can alter the plan of an almighty and all-powerful God. He said the earth is a gift, and we should be good stewards of it, but we could no more destroy the earth than that sand flea could have altered my travel plans. He said that true belief in an almighty and Holy God rejects chaos. On the other hand, nonbelief embraces a world governed by uncertainty and chaos. God created the earth and the universe in his own time and nothing will destroy it before he decides it's time to do so."

"I never considered it that way."

"It's a deep subject to consider, but enough about that. You're here now and that's all that matters. We can talk about the world ending all day, but I don't want to waste our time with that. Can I get you another cup of coffee?"

"I'll grab it. I have to visit the ladies room."

Colson grinned and relaxed. In the far distance offshore, the sky was turning dark where the ocean met the sky. There was probably a cold front approaching, and it would eventually merge with the moderately warm high pressure hovering above. It would creep westward as normal and dowse the shoreline with a cold rain before moving inland. The beach season would be officially over as the average temperatures would slowly drifted downward. Colson dreaded the winter, even in Daytona. Three to four months of being taunted by the sand and surf and not being able to lavish in the warmth of the Florida sun. He would miss the scent of suntan lotion and the sound of the ice-cream man playing his annoying "Twinkle, Twinkle Little Star" and the crowded beach roadway with country music, rock music, and pop music flowing from open car windows. The volleyball players, Frisbee throwers, and sandcastle builders would not emerge until spring break, and the sound of karaoke singers would not be heard from the tourist poolside parties on Wednesday afternoons. If only Beverly could stay.

She stuck her head around the doorframe and said, "Quick question for you, Major Colson."

"Anything."

"Do you really think Grant Parker was hallucinating when you found him?"

"Well, you heard all the crazy things he said."

"Uh, huh," she said looking over her sunglasses. She extended her arm out the door holding the Shrike. "I just happened to notice this little toy standing in the corner of the linen closet."

Colson looked at the tomahawk for a long moment and sighed. "I'm *so* busted."

ᑕᔕ Epilogue ᕼᕽ

C olonel Guerra stepped onto his office balcony
and lit a cigar. Small cars and people on
bicycles and scooters passed by on the street
at the foot of the prison wall below, dangerously weaving
around each other on their way to unknown destinations. He
took a long draw and blew out a thick cloud of smoke that was
instantly carried upward and over the roof. He walked to the
balcony railing and flicked ash off the end of his cigar as his
lieutenant stepped from the French doors with papers in hand.

"Colonel, I have the information about the American,"
the lieutenant said in Spanish.

"Who is it?" Guerra asked in a gruff tone.

"His name is Tom O'Connor," the lieutenant replied,
handing Guerra a booking report. "He is charged with
intoxicated driving and is in Quito for business."

"What is his business?"

"The hotel business. He was stopped leaving a dinner
party, where he had just closed a deal to purchase a parcel of
land in Guapulo."

Guerra's eyebrow shot upward. "A hotel magnet? We
will set the bail at one hundred fifty thousand."

"That much for intoxicated driving, Colonel?"

Guerra shrugged. "It may seem a bit excessive, but it will give us room to negotiate."

"Yes, sir," the lieutenant said, pointing at the bottom of the booking report. "He said this is the best contact number. He is very anxious to be released."

"Did you call our people in Fort Lauderdale about the other matter?"

"Yes, Colonel. The Inca was sent to Daytona, but they have lost touch with him and his men."

The lieutenant handed Guerra a large white envelope addressed to Colonel Ramos Enrique Guerra, Ave El Inca y 6 de Diciembre, Quito Ecuador, with no return address. Guerra tore open the flap and pulled out a folded piece of paper with writing in English. He handed it over to the lieutenant.

"You went to an American school. Translate for me."

The lieutenant took the paper and studied it while Guerra pulled a thicker piece of paper from the envelope. It was slick photo paper. The scene was of a narrow shoreline. An object sat on the shore that appeared to be a man-size pile of twisted dead wood, clearly weathered by the elements for years. A short Latino male with short buzz cut hair lay sprawled against the wood in an upright position and something was protruding from below his chin. Guerra slipped on a pair of reading glasses that he pulled from his pocket and focused. It was the head of a small axe or something similar with the back tip end buried deep in the man's throat. A stream of blood had run from the spot and stained his shirt neckline a dark red. To the man's right was Colson. He had grasped the man by the elbow and was pointing at a tattoo on the man's shoulder. Guerra jerked his head toward his lieutenant when he started reading the note. He read slowly through the translation.

"I entered your stinking country undetected before. Give me another reason and I will again."

"What is this?" said Guerra, pointing at the tattoo. The lieutenant took the photo and held it close to his face. He gasped and held the photo at arm's length.

"What?" demanded Guerra.

"That is the Latin King symbol. The man must be the Inca sent to kill Colson." The lieutenant began breathing heavy through his nose and cursed. "*Lapue filius.* I will notify our people in Fort Lauderdale immediately."

"No, you fool," Guerra barked and snatched the photo from the lieutenant's hand. He shook the photo in the lieutenant's face and shouted. "Do you not see this? Colson is a diablo. Let it go."

The End

About the Author

Chris is retired from the Cobb County Sheriff's Department in Marietta, Georgia where was assigned to the Undercover Narcotics Unit, DEA Task Force Atlanta Field Division, Fugitive and Fraud Units, and Internal Affairs. He held the rank of Deputy Sheriff Major in the Operations and Investigations Division. Chris currently works as a Police Officer with the Cobb County School District.

His first book *Code of Misconduct* "Conduct Unbecoming," released in 2012, received much acclaim in the literary industry and established Chris as a recognized professional author. Continued reader demand spawned his second work *The Nightmare Merchant* "Code of Misconduct II" which was released in 2014. *Mosquito Lagoon* "Code of Misconduct III" is a continuation of the exciting Grey Colson Crime Thriller Series.

Chris currently lives in Dallas, Georgia with his lovely wife Beverly and their dogs Marty and Bella. Chris and his family vacation in Daytona Beach each summer and can be found in the shade of their canopy, reading their favorite novels and plotting the next Grey Colson Crime Thriller.

www.authorcagriffith.com

CPSIA information can be obtained
at www.ICGtesting.com
Printed in the USA
LVOW08s0100080217

523549LV00001B/34/P